CRIMSON TEARS

WHEN ALL CONTACT is lost with the Imperial planet of Entymion IV, an expeditionary force led by the Crimson Fists Space Marines is sent to find out what is happening. Their investigations bring them into contact with the renegade Soul Drinkers Space Marines Chapter and the Crimson Fists ready themselves for war. With the Imperial troops engaged in combat, ancient evil forces take the opportunity to claim the planet for their own foul ends. Can the Soul Drinkers and Crimson Fists put aside their differences and unite to destroy their common enemy?

SOUL DRINKERS
SOUL DRINKER
THE BLEEDING CHALICE

MORE WARHAMMER 40,000
DAEMON WORLD
GREY KNIGHTS

A WARHAMMER 40,000 NOVEL

CRIMSON TEARS

Ben Counter

To Helen

A BLACK LIBRARY PUBLICATION

First published in Great Britain in 2005 by
BL Publishing,
Games Workshop Ltd.,
Willow Road, Nottingham,
NG7 2WS, UK.

10 9 8 7 6 5 4 3 2 1

Cover illustration by Adrian Smith.

A CIP record for this book is available from the British Library.

ISBN 1 84416 160 9

Distributed in the US by Simon & Schuster
1230 Avenue of the Americas, New York, NY 10020, US.

Printed and bound in Great Britain by
Bookmarque, Surrey, UK.

See the Black Library on the Internet at
www.blacklibrary.com

Find out more about Games Workshop
and the world of Warhammer 40.000 at
www.games-workshop.com

IT IS THE 41st millennium. For more than a hundred centuries the Emperor has sat immobile on the Golden Throne of Earth. He is the master of mankind by the will of the gods, and master of a million worlds by the might of his inexhaustible armies. He is a rotting carcass writhing invisibly with power from the Dark Age of Technology. He is the Carrion Lord of the Imperium for whom a thousand souls are sacrificed every day, so that he may never truly die.

YET EVEN IN his deathless state, the Emperor continues his eternal vigilance. Mighty battlefleets cross the daemon-infested miasma of the warp, the only route between distant stars, their way lit by the Astronomican, the psychic manifestation of the Emperor's will. Vast armies give battle in his name on uncounted worlds. Greatest amongst his soldiers are the Adeptus Astartes, the Space Marines, bio-engineered super-warriors. Their comrades in arms are legion: the Imperial Guard and countless planetary defence forces, the ever-vigilant Inquisition and the tech-priests of the Adeptus Mechanicus to name only a few. But for all their multitudes, they are barely enough to hold off the ever-present threat from aliens, heretics, mutants – and worse.

TO BE A man in such times is to be one amongst untold billions. It is to live in the cruellest and most bloody regime imaginable. These are the tales of those times. Forget the power of technology and science, for so much has been forgotten, never to be re-learned. Forget the promise of progress and understanding, for in the grim dark future there is only war. There is no peace amongst the stars, only an eternity of carnage and slaughter, and the laughter of thirsting gods.

CHAPTER ONE

ENTYMION IV WAS quiet.

Colonel Sathis couldn't even hear the insects here. The indistinct rumbling of his Chimera APCs, following some way behind his command vehicle squadron, all but drowned out the faint wind. Even the hoofbeats of the Rough Riders' mounts were louder than the sounds of the planet itself. Sathis could see the Rough Riders scattered up the sides of the valley through which his force was travelling, men from the 97th Urgrathi Lancers, whose supposedly obsolete methods of cavalry warfare made them excellently suited to scouting out unknown territory. And everything about Entymion IV was unknown.

Sathis took a practiced look at the terrain. He had good all-round visibility here, but further ahead that became less and less likely. 'Stop us here,' he ordered to the driver of his command-pattern Salamander.

The vehicle ground to a halt and the silence was almost total. Sathis climbed down from the Salamander as the engine's vibrations ceased. He took a breath of the air – every planet smelled different and he thought the air of Entymion IV was clean, quiet, as if it was old and proud and resented the marks of pollution that human habitation always left. The purplish sky overhead, the dark ragged ribbons of mountains before them, the thinly grassed valley slopes – it was easy to imagine that this was an unspoilt world. Of course, Entymion IV was nothing of the sort – Gravenhold was a large and populous Imperial city and large sections of the planet's surface were given over to the intensive agriculture that gave it such importance. But at that moment, Colonel Sathis imagined that there were perhaps some places the Imperium would never completely tame.

And always, the silence.

Sathis tried to imagine what was so damned important about this planet. The truth was hidden somewhere in segmentum-level economics. Entymion IV was a major agri-world and if the crop here failed it would have a knock-on effect across scores of other worlds. But a failure was a distinct possibility because the planet had fallen silent – completely silent, both to long-range astropathic communications and short-range vox and radio transmissions. If that meant something grave had happened to the planet's population then Sathis was to reach the capital, Gravenhold, find out what was wrong and report back. Entymion IV was certainly important, but Sathis couldn't imagine why such a bluster seemed to have blown up amongst the Administratum when the planet fell off the map. For the moment, the world was quiet.

Beneath the darkening dusk sky the tops of the valley slopes were knife-hard silhouettes. Ahead the terrain changed gradually, first becoming foothills and then great rearing slabs of rock. Colonel Sathis's immediate objective was to make his way through the Cynos Pass to the other side, where the way would be clear for a drive on Gravenhold. To do it he had the Steel Hammer detachment of the 2nd Seleucaian Defence Force, a formation of Chimera APCs teeming with almost a thousand battle-toughened and well-disciplined Guardsmen assisted by an artillery and anti-tank section, and enough bloody-mindedness to get them through anything. The Urgrathi cavalry were his scout force, and he was supported by tanks from the Jaxus Prime Siege Regiment. It was a fine force, compact and highly mobile. It was fortunate the right troops had been available, because the force had been assembled in a damned hurry by Guard standards.

'Everything alright, sir?' asked Sathis's driver.

'It's fine, Skarn,' replied Sathis. 'I don't want us hitting the pass at night. We should corral here and move on it at dawn. Get me comms.'

Sathis waited for a few moments while his Salamander crew raised the force's officers on the vox-net. Sathis had been on the planet for two days and one night, and he still didn't entirely trust it. The valley pass would be the best place by far for an ambush and at night the chances of such a thing happening increased drastically. Sathis had been in a similar position at the Hellblade Mountains years ago, when as an infantry lieutenant with the Balurians he had been pinned down for eighteen hours by a smattering of eldar troops who had the higher ground. He didn't want to end up in the same situation again – it could take just a few secessionists or rebels to force his advance to a halt and that wasn't in his battle plan.

He worked out the standard pattern in his head. The Seleucaians would form a formidable APC laager in which the men would spend the night, with the tanks and Sathis's command post in the centre while the Urgrathi rode patrols throughout the night. The few hours lost would be repaid with reduced risk to his force. Soon he could report back that all was well on Entymion IV, and he could go back to some real war or other.

'Marshal Locathan,' said Skarn, passing Sathis the vox handset.

'Locathan,' said Sathis brightly, knowing the grizzled old Jaxan tank commander would want to press on through the night.

'Commander?'

'We're going to wait out the night here. Go in with fresh men and daylight at dawn. Bring your tanks up past the Hammers and make sure your men get some sleep.'

Locathan was preparing to argue the point with Sathis when the first shot rang out.

THREE MONTHS BEFORE Sathis's force landed, all communication had been lost with Entymion IV.

Long-range communication, which was transmitted by psychic astropaths through the warp, died out without warning. Astropaths described a sudden dark blanket of silence falling, often in mid-sentence, which remained resolutely impervious to any attempt to penetrate it.

Entymion IV, and the whole Entymion system, was well-known in the sector for the vagaries of the warp space that lay just beneath its realspace, and so patchy communications were nothing new. Greater attention was paid when in-system communications dropped out as well, rendering the planet both deaf and dumb. Entymion's star was likewise prone to electrical disturbances and short-range comms had failed before, but a total silence was something new.

The Administratum, wary of losing whole agri-crops as transport ships could not organise landings on the planet, sent in a team to find out what was going on. The twelve-man surveyor team, which included an Arbites liaison to ensure punishment for whoever was to blame, entered the atmosphere of Entymion IV and was never heard of again.

The possibilities of rebellion, natural disaster or self-imposed quarantine had been raised and hopefully ignored. The Administratum could not risk ignoring them any longer. If Entymion IV stayed silent then billions of credits worth of food would never be harvested and delivered. Every scenario they created suggested resulting famines in the nearby worlds that relied on Entymion IV for sustenance. The Entymion Expeditionary Force was assembled rapidly and Colonel Sathis was given overall command, with orders to land on the planet, make his way to the capital Gravenhold, and bring back the news that all was well.

The consuls of the Administratum crossed their fingers.

Two days after making landfall on the relative safety of the great rolling plains beyond the mountains, the Entymion Expeditionary Force finally made contact.

* * *

ANOTHER BULLET SMACKED into the side of the Salamander before Sathis reacted.

'Taking fire!' he shouted and vaulted over the side of the Salamander as the rest of the crew took cover behind its high armoured sides.

He dropped the vox handset and scrabbled for it as shots whipped through the air above him and slammed into the vehicle's armour.

'...repeat? Colonel, repeat!' Locathan's voice was sharp and businesslike.

'We're taking fire,' said Sathis. 'Small arms, sounds close. Stand by.' Sathis reached over and switched the frequency to that of the commanding officer of the Steel Hammers. 'Commandant Praen. Commandant, do you have any men ahead of us?'

Praen's voice sounded surprised. 'Colonel? No, none of our lads.'

'Then who the hell is shooting? Get your forward platoon up here and give us some support!'

The gunfire suddenly thudded down heavier, chains of automatic fire juddering through the air and ripping plumes of dirt where they stitched along the ground.

'Get us back. Now, into cover.'

The driver, still hunkered down, ripped the Salamander into reverse and the vehicle lurched backwards. Sathis could see the fire now, streaking down above him from the top of the valley. A thick bolt of energy fizzed past and Sathis was sure he could make out the roar as it vaporised a chunk of the opposite slope. Heavy weapons, weight of fire – who was it? And how could they have hidden?

Something was shrieking down at them with a sound like a thousand voices screeching at once, the sound of metal carving through the air, layered beneath a dark stuttering of gunfire.

A force like a huge invisible hand slammed Sathis so hard against the side of the Salamander that his head cracked back and forth and he felt sure he would pass out. The purple sky whirled above him and for a moment it was beneath him, swinging down so he thought he would fall into it, tumbling forever.

The Salamander came to a rest on its side, gouging a deep furrow of earth as it slid to a halt. Sathis's vision swam back just in time to seen Skarn crushed beneath the lip of the armoured compartment and the hull. Another body fell brokenly past him – Lrenn, the gunner.

Sathis scrambled out, leaving his officer's cap behind in the wreckage. The ringing in his ears died down to be replaced with the sinister sound of bullets and lasfire thumping into the earth around him like rain, reports of gunfire and shouting filtering through from further away. He heard the whining of engines and looked up to see the craft that had strafed the Salamander – it was a sharp crescent shape, bladed and savage, that twirled upwards on twin white flames from its engines.

Rebels normally used obsolete marks of Imperial aircraft. This wasn't one of those.

The vox was still in the wreckage. The rest of Sathis's command squadron – a Chimera with a veteran squad from the Seleucaians and two more Salamanders – were retreating rapidly as volleys of enemy fire ripped down at them in white-hot ribbons.

Sathis's mind was in a whirl. He had been under fire dozens of times before, of course. He wasn't scared. He had been shot at, bombed, burned, betrayed and stranded. He had shrapnel in his leg from a rebel artillery barrage on Cothelin Saar, he had nearly died from a bayonet wound when the greenskins stormed his bunker at the Croivan Gap. He had joined the Planetary Defence Force at fourteen, been drafted into the Guard two years later, and killed and fought and eventually led for his Imperium, and he had earned every stripe on his sleeve. But he had never seen a silent planet become a battleground so quickly.

He had never fought an enemy that could get so close, so silently. He didn't think he could lead his men to fight an enemy they couldn't see.

He could see Rough Riders wheeling on the valley slopes, scattering as fire criss-crossed between them. There were silhouettes at the top of the nearest slope, but Sathis couldn't see if they were dismounted riders or the enemy.

Sathis began to run for the closest Salamander but a bolt of liquid fire tore down and bored right through the vehicle, turning its crewmen into guttering figures of flame, blowing its tracks out and sending a blue burning pool of promethium belching out beneath it. The sound and heat hit Sathis like a wall and he fell back onto the smoking earth, the flash of the explosion burned red against his retinas.

Sathis scrambled back towards the wreckage behind him, his nostrils clogged with the stink of burning grass and cannon smoke, his skin raw hot from the plasma flash.

This was worse than the Hellblade Mountains, worse than Cothelin Saar. Hell, it was the worst yet. It wasn't just pain, or fear, or the sight of his men dying, it was the humiliation. He had been caught cold, surrounded, beaten by an enemy that could pick its shots, that could wait to strike instead of being forced into battle against the superior Guard numbers and discipline.

For a moment he was back to his first actions, a boy soldier hearing hostile fire for the first time, seeing the first bloody bodies being dragged back from the battlements and seeing the look in his comrades' eyes that said: *I don't think we're going to make it out of this one.* Sathis had left the boy behind a long time ago but now he was back and with him the doubt, the fear.

A hand grabbed at him and Sathis knew he was dead.

He looked up at the aristocratic face of Hunt Leader Grym Thasool, commanding officer of the 97th Urgrathi Lancers, just before Thasool hauled him up off the ground and onto the back of his Urgrathi charger.

Sathis grabbed on tight to the elaborate tack that kept Thasool strapped to the back of the heavy, muscular charger. Thasool dug his heels in and the charger, bulkier and surlier than a Terran standard horse, shot forward, slaloming between the bolts of falling fire.

Sathis choked down the fear and confusion. He was an officer. This was where he earned that status.

'Get to a vox. Bring up the Hammers, get the... get the armour to pin the enemy down and counterattack...'

'Bloody xenos, sir!' said Thasool, wrenching the reins to haul his mount around the burning Salamander wreckage. He was heading towards the rear of the formation, where the Steel Hammers in their Chimeras would mount a massive counter-charge if someone could get there in time to give the order. 'Seen 'em before. The shadows, you see? They had to wait for the dusk. It's the shadows they hide in.' Thasool, Sathis knew, was utterly fearless, from a long line of aristo-cratic warrior-officers who had had all the cowardice bred out of them. He might have been recounting an anecdote over a glass of devilberry liqueur, were it not for the way he had to raise his voice over the gunfire.

A charger galloped by with a headless rider. Thasool charged on past a tangled knot of bodies, three or four men who had been caught by the same energy bolt and burned into a red-black mass in an instant. A horse lay sheared clean open by las-fire, shredded entrails smoking. Men were yelling. Rough Riders wheeled in confusion through a savage latticework of fire.

The sound of men dying was everywhere.

'Company, wheel twelve left!' bellowed Thasool. 'Close and give them the blade!' Sathis realised Tha-sool was giving orders through his unit's vox-net, trying to bring the scattered Rough Riders together so they could use the speed and strength of their charges to batter back at the enemy.

Riders in the green-and-gold Urgrathi uniforms were galloping heads down through the storm of fire, con-verging on their leader. They were as fearless as Thasool himself. Sathis didn't think he had ever felt greater respect for fellow soldiers than he did for the Urgrathi Chargers in that moment.

A figure coalesced from the dusk shadows at the foot of the valley slope. It was humanoid but its skin drank the light, so it seemed to be pure liquid blackness spilling through from another reality. As the weak sunlight hit, the features emerged – corded muscles, hands encased in sickle-like blades, the face hidden by straps and buckles as if it was trying to hold something in. It was tall and slim but powerful, moving quickly and smoothly as its skin shimmered between sickly pallor and pure blackness.

The thing made of shadow dropped and rolled between the stamping feet of the charger that rode at it. One curved blade flashed out and the charger pitched nose-first into the ground, throwing its rider. The figure seemed to flow over the ground to plant its blade between the rider's shoulder blades before melting back into the shadows.

Sathis let go of the charger's tack with one hand and took out his sidearm, a standard pattern autopistol. He could see more of the enemy. Figures flowed blackly along the lengthening shadows, blades cutting through the riders and their chargers as they swept down towards the valley floor.

The fire kept coming. The shadows further up the slope hid an army, and Sathis picked out a curve of glossy, beetle-black personal armour lit by muzzle fire. Enemy infantry with body armour – aliens if Thasool was right. Sathis spotted something flitting through the air out of the corner of his eye, something that left a glittering crescent of glowing black energy bolts as it passed. The enemy were everywhere, barely visible against the gathering darkness, just a suggestion of movement all over the valley slopes.

Thasool had his power sword drawn, a heavy thrusting blade encased in elaborate gold decoration.

A shadow congealed around the charger's feet – Sathis fired twice at the face that shimmered into view beneath him, its eyes sewn shut, a bloodied metal bar between its teeth. The shots went wide but Thasool swivelled in the saddle before spearing the thing through its throat. The sword's power field flashed and Sathis saw limbs broken beneath the charger's hooves in a wash of blood.

'Mandrakes,' spat Thasool. 'Scouts. We never forgot 'em, disgusting xenos assassins.'

'Xenos? You mean… Hrud? Tau?'

'Eldar,' replied Thasool grimly, slashing down at the black shape flowing towards them. 'The pirate kind.'

The charger rounded a bend in the valley and Sathis saw two forward Chimeras of the Seleucaian Steel Hammers, their veteran Guardsmen dismounted and firing disciplined volleys up the sides of the valley. Their officer – a Lieutenant Aeokas – saluted hurriedly as Thasool slewed the charger round to a halt in the cover of the nearest Chimera.

'We've got two hundred plus!' shouted Aeokas over the volley of las-fire. 'Hostiles on both sides. They've got us surrounded!'

'Comms,' said Sathis as he slid down off the charger. There was a body at his feet, a Seleucaian with a cluster of bloody crystal shards studded over his face and upper chest. The crystalline fire was like a rain of razors here. Sathis felt tiny fragments slicing into the exposed skin of his face and hands like papercuts. He heard a scream as a crystal shard pinned a Seleucaian Guardsman to the side of a Chimera through one bicep.

Someone handed Sathis a vox-handset. 'We're under attack!' he said, trying to keep his voice level. 'Praen, bring everything you've got forward for a counter-attack. Locathan, cover them and get that air power off us!'

'Understood. Saddle up and full charge!' ordered Praen, the engines of his Chimeras juddering behind his voice. Further back the sound of quad autocannons thudded through the air as the Hydra anti-aircraft tank began to fill the sky with shrapnel.

Lieutenant Aeokas yelled something at Sathis, but his voice was lost in a sudden shriek of white noise that blotted out even the gunfire. The air just behind the closest Guard squad's position blurred and puckered, warping the light as if something was scrunching up the background like a picture. A pinpoint of blackness in the centre of the disturbance flooded open like a dead pupil.

The first attacker out of the portal wore glossy purple-black armour with a bone-white face mask, wicked green eyes shining with malevolence, the plates of the armour swept into sharpened curves. Taloned gauntlets held a halberd with a blade that shone and rippled, shifting between one reality and the next. More followed, each one with a speed that, when coupled with the heavy armour and savage hacking weapons, made them as inhuman as the most horribly misshapen alien.

The Guard squad didn't even have time to turn and face them. Halberds bit through Seleucaian uniforms, cutting so cleanly that the bodies didn't even bleed until they hit the ground – they just fell, arms sheared off, torsos slashed in two, heads falling free, looking for all the galaxy as if they had never been alive.

Sathis had faced the eldar before, and he knew they were tricky, treacherous creatures who could turn from allies to savages without warning. But he had never seen anything like this.

The second Guard squad turned and fired instinctively. Las-bolts fizzed and burst against armour. More enemies were coming through the portal, these ones wearing lighter armour and carrying shard-firing rifles. They were spreading out and Sathis ducked down by the Chimera to shelter from the chains of shattering crystal, firing all but blind with his autopistol as the air was clouded with crystal shards.

Thasool waded in without a thought, vaulting down off his charger and stabbing left and right with his sword. He speared one enemy through the chest and lashed out at an armoured eldar, swiping off its arm. It stumbled to the ground, Thasool stamped down in its shoulder and, with a practiced downwards thrust, impaled it through the head. Las-bolts and crystal shots were streaking by him, shredding the hem of his hunt leader's greatcoat. Thasool ignored them. His men were dying and according to the code of the Urgrathi lancers, that meant Thasool was dying too, and physical danger didn't matter any more.

'Fall back and mount up!' yelled Aeokas, gesturing with his chainsword as he fired at the lighter-armoured eldar with his laspistol. 'Get us out of here!'

One of the Guardsmen, his uniform spattered with gore and grime, ducked the hail of fire and unlatched the rear ramp of the Chimera. Aeokas waved the surviving men towards the APC, half of them giving covering fire as the rest fell back.

For a moment Thasool was holding up the aliens on his own, cavalry sword flashing as he kept the armoured eldar at bay. Then one stepped forward into the arc of Thasool's blade, turning the power sword on the haft of its halberd. The butt of the halberd snapped up and cracked into Thasool's chin – the hunt leader stumbled back and the reverse stroke of the halberd brought the heavy shimmering blade carving up into Thasool's stomach, up through his ribcage and out in a crescent of blood. Another eldar stepped up behind Thasool and struck off his head so neatly it was like watching an execution.

A hand grabbed Sathis's shoulder and dragged him backwards into the body of the Chimera. The last Guardsman in was hauling an unconscious comrade with him and threw the body in after Sathis before clambering in himself.

'Go!' yelled Aeokas over the din of crystal fire shattering against the side of the Chimera. Sathis looked around and saw blood-streaked faces, eyes hollow with shock, some bringing their lasguns to bear to fire out of the back of the Chimera as the eldar followed them.

'We have to get to higher ground,' said Sathis, shifting the weight of the dying Guardsman off him. 'Get a vox-link to orbit so they can pick us up. And where the hell is Praen?'

There should have been several Chimeras full of vengeful Guardsmen here to bail them out. What was happening? Where had the xenos come from?

The answer was obvious. They had been there all along, waiting.

The driver of the Chimera was either brilliant or crazy; the engine complained loudly as the vehicle slewed round a bend in the valley, almost flinging men out of the back. Crystal rained down as eldar warriors on the slopes fired at the vehicle, lances of energy weapons bored deep smoking holes in the ground just centimetres away from the hull.

'There's an outcrop about half a kilometre up the valley,' shouted Sathis. 'It's defensible. We get there, raise the alarm and wait for Praen!'

The rear doors of the Chimera were still swinging open. Sathis half-expected to see the xenos fighter craft again, sweeping down on bat-like wings to stitch a line of fire through the Chimera. But instead he saw the first of Praen's Chimeras, kicking up a trail of churned earth as it sped down the valley after them.

Then, Sathis heard the sound. It was a thousand voices – more – all howling at once. It began quietly, a reedy wail somewhere beneath the gunfire and the engine and the breathing of the angry, wounded men around Sathis. But then it grew into a dull roar flowing down the valley like a wind, and grew further still until it seemed to be coming from everywhere at once, from the very earth and sky. Arcs of purple lightning crackled up the sides of the valley and pits of pure blackness were opening up in the air as the second Chimera roared past.

Then there were bodies almost tumbling out of the very air itself, out of holes in reality that opened above the valley floor. Dozens of bodies, alive and evidently human, pale and flailing. The Seleucaian Chimera zoomed past most of them, some disappearing under its tracks, a few somehow clambering over the bodies of their dead to cling grimly on to the hull. Sathis saw sparks as they tried to lever off panels to get inside. Sathis saw they definitely were human, half-naked and armed with shards of metal, bones, crude clubs. More were tumbling in the Chimera's path and Sathis saw the APC ride up over the mass of bodies, tracks whirring helplessly in the air as it lost traction.

The pause in its charge was all the enemy needed. Suddenly there were ten, twenty, more of them swarming over the tank. The APC's engines croaked horribly and it lurched forward, the throng forcing it over onto its side. A top hatch came off and as Sathis's Chimera zoomed away from the wreck he saw the feeding frenzy as the enemy got inside.

Emperor alone knew what the enemy were doing to the crew. It was too late for them now. But the whole valley behind Sathis's Chimera was choked with the enemy, a horde of them. The eldar did not attack like that – they used stealth and guile, moving their specialised elite forces into place before attacking. This was more like the headlong charge of the greenskins. This was all totally, totally wrong.

Lightning flashed down past the open rear hatch.

'Get us up the slope!' yelled Sathis. 'Higher ground! Now!'

He knew what had happened to the Seleucaian Steel Hammers. A massive horde of xenos attackers had flooded the valley, bogged them down, and probably killed them all. Locathan's tanks had probably suffered the same fate. If any had escaped it would have been in the opposite direction, back the way the convoy had come, towards the open plains. It was the better option, thought Sathis, but he didn't have the choice now.

The Chimera turned and ground its gears as it started up the slope. Pits of blackness were opening up in the air.

'Guns forward!' shouted Aeokas, and the able-bodied Guardsmen wrestled themselves into position so they could fire out of the back of the Chimera.

'Lasgun!' shouted Sathis, and someone handed him a well-used Triplex pattern lasgun, its barrel still hot from firing. He felt like a recruit again, the weapon heavy and sinister in his hands for the first time. Sathis had gone through the same basic training as any Guardsman and somehow he had always known deep down that, in the end, it would come down to how well he could shoot and fight just like the men under his command.

It was right. It was natural. One man fighting for the Imperium, and for his own survival. It was the way to fight an abomination like the one that was ambushing them on Entymion IV. Sathis pushed the doubt down further. He was an Imperial citizen sworn almost by definition to fight the Emperor's wars and meet his end uncomplaining, only grateful that he had been given the chance to live a life that meant something in this cold galaxy.

The Chimera was slowing as the slope got too much for it. More portals were opening up, irregular splotches of blackness like spatters of dark ink laid across reality.

More bodies poured out in a torrent. The eldar elites had jumped down in a regular practised formation, like grav-chuters dropping from a transport plane. This was a rabble, herded into the portal somewhere else to be thrust unceremoniously out into battle. They were armed with knives, clubs, iron bars and the occasional low-powered laspistol some civilians owned. There were straps buckled over their eyes and their cheeks were slit so their mouths were wide red flapping grimaces.

And they were not eldar. They were human.

The good men and women of Entymion IV.

'Fire!' shouted Aeokas, but he needn't have bothered. Lasgun shots spattered out in a fan, punching red holes through the mass.

They were getting closer. Sathis pulled the lasgun's trigger and the gas kick from the power converter was familiar; he could imagine the rectangular bruise below his shoulder in the morning. Not that there would be a morning.

The enemy were getting closer. Sathis could see their pale, malnourished bodies, the rags they wore around their waists, the scars and crude self-made tattoos on their naked torsos. Another las-volley chewed through them but those behind were climbing over the dead so that they rose up like a wave about to break.

A metallic shriek signalled the end of the Chimera's gearbox. Sathis heard the top front hatch open and more las-shots open up as the driver added his laspistol to the carnage.

Brave chaps, thought Sathis. All of them. Such a shame.

Sathis hauled himself forward out of the Chimera. The APC was stuck now and it was no more than a tomb. The horde was close enough for him to smell the sweat and blood. Outside the APC their howling was the only sound. He couldn't even hear his own voice as he ordered the Guardsmen out of the APC.

The Seleucaian Guardsmen dropped out of the rear hatch, Aeokas yelling to leave the wounded. Sathis flicked the lasgun selector stud to full-auto, knowing that it didn't really matter if the power pack ran out now.

It was strangely comforting, he thought, to know that he was going to die. The certainty was warm and encouraging. An officer could rarely be certain about anything – he had to have fall-back plans, contingencies, reserves. Now, he could concentrate the last few seconds of his life on killing as many of these alien-loving scum as possible.

The Guardsmen were going to make a stand on the ridge. Good for them. Sathis clambered up on top of the Chimera as the horde surged closer, las-bolts still blowing sprays of blood from them. One ran forward and tried to jump up after him but Sathis shot him through the throat, imagining his old parade-ground instructor clapping him on the shoulder for such a good shot.

Sathis looked up and saw the valley stretching out behind him. It was thronged with crowded white bodies, like squirming maggots. Thousands of them. Hundreds of thousands. No wonder Entymion IV had fallen silent – its population was insane.

The eldar were waiting on the slopes and watching them, almost invisible, their dark armour mingling with the lengthening evening shadows. Their plan had simply been to stop the convoy and break it up, so that when their horde of slave-soldiers arrived the end would come the quicker.

They probably thought they had won. But no alien could win against the Imperium. Trillions of citizens, billions of soldiers, thousands of forge-worlds pumping out tanks and guns and spaceships, the Imperial Navy, the Adeptus Ministorum to marshal their faith, the Adeptus Terra to guide them – all the eldar had done here was to make them all angry.

Portals were opening up over Aeokas and the Guardsmen. Their lives were measured in seconds now. Aeokas would lead them to the last, not because he had to, but because there was no meaning left in his life except to lead his men in dying.

The horde were scrumming around the Chimera now, trying to clamber onto it. Sathis kicked one in the face and shot another, wishing he had a bayonet. He sprayed a fan of las-fire that knocked two or three more off the Chimera.

The evening sky was now a deep, vibrant purple. The distant mountains were silver-edged teeth of black in the distance. What did the eldar want this world for? Why was it so important? Why here, and not somewhere out on the frontier where the Imperium might never intervene? Why not some fat sweating hive world where the xenos could herd millions of under-hivers through their portals without anyone even noticing? Why here? Why Entymion IV?

A handmade knife plunged between Sathis's shoulder blades. Sathis's hand spasmed and he dropped the lasgun as more of the subjugated humans surrounded him. Something heavy and metal slammed into his ribs. His vision swam as the blood flowed out of him.

Colonel Sathis's world ended on the slopes of Entymion IV. And even as he died, he knew that his death would not be the last.

CHAPTER TWO

LIFE, IF YOU knew how to look, was a field of stars. If you could see past the mundane backdrop of the galaxy and tune in to the lights that everyone carried around in their minds, then you would see a million shining beacons of humanity. Most were virtually static, milling around in cities on tight endless circuits from homes to manufactoria and back again. A few ranged over their worlds, aristocrats or lawkeepers, criminals or wanderers. Some orbited planets in smugglers' scows or planetary defence platforms, and some zipped between worlds on spacecraft – they were the soldiers, the messengers, the adepts, the Imperium's lifeblood pumping through the arteries of space.

This particular system, Diomedes Tertiam, was well-populated so the task would be difficult. There were about twenty-three billion inhabitants spread across two hive worlds and a multitude of colonies and off-world stations. How was it possible to sort one life-light out from all these?

It was certainly the right system. One of the hive worlds sported the psychic scars of sudden, inhuman violence. All hives were shaded with the mental crimson of bloodshed but that was like a dull glow, almost comforting in its normality, signalling that the under-hivers were culling each other as effectively as they had ever done.

But one hive was different. Bright slashes of carnage were still written across the upper spires of one particular hive, throbbing with the shock that had yet to wear off, seeded with the residue of death and watered with intense white fear that ran like foul water down the levels of the hive.

There. It had happened there. It matched up with what they already knew, and confirmed they were in the right place.

There was another world, equally important as a landmark in their quest. It was a smaller planetoid where the lives were penned into tight regular clusters – they barely moved, and so they formed geometrical ranks rising in pyramids from the surface. Prisoners in their cells. A prison-world, the sinkhole for the most dangerous criminals that the Diomedes Tertiam could produce. Beneath the upper levels were empty spaces in the pattern, larger cells with no prisoners. The life-lights present on those levels flickered with pain or throbbed dully with desperation. Glowing splashes of death were overpowered by the ice-cold rime of suffering.

Interrogation cells. Highest security. And one of them was full of bright lives, milling around as they made preparations. Reinforced doors, adamantine

restraints, medical servitors to deliver massive doses of
hypno-sedatives into the prisoner to be kept there.
They knew what they would have to hold, and they
knew what it could do. Perhaps they had been to the
hive and seen the results first-hand – either way they
would be under no illusions. They were preparing to
receive one life-light that could never again leave the
pattern of the prison world. It would grow dim and die
there.

The view pulled out again. The object of their
scrutiny would not be there, but the knowledge of the
prison world helped pin it down. Seen from a distance, the system had patterns of its own. Some lives
– smugglers, fleeing criminals, deep system patrols –
moved seemingly at random around the planets and
their star, but most followed fairly regular routes
between the worlds. Thin arteries picked out by the
psychic echo of those who plied them, the standard
routes were relatively safe and well-patrolled. That
meant the highest chance of getting their prisoner back
if he escaped. That meant he would be there, somewhere.

The collective scouring intelligence lined up the
violence-marked hive and the prison world, and
found a thread that connected them – a short,
straight, direct route with few travellers but plenty of
static waypoints where monitoring stations were
marked out by the lives of those who kept watch.

There. It had to be. The secure route the system
authorities used to transport their prisoners. It was
probably watched over by the Adeptus Arbites,
watching out for treachery or incompetence. Perhaps
some of those hard, bright, disciplined points of
light were the life-echoes of the Arbites officers, stern

and upright, giving leadership to the Imperium's policing.

The watchers had killed more than a few Arbites in their time. They had not relished it, but it was necessary. The Arbites were just one arm of the Imperium, just one cog in the huge machine that ground Mankind down into a helpless, pliable mass of weakened minds. The lights of the population were dim and dying, susceptible to rebellion or suggestion from dark powers. If more men and women of the Imperium could see the population as the watchers saw them, then perhaps the Imperium would be no more and there would be freedom. Or perhaps just mindless anarchy – they all knew the solution for the galaxy would not be an easy one.

These were all questions for another time. Together the watchers peered down closer at the inter-system route between the hive and the prison planet. The prison planet, they noticed, was small and its gravity would be low. That way the prisoners' muscles would be wasted and stringy after a year or so, making it more difficult to escape if they got onto a ship or made it as a far as a standard-gravity world. It was an old trick, and it worked. It probably wouldn't work on the prisoner they were surely transporting at that moment, though. There would be no choice but to restrain him permanently, and kill him when they were done with him. This was because their prisoner, in body and especially in mind, wasn't really human.

One ship carried several hundred despairing souls. The result of an underhive sweep, rounded up to fill some conviction quota. Another had a few hard-bitten criminal minds sedated and kept in restraints. Killers. Seditionists. The Imperium's worst, as much a result of the Imperium as the bustling hives and iron-hard discipline of the Arbites. Interesting, but not what they were looking for.

One ship was small, holding barely a dozen life-lights. It was the crew that gave the first clue. They were afraid. Fear was a strange thing that made a soul stronger and weaker at the same time, and you couldn't hide the stain it left on your soul. A thin, reedy flicker hovered at the heart of their minds, fluttering away behind everything they did. They were afraid because they knew their ship could be scuttled at any moment if their prisoner looked like he could escape; their lives were not valuable enough to be spared if it looked like they might lose their cargo. They were afraid, too, that they would do something wrong in the long, complicated dance of red tape that surrounded the transport of a prisoner like this. Adepts from a dozen organisations would have to be notified, and each would have to ratify some part of the process. Maybe even the Inquisition would be involved, demanding one of their observers be present, perhaps even insisting on conducting some interrogations of their own.

The Inquisition would have a lot of questions to ask the prisoner. Most of them would be about the watchers themselves.

Most of all, of course, the crew were scared of the prisoner himself.

A hard red-white point of boiling hate, so sharp and stark it looked like it had been nailed into the backdrop of space. A bullet wound of madness. The depths of primal emotion had bubbled up to the surface and swallowed the conscious mind. It was unmistakable. Even from this distance, even with only the psychic residue to go by, there could be no doubt. This was their man. The violence on the hive had been of such intensity that only several men like this could be responsible. Most of them had escaped to ply their carnage in some other system, but something extraordinary had happened at Diomedes Tertiam – one of them had been captured. Probably at great cost, he had been subdued, restrained, processed through many layers of bureaucracy, and assigned a grim drawn-out death of interrogation on the prison world. It was extraordinary, one in a million. But it had happened. And it was the chance the watchers were looking for.

The hating soul writhed in its restraints. At its heart it was a paradox – everyone was, but the paradox here was stark and obvious. It was boiling over with hatred, the uncontrolled outpourings of a broken and degraded mind. But all that was doubly dangerous because it was bound in the iron-hard bands of discipline – that same discipline that bound the soul of every Space Marine.

THE CERTAINTY WAS enough to break the contact. The Diomedes Tertiam system snapped back, the billions of life-lights whirling away into the distance as Sarpedon's perception pulled back from the psychic landscape.

The swirling blackness dissipated and Sarpedon was back in the chamber on the *Brokenback*. Librarian Gresk sat just across from him, sweat running down his dark skin. The Chapter's third Librarian, Tyrendian, sat stock-still and meditative, his breathing controlled. He looked too young and handsome to be a Space Marine, let alone a battle-hardened outcast like a Soul Drinker.

Each Librarian did things differently. Gresk's power tuned into the metabolisms of his fellow Marines, quickening their reactions and movements to make them more effective fighting machines. Tyrendian's psychic power was raw and unchannelled – he hurled lightning bolts across the battlefield. Sarpedon, meanwhile, was a telepath who could transmit but not receive, and so he sent hallucinations and unwanted primal emotions straight into the minds of his enemies. And just as they differed on the battlefield, so the three used their own techniques and skills when it came to the meditation.

Sarpedon had found a large, lavish ballroom in one of the spaceships that made up the twisted hulk of the *Brokenback*. It was dim and shadowy now, its chandeliers burned out and its furnishings mouldering. It was large, dark and quiet, perfect for the meditations.

Gresk shuddered and leaned forward over the table. He had focused his power inwardly, forcing his mind into ever-faster cycles of activity until he had projected his perception out into space and into the Diomedes Tertiam system. It took its toll – Gresk's breathing was heavy and laboured. Gresk was old, and meditation was a paradoxically exhausting activity for him.

'It was him,' he said.

'He was further gone than we thought,' replied Sarpedon. 'You felt the hatred. I couldn't feel anything else in him.'

'But it was definitely one of them. One of our own.'

'Yes, yes. It was.' Sarpedon shifted uncomfortably. The meditative session had lasted several hours and, even without his power armour, he had become stiff and aching. 'They have almost put him past our reach. We will have to be quick.'

'Perhaps it is best to leave him be,' said Tyrendian.
The Librarian's eyes slowly opened as he brought himself out of the trance. 'There is nothing in this brother
that can be reasoned with. He is just an animal now.
Think what Tellos himself would be like! Perhaps it is
better to let him run amok. The Imperium will find
him and put him down.'

'Think, Tyrendian.' snapped Gresk. 'Tellos had the
run of this place. He knows the *Brokenback* better than
any of us. He might know how to hunt it down, or
cripple it. Even Techmarine Lygris doesn't know what
all its strengths and weaknesses are. If the Inquisition
got to Tellos it could be the end of us.'

'And if we go after him, Gresk, we might deliver ourselves to the Inquisition regardless. Don't you think
they're after him, too?'

'Enough,' said Sarpedon. 'We haven't got that close
yet. We will make the most of the lead we have. Thank
you for your meditations, brothers. Now rest and prepare. If we recover this one we might need both of you
to break him open.'

Sarpedon stood up from the table, and an ignorant
observer would see for the first time one of the reasons
the Soul Drinkers were excommunicate. Sarpedon was
a mutant, an obvious and powerful one. Eight segmented arachnoid legs sprouted from his waist, a relic
of the Chapter's most shameful actions. Taking advantage of a schism between the Soul Drinkers and other
Imperial authorities, the Daemon Prince Abraxes had
corrupted the Marines' bodies and very nearly done
the same to their souls. Abraxes was dead and the Soul
Drinkers were treading the long path of redemption,
outcast by the Imperium they had once served but
sworn to fight the powers of Chaos that had so nearly

claimed the Chapter itself. The mutations remained, and though Apothecary Pallas was well on the way to halting the degeneration they were causing, they would never be completely cured. Most of the Soul Drinkers had mutations somewhere, but none so dramatic as Sarpedon's own. As Chief Librarian and de facto Chapter Master of the Soul Drinkers, Sarpedon was their greatest hero and their greatest failure. It was he who had led them into the Chapter War that left so many of their own dead at a brother's hands, who had almost led them into the worship of Abraxes's patron god Tzeentch, who had left them with a mutative legacy that had almost claimed all their lives.

And Sarpedon was responsible for Tellos. That might be his greatest failure.

Sarpedon activated the vox-bead in his throat with an unconscious impulse. 'Lygris?'

'Commander?' Techmarine Lygris's voice crackled through the vox.

'We've got a location. A transport heading for the prison planet in the Diomedes Tertiam system. Get some sensors on it and put us on our way. I'll need intercept plans.'

'Understood. Boarding torpedoes?'

'No, it's a well-policed route. They could be shot down. Use one of our Imperial ships. We'll send in the scouts.'

There was a slight pause. 'Understood.'

'This is what we trained them for, Lygris.'

'Can they handle one of Tellos's men?'

Sarpedon smiled. 'Ask Karraidin.'

It was all the answer Lygris needed. The hoary old Captain Karraidin, the Chapter's hardest-bitten assault officer, was the Soul Drinkers' new Master of Novices

and he was an even harder taskmaster than Sarpedon
had expected. The scout-novices had hated him when
they were first recruited, now Sarpedon knew they
would follow Karraidin through the Eye of Terror
itself.

Gresk had stalked off through the decaying finery of
the ballroom, beginning the long trek through the
hulk to his cell where he would run through mental
exercises to recover his strength. Tyrendian had stayed
behind, contemplating the once-beautiful gilt murals
that covered the room's walls.

'Aekar would have been so much better at this,' said
the Librarian quietly. Tyrendian seemed to say everything quietly.

'We did well enough,' said Sarpedon. Aekar had died
of psychic feedback while probing the atmosphere of a
world where the Soul Drinkers had fought the Daemon Prince Ve'Meth. The rest of the Chapter's
Librarians had been killed in the subsequent battle
against Abraxes, on Stratix Luminae, or from uncon-
trollable mutation. Now Sarpedon, Gresk and
Tyrendian alone made up the whole Chapter Librarium.

Tyrendian turned to Sarpedon, his face was normally
unreadable but there was something earnest in it now.
'We all need to know you understand the risks, commander. The Imperium is hunting Tellos as closely as
we are. We will put ourselves in plain sight if we move
on him.'

'I can't leave one of our own out there,' replied Sarpedon. 'Tellos is my responsibility. I was the one who let
him get so far.'

'You,' said Tyrendian. 'Not us. You have led us this
far, commander, but remember this Chapter is still

bigger than you. We have the scouts and the novices to protect, too. We only have – what, four hundred Marines left? And just the three of us Librarians. We cannot afford another Stratix Luminae.'

Sarpedon nodded sadly. 'You're right. A Space Marine Chapter should consolidate after our losses. Build up a scout company, fortify, re-equip. But Tyrendian, the Soul Drinkers are not a Chapter any more. We are not an army. We are nothing but the principles that bind us together, and one of those principles is that a brother is a brother and we have a responsibility towards him. If we can get Tellos and his Assault Marines back then we have to try. And if we can't, it is our responsibility to see that the Dark Powers do not get him first. Besides, Gresk is right. If the Inquisition gets hold of Tellos they could hunt us down.'

'We might not survive, Sarpedon. You know that.'

'If we forget why we are fighting then we will be just one more band of renegades. Remember what we once were, Tyrendian. We fought for the Imperium to prove how superior we were. Now we fight because it is the work of the Emperor. Rogal Dorn was the man he was because of the strength of his will. We have to be the same.'

Tyrendian shrugged. 'We could leave. Take the *Brokenback* to the other side of the galaxy. Tellos is the Imperium's problem.'

'The people of the Imperium have to live with a corrupt regime that would see them dying before it admitted it was wrong,' replied Sarpedon. 'They don't deserve Tellos butchering his way through them as well. He's our problem and I intend to see that we solve it.'

For a moment it looked like Tyrendian would say something in reply, but whatever it was he bit it back.

'The scouts will have to be everything we hope they are,' continued Sarpedon. 'How are the Librarium recruits doing?'

Tyrendian thought for a moment. 'Scamander will join the Librarium eventually. Nisryus too, perhaps. None of the others are strong enough to be certain, but there may be a couple of capable psykers still amongst them.'

'I want Scamander going in with Eumenes's squad.'

'Then we'll see if I'm right.'

With that, Tyrendian left. The Soul Drinkers' Librarians, even before the Chapter's excommunication, had served as advisors to the Chapter Master, always open and honest with their advice. Sarpedon was glad there was one still left who felt he could speak his mind. The Soul Drinkers had followed Sarpedon almost religiously since the schism and he knew that he needed a foil for his command. The Primarch on whom the Soul Drinkers' geneseed was modelled, Rogal Dorn, had himself been wilful and headstrong. That was his strength, but also his weakness, a weakness shared by every Chapter Master since and compensated for by the counsel of the Librarium.

What if Tyrendian was right? Sarpedon could tear the Chapter apart, pursuing battles they couldn't win. But what else was there? How many times had Sarpedon sworn to die in the service of the Emperor? What would the Soul Drinkers themselves say? They would walk into hell if it seemed the best way to do the work of the Emperor and bring the fight to the forces of Chaos. But then, Tellos had once been the same.

These were questions for later. Sarpedon had to brief the scouts for their first true mission, one that would go some way to deciding the Chapter's future.

THE DESTRUCTION OF the Entymion IV Expeditionary Force did not go unnoticed. The sketchy reports from orbit showed a massive enemy force cutting Colonel Sathis's command to ribbons in a matter of minutes. No one had any idea anything like that could be present on the planet – any potential resistance had been expected on the plains outside Gravenhold, consisting of rebellious guerrilla fighters or, in the worst case scenario, household troops and rebellious Planetary Defence Force units commanded by Gravenhold's hereditary aristocracy.

The reality had been impossible to understand. The sheer numbers were dizzying. A minimum of ten thousand enemy soldiers had packed the valley, having seemingly appeared from nowhere. Warpcraft or hitherto unknown xenos technology were the only explanations for the sudden appearance of the army. Worse, the only place an enemy could have mustered an army of that size was from the population of Entymion IV itself.

The Adeptus Terra had to assume that Entymion IV was under the control of a hostile force, a moral threat, something that could use Imperial citizens as a weapon against the Imperium.

The message reached the dusty ancient halls of Terra itself. Lord Commander Xarius, hero of the Rhanna Crisis, was swiftly appointed command with orders to recover the planet at all costs. Xarius appropriated all the available Guard units for several sectors around and had, in a little under two months, assembled a force that most commanders would need years to pull together. The entire Seleucaian Fourth Division, more that seventy thousand men, demanded that Xarius take them to Entymion IV to avenge the dead of their brother regiment. Xarius also brought the regiment with which he once served, the elite heavy infantry of the Fornux Lix 'Fire Drakes'. The sector battlefleet was less rapid to answer the call but still seconded a cruiser, the *Resolve*, and escort squadrons along with a fleet of transports to get Xarius's army to the Entymion system and maintain a blockade to keep the rot on Entymion IV from spreading.

Xarius was a hard and unrelenting man, especially with himself. He called in every ally and favour he could to bring the army together, but if he wanted a rapid, effective invasion of Entymion IV then he had to have a cutting edge. The Seleucaians and the Fire Drakes were tough troops but they weren't the tip of the spear, the surgical strike-capable assault troops he needed to crack open Gravenhold. For a moment he paused before he ordered the troop-laden fleet to move into the Etymion system. He had seen the hazy, flickering sensor images of what had happened to Sathis. He knew he needed an edge before he would send a hundred thousand Imperial lives into the teeth of that kind of war.

At the last moment, answering the request of the Senatorum Imperialis itself, a strike cruiser arrived then left just as suddenly, leaving behind several Thunderhawk gunships carrying the men Xarius needed to lead the charge on the walls of Gravenhold. Those men were the Space Marines of the Crimson Fists' Chapter.

* * *

GRAVENHOLD WAS A masterpiece.

It was an old city that had survived the best efforts of the Administratum to Imperialise it. The existing histories of Entymion IV had the city dating back to the Great Crusade, and the city now standing on that site was several hundred years old. Some passing fashion for simple pale elegance had coincided with a drive by the planet's aristocracy to build themselves a capital worthy of the name. The result was Gravenhold as it now stood. Broad decorative arches straddled mosaiced thoroughfares that ran between the grand exchanges and trading-houses of the nobles. The River Graven that cut through the city from east to west was straddled by several bridges, each a work of fine decorative engineering, the most impressive being the Carnax bridge that connected the government district to the city's wealthy north.

Each estate in the north was like a city of its own in miniature, as if the aristocrats who once ran the planet liked to imagine themselves as the monarchs of tiny empires. The senate-house where the Gravenhold's plutocratic government once met was a handsome circular building, all columns and galleries, located on a bend in the river so the Graven almost surrounded it like a moat. The city's amphitheatre dominated the southern portion where the houses of the workers and minor adepts became picturesque slums, winding streets raidating away from the arena.

It was a shame, reflected Commander Reinez, about the mills. The large, ugly buildings were typical of the kind the Administratum inflicted on cities under its ultimate control, as Gravenhold had been. The knotted industrial piles were crammed up against the eastern wall, and around them were encrustations of shanty towns where an unwelcome underclass of sub-menial workers had taken root over the last few decades. The spaceport just beyond the eastern wall was an eyesore, too, a network of concrete landing hubs and maintenance yards that sprawled obnoxiously on the city's doorstep.

All this information was of secondary importance to Commander Reinez as he looked over the city from the south-western gate chapel. His Space Marine's eye had first noted the military implications of invading Gravenhold. He had seen worse places for cityfights – immense urban hives, crumbling hollow city-corpses riddled with craters and enemy foxholes, even cities seething with the influence of Chaos right down to the very stones. But Gravenhold had been built with an eye towards defensibility – certainly the city's walls were firm and unbreached, the gates easily-defended. The River Graven was as big an obstacle as any. And, like every city Reinez had fought over, the most well-ordered streets could become warrens of barricades and firing points without notice, suddenly plunging a placid cityscape into an unending labyrinth of warfare.

But what struck Reinez most was the same thing that had puzzled everyone since Cynos Pass. The city was, as far as his augmented and well-trained eyes could see, deserted.

Sergeant Althaz hurried up to Reinez, the pre-dawn light casting a greyish sheen over his dark blue power armour. 'The lower levels are clear, sir. The chapel is secure.'

'Good. Tell the Guard command the gate is theirs.'

Althaz saluted. 'Yes, sir. For Dorn.'

'For Dorn, sergeant.'

The gate chapel was a finely-made temple that formed the end of the city's wall just before the south-eastern gate. Its clergy had once performed rites to bring the Emperor's blessing on those passing through the gate below, casting holy water from the marble balconies and making benedictions on those who stopped at the city's threshold to pray. The chapel was now abandoned but perfectly intact, pale grey marble cherubs held up the ceiling of the top floor where Reinez stood, flanked by High Gothic inscriptions cut deeply into the walls. There was room enough in here for a congregation of a couple of hundred, kneeling before an altar of carved obsidian, their faith focused by the aroma of incense from the censers on the ceiling and the way the sunlight fell in shafts between the columns around the balcony.

The chapel covered several floors, down to the ground level where the city's population once walked out to begin the journey to the fields to the south. The chapel itself was the top floor, with the belfry just below, then a winding spiral staircase connected half-floors and mezzanines down to street level. Three squads of Crimson Fists held the chapel: Reinez's own command squad, Althaz's Tactical squad, and the Devastator squad of Sergeant Caltax. The Crimson Fists were the lynchpin of the first Imperial drive on Gravenhold – the heavy infantry of the Fire Drakes Guard regiment would enter the city through the south-eastern gate, and the Crimson Fists had to keep that gate open at all cost. If the enemy turned the broad thoroughfares beyond the gate into a killing zone, using the towering administrative blocks as firing platforms, then even the tough Fire Drakes would be thrown back in disarray. The Crimson Fists were to prevent that from happening.

Not that any enemy had yet shown his face. The invasion force had landed in the hinterland of Graven-hold itself, but neither the southern landing fields of the Fire Drakes or the Seleucaians to the city's east experienced any kind of resistance – Entymion IV was quiet and welcoming. The only hint that anything was wrong lay in the complete abandonment nature of the small settlements outside the capital, some left with food decaying on tables.

The Imperial forces had warily approached the city, every Guardsmen watching for omens of bad luck that would confirm his suspicions that the city was one big trap. The veterans of the Seleucaian Fourth Division had successfully invested the spaceport through which the eastern thrust would be mounted, while the Crimson Fists had taken the chapel with nothing more than a handful of orders and the cold-blooded efficiency that was the legacy of Rogal Dorn.

Reinez knew better than to assume the Imperial drive would be uncontested. But he also knew he was above the superstitions of the Imperial Guardsmen who saw imminent death in every shadow and idle remark. The population of Entymion IV had been corrupted and made rebellious by xenos or Chaotic influence, that didn't mean the heretics would contest their city. They might have abandoned the place, perhaps left a few booby traps to keep the troops busy for a while, intending to make their stand in the mountains or the rugged, untamed forests that straddled the planet's equator.

Either way, no matter how Reinez might want to get to grips with the enemy here, the Crimson Fists had a job to do. When the gate was forced, the Fire Drakes had taken their section of the city and Gravenhold was back in Imperial hands, then they would worry about taking back the rest of Entymion IV.

As if on cue, alert-runes flashed on Reinez's retinal display.

'They're in the wall,' came a vox from Caltax two floors below, just beneath the belfry floor. Then an explosion rocked the chapel and sent the limbs of stone cherubs raining from the ceiling. Deep cracks snapped through the floor and ceiling and the whole chapel shifted suddenly as if it was about to topple into the gateway.

The Fire Drakes were making their move even now. Chimera APCs, a handful of support tanks, and hundreds of men were marching across the city's threshold, relying on the Fists to support them. The enemy had struck at the Fists first, so that when the real slaughter began there would be no one to stop it.

Bolter fire chattered up from below, from the belfry level with its huge adamantium bells, from the crypt floors with entombed clergy.

'Caltax! What are we fighting?' Reinez jumped down the flight of stairs to where his own squad was stationed, in the main chapel with its rows of pews and grand lectern. They were fanned out with bolters ready, prepared to sell their slice of the gate chapel dearly. Already the chemical tang of gunsmoke was in the air.

Bolter shots rang off marble. Blades clashed with ceramite armour. The fight was inside the chapel, but that made no sense. The city wall was made of solid stone blocks several metres thick – there was nowhere for the attackers to have come from.

'Marines!' yelled Caltax over the vox. 'Traitor Legions!'

Then the back wall of chapel fell in, the stone blistering and rotting to reveal a cavity melted deep through the rock. And the Chaos Marines poured in.

A storm of bolter fire filled the chapel floor. Black wooden pews were chewed into kindling. Marble columns became clouds of spinning shrapnel. The world snapped into slow motion, a result of the combat-hormones now pumping through Reinez's body. The enemy were Space Marines, the worst of the worst, those who had turned their back on the Emperor and given themselves to the dark gods. Their armour was deep, vibrant purple, trimmed in bone. They carried chain-blades and bolt pistols, and they were adorned with body parts – hands, heads, ears, skins – nailed to the plates of their armour. Few wore helmets and their faces were pale, drawn visions of soulless malice: eyes wild, hair unkempt, skin tight and scabby. One had eyes that stared madly from stalks jutting from sockets, another moved on cloven hooves with legs that were jointed the wrong way.

The storm of bolter fire tore one Traitor Marine to shreds and ripped the arm off a second. But there must have been a dozen piling into the room. Reinez's senses were working faster than his body and he fought the inertia of his limbs to draw the heavy thunder-hammer from its scabbard on his back and charge through his squad into the fray.

Marines. Chaos Marines. No one had suggested it might be this bad.

Then he saw the golden chalice symbol on the shoulder pads of the enemy Marines, and Reinez realised how bad it really was.

The two sides clashed and the chapel was suddenly a mad, swirling cauldron of violence. Chainblades drew showers of sparks against ceramite. Reinez saw Brother Alca die, his head cracked against the stump of a pillar, skull split open by a traitor's boot. A Chaos Marine was impaled through the shoulder joint of his armour by Brother Paclo's bayonet – Paclo heaved the Marine into the air and fired half a clip of bolter shells through the traitor's ribcage.

Reinez's hammer slammed into the mass of enemies. He didn't care which of them he hit.

A Fist fought with his combat knife against a Chaos Marine with a chainsword. The chainsword won, carving off the Fist's leg before spearing through his gut.

Reinez struck again and felt ceramite break. He could barely see anything – the air was seething with smoke, gunflashes, debris and sprays of blood. The sound was immense – men screaming and yelling, gunfire, the shriek of chainblades, the thunderous strike of his hammer.

The world howled and fell apart. The ground fell away. Everything tumbled end over end, darkness alternating with the shafts of sunlight, purple and blue armoured bodies falling past one another.

The floor of the chapel had given way. Reinez realised this just as he landed two floors down, in the belfry.

Reinez had suffered worse. He had come through this horror and confusion before, and always survived, always been there at the end to drag some victory from the jaws of Chaos. He was the first up – he had to be, otherwise a single bolter shell or well-placed chainblade thrust could kill him on the ground.

Sounds filtered through the white noise of shock. A gunfight on the lower levels was sending stray bolter shots up to ring a strange rapid crescendo from the half-dozen massive grey metal bells hanging in the room. A stairway ran around the inside of the column that made up the chapel building at the end of the city wall. Crimson Fists were pressed against the wall, firing almost blindly down at enemies on the levels below. Reinez had landed badly on a platform stretching across the stairway, level with the bells – many Marines must have fallen past him to the bottom of the shaft.

Reinez dragged himself to his feet. Bolts of pain shot through him but they were comforting – none of his injuries were too severe. He could forget them.

His thunder hammer vibrated gently in his hand, its power field eager to crash into another enemy. A Chaos Marine, half his face a massive oozing wound, ran at him before Reinez could take proper stock of his situation.

The Marine knocked Reinez back onto one knee, slashing with his chainblade before trying to bring his bolt pistol level with Reinez's head. Reinez grabbed the gun wrist with one hand and lashed out with the hammer, knocking the Marine's legs out. He used the momentum to bring the hammer back up again and let it fall in a slow, brutal arc, slamming into the Marine's head and carrying on through the skull into the floor. Reinez had to haul on the hammer to keep it from carving through too much of the platform and bringing the whole thing down.

'Commander!' yelled someone behind Reinez. He looked up from the dead Chaos Marine to see Sergeant Caltax clambering up the last flight of stairs to reach

Reinez's position. 'There're at least twenty of them, sir. Came in through the wall. Half my men are down or cut off.'

'Take everything you can and win back the stairs.' Reinez glanced around, several of his squad were on their feet around him. Brother Paclo's crimson gauntlets glistened with the blood of the Marine he had killed, Arroyox had probably broken a leg but was living with it, and Kroya was calmly finishing off a wounded Chaos Marine at his feet with a bolter round to the neck. 'We'll force them down to Althaz, crush them between the two.'

Caltax nodded quickly. He turned back to yell down at his men. 'Force them back! Get that heavy bolter to bear and–'

Reinez barely saw the blade. It was too quick to see, the only evidence of its passing the sudden sharp crescent of blood and the way Caltax's head rolled sideways to fall free of his neck.

The enemies of the Imperium took infinite forms and Reinez had fought thousands of them. Savage orks. Heathen eldar. The robotic constructs of dead empires, mindless hordes of ravenous aliens, the dead come back to life, Emperor-fearing citizens seduced into rebellion, the legions of Chaos itself, and more besides. He had come to recognise when a foe was something he couldn't face himself, a sixth sense that had kept him alive long enough to rise through the ranks of the Crimson Fists.

The sixth sense was screaming now. The thing that had killed Caltax paused for a fraction of a second and Reinez took that time to evaluate it as an opponent. From the waist down it was a Space Marine, in the purple of the Chaos Marines now sheened with blood.

But its upper half was different. Its torso was so packed with muscle it seemed about to burst, and its skin was so pale and translucent that Reinez could see the thick bundles of muscle and white tendons bunching up beneath. The skin was covered in threadlike white scars, thin and neat enough to mark the surgical implants that turned a recruit into a Marine. But if this thing had once been a Marine it wasn't any more – its head turned towards Reinez and all the Crimson Fist could see in that face was hate. The eyes were black pearls staring from between strands of unkempt black hair, the teeth bared and bestial.

Reinez barely had to think it and his bolter hand squeezed the trigger, pumping two shots into the Chaos Marine. There was no blood, just puckered white wounds appearing in the skin. The flesh flowed around them, sealing off the wounds as if they had never been there.

Mutant. A powerful one – fast, strong, and bullet-proof. The only way to kill it was to tear it apart piece by piece, and Reinez didn't know if he could do that.

The Chaos Marine charged. Reinez saw its weapons were not swords it held, but chainblades jutting directly into the severed stumps of its wrists. It had no hands, because it didn't need them – it existed to kill.

Reinez put everything he had behind his thunder hammer, swinging it low into the Marine's unarmoured midriff. The Marine twisted as it ran, moving out of the arc of the hammer's head. One blade speared towards Reinez's face and Reinez, dropping his bolt pistol, dropped to one knee and grabbed the Marine's bare arm.

His fingers sank into inhuman flesh that closed over them.

Reinez turned to match the momentum of the Chaos Marine, planting his foot on the floor and adding his own weight to the Marine's charge. The two careered headlong together, slamming into the stone wall of the belfry.

Reinez couldn't defeat this enemy. Everything he had learned in decades of service had told him that. But he could kill it, if he paid a high enough price .

Reinez felt them smash into the wall and keep going, the stone blocks ripped out of the wall before them. The light that swept over him was the dawn light of Entymion IV – they were several floors up, just empty air between them and the ground.

The south-eastern gate whirled around Reinez as he tumbled downwards with his enemy.

A broad avenue ran between the two gatehouses, one of which was taken up by the gate chapel. Statues of devout pilgrims and past aristocrats lined the avenue, figures rendered in multicoloured marble with details picked out in gilt. Down this avenue were advancing the Fornux Lix Fire Drakes, hundreds of men moving warily in their body armour and gas-helms, between rumbling Chimera APCs and Hellhound support tanks.

They knew that something was wrong. They had heard the storm of bolter fire. Some of them were even now scattering into cover, knowing that they might be next. Many of them turned and watched as Reinez and the Chaos Marine burst out through the wall of the gate chapel and tumbled the long drop to the ground.

Reinez clung to the Chaos Marine, feeling the muscle squirming beneath his gauntlet. This creature would die with him. No Space Marine feared death – but every one feared dying without doing their duty to the God-Emperor. Reinez inwardly rejoiced that he would not have a pointless, unsung death.

The dark green oblong of the Chimera whirled up towards him, and with a scream of torn metal Reinez and the Chaos Marine smashed into it like twin meteors.

Reinez's vision blurred and swam. He was in a deep sharp pit of shredded metal, the tall towers of the administration district swirling high above him. The pallid bulk of the Chaos Marine hauled itself over him, blocking out the blue-grey morning sky of Entymion IV.

The Chaos Marine looked down at Reinez. There was no soul in its eyes. It raised an arm above its head, ready to piston the long rusting chainblade down through Reinez's throat.

Reinez ripped his pistol hand free of the wreckage and emptied the magazine into the Chaos Marine. The shells ripped through it, tearing bloodless wounds so deep Reinez glimpsed lungs and veins pulsing before the wounds closed up. The Marine reeled, its weight falling back off Reinez.

The half-second it bought him was enough. Someone shouted an order and suddenly dozens of las-shots were slashing through the Marine, battering it back. It roared horribly and launched itself off Reinez, into the shelter of the wrecked Chimera.

Reinez tore himself free. His thunder hammer was still in his hand – its power field ripped through the torn metal and Reinez was free.

More las-fire. Thudding into the Chimera, splintering the stone of the chapel tower, fizzing trails of superheated air.

The Fire Drakes weren't just shooting at the Chaos Marine. They were firing everywhere, and that fire was answered from the tower blocks surrounding the Fire Drakes' entry point.

Reinez could see the enemy. They had infiltrated the tower blocks in their hundreds, firing from dozens of windows. They were tiny pale shapes – even from this distance Reinez thought they looked human. The fire was small arms – lasguns and autoguns, with a few heavy stubbers sending chains of fire rattling down. The Chaos Marine attack had been the first move in a massive counter-attack.

The gunfire was like hot, deadly rain. If the Crimson Fists had still held the chapel, Caltax's Devastator squad would have sent heavy weapons fire ripping through the administration towers. But the Fire Drakes were now trapped beneath the weight of enemy fire, pumping useless lasgun shots up at the windows.

Reinez saw a Hellhound's flamer tanks blow, swallowing up several men and an officer in a mushroom of flame. 'Scatter!' yelled Reinez at the Guardsmen, hauling himself out of the Chimera's wreckage. 'Get to cover! Now!'

The Fire Drakes nearby heard him, running heads down to take shelter behind statues or at the foot of buildings. There were bodies already scattered – flailing forms fell from windows where a lucky hit brought down an attacker. One landed wetly nearby and Reinez saw they were indeed human, naked to the waist, their faces wrapped in leather straps and their skin pierced all over.

Cultists. Heretics. The lost and the damned, beyond all hope. Which meant that there was no hope for Gravenhold, either.

The Chaos Marine reared up monstrously and lashed out, taking off a Guardsman's head and bisecting a second man. Reinez hefted his thunder hammer and prepared to die there, beating back the thing that could wreak bloody ruin through the Guardsmen.

He charged, and fell. Pain rifled through his body. His vision greyed out and he looked down to see a shredded mess of blood and ceramite where the armour around his foot had split – the adrenaline and combat hormones had blocked out the pain and he hadn't even noticed.

Reinez dragged himself towards the Chaos Marine, las-fire boring through the paving around him. The Chaos Marine was heading for the closest tower block – there were other Chaos Marines in the lower storeys, rattling bolter fire down at the Fire Drakes.

Reinez knew he wouldn't reach the Chaos Marine, but he had to keep going. Because this wasn't just another traitor to him, as foul as that was. This was something even worse.

Reinez recognised the golden chalice the Chaos Marines bore on their shoulder pads. He knew that purple and bone livery.

'I know what you are!' yelled Reinez, trying to prop himself up on his thunder hammer. 'I know! Traitors to the blood of Dorn! Excommunicate and damned!'

The Chaos Marine seemed to hear him. It looked round, once, but Reinez couldn't read the expression on its face. Then it was gone into the shadows of the nearest building, and a scattering of las-fire threw Reinez back onto his face.

Engines roared nearby. Tracks chewed into the paving slabs.

'Medic!' someone yelled. Hands reached down and Reinez felt himself hauled by several Guardsmen into the back of a Chimera, a medical officer with hands full of blood packs leaning over him.

'I don't need blood,' he said bitterly. 'Help your men.'

The medic, who had probably never seen a Space Marine before in the flesh, turned back to men moaning in the back of the Chimera. Reinez didn't need a medic, he had survived much worse. He would be back on his feet within the day with the attentions of a competent Apothecary. His pride was more injured than his body. He had been prepared to die, and he had failed. He had come face to face with the traitors who had left a stain on the name of Rogal Dorn himself, and they had escaped.

But he would redeem himself. Because as soon as he was back with his battle-brothers, he would contact the Chapter Master of the Crimson Fists and tell him that he had found the Soul Drinkers.

CHAPTER THREE

EIGHTY PER CENT of the Fornux Lix Fire Drakes made it out of the south-eastern gate, falling back in good order. They regrouped and by nightfall had counterattacked with armour and Hellhound flame support tanks, fighting bitterly through the lower floors of the closest tower blocks until they had a foothold just inside Gravenhold.

As the attack had got under way, the surviving Chaos Marines had melted away into the city, taking their dead and disappearing. As they were ordered to pull out of the chapel, the Crimson Fists reported the supposedly solid city wall that backed onto the chapel was riddled with a warren of tunnels. Before they left, the Fists used some of the Fire Drakes' demo charges to bring the whole gate chapel down, sealing off that avenue of attack. But they had killed only a handful of the traitors in the few minutes of the gunfight – the enemy had now melted back into the city, ready to burst out and strike at the invading Imperial forces.

Captain Reinez survived. While the Crimson Fists' Apothecary tended to him, he demanded a high-level astropath from Lord General Xarius and got it. He sent an astropathic message to the Crimson Fists' Chapter Master on the Chapter fleet several sectors away, and informed him that the Soul Drinkers were in Gravenhold. Shortly afterwards Reinez ordered his remaining Marines to withdraw from Gravenhold to the Fists' command post south of the city, and to await further orders.

The Seleucaian Fourth Division's drive into the west of the city went better, at first. Even as the enemy were turning the canyons of tower blocks into a killing zone for the Fire Drakes, the Seleucaians moved in rapid order through the massive landing decks and maintenance sheds of the city's spaceport. Access to the city was through a series of huge arches cut into the wall, leading to the dark industrial mill district crowded into the eastern edge of Gravenhold. Xarius's own Baneblade super-heavy tank formed a command post in the centre of the Seleucaians, and from its heavily armoured interior Xarius listened to the desperate reports from the south-eastern gate as his own side of the pincer rolled rapidly through the abandoned spaceport unopposed.

The enemy were behind them. The fuel sumps had been drained and, risking the suffocating and flammable fumes, the Gravenholders erupted from beneath the ground to swarm over the rear echelon elements following the main body of Guardsmen into the city. Medical units, artillery, half-tracks loaded with ammunition, fuel and food, the small Adepta Sororitas preceptory that administered to the division's spiritual health – they fought a savage close-quarters battle they were ill-equipped for.

Xarius turned the formation around to strike back but by then all order was gone. The tanks at the forefront were held up by the infantry that had been marching behind them. The heavy guns were useless with so many Imperial units mixed up in the melee. Somehow, Xarius forged a meaningful counterattack from the chaos and sent several thousand men and scores of tanks rolling into the enemy.

But the damage was done. The Seleucaians won back uncontested landing pads streaked with blood and burning vehicle sheds draped with the bodies of their support units. The enemy left their dead and headed back underground. Xarius forbade reprisal attacks down the miles of filthy fuel tunnels. Those who disobeyed never returned, many drowned or incinerated when the tunnels were flooded again.

The Seleucaian thrust never got into the city. Night fell over the spaceport on the first day, Entymion IV's evening sun reflecting off the sheen of clotting blood that marked where the enemy had torn Sisters Hospitaller and divisional file clerks apart in the melee. There were hundreds of the enemy dead, but no one had any illusions that there weren't plenty more where they had come from.

THE ENEMY. WHEN the stream of wounded finally ran drier, divisional medics received some relatively intact corpses to examine. Xarius himself made sure he was present, the dissections carried out in the shadow of his Baneblade.

Beneath powerful arc-lights the enemy was revealed.
It was quickly established that they were human. They
seemed heavily worked and borderline malnourished,
their skin was pale from a lack of light suggesting an
almost completely underground or nocturnal existence. The faces of some were wrapped in thick metal
straps buckled around their heads, others were so covered in self-inflicted scars that they formed masks of
scab tissue. A couple had the skin of the face entirely
removed – the more extreme mutilations should have
led to rapid sickness and death, but these had survived.

Their bodies were scarred, too. Most were pierced.
Some had evidently carved messages into themselves,
either in too eccentric a hand to read or in a language
foreign even to the Sister Dialogus who was brought in
from the survivors of the preceptory.

The dissection continued and the evidence mounted.
The enemy had enlarged hearts or apparently superflu-
ous organs grafted into them. Many had been
repeatedly cut open and sewn back together with crude,
almost frenzied stitches.

But they had survived. They should have been killed
by whatever procedures they had suffered, yet these
men and women had survived long enough to die
beneath the lasguns and tank tracks of the Seleucaian
Fourth Division.

The weapons were mostly the expected mix of lasguns and autoweapons looted from the Planetary
Defence Force supplies, with a few hunting rifles and
other aristocratic pieces thrown in. But there were
some of apparently xenos design, too – some kind of
rifle made of irregularly-shaped material like hardened
black glass, that fired streams of razor-sharp crystal

shards. A stubby bulbous weapon that looked somehow organic, which shot bolts of blackness that
burned through armour. Some of the rebels had glossy
black armour plates, like segments of beetles' cara-
paces, fused with their skin.

Aliens, the rumours had said. Some kind of corruptive xenos influence had taken hold of Gravenhold. It
was clear by now that the enemy was the one-time
population of the city and that they had sunk far too
deep to ever redeem themselves. There were even
reports of Traitor Marines from the Fire Drakes, but
inevitably no bodies had been recovered to confirm
them. Xarius watched the gruesome dissection silently
as the divisional medicae peeled back the layers of
horror, and thought how the enemy must have been
begging their gods for him to send in spearheads of
Guardsmen for them to ambush.

But Reinhardt Xarius had been an Imperial soldier
for his entire life and a commander for most of it. He
knew exactly what advantage the Imperium had. They
had determination, tenacity, bravery and above all,
numbers. He spent the rest of the night working out
defensive strategies for the troops camped in the spaceport and the south-eastern gate, but he knew that the
next day his first task would be to demand all the sector authorities send him every reinforcement they
could.

The enemy knew the city, and the Guard would have
to kill every single one of them to winkle them out.
But the Imperium's crucial advantage was that they
could muster enough Guardsmen and tanks to do
exactly that.

* * *

WHEN THE PLANET Veyna was annexed by the Imperium in 068.M41, it was a Halo Zone world marked out only by the lakes of liquid nitrogen at its polar caps and the small civilisation that clung to survival near the equator. These people were the descendants of settlers from the Scattering, the great drive of colonisation that seeded the galaxy with humanity after the discovery of warp travel. Veyna was one of the many worlds that had been forgotten for thousands of years, cut off by the Age of Strife and bypassed by the Great Crusade, only to be rediscovered in the second half of the forty-first millennium.

There were hundreds of worlds like Veyna. Most of them never even had names. Isolated and backwards, feudal or blackpowder-level worlds, gradually drawn back into the fold by the ravenous Imperium that considered itself to own every community of humans in the Galaxy – including those they hadn't discovered yet. Normally Veyna would be given an Imperial designation and perhaps a handful of hardy activists from the Missionaria Galaxia to convert the heathens, and then left alone aside from the occasional tithe demands from the Administratum. The Imperium would add a handful of new citizens to the immense population labouring and fighting under the aegis of the Emperor, and the people of Veyna would have been granted theoretical protection against the many ravening forces that might creep across the galaxy to consume them.

But Veyna had its polar caps. It was cheaper to ship pure liquid nitrogen from Veyna's polar lakes than to manufacture it, and so Veyna's only natural resource was quickly claimed by the Adeptus Mechanicus for the factoria on its forge-worlds.

The only habitable land was earmarked for the great processing plants and spaceport that the Mechanicus would need to take their harvest from Veyna. The natives were displaced, offered one-way passage to the closest forge-world where they would live short but productive lives in the lightless workshops and factory floors. Slow death in the name of the Emperor beckoned them, and they were assured by the missionaries that they would do better to die young for the Lord of Mankind than to die old heretics.

Most believed them and the civilisation of Veyna disappeared overnight, herded into the bellies of Mechanicus cargo ships. Many survived the trip only to die in industrial accidents or simply get so ground down by the unrelenting toil until it was difficult to tell the living from the dead. The last of them survived long enough to see the dregs from other worlds, more slaves in all but name, brought in to replace them at the machine face. Each one was just one more link in the endless chain of suffering that greased the wheels of the Imperium with the blood of the hopeless, and as they themselves prepared to die they longed for the brutal frozen haven of Veyna.

But some did not agree.

The hardiest and proudest of the Veynans survived out on the tundra, raiding and harassing the Adeptus Mechanicus garrison, sabotaging pipelines and space-craft before disappearing into the wilderness. Sporadic tech-guard patrols could do little against an enemy that could live off the tundra and disappear at will.

Within thirty years of the first shipment the polar lakes were drained and the Adeptus Mechanicus withdrew from Veyna. The only survivors of the once-proud Veynan civilisation were by then the

dwindling tundra raiders who saw their chance as the
Mechanicus evacuated their equipment and personnel. They stowed away on cargo ships and hijacked
shuttles, determined to take revenge on the Imperium
by attacking the valuable cargoes travelling the ill-
guarded space between outlying systems. The Veynans
would become pirates, waging a symbolic war to honour the memories of their dead.

The Mechanicus convinced the Imperial Navy to nip
this threat in the bud. The Imperium did not want one
more nest of pirates preying on vulnerable space traffic. A squadron of escorts was diverted to surround the
Mechanicus ships and destroy those Veynans who had
taken the crews hostage. The Navy offered an ultima-
tum. The Veynans could free their Mechanicus
hostages and abandon the ships they had taken, to be
taken into custody, given the opportunity to renounce
their sins in the sight of the Emperor, and be executed.
Otherwise, they would be blown out of space, hostages
and all.

The escorts had been about to open fire when the
Brokenback arrived.

THE TRANSPORT SHIP'S outer maintenance corridors
were as cold as the Veynan winter. Eumenes saw his
breath coiling in front of him as he clambered down
through the ragged metal hole bored by the boarding
pod and drew his bolt pistol.

He had braved those Veynan winters as a boy, all but
naked on the tundra. Now he had an enhanced metabolism and augmented organs so new he still ached
from the operations to implant them, and wore a carapace of padded semi-powered armour. Cold couldn't
kill him any more. It felt like nothing could.

Eumenes's enhanced vision picked out details from the darkness. Steel struts, heavy segmented pipes, spurts of coolant, the occasional inscription promising to honour the ship's machine-spirit if it kept working. One wall was the curved metal skin of the inner hull surface. The thrum of the ship's engines rumbled through everything.

'Squad Eumenes down,' voxed Eumenes, the feel of the vox-bead still unfamiliar in his throat. He had been trained with all this equipment over and over again but it was still relatively recently that he had taken up all the equipment and augmentations of the Space Marine he would one day become.

He would be a Soul Drinker. He had prayed for salvation from the souls of his dead ancestors on Veyna, and they had led the Soul Drinkers to him. He and the other scout-novices were recruited from those who had suffered at the hands of the Imperium, and none had a bigger grudge than Eumenes. One day, he would lead his excommunicate brothers against the darkness that grew from the Imperium like cancers in a sick body.

Eumenes had memorised the likely layout of the transport ship. Each ship was different but the transport was built around a plan that meant the differences would be minor. He heard the feet of his scout squad hitting the floor behind him and he began to lead them forward into the closest access duct.

'Selepus, get up here,' said Eumenes. 'I want you up front.'

Selepus, thin-faced and quick, was instantly at Eumenes's shoulder. 'If we get a contact, I'll keep it quiet.'

'Good man.'

Scamander, the Librarium novice, was last out of the boarding pod. Eumenes's six-man squad wore dark purple carapace armour over bone-coloured under-suits. Since they weren't physically full Space Marines they could not yet wear the armour of a full battle-brother, but it had its blessings – it meant they were smaller and quieter, perfect for sneaking into an enemy spacecraft.

The squad moved quickly and quietly through the inner hull skin and into the ship proper. Selepus was on point, his monomolecular fighting knife in his hand and his bolt pistol holstered. Selepus was more dangerous that way. Scamander brought up the rear. He was there in case the plan went wrong and they needed some psychic artillery.

The transport was cramped but well maintained. A niche in the wall held a libation of scented machine-oil and a prayer typed out in binary, forming a tiny shrine to the ship's machine-spirit. Selepus ducked around the corner up ahead, and waved the rest of the squad forward.

'Crew quarters ahead.'

Eumenes nodded, and the squad moved on.

The corridor opened into a low-ceiling room, parti-tioned by columns and low walls. It was divided into a kitchen and mess, dormitories with rows of bunks, a small shrine with a gilded icon of an Imperial saint, and an area with seating and a few books.

Selepus had killed the first contact before Eumenes even noticed him. It was a menial in grease-stained coveralls, with half of his head shaved and the other half covered in long braids. Hive gang stock probably, press-ganged or con-scripted into menial service. The man's head lolled back too far as Selepus drew his knife through his throat from behind – the menial had been sitting at one of the mess tables, eating a bowl of something grey and stringy.

Selepus lowered the body silently to the floor. The squad spread out through the crew quarters, Nisryus, Thersites and Tydeus flanking Scamander.

Once the sweep was done, Eumenes had the squad pause.

'Anything, Nisryus?'

Nisryus's own grudge with the Imperium was that it had murdered his family. Nisryus had narrowly avoided being burned at the stake, he had been the son of an aristocrat whose family hid the psyker-taint in their bloodline. Nisryus had watched his family scourged and burned alive. It was the Soul Drinkers's attack on the Sothelin prison world where the executions were held that saved him. The Soul Drinkers had drawn may recruits from the rebels held prisoner on Sothelin, and Nisryus was one of those who had proven able enough to take on the mantle of Chapter novice.

Nisryus closed his eyes. His precognitive powers were immature, but he was strong enough to use them without risk of corruption. His eyes were too old for his face, surrounded by crow's feet, and they wrinkled up as he concentrated.

'He'll think we're enemies,' said Nisryus. 'To him, everyone's an enemy.'

'And the crew?'

Nisryus shook his head. 'I can't see them. His presence blocks them all out.'

It made sense. From what Sarpedon had said, the strength of the captive's emotions had broadcast his location to the Librarium from several systems away. It was a miracle Nisryus could see anything at all.

Selepus indicated a narrow archway leading towards the stern. 'Cargo bay that way.'

'Let's go.'

BEFORE EUMENES'S TIME, when the Soul Drinkers still fought under the Imperial banner, the Great Harvest was held every decade to bring new recruits into the Chapter. Since the Chapter had been fleet-based, the Great Harvest saw them visiting scores of planets over the course of a year, picking a handful of the best and youngest warriors and running them through a brutal meat grinder of a selection process. Those the Chaplains selected as suitable were given endless psycho-doctrination sessions, surgical implants and enhancements, and intensive combat drills. They lived as novices, attending upon the Marines to forge respect for the soldiers they would one day become.

The Soul Drinkers had finally begun to arrest their genetic decline a little more than a year ago, and had restarted the Great Harvest to recover the losses they had suffered at the hands of both Chaos and the Imperium. The Chapter, now residing on the space hulk they had christened the *Brokenback*, travelled to worlds where rebellion had flared against Imperial repression. Their new recruits came from the ranks of those who had dared to stand against the Imperium, not because they thought they would win but because they valued their freedom more than their lives. They saved the best of them from corpse-strewn battlefields or Imperial prison ships, from desperate last stands and mass executions. Eumenes had been rescued from the last stand of the Veynan rebels, Nisryus from execution as a psyker-witch. Scamander had been saved from the duelling pits of Thrantis Minor where he had been sentenced to die in the arena for joining a movement in support of the planet's persecuted psykers. There were just over a hundred fighting novices in the Chapter now, and Master of Novices Karraidin had judged many of them ready to take up active duty alongside their battle-brothers.

They were not yet fully Space Marines – there were many more surgical adaptations to take place before then – but in a sense they never would be. The Soul Drinkers had spent almost all of their history as Imperial lapdogs and only the leadership of Sarpedon himself had brought them into the light. Sarpedon had decreed that the Chapter's novices would no longer undergo the rigorous psycho-doctrination that all Soul Drinkers before them had. The novices would fight as the Chapter's existing Marines did – because they were in a battle worth fighting, against the forces of Chaos instead of at the whim of the corrupt Imperium. Not because endless sleep-training had broken their free will.

The scouts were the future. There were only around four hundred Soul Drinkers left and the scout-novices would be the ones to repopulate their ranks. It was a new Chapter being born from the ashes of excommunication. An army of free men, fighting because it was right.

No wonder the Imperium feared them.

THE LAST FEW crewmen made their stand in the engine block.

The adept, on secondment from the Officio Medicae hospital on Diomedes Tertiam, clutched his slim black case to his chest with one hand while the other held a shaking laspistol. The case contained his medical implements with which he had been carrying out tests on the prisoner.

It was a fascinating subject, after all. But now all that was forgotten.

Most of the crew were probably dead. The bridge hadn't answered the ship's vox. The adept himself had seen some of the ship's crew lying with slit throats. He had seen one of the invaders – quick, shaven-headed and wearing heavy purple armour that didn't slow him down one bit, firing rapidly with a bolt pistol and blowing a menial's torso apart.

The adept and two of the ship's armsmen had fled here, to the engine block, where they had taken up a vantage point on the gantry halfway up one of the generatorium stacks. Even a small ship like this needed vast amounts of power for its sub-warp engines and the result was this cavernous space, dominated by the engine stacks. The vantage point was excellent; they could see across the oil-stained floor of the engine block below and the solid humming mass of the engine tower protected them from behind.

One armsman, an excellent shot who had sniped tharrbeasts for sport on the ash wastes of Diomedes Tertiam, scanned for targets, pulling back the hood of his pressure suit to get an unobstructed view through the sights of his long-las. The other armsman stuck close to the adept and racked the slide on his shotgun.

For a moment there was silence except from the adept's shuddering breath. They would be safe here – they had plenty of ammunition and no one could sneak up on them. The armsmen would protect their adept. It was their job. Whoever it was who had taken the ship, they would suffer when the ship's autopilot brought it to the orbital checkpoint where their prisoner was to be transferred out. The adept only had to survive for the half hour or so before that happened, then security troops would storm the ship and save him.

He was an old man. He wasn't supposed to do this kind of thing any more. But he felt the comforting weight of the laspistol in his hand. No one could get him here. The armsmen would die first. But it wouldn't come to that.

'Movement,' said the armsman with the rifle. 'I've got it...'

That was when the adept burst into flames.

SCAMANDER'S BLOOD RAN cold. It always did when he used the power the Emperor had given him. It took all the fire in his soul and siphoned it out into the outside world where it took the form of leaping flames that appeared as if from nowhere. But it had to come from somewhere – somewhere inside Scamander, in the depth of betrayal he had suffered. The Emperor had looked out from his Golden Throne and granted Scamander pyrokinetic powers with which to scourge the Emperor's enemies, and yet the Imperium had condemned Scamander, that same Imperium that claimed to do the Emperor's work.

He remembered that betrayal and let it flow from the depths of his soul and out through his outstretched fingers, through the air to the cluster of figures huddled on the gantry above.

Bright orange flame blossomed. A man screamed as his clothing suddenly caught fire. Scamander forced the fire out of himself, feeling a psychic cold like a spiral of ice coiling down through him. He played the fire across the other targets, too, a pair of armed crewmen. One of them had seen Scamander and had been preparing to shoot, but that only made the psychic path between him and Scamander shorter. The sniper spasmed as fire boiled up from inside his lungs – he flailed and toppled over the gantry rail, falling to the floor far below.

Scamander let the fire fall. His frozen breath glittered as he exhaled, crystals of ice were hard slivers in his mouth. He couldn't use his power for long periods of time yet, and would have to train long and hard to become living artillery on a par with Tyrendian.

With the psychic flame gone, the adept and the second armsman were wreathed in black smoke as the fire guttered. They were no longer screaming.

'Are they dead?' asked Thersites, who was hunkered down behind Scamander covering the approach behind them.

'Better check,' replied Scamander, panting with the effort. He was radiating cold.

Thersites nodded and hurried towards the stairway leading up to the gantry. A quick glance told him the armsman on the floor was very dead indeed – Scamander had felt the man die, his death a flicker of feedback as the flame coursed through him. The other two might need a bolt shell to be sure.

'Eumenes? We've got the last of them in the engine block. They're gone,' voxed Scamander.

'Understood. Get back to the engine block entrance and be ready to fall back to the pod. How are you?'

'It took a lot out of me. But Thersites is covering me.'

'You rely too much on your power, Scamander. There won't always be another scout there to back you up. It doesn't matter how many men you can burn, as long as it leaves you vulnerable you're better off shooting.'

'I have to learn, Eumenes…'

'And I have to lead. The galaxy hates us enough without you knocking yourself out trying to incinerate everything.'

'Of course. Of course you're right.'

'Good. Stick to your gun except in extremis. Now get back to the pod, we're entering the cargo hold.'

No wonder Nisryus had been all but blinded. Eumenes didn't have his fellow scout's precognition, but even he could feel the force of raw emotion that bled out of the captive.

The cargo hold was mostly empty, with a few crates and void-boxes piled up against the walls to leave a single wide space. In the centre of that space was a metal frame, evidently purpose-built to hold an oversized human figure spreadeagled, angled forward so it was forced to stare at the floor. A block of steps led up to a pulpit overlooking the prisoner's back. Several jointed armatures reached out from the pulpit, each tipped with a syringe or scalpel.

The captive was two and a half metres high. He was stripped naked and his body was so crammed with muscle that it seemed ready to burst. Dark grey oblongs under the skin of the pectorals and abdomen marked where the black carapace had been implanted, and neuro-jack sockets in the biceps and chest once linked the captive's nervous system to his power armour.

His torso was covered in scars. Many were thin white surgical scars, showing where organs had been implanted or internal injuries had been healed at the

Chapter apothecarion. Others were thick wounds, many recent, plastered over with the fast-forming scab that resulted from a Space Marine's augmented blood. Other, fresher surgical scars covered his back – the crew had been busy taking samples and testing the captive's metabolism to see if he really was who they thought he was.

A Space Marine. A soldier of the Adeptus Astartes, one of the legendary giants of the battlefield that every Imperial citizen had heard of but so few had ever seen. They were the stuff of stories, the fabric of the Imperium's legends, and now there was one here, mad and captive.

But more than that. The prisoner was that rarest of creatures – a renegade Marine, one that had broken his psycho-doctrination to rebel against the Imperium itself. A Soul Drinker.

A Soul Drinker gone mad.

The prisoner looked up. A rope of spittle hung from his lower lip. His eyes looked heavy and exhausted. But as soon as he saw Eumenes crossing the cargo bay towards him something woke up inside him. Eumenes saw the Marine's hair, once shorn close, was growing out – sweat and grime had turned it into rat's tails. He was unshaven, too.

He growled and the frame shook as he tried to break free. Runnels of dried blood crusted the manacles around his wrists and ankles.

'Brother,' said Eumenes carefully. 'We have come to take you back.'

The rage in the Marine's eyes died for a moment. 'I have no brothers,' he said.

Eumenes had not seen the battle on Stratix Luminae. That had been before he and the other novices were recruited. But he had heard that it was terrible indeed, and at its climax the Soul Drinkers had been forced to leave behind more than thirty Assault Marines under Sergeant Tellos. Tellos, they said, had gone mad in the battle, and he had taken with him the Assault Marines who had chosen to follow him.

The Chapter had known better than to assume Tellos and his battle-brothers had died. But it was still a shock when the scattered reports of renegade Marines from across the Imperium, filtered through the many cogitators on the *Brokenback*, had indicated that Tellos was not just alive but possessed of a mindless lust for destruction. He and his Assault Marines had blazed a path of destruction, indiscriminate and pointless, raiding Imperial settlements and killing anyone they found. On Diomedes Tertiam one of them had been captured and that Marine was here, being transported to the system's prison planet.

But he would never get there. Sarpedon needed him, because he might know where Tellos was headed next.

'Nisryus,' said Eumenes. 'Is there a Marine in him somewhere?'

Nisryus walked forward carefully. The Marine looked at him with undisguised hate. Nisryus held out a hand, gingerly probing the emotion that saturated the cargo bay. Those emotions echoed backwards as well as forwards, giving Nisryus limited precognitive powers – here, they were strong enough to hint at the mental landscape hidden within the Marine's madness.

'Just,' said Nisryus.

'Good. Selepus, Tydeus, unclamp the frame and take it back to the pod. We need to be out of here before the checkpoint.' Eumenes flicked on the vox. 'Scamander, Thersites, get back to the pod. We're done.'

Soon the scouts would be gone and the ship would be devoid of life when it was recovered. The system authorities would believe that their prisoner had escaped and killed the crew, before disappearing. They would scour the nearby intrasystem space for a saviour pod or shuttle that the prisoner might have used to escape. They would, of course, never find him.

The lost battle-brother would not be broken for the good of a corrupt Imperium. Instead, he had an appointment with his Chapter Master.

CHAPTER FOUR

SARPEDON LOOKED ACROSS at Brother Lothas. He was reminded that all the Soul Drinkers had very nearly fallen as far as Lothas, and Sarpedon had led them to that brink.

Lothas had been sedated and taken to the apothecarion, located inside a hospital ship that made up part of the *Brokenback*'s immense bulk. His wounds had been healed and he had been cleaned up, but he still looked every inch the monster Eumenes had found. Unbound but separated from Sarpedon by a near-invisible power field that crossed the interrogation cell, Lothas almost vibrated with pent-up energy.

Sarpedon was alone in his half of the cell, but he knew that Chaplain Iktinos and other senior Soul Drinkers were watching. Lothas didn't know that, however. Sarpedon wanted this to be man to man, a soldier to his commander, face to face.

'I have seen the records of your service with the Chapter,' said Sarpedon. 'Eleven years as a son of the Emperor. Assault honours at Diocletian Dock. Purity Seal granted after the Quintam Minor. Sergeant Grae-vus recommended you as leadership material after the Chapter War.'

Lothas spat into the power field, which flashed slightly and fizzed. Sarpedon ignored it.

'It is said that Tellos valued you very highly.'

Lothas paused at that. Tellos, the most severely mutated of the Soul Drinkers except perhaps Sarpedon himself, had been a heroic and skilled Assault Sergeant before the Chapter's downfall and a talismanic, seem-ingly unkillable soldier after it. Assault Marines who had lost their sergeants had often chosen to follow Tel-los into battle, he was a symbol of the Soul Drinkers' triumph over corruption and perhaps the most natu-rally gifted warrior the Chapter had. Lothas had probably all but worshipped the man.

Then, on Stratix Luminae, Tellos and his Assault Marines had gone insane.

'Is Tellos still alive?'

Lothas clenched and unclenched his fists. His desire to break through the power field and strangle Sarpe-don was palpable. 'Tellos can't be killed,' he growled.

'Was he with you on Diomedes Hive Prime?'

'Ha! If he had there wouldn't be a Hive Prime! We are the seeds of destruction. We are the new scourge. Some of us he scattered. Some of us still follow him.'

'Why follow him? Why not return to your Chapter?'

'Because you were weak!' Lothas lunged forward and punched the power field, sending out a red flash and a spray of orange sparks. The field was configured to administer a neural shock on contact but Lothas's enhanced metabolism shrugged it off, he hardly seemed to notice.

Sarpedon was physically stronger than perhaps any of the Soul Drinkers, a legacy of Abraxes's mutations. Presumably the weakness Lothas mentioned was mental. 'What could Tellos do, Lothas, that we cannot?'

Lothas sneered. 'He could see beyond. There are billions of vermin in this galaxy wasting their lives fighting for an empire that doesn't care about them. Do you think you are any different? What can you do? You are fighting a war you can never win, as if you could destroy Chaos, cleanse the galaxy, with four hundred mutants and a space hulk!'

Sarpedon knew it would do no good to argue with Lothas. He wanted the man to rant at him to tell Sarpedon everything that was bubbling over in his mind. 'So why does Tellos fight?' he said calmly.

Lothas barely needed prompting. His eyes were afire like a preacher's. 'To fight! Because there is no right and wrong, there is no freedom, there is no Emperor's light! The only meaning in life is to leave a scar on the galaxy that will never heal. In the moment of destruction is exultation, and Tellos taught us to make that moment last forever.'

Sarpedon leaned forward, one bionic leg clicking on the pitted metal floor. 'Pure destruction. Nothing else.'

'Pure,' said Lothas. 'True purity. None of the excuses, none of the limitations. These are the things that make you weak. Everything you could be is bound up in this crusade that you cling to.'

Sarpedon guessed that Lothas was repeating Tellos's own words. Lothas had no will left of his own, only the seeds planted there by Tellos after Stratix Luminae.

Perhaps he had been corrupting them even before that, on the *Brokenback*, under Sarpedon's nose.

'But it will have to end, Lothas. Everyone dies eventually.'

Lothas shook his head, smiling grimly, revealing broken teeth. 'No, Sarpedon. The bigger the scar, the longer you live. And Tellos will live forever, because after Entymion there will be no greater scar.'

Sarpedon leaned back on his hind legs. 'Is that all you see? Purposeless destruction?'

'I see you lying to yourselves. You will die as if you were never here while we will let the galaxy burn. I see a universe so drowned in blood that it will never forget us. Blood, Sarpedon. Blood for the Blood God.'

Sarpedon rapped sharply on the door behind him. He could hear Lothas's breathing, heavy and deliberate, as the door ground open and Sarpedon walked on his eight clacking talons out into the corridor beyond.

The cell was located in the belly of an Imperial battleship, an old mark that had seen service well before the Gothic War. The black iron formed an oppressive vaulted ceiling and false columns down the walls. Dozens of brig cells led off on each side – a ship this size might have had twenty thousand crew, with its own criminals, police force and prison. With the addition of the power fields set up by Techmarine Varuk, it was secure enough to hold a Space Marine.

Chaplain Iktinos, as normal wearing full armour and skull-faced helmet, was standing just outside the door. The door clanged shut behind Sarpedon.

'He's gone,' said Iktinos.

'But Tellos might not be. We have a name: Entymion. Probably a place, maybe a person.' Sarpedon thought about the immense size of the Imperium and the difficulty of finding out what one word meant amongst those thousands of worlds and trillions of people. 'I'll put Techmarine Varuk on it.'

'If only we still had Solun,' said Iktinos.

Solun had been a specialist in information. The mem-banks implanted in his armour had given him a formidable capacity for processing information. He was dead now, left beneath the surface of Stratix Luminae.

'What about Brother Lothas?' Iktinos's voice was grave. He already knew the answer.

'Shoot him,' said Sarpedon. 'Incinerate the body.'

Iktinos turned aside and Sarpedon heard him voxing Sergeant Locano, whose Marines would function as a firing squad. It was Iktinos's duty to administer the final rites to a condemned battle-brother, not that Lothas would appreciate it.

Yet again a battle-brother would die a death that had nothing to do with the Emperor's will. Sarpedon had lost too many that way already. It was time to lead his Marines into a fight that meant more than survival.

Tellos was a force for Chaos now. The Soul Drinkers had created him, they would bring him back, or they would destroy him trying.

'This is Wing Epsilon out of the *Resolve*, reporting on G-Day plus seven.' The voice was weary, vox-echoed from some flight officer who had badly needed sleep after a long, hard sortie. 'Seven Marauder fighter-bombers with three Thunderbolts flying cover approached Gravenhold from the south-east and broached enemy airspace in good order. Anti-aircraft fire was sporadic until within one point five kilometres of the target, when flak-batteries of the same pattern

Ben Counter

assigned to the Entymion IV PDF opened fire. Thunderbolt Epsilon-Red suffered minor flak damage. Marauder Epsilon-Green suffered the loss of the starboard waist gun and two crew casualties.'

There was a pause, perhaps as the officer remembered the dead and wounded. 'The target co-ordinates were for Gravenhold's sporting arena. The target was well-lit by tracer bombs and clearly visible amongst the surrounding buildings. Marauder Epsilon-White began the bombing run. Epsilon-White's radio transmissions became erratic. Epislon-White overshot the target and Epsilon-Green took the point for the bombing run before suffering heavy damage from Epsilon-White's tail armaments.'

Another pause. The officer took a couple of breaths. 'Epsilon-Green was lost with all hands. The Marauders Epsilon-Blue, Black and Grey began transmitting erratically. As squadron commander I ordered all craft to withdraw from the target area and return to the *Resolve's* ground base. Only Thunderbolt Epsilon-Red and the Marauders Orange and Indigo responded to this order. Um... I was on Epsilon-Indigo. The... the transmissions... I considered the transmissions coming from the rest of the squadron to constitute a moral threat. I... I lost control of Epsilon-Indigo. When I returned... when I regained control the Marauder was over the north of the city. Its bomb load had been dropped, I don't know where. Crewman Trevso was still alive, I think I had, um, executed the other four, or perhaps they had turned on one another, I don't know... Trevso and myself turned Epsilon-Indigo back towards the ground base. There was no further anti-aircraft fire and we landed successfully. Crewman Trevso and myself were separated upon landing and taken to separate monitored medicae-cells where I was asked to make this report. I haven't seen Trevso and I don't think the rest of the squadron came back...'

Lord General Xarius flicked off the recording. He had heard enough. The same kind of thing was happening all over Gravenhold. The place was crawling with moral threats. He leaned back in his chair, wishing there was enough room in the sunken command office to stretch out in. He was an old man now, he needed to get out and stretch his legs.

The inside of Xarius's Baneblade was plush compared to a front-line tank, but it was still cramped. Gunners sat in cradle-seats, suspended almost upside-down, thick cables running from their skulls into machine-spirit ports. The Baneblade's enginseer stood at the command pulpit, the thin metal tines that had replaced his fingers working on the keyslate in front of him as he adjusted the tank's systems and typed binary prayers to the Machine God. Xarius's flag-commander Hasdrubal was near the Baneblade's brutal sloping prow, watching the pict-screens that formed the eyes of the super-heavy tank. The flag-commander was a man perfectly suited to his job, good at repeating Xarius's orders in an ear-splitting yell and filling in the gaps with his own common sense. Servitors hung in two rows, massive bronze-cased arms contrasting with their grey dead flesh. They were still now, but when the Baneblade was in combat they would haul the massive shells into the breech of the tank's forward gun. Up in the turret, perched on top of the Baneblade, more gunners and loader-servitors waited for the next time Xarius ordered the tank to move.

Right now it was still parked in Gravenhold's space-port. It was comparatively safe there, since the makeshift mortars that the enemy sometimes fired from the eastern wall could not penetrate the Baneblade's massively thick armour.

Gravenhold. Xarius would have to take every stone of the city the hard way. After the initial thrusts on the city had been repulsed, he had asked for reinforcements and got them: fighter and bomber wings from the naval cruiser *Resolve*, the reserve elements of the Fornux Lix Fire Drakes, and the Algorathi Janissaries to reinforce the Seleucaians in the west of the city. But they weren't enough to break into the city and crack open the hard core of rebel resistance. Armoured thrusts were surrounded and cut off, infantry assaults charged only into empty buildings while their flanks and rear echelons were swamped by cultists. The Naval bombing runs were supposed to have reduced the enemy strongholds to rubble, but they had found it hard to pin down the enemy, even when warpcraft was not ripping the minds out of their crews.

Emperor's teeth, they didn't even know what they were fighting! The Seleucaians had been grinding slowly through the industrial sector in the west of the city and many men were swearing that they has fought xenos there – probably eldar, maybe something else, highly-trained and lethal. The human enemies, on the other hand, fought in desperate hordes, and the priests who heard the Guardsmen's confessions had reported to Xarius that the hand of the dark gods was laid heavy on Gravenhold. There were even Traitor Marines in their somewhere, waiting to launch terror strikes the moment the Guardsmen got too deep into the city. The enemy, whatever they were, had the run of the city and knew it inside-out to the extent that they could appear and disappear at will, laying ambushes and confounding Imperial patrols.

Chaos. Chaos and aliens. Xarius shook his head and tried to remember the many enemies of both that he had fought. Aliens were lying and devious, Chaos was abominable and destructive. Sometimes, Xarius thought he would give anything for an honest enemy.

Nothing in Gravenhold made sense. Whatever was killing his men in the massive ugly mills, or forcing the Fire Drakes to buy every inch of the south-eastern district in blood, it wasn't made up of the rebels and degenerates Xarius had fought so often. Something very, very terrible had happened to the city and Xarius had only just scratched the surface of it. There were hints of it in the battlefield reports he had piled up on the desk that took up much of his command office – the statements from soldiers who had fought super-fast xenos killers or mind-warping heretic sorcerers. Amongst them was an old archaeological intelligence report that suggested Gravenhold's supposedly solid outer walls were actually honeycombed with thousands of cramped tunnels. The same report had conjectured that Gravenhold was built on the site of several pre-imperial settlements. Emperor only knew what was lying under the streets, and how the enemy was using it to avoid the Naval and artillery strikes that should have pounded them into submission.

'Lord general?' Flag-commander Hasdrubal looked down into Xarius's command office. His voice was clipped and nasal, typical of the sleep-taught diction of the Seleucaian officer class.

'Hasdrubal. What is it?'

'Developments at the south-eastern gate, sir.'

'Are the buggers counterattacking?'

'It's not the enemy, sir. We've got it on the holo.'

Xarius grunted in annoyance and switched on the tactical holomat, which unfolded from a brass-cased console like a metallic flower. The old machine shuddered and a flickering three-dimensional map of Gravenhold appeared in the air. Xarius oriented it so it was lying on one edge and he could see the whole plan of the city. He noted the arena, surrounded by the southern hovels and stubbornly still standing after the destruction of Squadron Epsilon. Enemy contacts were sinister yellow triangles, covering the industrial and administration sectors. Massive swathes of the north and centre of the city hadn't even been touched by Imperial forces, and the map was infuriatingly featureless in those areas.

Xarius spotted the new development straight away. 'What are these?' he said, pointing to a cluster of dark blue squares that had appeared just outside the south-eastern gate, forming an island in the Fire Drakes' rearward supply areas.

'That's the thing, sir,' said Hasdrubal with a smile. 'They're Thunderhawks.'

COMMANDER REINEZ WATCHED the Thunderhawk gunship descend, its downthrust throwing up a wall of dust and debris off the hastily-cleared landing zone, battering the barracks tents and medical posts of the Fornux Lix regiments. The Thunderhawk was painted in the dark blue and crimson livery of the Crimson Fists, and bore the personal heraldry of the Chapter Master himself.

Reinez's squad stood to attention. Four of them had been lost in the Soul Drinkers' attack – Caltax's squad had suffered worse, including the death of Caltax himself. Sergeant Althaz's squad had held the lower floors bravely but had still lost two Marines. Reinez and the six surviving Marines of his squad saluted as the Thunderhawk touched down, joining the four others that had already made landfall, and the deployment ramp ground open.

Chaplain Inhuaca stamped down the ramp, black armour polished and gleaming, the silver skull of his helmet face mirror-bright. The dark red tabard over his armour matched the traditional red gauntlet of the Crimson Fists and at his waist hung the crozius arcanum, an eagle-topped icon that served as both weapon and badge of office. Censers mounted on Inhuaca's backpack released strong, spicy incense that cut through even the swirling dust of the Thunderhawk's landing. A pair of servitors tramped along behind Inhuaca bearing two banners, one was Inhuaca's personal heraldry, and the other was that of the Chapter Master. Inhuaca's banner showed a skull burning with silver flames, over a field shaped like a gauntlet to symbolise the hand of Rogal Dorn that was recovered after his death. The Chapter Master's heraldry was the red gauntlet with laurel wreath that had been carried by successive Chapter Masters for three thousand years.

Inhuaca's squad followed him. They were Tactical Marines with dark red robes over their armour – veteran battle-brothers who had been inducted into the Chaplain's seminary, and from whom would eventually be chosen a successor to take up the crozius when Inhuaca was gone.

'Commander,' said Inhuaca, his voice steely and stern through the rictus of his skull-mask. 'Well met.'

Reinez inclined his head respectfully. Inhuaca was a senior member of the Chapter, and this day he carried the authority of the Chapter Master with him. 'Well met, Chaplain. I think Entymion IV could do with some spiritual strength.'

'The Chapter Master was most concerned with your report. He asked me to confirm it with my own eyes.'

'Of course.' Reinez turned to his squad, still at attention behind him. 'Paclo!'

Brother Paclo picked up the ammunition crate at his feet and walked up front. Reinez opened the crate and took out the item inside.

He held it up for Inhuaca to see. The Chaplain inspected it for a few moments, no emotion visible through the opaque green eyepieces of his skull-mask.

It was a shoulder pad, ripped from a suit of power armour. The purple ceramite was chipped and bullet-scarred, but there was no mistaking the symbol painted onto it. The golden chalice of the Soul Drinkers.

'Then it is true,' said Inhuaca at length. 'The blood of Dorn itself has become corrupted.'

'Mutants and traitors, Chaplain,' said Reinez. 'I saw them with my own eyes.'

'And you will have your chance to avenge the honour of Rogal Dorn, commander.' Inhuaca took a rolled parchment from his robes and handed it to Reinez, it bore the Chapter Master's seal in crimson wax.

Reinez unrolled it and read quickly.

'The Chapter's instructions are simple,' said Inhuaca as Reinez read. 'You have the second battle company along with myself, armour and support units. Your mission is to locate the Soul Drinkers in Gravenhold, cripple them and prevent their escape from Entymion

IV. If he is here, you are to bring back the head of Senior Librarian Sarpedon.'

'The second company? But what of Captain Cazaquez?'

'The Chapter Master decreed that as the first to face this enemy you were best to preside over their destruction. Captain Cazaques is agreed upon this and relinquished command of the second company. I and my retinue shall act in the Chapter Master's stead regarding the interpretation of his orders but shall defer to your command in all other things. This is the will of the Chapter. The blood of Dorn must be made pure, commander.'

Reinez kneeled, as he would before the Chapter Master himself. The servo-assisted brace encasing his wounded foot whirred to compensate, reminding him that in the moment of retribution he had been found wanting. With a whole company under his command, he would not fail like that again. 'By my honour as an Astartes and an inheritor of Rogal Dorn, I submit to my Chapter Master and am bound to the will of the Crimson Fists,' said Reinez, following a traditional Chapter form.

'Good. Arise, commander, I am under your orders now.'

Reinez was under no illusions as to how important his task was. The Crimson Fists were still rebuilding themselves after the disaster that had destroyed their fortress-monastery on Rynn's World, and were barely above half their peak strength. The second company, a flexible battle-company with a hundred Marines and enough firepower and expertise to equal ten times that number of Guardsmen, represented an enormous slice of the Chapter's fighting strength.

But it made sense. Reinez had felt it when he first saw that golden chalice on the shoulder pads of traitors, and he still felt it now; the Soul Drinkers were an abomination in the face of Rogal Dorn. Their continued existence prejudiced the Crimson Fists' place as defenders of the Imperium as much as the Rynn's World disaster had done. Every moment the Soul Drinkers abused Rogal Dorn's legacy was a moment of defeat for all Dorn's sons.

No doubt the other Chapters that bore Rogal Dorn's geneseed – the Imperial Fists, the Black Templars – would have felt the same. At full strength and with the backing and respect of the Adeptus Terra, they probably would have believed they were the proper choice to act as executioners in Dorn's name. But they were not here. The Crimson Fists were, Reinez was, and it was a responsibility he welcomed.

'Your first task,' said Reinez, 'will be to assemble the battle-brothers and ensure they understand the nature of this enemy and moral threat it poses. You can speak to their souls as I cannot.'

Inhuaca inclined his head in acceptance. 'And you, commander?'

'The Soul Drinkers deserted the Imperium in their entirety and they may have more than one company at their disposal. I am going to secure us some allies.'

THE SELEUCAIAN REINFORCEMENTS had included, at Lord General Xarius's specific request, a great deal of armour. Demolisher siege tanks for turning Gravenhold's picturesque architecture to rubble, Basilisks and Griffons to shell anything that looked suspicious, Hellhound infantry support tanks to fill streets and alleyways with burning promethium. Xarius's battle plans called for plenty of tanks, even hard-bitten, heretics thought twice about fighting on when faced with las-proof armoured hulls and saw their comrades crushed beneath rumbling tracks. But while a soldier could scavenge food and ammo from the battlefield, and even fight on with a bayonet if it suited the Emperor's will, a tank could not drive on unsupported.

The coming drive into Gravenhold needed fuel and ammunition. It needed spare parts. The most valuable part of the force's Naval component wasn't the *Resolve* or its Marauder fighter-bomber squadrons, it was the dozens of supply ships. Fuel landers disgorged bellies full of promethium into hungry tanks, armoury shuttles dropped off loads of Griffon shells and lascannon batteries. Xarius knew, as all the best commanders did, that an army starved of support was just a herd of helpless men at the mercy of the Emperor's enemies.

Most of the craft made landfall at the Imperial-held spaceport, where the rearward elements of the Seleucaians and the newly-arrived Algorathi Janissaries bullied Officio Munitorum adepts over who got which crates of ammunition, rations and medical supplies. A few landed to service the Fornux Lix Fire Drakes, although that particular regiment was known for its self-sufficiency and ability to do with men what most regiments had to do with tanks. Some wounded officers left on the support craft, heading up to the medical suites up on the *Resolve* where the conflict had yet to reach, although most wounded men had to make do with the casualty posts manned by regimental medics and Sisters Hospitaller.

Just after midnight, a few minutes into G-Day plus eleven, two fuel transports went off-course and veered eastwards, away from the spaceport and over the stony mass of Gravenhold. It wasn't the first time – some transports had been lost to the warpcraft that had so confounded the Marauder squadrons, others to old-fashioned malfunctions or human errors as there were in every war.

No one, including Lord General Xarius, thought much of it. The Officio Munitorum factored in such losses: a few aircraft, a tanker full of promethium, a spacecraft that was mass-produced on a dozen forge-worlds. No great loss.

Except they were not lost. Over the centre of Gravenhold, in the very shadow of the senate-house, the two wayward craft came in to land.

TECHMARINE VARUK PRESSED his bolt pistol hard against the side of the pilot's head.

'There,' he said coldly. The mechanical servo-arm attached to the backpack of his power armour pointed at the wide avenue beneath the ship, between the senate-house. 'Land us there.'

The terrified pilot shakily brought the lander down between rows of buildings that rose like marble cliff faces. This district had housed the offices of Entymion IV's ruling senators, and the streets had served their horse-drawn carriages and sedan chairs along with long trains of scribes, assistants and hangers-on. There was no one there now, and barely anything to indicate the malice that infested the city. The windows were dark and doors hung open, and just down the road the paving was scarred with a long burned crescent leading to the smouldering wreck of a Naval fighter craft. Aside from that, nothing.

The lander was only just wide enough for the avenue. The pilot, some Officio Munitorum lower adept, had no doubt landed the craft in worse terrain than this but never with a Space Marine threatening to blow his brains out. The lander's stubby wing scraped down a building, knocking down chunks of masonry and splitting the columns that held up a carved pediment. The ship's proximity alarm made an annoying pinging noise as the landing gear descended automatically, crushing a wrought iron streetlight.

The lander settled uncomfortably on the paved surface of the avenue.

'We're down,' said the pilot. He was pale and in poor shape, sweat rolling down his face and gathering in the folds of his neck. The shirt of his Munitorum-issue uniform hung open over his ample belly and the vest underneath was dark with perspiration.

'Open us up,' said Varuk. 'The lower hatches.'

The pilot scanned the instrument panel as if seeing it for the first time, then flicked a couple of switches.

'We're down,' came Graevus's voice, voxed from inside the lander's cavernous fuel tank. Through the lander's front window Varuk saw the first couple of squads hitting the ground and spreading out under the nose of the lander, taking cover behind the landing gear and closest columns.

'Good,' said Varuk. He took his bolt pistol away from the side of the pilot's head and holstered it. 'Stay here.'

Varuk pulled himself through the rear hatch of the tiny cockpit, clambered down the short access ladder and found the lower hatch open. He swung out onto the ground below and took his first breath of Enytmion IV's air. It stank of fuel from the lander. Not a good omen.

Squads Graevus, Salk, Luko and Corvan were on the ground. Apothecary Pallas and Librarian Tyrendian were with them. The second lander, a larger ammunition carrier, was landing at the intersection a hundred metres away, crushing a grand ornamental fountain beneath its weight as it came down. As a Techmarine, Varuk was a specialist in machine-lore, and to his trained eyes the landers were both ugly, inefficient things. Watching the ammo carrier shifting its ponderous bulk onto its landing gear reminded Varuk of the high risk Sarpedon had taken – trusting the better part of the whole Chapter to these crude machines that might have been shot out of the sky, or simply crashed through mechanical failure, at any moment.

Before the ammo lander was fully settled the rear loading ramp was down and, instead of crates of lasgun power packs and autocannon shells, Soul Drinkers dropped out onto the ground. Sarpedon himself was first out. Sergeant Krydel's squad followed close behind and ran ahead to secure the intersection along with Squads Dyon, Kelvor and Praedon. Iktinos was next out, along with a mob of more than forty Soul Drinkers who had lost their officers and chosen to follow the Chaplain as they had done on Stratix Luminae. Varuk himself was one of the last out: he was accompanied by the remaining specialists, Apothecary Karendin and Librarian Gresk, and the two scout squads under Senior Novices Eumenes and Giryan.

More than two hundred Soul Drinkers, including most of the Chapter's officers and specialists. Those left on the *Brokenback*, including the senior Techmarine Lygris, had simple orders: don't get spotted, and be ready to carry on the Chapter's work if the force on Entymion IV failed to return.

'Varuk! Are we alone here?' The vox was from Sarpedon. Varuk checked the dataslate mounted on the back of his wrist as the clamp on the end of his servo-arm rotated away to be replaced by a bundle of sensor tines.

He waited a few moments as the screen of the dataslate swirled with interference.

'Nothing,' he said at length. 'But it might be these buildings.' Varuk wasn't used to being the lead technical specialist in the field. Lygris normally took that role, but as effective captain of the *Brokenback* he was more valuable in space, keeping the space hulk hidden in the darkness outside system space.

Sarpedon switched to the all-squad channel. 'Sarpedon to all squads, we need hard cover. Get to the chamber mercantile alongside the senate-house.'

There was a sound like a lightning strike and Varuk saw Sergeant Graevus shattering the heavy wood door of the closest building with his power axe. A hardy close combat veteran, Graevus bore one of the Chapter's more obvious mutations in the form of his grossly enlarged and powerful hand. 'Through here!' he yelled and led his Assault Squad into the building.

'What do we do about the pilots?' asked Varuk.

Graevus glanced back at the lander. 'They can fend for themselves.'

Varuk followed Graevus through along with Squad Luko, the massive armoured bodies of the Space Marines only just fitting through the frame of the broken double doors. Varuk's eyes adjusted to the darkness instantly and he was almost stopped in his tracks.

The building had presumably once been a meeting-hall or council chamber where Gravenhold's ruling class had negotiated over control of the trillions of credits' worth of agricultural produce that Entymion IV exported. Now, it was something quite different.

A pedestal of deep green stone stood topped by a throne rendered in black metal, twin crescents rising from the back like huge sickle blades. Seating had surrounded it in concentric rings but the seats had all been torn out and replaced with heavy metal rings hammered into the floor. Each ring fastened a set of manacles to the floor, and Varuk could imagine hundreds of hunched forms kneeling in chains before whoever had sat in the throne. There were deep scratch marks on the tiled floor, dark brown with dried blood. There were more manacles on the pedestal where the enthroned creature had kept slaves or captives chained at his feet.

The walls had been stripped of whatever decoration they previously held, and were now covered in a deep black and silver mural. Heavily stylised beings, tall and slender and wielding curved blades and whips, stood over endless rows of human figures kneeling with their faces turned to the floor. Complex, curved lettering ran in friezes, spelling out some xenos language.

Varuk looked upwards. Hundreds of severed human hands hung from chains from the ceiling.

'By the throne,' said Sergeant Luko, making the sign of the aquila with his lightning claws.

'Grox-born xenos,' spat Graevus. 'Heathens.'

'We've found something,' Luko was voxing. 'Looks alien.'

'Recent?' came Sarpedon's reply from outside.

'It's been here a while.'

'Then we've probably found this world's source of corruption. But it's Entymion's problem, keep moving.'

'Understood.' Luko jogged to the far side of the room, activating his lightning claws and tearing out the far door. Beyond was the massive stone construction of the chamber mercantile, a semi-circular building in the shadow of the senate-house. It was fronted with massive columns carved to look like giant stacks of archaic one-credit coins and covered in sculptures of stern-faced adepts holding scales and quills. Gravenhold's commodities were once traded there between the various power groups – now the windows were dark and there were a few smears of long-dried blood on the front steps.

Varuk caught something moving at the edge of his vision, his ocular enhancements magnifying the small, sudden motion.

'Contact,' Varuk voxed to the three squads beside him.

'How many?' asked Graevus.

'Not sure.'

'I didn't see anything,' said Corvan, whose Assault Squad was right at the doors.

Sarpedon's Marines were crossing the street, already securing the steps and the shadows beneath the chamber mercantile's pediment.

'Be advised,' Sarpedon was voxing, 'Novice Nisryus reports possible hostiles.'

Nisryus – the precog. Varuk was not seeing things after all. The shape had been dark and darting and though Varuk was sure he had seen it, it had dissolved into the shadows before he could focus on it.

Varuk unholstered his bolt pistol again. Luko led the way across the street and Varuk folowed close behind. He could taste it, the alien wrongness of the place, the eyes upon them.

A Marauder squadron streaked overhead and as Varuk watched, one of the craft banked sharply and lost control, locked in a death spiral. He could feel a dark, sinister pulse beneath his feet or perhaps in the back of his mind, waves of faint madness. There was something terrible underneath Gravenhold, something that had snared Tellos, knocked that Marauder out of the sky, perhaps even drawn the Soul Drinkers themselves to the city.

'Heads up!' came Sergeant Krydel's voice over the voice. 'Charges set!'

In a plume of fire and rubble, the stone doors were blown off the front of the chamber mercantile and Sarpedon was leading the way into the building, ready to face any heretic or alien that might be waiting for them.

Varuk could see the scout squads following Sarpedon, Novice Nisryus hollow-eyed and intense. He could see it, the evil all around them. What was happening on Entymion IV? What did it want with the Soul Drinkers?

Varuk followed Luko into the shadows of the chamber mercantile, and Gravenhold swallowed them all whole.

CHAPTER FIVE

'THE THING ABOUT Space Marines, Threlnan, is that they're all brainwashed psychopaths.' Lord General Xarius walked lopsidedly with a cane. His troops tended to assume it was an old war injury but the truth was Xarius was an old man and his hip was giving out.

'Sir?' Colonel Threlnan was a large and brutal-looking man who looked almost comical following on the smaller, almost feeble-looking Xarius.

'I'm glad they're here, certainly,' continued Xarius. 'The Crimson Fists were an essential part of the battle plan. But you see, now the first battles have been fought I'd rather have a few more decent men who can be counted on to follow orders and run away like proper soldiers.'

The two were walking through the spaceport, where the maintenance sheds and docking clamps were over-run with supply yards, machine pools and endless dark green tents in which the Seleucaians snatched a few hours of sleep before being rotated back into the city. One of the landing pads had been appropriated by the Algorathi Janissaries and several units of them, in their archaic uniforms with bullion and epaulettes, were drilling on the cracked concrete surface. The Janissaries were a museum piece, their previous duties had involved the pacification of backwards worlds and they still fought as if forming a square and fixing bayonets could win a battle.

'Marines are good for morale,' said Threlnan.

'Hah! That they are, as long as they're fighting on the same side. Don't look at me like that, Threlnan, I know what they're like. The Dark Angels were supposed to spearhead our assault on the Dragon Archipelago on Balhaut, and when the order came down they were nowhere to be seen. Off fighting their own little war, never mind the men dying in the surf to win a beach the Marines should have taken. Never mind the rest of us lesser men.

'No, when they do what they're told they're the best, I know that. But just because we've suddenly got a company of Crimson Fists doesn't mean they'll fight where I tell them. They should be helping the Fire Drakes get a decent foothold in the south but I can't even contact the Fists' commander. They've got some private war here, Threlnan, and you're a fool if you're hoping it will coincide with ours.'

'I still think we should do our best to get them onside, lord general,' said Threlnan. He nodded in return to a salute from a group of Seleucaians loading ammunition onto a Leman Russ battle tank. 'They're the best soldiers the Imperium has.'

'Soldiers? I hardly think they fit that description. Do you know how they make them, Threlnan? No, of course you don't. They find some barbaric planet where children fight before they can walk, and they hunt down the most bloodthirsty killers. They recruit them when they're twelve, thirteen, fourteen, with all that hate and that arrogance, just at the age when you think you're bulletproof and nothing can kill you. Then they keep them like that, give them a gun and some armour, and point them at the nearest enemy. They're not soldiers, colonel, they're maniacs. They won't answer to anyone save their own kind. And have you seen how they fight? They find the closest enemy and try to cut them up with swords.' Xarius shook his head. 'Madness. Just madness. Just so there can be something to carve on the cathedrals and put in children's stories. Now I've got a hundred of them just waiting to bend all my battle-plans out of shape.'

They walked for a few moments. Xarius watched the troops going about the real business of war: tending to the wounded, keeping the tanks running, distributing rations and ammunition. 'At least with soldiers,' he mused almost to himself, 'you know they'll fight until they break and then run away or hide in a fox-hole. You know when it'll happen so you can pull them out before they break. You know when they think they're safe they'll go off drinking and whoring, you know they'll brew rotgut and steal rations and gamble and get into knife-fights. You can plan for those things, Threlnan. Space Marines you can't plan for.'

A mortar round landed somewhere on the space-port, throwing up a cloud of smoke and debris. There were still rebels hiding in the looming curve of the outer wall, using the tunnels to move. The Seleucaians were putting teams into the tunnels but they were short-lived, and there were too many places for the enemy to hide. Most of the soldiers were content to ignore the mortars and hope they never ended up a tunnel rat.

'We can do this without the Marines,' said Threlnan. 'An armoured thrust will puncture the heart of this city. Move up artillery and pound whatever's in front, then do it again. Keep going until we've driven them onto the Fire Drakes.'

Xarius sighed. 'I know. Armour, and lots of it. Followed up by plenty of poor dead boys. How long until the artillery train is down?'

'Departmento Munitorum says it'll be available within forty-eight hours. They're loading the landers now. Medusas and Basilisks, plenty of mobile firepower.'

'Good. Keep your boys in good spirits, Threlnan. Tell them they're going to get a chance to take the fight to this enemy, to do what they're trained for, fight the Emperor's fight, all that.'

'Yes, sir.' Threlnan saluted and walked off towards his staff tent, where he would finalise the plans for the drive into the heart of Gravenhold. Emperor alone knew what they would find, but Xarius knew he had the galaxy's ultimate weapon – tens of thousands of soldiers, none of whom the Imperium would greatly miss. What did they matter when there were trillions without number under the aegis of the Imperium? Xarius looked at them, fresh-faced near-recruits and scarred veterans alike. None of them deserved to die in Gravenhold, but a lot of them would. They were the fuel that kept the Imperium going, of course – without their sacrifice the Empire of Man would fall to ravening aliens, heresy, and worse. But that he should be the one to condemn them all! Him, one man out of all those trillions to have the deaths of so many laid at his door!

That was why he was a lord general, of course. Few men could understand the burden of command. Fewer still could handle it. That was what separated a Guardsman from a Space Marine; the Marines didn't understand death. To them it was nothing, just a stage in universal justice delivering heroes to the Emperor's side and heretics to the many hells of the Imperial Creed. But Xarius knew that death was the end. He was facing his own death and he felt the impending deaths of his men as keenly as his own. When you died, you turned to dust, and no matter what the preachers said the Emperor never noticed.

For the Emperor, he thought. In the hope that He might one day do something for them.

For the Emperor, they would all die.

NEITHER PILOT SURVIVED. As they tried to raise someone, anyone, on the long-range vox they were swamped by pale-skinned, half-naked enemies, faces marred by ugly piercings and masks of leather and metal, bloody hands prying off hatchways and hull plates.

Pilot First Class Edorin managed to open up a vox-channel to the *Resolve* just in time for them to hear his screams as he died, his ammo lander lurching off the ground as he desperately gunned its takeoff engines in an attempt to take flight and escape. The yowlings of his killers sounded through the vox, bestial and inhuman, before the lander turned slowly over and fell back into Gravenhold's streets. Its fuel cells ruptured and burning promethium poured out onto the road before igniting and immolating both

Pilot First Class Endorin and the insane cultists who had killed him.

Pilot Second Class Kallian lasted a bit longer. He opened a vox-channel while his fuel lander was still intact, but he couldn't take off – enemies were jammed in his landing gear and tearing open transmission lines. He broadcast feverishly to anyone who could listen as he drew a sidearm he had never fired and hoped it would let him take a few of them with him.

He had been hijacked by Traitor Marines, he said to anyone out there who could hear him. Mutants. Heretics. There were hundreds of them, and they were in the city, last seen in the mercantile district by the senate-house. He described the purple and bone of their armour, the mutations he had seen, their cold-bloodedness and determination. Now he was useless, and the Traitor Marines had sent near-naked Gravenholder cultists to come and finish him off.

Then they tore the rear cockpit hatch out. Pilot Second Class Kallian saw the straps and spikes they wore like bridles and blinkers, the patterns of the wounds on their skin, the bloodstained rags they wore and the crude weapons they carried. He took aim and fired.

He had never fired the autopistol he had been given as a sidearm. He had never cleaned it, either. The weapon jammed solid in his hand.

Pilot Kallian died a short and bloody death, not knowing that his frantic vox-transmissions had been received. But they had not got through to the receivers on the *Resolve*, or to the command posts of the Seleucaians or Algorathi Janissaries at the spaceport.

Instead, they had reached the comms post of the Fornux Lix Fire Drakes.

'How LONG AGO was this?' Reinez held the printout in his massive gauntlet and glared down at Lieutenant Elthanion.

'Twenty minutes,' replied Elthanion. He was something of a rarity, a genuine assault veteran who had both the tenacity to survive up-close combat and the level-headedness to become a worthwhile officer. He was the front-line commander for the Fire Drakes, with Colonel Savennian a figurehead and administrator. Elthanion's bionic eye and mouthful of broken teeth told Reinez everything he needed to know about the man.

'Do we know where?'

'Naval command say there were two landers that went down by the senate-house. They weren't destroyed on impact so it looks like one of them was our man.'

Reinez glanced through the body of the transcript. The pilot had evidently been terrified. As a Space Marine, Reinez was always vaguely mystified to see a man's fear laid out before him. To think that the threat of physical harm should drive a man to babbling near-incoherence – it reminded Reinez of why the Imperium needed the Space Marines. They were the Emperor's chosen, and they knew no fear. But the dead pilot had at least been lucid enough for Reinez's purposes.

'Lieutenant, you remember what I said to you earlier?'

Elthanion nodded. 'That we are on the same side. And that you and your men can take the fight to the enemy as we alone cannot.'

'Do you believe it?'

'My men are some of the toughest in the Guard, commander. I have the greatest respect for them. But yes, I believe what you said.'

'Good.' Reinez crumpled up the transcript. 'I need Colonel Savennian to give me command of his fastest and hardest-hitting elements. Your Armoured Fists units. Your veterans. Assault specialists. Tanks.'

'You're going in?'

'There is no choice to be made, lieutenant. We have only one shot at this enemy. My Marines can take it but only with your support. Will your men fight alongside us?'

Lieutenant Elthanion paused. No doubt he was thinking about the thrust the Crimson Fists and Fire Drakes would have to make into Gravenhold., further than they had gone before into the city's most important district where the enemy no doubt held sway. But he was also thinking about the chapels he had worshipped in with their statues of Astartes heroes, the stories the preachers had taught him of the Space Marines who won the Imperium for Mankind and put normal men to shame. He was thinking about the legends he had read, and of how he might be a part of one of them.

'Yes, they will fight,' he said.

'Excellent.' Reinez held his hand out to shake, Elthanion took it, and Reinez had to make a conscious effort not to crush the man's hand with his instinctive strength. 'The colonel will relinquish command of his forward assault units and have the force assembled within two hours. We will move then with or without the Fire Drakes.'

'You will not be failed, commander. You have my word as an officer.'

Elthanion saluted, turned on a heel and strode off. He would keep his word. Secretly, somewhere deep inside him, he had longed to fight alongside the Emperor's chosen. Reinez had seen it before. He knew that Lord General Xarius would not allow his Guardsmen to be diverted into the Crimson Fists' war – but Xarius wasn't there, and he didn't know. Gravenhold was damned and for Reinez the only thing worth fighting for on Entymion IV was the destruction of the Soul Drinkers. If he had to spend the lives of every Guardsman here to achieve that goal, he would do it.

If the Guardsmen could understand what it meant to be a Space Marine – the traditions and principles they were protecting, then they would gladly lay down their lives.

'Reinez to all units,' he voxed. 'We have them. Prepare to move.'

NIGHT WAS FALLING. They all knew they were being watched.

The chamber mercantile was a long, curved high-ceilinged hall, its broad, mosaiced floor broken by dealing-tables and auction-pulpits, heavy carved wooden thrones for important delegates, fenced-off pens for display livestock, small side-offices for scribes and adepts and ledger-stations with script-servitors still bent dormant over well-thumbed account books.

The Soul Drinkers had secured the building quickly, the scouts searching the offices and private dealing rooms, and it was again deserted. The Marines had taken up defensive positions behind the stone columns and hardwood dealers' desks, and settled in until they understood their surroundings better.

Sarpedon's gamble had paid off. Whatever force had summoned Tellos to the planet had recognised the Soul Drinkers and hadn't attacked them on sight as they would have any Imperial troops. The landers they had taken down to the city had been swamped and destroyed by cultists who had waited for the Soul Drinkers to be clear before attacking. But clearly the enemy did not fully trust the Soul Drinkers just yet, because they were watching.

Scout-Novice Nisryus could feel them all around. He knew a second before when they would show themselves and so only he had seen them clearly – xenos, probably eldar, wearing close-fitting elegant armour and lurking on the rooftops or between the columns of nearby buildings. They were silent and almost invisible, and Nisryus guessed at several dozen of them moving just out of sight, both alien and human, able to melt into the city apparently at will.

Sarpedon knew they were testing the Soul Drinkers, waiting for them to make some move that would mark them out as the enemy. Sarpedon wasn't going to give them that chance. He sent out patrols to monitor the closest buildings and maintain a perimeter, and sent the scouts up onto the chamber mercantile's roof to keep watch. The xenos had not tried to destroy the Soul Drinkers as they landed so they must suspect they were here to join their cause, but that didn't mean Sarpedon could risk breaking the fragile truce by tearing up the city looking for an alien to interrogate.

Eldar. That made things more complicated. The eldar were deceitful, untrustworthy and arrogant in the extreme. The Imperium had stopped short of a campaign of genocide against them because the eldar were an ancient race and knew secrets about the galaxy that the Imperium wanted to know – and the eldar were as implacable foes of Chaos as the Imperium itself claimed to be. But they were still aliens, heathens and pirates. Sarpedon had fought them before and he remembered a species who would gladly lead a billion humans to their deaths to save one of their own. Sarpedon didn't blame them for not trusting the Soul Drinkers, he would certainly never trust the eldar.

The uneasy quiet was broken by the crackle of the vox from Squad Eumenes on the roof.

'THEY'RE APPROACHING,' VOXED Eumenes, peering through his magnoculars at the plume of dust and smoke to the south-east. Small arms fire was spattering, tiny flashes of auto- and las-weapons through the smoke. 'Looks like armour and troop carriers.'

'Xarius is driving on the city at last,' voxed Sarpedon in reply.

'Doesn't look like it, commander,' said Eumenes. He handed the magnoculars to Selepus, who kneeled beside him behind the marble parapet of the building's roof. Without them Eumenes got a better sense of the approaching force. 'It's on a narrow front and it's moving too quickly. I don't think this is in Xarius's battle plan.'

'Marine armour,' said Selepus, sharp-eyed as ever. 'They've got Vindicators and Rhinos.'

Eumenes smiled. 'It's the Fists,' he voxed.

BULLETS THUNKED INTO the side of the Rhino APC, sounding like massive fists battering the vehicle as it churned through Gravenhold's streets. Las-bolts whined in reply, and vehicle-mounted autocannons thudded shells into the buildings on either side.

Reinez's squad, cramped in the hardened passenger compartment of the Rhino, had been through infinitely worse. Reinez stood and threw open the Rhino's top hatch, three of his Marines stood with him, bolters ready to counter any fire that came their commander's way.

The street was full of churning engine-smoke. The Rhinos carrying his strike force thundered alongside Chimeras and Leman Russ tanks stencilled with the insignia of the Fornux Lix Fire Drakes, the monstrous roar of their engines punctuated by gunfire streaking in from the buildings on either side of the broad avenue. The towering buildings of the administration district had given way to marble and white stone, carved friezes and statues, monuments and columns. The enemy had been caught cold by Reinez's bold gambit, and the force he had assembled: eleven Rhino and Razorback APCs, several Vindicator and Predator support tanks and the Fornux Lix armour of a dozen Chimera-mounted squads and half as many Leman Russes and Hydra flak-tanks were driving at prodigious speed through Gravenhold. Reinez could see the indistinct figures of enemy troopers in the windows and on the rooftops, firing at the vehicles as they roared past. The Fire Drakes had lost two Chimera squads to rocket launchers and small arms, and one Crimson Fists' Predator was stranded, crippled beneath the south-east gate.

'How much further?' he voxed on the Fire Drakes' channel as the convoy tore through an intersection, gunfire stitching lines of scars across the road.

'Five minutes,' came the reply from Lieutenant Elthanion, who was in a Chimera at the front of the convoy. Behind his voice on the vox was the roar of a

Vindicator shell blowing the front wall out of a building. Reinez saw the thunderhead of dust and debris blooming up ahead.

'Good. Crimson Fists, prepare to disembark! Assault units, we're going in hot! You are the spearhead!'

A chorus of acknowledgements sounded over the Fists' vox channel from the sergeants under his command.

'In the name of Dorn and the immortal Emperor,' intoned Chaplain Inhuaca over the vox. 'By the Hammer of the Primarch and the Sword of Him on Earth, through pain shall we know Him, through death shall we exalt Him...'

As Inhuaca's prayer echoed through the vox, autogun shots spanged against the upper hull of the Rhino. Reinez's Marines returned fire, snapping off bolter shots. The massive architecture of the merchant's district loomed and the weight of fire increased. Pallid figures scampered between the buildings, silhouettes against the roofline or scraps of movement in the near-dark shadows. 'Faster!' yelled Reinez, banging on the roof of the Rhino. A bolt of pure blackness whipped down from a rooftop and blew the track off a Leman Russ. Reinez's Rhino slewed wildly to avoid the wreck. A Chimera up ahead overturned spectacularly as the convoy gunned engines and made a final charge towards the objective.

Every gun was blazing now: sponson-mounted heavy bolters, Marines' boltguns, even the lasguns of the Fire Drakes taking pot shots from their Chimeras. A tank commander leaned out of the turret of his Leman Russ and loosed off a plasma pistol shot. A battle cannon ripped the heart out of a building, sending broken bodies flying from the upper floors. Hot trails of gunfire streaked through the gathering darkness, and the streets were illuminated by the massive muzzle flashes of the tanks' autocannon.

The resistance was fearsome. But Reinez had fought through worse. The shock of the attack, the element of surprise, had achieved what Xarius's initial thrust on the city had not. The enemy were just humans, unaugmented heretics, amateurs and fanatics who were breaking against the sheer resolve of the Adeptus Astartes.

The curved mass of the chamber mercantile appeared down the next avenue, ornate and imposing. The convoy passed an overturned Predator battle tank and another burned-out Chimera as the convoy gunned down the avenue, Reinez's bolt pistol kicking as he fired into the shadows. Reinez saw Inhuaca, standing proud from the top hatch of his Rhino, the crozius in his hand crackling blue-white in the gunsmoke and flying debris.

'KELVOR, DYON, give me a firing line at the windows. Graevus, Krydel, counter-charge. The rest of you, I want a crossfire, massed bolter fire.' Sarpedon stood in the centre of the chamber mercantile as his Marines scattered to take up defensive positions. 'Luko, where are you?'

'The street to your left flank,' replied Luko over the vox. 'We've got movement everywhere, xenos crawling all over the damn place.'

'They're not our problem right now. Get behind us and keep the route out of here clear.'

Librarian Tyrendian stomped up, his force sword in his hand. 'Where do you want me?'

'With Graevus.'

Stray shots were spattering in through the front windows and the roar of engines set the massive marble architecture and hardwood fittings trembling.

'For Dorn!' yelled Sarpedon, his eight legs taking him swiftly towards Squad Dyon hunkered down beneath the front windows. 'For the Emperor and for freedom!'

None of them had asked why they weren't falling back. They all knew why; the Soul Drinkers weren't running any more.

'...count ten Rhinos, support armour, at least eight Chimeras, probably Armoured Fist squads...' Eumenes was voxing from the roof. 'First coming in now.'

A Chimera in the colours of the Fornux Lix regiment slewed to a halt outside the chamber mercantile's ruined front doors. Guardsmen in heavy flakweave body armour were piling out of the back.

'Wait for the Fists,' voxed Sarpedon, the psychic circuit of his aegis hood heating up as his telepathic powers boiled below the surface of his mind.

THE FIRST CHIMERA shrieked to a halt.

'We're there!' voxed Elthanion. 'Fire team seven down!'

Fire was hitting the convoy hard from behind, xenos energy weapons now, bolts of power that sliced through hulls.

'This is the place,' relayed Elthanion as the squad reported their location. 'Suggest we give 'em a taste of battlecannon!'

'No!' ordered Reinez, flicking on the energy field of his thunder hammer. 'They're not that easy to kill, the rubble will just give them cover. Just back us up and

pin down their flanks.' Reinez switched to the Fists'
vox-channel. 'Second Company, charge!'

THE FIRST RHINO tore through the front wall of the
chamber mercantile in a waterfall of shattered marble,
riding high on a wave of rubble and plunging into
Squad Kelvor. Soul Drinkers disappeared beneath its
tracks as the rear and side hatches swung open.

Squad Dyon opened fire as one. Bolter fire riddled
the side armour of the Rhino and shredded the first
man out, an Assault Marine in the dark blue and red
colours of the Crimson Fists. The rest of the Fists
leaped out and Sarpedon saw a chainblade dispatch
one of Squad Kelvor, another sliced the leg of Sergeant
Kelvor himself.

Bolter fire streaked in from the rear of the hall as the
Fists dived into Squad Dyon, blades shrieking. Sarpedon jumped forwards and stabbed with his force staff
like a spear at the closest Assault Marine, the aegis circuit burning white-hot as he focussed his psychic
power through its tip.

The press of power-armoured bodies turned the
blade aside and the butt of a chainsword smacked into
the side of Sarpedon's head. Sarpedon reeled, reached
out with his free hand and grabbed the edge of the
Crimson Fist's shoulder pad. He planted his legs
firmly, talons cracking the tiled floor, and threw the
Assault Marine clear over his head. He reared up on his
hind legs and plunged the force staff two-handed
through the Marine's chest, psychic energy discharging
in a bright white flash that split the Marine's breastplate in two.

Another Assault Marine squad was vaulting in
through the front windows, then another. A section of

the front wall blew in to a Vindicator shot, scattering chunks of masonry all over the place. A wall of bolter fire ripped in through the gap followed by two units of Tactical Crimson Fists Marines – one carried a flag depicting a red gauntlet surrounded by lightning strikes, the standard of the Crimson Fists' Second Battle Company.

'Graevus! Now!' voxed Sarpedon frantically as a bolt pistol shot punched through one of his back legs and Brother Thorinol's severed head smacked into the wall beside him.

From the darkness in the back of the hall, lit by the strobing gunfire, Sergeant Graevus led the charge.

EUMENES SPOTTED A Guard officer cut down as he directed his troops, head snapped back by a shot from Sniper-Novice Raek of Scout Squad Giryan. A detonation from below shook the building and several of the scouts were knocked to their knees.

'The Guard are trying to flank us,' said Eumenes, lining up a bolt pistol shot and firing. His first went wide, his second blew the leg off a Fire Drake toting a grenade launcher. The Guardsmen were swarming all over the place, jumping from the Chimeras to take up cover beneath the thick columns and ornate statues that lined the front of the buildings. Las-fire was streaking up at the scouts, tearing chunks out of the lip of marble sheltering them.

'Giryan! Take the right, I'll take the left!' shouted Eumenes. The two squads broke up and headed for the sides of the buildings, where the chamber mercantile was separated from the neighbouring buildings by narrow alleys. Eumenes skidded to a halt and glanced down into the alley, drawing his head back from the replying barrage of las-fire. 'Scamander!' he yelled. 'Give us some room to work!'

Scamander dived into cover beside Eumenes. He took a deep breath and held out his hands over the edge, the spaces between his fingers glowing with licks of flame. There was a flicker of heat in the air and suddenly a rush of fire blazed down indiscriminately, pouring like liquid over the Fire Drakes massed below.

Scamander grimaced as his mental energy poured out through his mind. He let out a long juddering breath that was white with frost crystals as all the heat bled out of his body, and was multiplied by his psychic focus to turn the valley into a blazing orange furnace.

Men were screaming. An officer was shouting for calm, firing warning shots. Ammunition from a grenade launcher cooked off in a deafening crescendo of explosions. Flesh sizzled and popped.

'That's enough, novice!' ordered Eumenes before Scamander drained himself completely.

Scamander shuddered and the flame stopped falling from his hands.

'Squad, move!' called Eumenes. Scamander was falling backwards, exhausted, as Eumenes vaulted over the parapet and dropped into the alleyway.

There was nothing to burn in there now Scamander's psychic fire had been withdrawn and only bodies were blazing. Eumenes landed well enough to snap off a shot that took off the officer's hand, Selepus dropped straight as a dagger behind the officer, stabbing his combat knife through the man's neck and turning to plunge it into the chest of the Guardsman behind him. Nisryus followed, then Thersites and Tydeus. Tydeus fired a round from his grenade launcher, filling the least charred end of the alley with smoke and shrapnel, throwing two Fire Drakes out onto the street. Scamander was last, landing badly, his body limp with exhaustion. He would recover in a few moments, but for those few moments he was vulnerable.

The sound of a tank rumbled close. 'Hellhound,' said Nisryus. 'They're going to smoke us out.' His stilted body language told Eumenes that Nisryus's precognitive powers were kicking in.

'They wish it was that easy,' said Selepus, knife still in hand in preference to his bolt pistol.

'They think we'll fall back,' said Nisryus. 'So they can follow us.'

'Then we won't,' said Eumenes. 'Tydeus! Cover us! Let's move!'

THERE WAS NO room to bring pistols to bear in the savage press of armoured bodies. Sergeant Graevus wielded his power axe with his left hand and punched with his mutated right, the close quarters magnifying his strength as every blow struck a Crimson Fist.

He was surrounded, he was all but blind. The air was full of shrapnel and smoke and even his enhanced hearing couldn't make sense of the screaming din. Gunfire, yelling, shrieking chainblades, the blade of his own power axe biting into ceramite, bones snapping, thunderous explosions as the Guard armour continued to demolish the far end of the chamber.

He was drowning in a sea of bodies. Soul Drinkers and Crimson Fists fought in a brutal scrum. It was ugly and savage with no room for skill – but if the Crimson Fists piled into the chamber the weight of their gunfire would scour the Soul Drinkers off the face of Entymion IV. Graevus had to stop them. He had to buy his battle-brothers time.

Graevus shoved with his right and an Assault Marine stumbled back, opening up enough space for a good swing of Graevus's power axe. Another blue-armoured arm punched out to block his blow and the axe blade severed it above the elbow in a flash of sparks. The Assault Marine regained his footing and lunged with his chainblade, Graveus turned it with the haft of his axe and suddenly they were face-to-face, wrestling, Graveus's face reflected in the red eyepieces of the Marine's helmet. He saw his own gnarled veteran's face was spattered with blood.

Bodies pressed in around him. A bolt pistol rattled off its whole magazine and someone slumped against Graevus, held upright by the press – he couldn't tell if it was a Fist or a Soul Drinker who had died.

The Assault Marine had his arm around Graevus's neck and was dragging him down. Graevus shifted his weight and reached down with his deformed hand, its enlarged, elongated fingers wrapping around the Marine's leg armour. He pulled and the Marine was pitched onto his back, Graveus on top of him, Graevus forcing a knee onto the Marine's chest and punching again and again, the ceramite denting and cracking under the huge mutated fist that pistoned into the Assault Marine's face and chest.

Someone kicked Graevus in the head and a chain-blade just missed a slice at his head. Graevus swung his axe wildly, the power field carving a shining blue arc. He couldn't tell if he had hit anything. The world was just a mass of armoured limbs and the deafening scream of a fight he couldn't win.

There was something else. Held high above the melee, tattered by gunfire, was the banner. The battle standard of the Crimson Fists Second Company. The image brought home the fact that the Fists hated the Soul Drinkers so much they had sent an entire battle company after them, the Fists, who were themselves severely depleted, had been willing to risk perhaps half of their fully-trained veteran manpower on destroying the Soul Drinkers.

The standard.

The Marine beneath Graevus hadn't tried to kill him in the last few seconds so Graevus assumed he was unconscious. Graevus swung again, trying to clear a space in front of him. The Soul Drinkers of his squad behind him rattled bolt pistol shots over his shoulder to batter back the Crimson Fists and suddenly there was a space in front of him to charge into, swinging a lighting-quick figure-eight with his axe. A chainsword shattered somewhere in the throng and sparks showered where the axe's power field met ceramite.

Graveus couldn't tell his battle-brothers apart through the veil of shrapnel and smoke. He could barely tell friend from foe. He just hacked and barged forward, the weight of his brothers behind carrying him forward. There were dead Marines beneath his feet and the floor was slick with blood. A Soul Drinker fell to a plasma pistol blast from a Fists' sergeant; Graevus ignored him, concentrating on pressing forward.

A lightning bolt split the air above him and a Fist was thrown into the air as if from a catapult, electricity arcing off him. Graevus glanced behind him and saw Librarian Tyrendian backing them up, his aristocratic face lit by the flickers of power playing around his head.

Graevus saw a Crimson Fist in lighter blue armour, a high aegis collar obscuring his helmeted head, his armour inscribed with protective sigils. A Crimson Fists' Librarian.

The Fists' Librarian raised a hand and dark ripples flowed from his fingers. They punched through the air in writhing darts and Graevus saw them swirling around Tyrendian, forming tendrils of shadow that tried to snare his arms and drag him down, envelop his head and blind him. Blue-white power flickered around Tyrendian's hands and with a blast of electricity the shadows were suddenly shredded.

Graevus was caught in the middle of a psychic duel. It meant he was in an even more dangerous place than before, but he couldn't worry about it now.

A bolter shot hit his greave and almost pitched Graevus onto his face. Splinters of ceramite were driven into his shin but he strode through the pain. The world was dissolving into dark chaos, with only the Battle Standard of the Second Company to focus on. Another lightning bolt slashed by from Tyrendian and the Crimson Fists' Librarian sent black tendrils spiralling through the air, lashing out at Soul Drinkers, ensnaring flailing limbs. Graevus saw the wounded Sergeant Kelvor ducking in front of him, only to have his chainsword snatched out of his hand by the shadow tentacle, another snagged his remaining ankle and threw him on his back. A Crimson Fist loomed over Kelvor but Graevus put his shoulder down and barged into the Fist, knocking him back into the throng to disappear between the jostling bodies.

Kelvor was back on his remaining foot and firing with his bolt pistol, but the momentum of Graevus's charge was gone and the crowd pressed in again. Graevus, back-to-back with Kelvor, held his power axe like a quarterstaff and blocked a chainblade strike. He took a bolt pistol shot to the chest, his internal breastplate of fused ribs cracking, compressed gas spraying from his armour's ruptured exhaust.

Lightning tore past Graevus and suddenly Tyrendian himself was in the press beside him, purple shining in the strange light pulsing from his temples.

The Fists' Librarian was fighting through the melee, too. Two psykers, lit up to one another like beacons on the battlefield, each one an affront to the other. It was inevitable they would ignore the rest of the battle to kill one another.

Bolter fire ripped in a disciplined volley from the Soul Drinkers in the rear of the chamber mercantile, thudding into the bodies of the Crimson Fists trying to force their way in. The battle standard dipped as the Marine holding it fell, only for it to be snatched up again by another Fist. Return fire streaked over as Crimson Fists pulled back from close combat to snap fire back, and the press eased off around Graevus.

There were too many Crimson Fists. A whole company could tear the building down if they had to. The bolters of the Soul Drinkers had bought a few seconds, and Graevus had to use them now or he might as well roll over and die.

Tyrendian and Graevus charged as one, Graevus's axe and Tyrendian's force sword hacking to force a path through the Crimson Fists. Someone swung a power sword at Graevus and it met the head of his axe in a terrific spray of sparks – Sergeant Kelvor dived on the attacker and Graevus pressed on.

Tyrendian broke free and sent a bolt of psychic lightning straight into the ground, knocking back the closest Fists and clearing his path to the Librarian. Hands of shadow were reaching from the ground but Tyrendian kicked free of them, the Crimson Fist

Librarian stopped projecting his power and drew his own force sword, a long rapier of burning light, putting up a guard just in time to turn Tyrendian's lunging strike.

Graevus's head whirled. He was all but surrounded now, only momentum keeping him going. He could see the Marine who carried the Second Company's standard. The bearer was standing on the slope of rubble that had once been the chamber mercantile's front wall, holding his bolter in his free hand and firing off rapid volleys into the Soul Drinkers taking cover behind rubble and furniture in the back of the hall. The Fist's white-painted helmet and the golden honour studs marked him out as a recognised veteran, someone who had lived through the Rynn's World disaster and come out driven by bitterness and vengeance.

The battle was lit in staccato flashes as force swords clashed, Tyrendian's sword and the Librarian's rapier clashing and discharging their pent-up psychic power into the air. The Librarian saw an opening and lunged – Tyrendian sidestepped and closed the gap, trapping the Librarian's head in the crook of his elbow and kneeing the Crimson Fist in the face. He dropped his sword and with his free hand ripped the Librarian's helmet off, revealing a dark-skinned face distorted with effort.

Tyrendian threw the Crimson Fist backwards and before the rapier could be brought to bear Tyrendian held out both hands on either side of the Librarian's bare head. With a final yell of effort, power leapt from Tyrendian's palm and a lightning bolt ripped right through the Fists' Librarian's head, coursing into Tyrendian's other hand to form a continuous current of looping psychic power.

The Crimson Fists' Librarian was bathed in hot blue light as he threw up a psychic shield to keep his mind from being shredded. But Tyrendian, while he lacked subtlety in the application of his psychic talents, had immense reserves of raw power. The Crimson Fist spasmed wildly, foam spattering from his lips, his force sword falling from his shuddering hand.

The Crimson Fist's head exploded in a massive wash of psychic feedback, ripping out from him like the shockwave from a bomb blast. The Fist's body was ripped apart in a welter of gore and a storm of shattered ceramite, throwing Crimson Fists and Soul Drinkers onto the ground. The sound was like a thousand screams, a psychic death cry that speared straight into the mind of every Marine.

It felt like Graevus had run into a wall of solid force. He was battered backwards and fell to his knees, the Librarian's death a spear of white noise transfixing his mind.

He forced his eyes open, the scream still reverberating through his head. A huge hole had been blasted in the middle of the battle at the breach, with Soul Drinkers and Crimson Fists thrown to the ground or blasted back out onto the street.

The standard bearer was on his knees.

Graevus forced himself to his feet. He ran the last few paces as if in slow motion, his limbs complaining, every breath agony through his cracked ribs. Fallen Crimson Fists reached out to grab him but he hacked down on either side of him with his axe; he sliced off a hand, kicked a Fist out of his way. A Soul Drinker at the back of the chamber mercantile saw what he was doing and bolter fire snapped over his shoulder, beating back the Crimson Fists' Assault Marines who tried to reach him.

The standard bearer was on his feet. Graevus knew he only had one shot. He swung back his axe and dived, bringing the axe in a glittering arc heading for the Crimson Fist's neck.

The Marine brought the haft of the standard up to block the blow, just as Graevus knew he would. The axe blade carved downwards, passing under the standard and cutting clean into the Marine's waist. Graevus felt the blade jarring as the power field forced its way through the ceramite of the Marine's abdominal armour, sliced through his spine, and passed clear out the other side.

The Marine's upper half toppled to the ground. Vermilion blood fountained. Graevus caught the standard as it fell, the banner falling over him like a shroud.

The Librarian's death throes had cleared the space for Graevus to take the banner, but it had also removed the brutal melee that was blocking the Crimson Fists' route into the chamber mercantile. Two squads of Crimson Fists were even now scrambling over the rubble into the hall to bring their bolters to bear.

Graevus knew they would get in. There were just too many of them. The Soul Drinkers could not outgun the Crimson Fists, the only way to beat them was to break their spirit. Space Marines were the most unbreakable troops the Imperium had, but the Soul Drinkers had no choice.

Graevus had struck one blow by snatching their standard. If he made it out of the chamber mercantile alive, he would strike another. And as he ran through a storm of bolter fire, he prayed that Sarpedon would strike the third.

His prayers were answered, because that moment the hell began.

CHAPTER SIX

'THEN WHERE THE bloody hell is he?' snapped Lord General Xarius. He stood up sharply, ignoring the familiar pain in his hip, and knocked the makeshift table of ammo crates so several of Colonel Threlnan's situational maps fell onto the floor.

'We're not sure,' came the vox reply from Hasdrubal. Hasdrubal, the flag-commander of Xarius's Baneblade, functioned as Xarius's adjutant mainly because he was there. Xarius didn't maintain a personal staff of his own, preferring the resources to go to the front line where they might actually make a difference. 'He's commanding a force of armour in the south of the city but Colonel Savennian says he doesn't have an accurate location for the convoy.'

'St. Aspira's teeth!' hissed Xarius into the vox-set. Colonel Threlnan and his adjutant officer looked up in surprise at the minor blasphemy. 'Tell me the Crimson Fists haven't gone with him.'

'We're… again, we're not sure…'

'Find out. Get an eye in the air, a Thunderbolt or something.' Xarius flicked off the vox-channel.

'Trouble?' said Threlnan.

'Lieutenant Elthanion and half the Fire Drakes just drove into Gravenhold without thinking to mention it to anyone else.'

'Couldn't Savennian order them back?'

'Damn it, Threlnan, how do you think I got where I am today? By making sure I sure as hell know what kind of men are supposed to be fighting for me. Colonel Savennian earned his rank by being the half-brother of the governor-regent of Fornux Lix. He's a politician. He's only there because protocol needs a colonel's signature on everything. It's Elthanion that runs that regiment and he's swanned off.'

'Where does that leave all this?' Threlnan indicated the maps and plans Lord General Xarius had been poring over before Hasdrubal had informed him of the Fire Drakes' unauthorised mission. They were the troop dispositions of the Seleucaian and Fornux Lix troops and those Algorathi units who had been rotated into the field. They also described the troop movements that would lay the foundation for the next phase of the war for Gravenhold. A huge drive into the city, masses of infantry and armour, moving forward according to intricate patterns to bring massed firepower against every intersection and likely strongpoint. Other plans were backups, describing how forces were to react to bottlenecks or bypass potentially fortified strongpoints.

They relied, of course, on Imperial forces rolling in from both directions, splitting the enemy forces. That meant the Fire Drakes had to play their part, winning the whole administrative sector and then the governmental quarter culminating in the senate-house itself. It was a goal they could not achieve if they were storming about the city getting killed in some private war.

'It leaves all this a mess,' replied Xarius. 'The Departmento Munitorum say they can't get us any more Guard units. If we lose the Fire Drakes then we don't have a battle plan. We just let this city bleed our forces dry until they pull us out.'

Threlnan shook his head. 'If they didn't care so much about getting this damn city back the Navy could have just have fragged it from orbit...'

'No one could care less about the city, Threlnan. The reason we haven't hit it from orbit is that an orbital strike would have levelled the city and left the enemy intact. They're underneath it, hiding. There are sewers and ruins and Throne knows what down there. We'd just be giving them a ruined city to hide inside. Our men are not dying just because someone admires Gravenhold's architecture, colonel, they are dying because that's the only way we can get this planet back. I would thank you to remember that.'

Threlnan was about to answer, but the vox-set bleeped. Xarius picked it up.

'Lord general?' It was Hasdrubal. 'The auspex crews on the *Resolve* are picking up activity near the senate-house. Plenty of it, too. It's lighting up all the sensors.'

'The Fire Drakes?'

'Yes, sir. Them and the Crimson Fists.'

'The Fists? Wonderful. Now we've got two armies running wild.' Xarius rubbed his eyes, trying to force back the headache that was building behind them. 'How many?'

'It looks like all of them, sir.'

THE BURNING WRECK of the Hellhound filled the streets with billowing red-black smoke, choking back the dozens of Guardsmen who must have thought they were facing a force with massive numerical superiority. In reality it was just the six men of Scout Squad Eumenes, snapping off bolter shots while Selepus dragged any Guardsmen who got too close into the shadows and slit his throat. Eumenes himself was crouched down beside Novice-Librarian Scamander, directing the bolter fire through the smoke. He hadn't received all the implants of a full Marine but his eyesight was still considerably augmented. It cut through the smoke so his scouts were shooting at Guardsmen who couldn't fire back. From the cover of the rubble by the entrance to the alleyway, Scout Squad Eumenes was holding back the Fire Drakes troops who were supposed to be surrounding the Soul Drinkers and attacking from the back of the chamber mercantile.

A unit of Guardsmen, veterans with melta guns and plasma weapons, was moving rapidly around the pool of burning promethium to pin down the scouts. Eumenes indicated them with a sharp stabbing hand signal and Scamander, now recovered from his exertions, holstered his bolt pistol. He took a deep breath and raised his hands, teeth clenched with effort as he coaxed a long tongue of flame from the blazing wreck.

The flame lashed out like a whip, wrapping around three of the veterans and setting their fatigues ablaze. They fell to the ground, rolling in an attempt to put the flames out but Scamander concentrated on them instead, making the flames grow until the superheated air scalded their lungs and stopped their screams. The other Guardsmen ran for cover on the far side of the street – in retreat and unable to return fire, they were wide open to the volley of bolt pistol shots the rest of the squad snapped off at them. One was struck in the back of the head by a well-placed sniper shot, sending him somersaulting forward.

Scout-Sniper Raek ran from the still-smouldering alleyway and hit the ground by Eumenes. His armour was charred and smouldering, and the supressor on the end of his long sniper rifle was dull red with heat. His face was dark with grime and bled from a dozen minor shrapnel wounds. 'Squad Giryan's falling back,' he said. 'The Guard have got the alley on the far side.'

'Losses?'

'We've lost three. Including Giryan.'

'Get to the back of this alley and keep them away for as long as you can, we need that street clear.' Eumenes switched to the command vox-channel. 'Sarpedon, this is Eumenes. We've lost Squad Giryan and the Guard are going to flank us.'

The vox-net was full of static and background bolter fire. 'Fall back,' came the reply. 'All squads, retreat to the senate-house. Luko, Eumenes, cover us. For Dorn!'

SARPEDON WAS A telepath. He had always been extremely powerful, powerful enough to join the ranks of the Chapter Librarium, and following his mutation his mental strength had grown to heights rarely achieved by even the most renowned Librarians of the Adeptus Astartes. But he was a telepath that could only transmit, not receive – he made up for this flaw with raw power, and the intensity of the images which he forced into the unwilling minds of his enemies.

The power was referred to as the Hell. In the carnage of the chamber mercantile, it was a vision of corruption. If the Crimson Fists wanted to find Chaos amongst the Soul Drinkers, then Sarpedon would give it to them.

Tortured daemonic faces howled from the shadows. The ceiling of the chamber dissolved into a swirling black cloud from which huge taloned hands reached down, blazing with corruptive power, pulsing with waves of decay. Sarpedon ripped out of his memory every daemonic abomination he had encountered in his long career as a Space Marine and painted them on the walls of the chamber mercantile – sorcerous runes that refused to be read, raw naked souls burning in the madness of the warp, scabrous daemons capering in the darkness, voices that whispered blasphemies from every direction.

The Soul Drinkers had all trained with Sarpedon, subjecting themselves to the full force of the Hell in the depths of the *Brokenback* so they would be able to tell Sarpedon's illusions from reality. The Crimson Fists had not.

They had seen Graevus snatching their standard from under their noses. Now they faced this daemonic assault, as if a horde of daemons was suddenly manifesting from thin air all around them. The Emperor himself had decreed that a Space Marine should know no fear and the Crimson Fists were no exception, but it wasn't fear that Sarpedon needed. It was just that one moment of doubt, the realisation that they might be fighting something they couldn't beat, something that could steal their sacred standard and conjure daemons all around them. It wouldn't last long, but it did not have to.

'For Dorn!' Sarpedon yelled again, and broke cover, followed by Squad Dyon and the remains of Squad Kelvor. Graevus was already heading in the same direction with the scattered brothers of his squad, Tyrendian just behind him. The Crimson Fists poured bolter fire after them and Sarpedon saw one of Graevus's Marines struck down by a bolter round through the neck, but the Crimson Fists weren't following, not yet. For a couple of seconds they would pause at the breach, unsure whether they should dive into the fight or hold back in the face of superior opposition.

The Soul Drinkers were falling back through the exits in the back of the hall, the many smaller entrances once used by the lesser adepts and retainers. Sarpedon reached the back of the hall, running past Squads Corvan and Praedon who were lined up behind the heavy wooden fixtures of the chamber to provide covering fire.

'Get out!' Sarpedon yelled as he ran past, his eight talons splintering the mosaics on the floor.

He was forcing every foul image out of his mind and into the storm of illusions behind him, as much to cloak the Soul Drinkers' retreat as to keep the Crimson Fists back. Already the Fists were advancing – they were mostly veterans who had seen worse things before and after Rynn's World than anything Sarpedon could conjure up and the ruse had only worked for a few seconds. But already most of the Soul Drinkers were out into the street behind, heading for the senate-house under cover from Eumenes and Squad Luko.

Sarpedon burst out into the street. The air was full of smoke and las-fire was streaking down at him now, whipping by from one end of the street where the Guard had got men through the alley. Squad Luko was gathered on the steps keeping up a volley of bolt pistol fire. Squad Dyon's Tactical Marines took their place and their more effective bolter fire battered back the Guardsmen already sheltering behind a pile of their own dead.

Squads Corvan and Praedon were out, followed by volleys of fire from the Crimson Fists. Two battle-brothers from Squad Praedon were caught and tumbled down the steps – one had lost the better part of his leg but the other had suffered a massive head shot. The still-living Marine was hauled to his feet by Sergeant Praedon as the Marines made a break for the buildings opposite where the rest of the Soul Drinkers were already taking cover.

The Guardsmen at the alleyway scattered, but not for cover. With a roar of collapsing masonry, a Leman Russ Demolisher ripped out through the alleyway, shunting aside massive piles of rubble with the huge dozer blade fitted to its front. The turret turned and the huge main cannon fired, blowing a tremendous hole in the front of the building opposite. Sarpedon was almost thrown to the ground.

'Get out of here!' yelled Sarpedon to the Marines still in the street. 'Move! They're coming through!'

Guardsmen were pouring through the widened alley, using the Demolisher for cover. A bolt from Squad Dyon's plasma gunner streaked into the side of the Demolisher, blowing the side weapon off in a welter of fire and sparks, but it wouldn't help much.

Sarpedon was out in the middle of the road, running and shooting. All the Soul Drinkers were out of the chamber mercantile and were making a dash for the buildings opposite.

'Varuk!' yelled Sarpedon into the vox. 'Now!

Somewhere in the complex of buildings, Techmarine Varuk activated the detonator signal keyed to receivers in bundles of krak grenades hidden against the back wall of the chamber mercantile.

The wall of force hit Sarpedon before the sound did, a blast of expanding air like a shove in the back. His eight legs kept him upright but the sound was deafening, followed by the blinding cloud of dust and debris that billowed across the street as the rear wall of the chamber mercantile collapsed.

Sarpedon kept going, the pre-filters in his throat keeping the choking marble dust out of his lungs. The Fire Drakes were protected by respirators and as they recovered they kept up their las-fire, sending scarlet streaks of laser through the dust, but it wasn't enough to slow the Soul Drinkers down now. Sarpedon thudded into the side of the building and scrambled along the front, finding the huge jagged hole the Demolisher had blown and pulling himself inside.

The Crimson Fists would be slowed down by the explosion, but nothing else. It took a great deal more than a well-timed booby trap and some flying masonry to dissuade a Space Marine. At the most, it bought the Soul Drinkers a minute or so more time to get out, and Sarpedon knew they had to make the best use of it they could.

The plan was simple. With the Fists and the Guard broken up and slowed down at the chamber mercantile, the Soul Drinkers were to retreat, force their pursuers to follow them through offices and meeting-halls, until they got to the senate-house.

The senate-house. The location Sarpedon had chosen for the Soul Drinkers' last stand.

No HUMAN WOULD understand the thoughts that went through the mind of the alien.

On one level, they were driven by the same desires that defined the actions of all living things. To survive. To achieve, and attain superiority. To stave off suffering. But below that layer of instinct was something else entirely, something that was made up of both pride and desperation, an obsessively free will and a grim pre-ordained, almost biological imperative to prey on lesser species. The alien was monstrously proud, and yet he acted out of fear. He was cruel to the point of abstraction, as if the infliction of suffering fulfilled an aesthetic ideal – and yet every cut and kill was in deference to forces it could not control and that it had to bow before, no matter how it refused to accept the domination of another. A human could not possibly understand all the contradictory layers that made up its consciousness. All they ever saw were the results: the dead, the enslaved, the broken.

This was what it meant to be one of the eldar, the galaxy's chosen race, the heralds of creation, the masters of reality. Freedom and enslavement, cruelty and deference, arrogance and desperation. The minds of the eldar were based on an unending cycle of cause and contradiction that would drive the primitive-minded humans insane.

Akrelthas of the Kabal of the Burning Scale crouched down behind the elaborate carving that jutted from a corner of the rooftop. Only the faintest of evening light remained and night was rolling across Gravenhold, but there was plenty of illumination below.

Muzzle flashes and explosions lit up the streets of Gravenhold's ruling district as bright as day, and Akrelthas could clearly see the human soldiers gunning each other down, tearing each other apart.

There were two sides to the conflict but Akrelthas had to look carefully to see how the fight was playing out, because to Akrelthas they all looked the same.

Akrelthas leaned forward, the interlocking beetle-black plates of his armour flexing over his close-fitting bodysuit. He left the splinter rifle slung on his back as he crawled a little way down the wall like a large and spindly spider – they couldn't see him up there. He had been watching them here before the fight had begun and they hadn't seen him then, when they had been on the lookout. They were all but blind, these humans, blind and stupid. It was only their sheer numbers and wide distribution across the galaxy that meant the species had survived this long.

The unarmoured humans were fit only to fight the subjugated warriors who had once made up the population of this city. They were beneath eldar notice, no better than cattle driven forward to die. The armoured humans, however, were something else. Their specialisation approached the skill of the Kabal's own incubi – these humans were shock troops, built to fight with up-close savagery. It was crude but beautiful, for the sight of such destructive power brought to bear in one place pleased Akrelthas's aesthetic senses as much as a well-placed blade strike or a horde of slaves bent down beneath the lash.

It was nothing compared to the honed prowess of the Kabal, of course, but it was impressive nonetheless.

Akrelthas had a job to do. His master, and the mistress above them all, wanted information. Gravenhold was a complex pattern of forces, both military and metaphysical, and the Kabal had to know everything it could about the human armies and how they interacted. The purple-armoured humans were an independent force, their motives unknown, their allegiances undecided. If the Kabal's plans were to unfold in such a way as to please She-Who-Thirsts, then those questions had to be answered.

The unarmoured humans – the Imperial Guard, whose billions of soldiers marched to their deaths to maintain some hopeless vision of humanity's future – and the blue-armoured soldiers fought together. That much was simple enough. Those in blue and those in purple were Space Marines, soldiers vaunted as heroes of legend by the rest of humanity, and which were in reality just another bludgeoning weapon the Imperium of Mankind used to clumsily imitate the true patterns of warfare. Akrelathas watched as the Marines in blue surged forward out of the contested building, their gunfire throwing a purple Marine to the ground. The fallen Marine was set upon and quickly despatched where he lay, the ugly chain-toothed weapons of the Marines cutting him in two on the ground.

The two armies of Marines were not allies, then. This would interest the Kabal greatly. This was the sign Akrelthas had been told to look out for, it meant that both forces of Marines would play their assigned part admirably well in the eldar victory.

Akrelthas sprang lightly back up onto the roof, glanced once more down into the melee where humans killed one another to unknowingly exalt She-Who-Thirsts, and sprinted off into the gathering darkness.

* * *

CHAPLAIN IKTINOS LED the charge through the offices of Gravenhold's proxy cardinal. Where once Gravenhold's great and good had come to beg counsel or indulgences from the Ecclesiarchy's representative, now the armoured boots of the Soul Drinkers crunched through scholars' cells and racks of illuminated scrolls. Pistol fire from more than twenty Crimson Fists Assault Marines, who had used their jump packs to take the first floor of the building, streaked down from the first floor balcony, where the grand staircase lead up to the chambers once occupied by the Proxy Cardinal's own staff.

Iktinos didn't yell the devotional prayers a Space Marine Chaplain was supposed to as he drew his Crozius Arcanum and headed for the stairs. He didn't have to. He was the spiritual heart of the Soul Drinkers – the only Chaplain the Soul Drinkers had, the principal advisor to Sarpedon and the spiritual mentor to every Soul Drinker.

Brother Falcar, who had fought under Sergeant Hastis before Hastis's death on Septiam Torus, dived in front of Iktinos, taking the full blast of a plasma gun shot that was meant for the Chaplain. Falcar was thrown off the grand staircase, a smoking hole ripped through his torso.

More Soul Drinkers surged forwards, taking volleys of bolt pistol fire. Some fell, tumbling down the stairs, others sprinted ahead to come to grips with the first of the Crimson Fists.

Iktinos's crozius arcanum blazed, its power field reacting with the veil of shrapnel hammering down. Another Soul Drinker fell shielding Iktinos – Brother Thorical this time, whose squad leader had been the late Sergeant Givrillian.

Iktinos charged up into the Crimson Fists, crozius shattering ceramite and bone. He did not feel the hot fury of a warrior or the dry desperation of a man fighting for his life – he fought deliberately and calmly, knowing the Soul Drinkers around him would hold off the chainblades and bolter shots that were meant for him. On Stratix Luminae, when the whole Soul Drinkers Chapter had faced destruction, he had forged a bond between him and the Soul Drinkers who followed him. They had died to keep the Chapter's figurehead alive. They had walked into the jaws of death because he was leading them.

A Crimson Fist drove his chainsword through the shoulder of the Soul Drinker who pulled him out of Iktinos's way. Another Fist fell back, one side of his helmet's faceplate blown off by a bolter shot.

The Crimson Fists Assault Captain was in front of Iktinos now. Iktinos recognised him – Assault-Captain Arca, one of the Second Company's real veterans. Iktinos had met him briefly when the Chaplains of the Imperial Fists' successor Chapters had gathered at Rynn's World. That had been before the Crimson Fists' fortress-monastery was destroyed, before the Soul Drinkers were excommunicated.

It was a long time ago.

Arca must have recognised Iktinos, because the Fist paused for a second. In the middle of the melee at the top of the stairs, the two Marines regarded each other for a moment. One thought how such a brave and noble man could still fight in the name of a corrupt and monstrous Imperium. The other wondered how a guardian of the Chapter's faith could have fallen so far into corruption and rebellion.

But then the moment was gone. And the fury of their combat lit up the building like a lightning storm.

'THREE SHOTS. LASCANNON. Then we're clear.' Nisryus, his eyes glazed with concentration, crouched with his back against a half-ruined wall, the rest of the scouts hunkered down behind him. The shouts of the Fornux Lix Guardsmen and the hissing las-fire filtered through the background of rumbling tanks and falling masonry as the Guard units advanced.

On cue, three fat bolts of crimson energy hissed overhead, sending out a wash of stinking ozone.

Nisryus hadn't been wrong yet.

'Now!' yelled Eumenes and the scouts ran forward, crossing the gap in cover. Tydeus fired a grenade to cover them and the scouts made it to the cover of the next ruined building intact. The Guard's Demolisher siege tanks were rapidly reducing the district to rubble, blasting siege cannon shells into the buildings in the hope of slowing down the Soul Drinkers so the Crimson Fists could force a stand-up fight. The scouts, in return, were doing their damndest to hold up the Guardsmen, and Eumenes had little doubt that his handful of scouts were the only obstacle between the Fornux Lix Fire Drakes and a complete encirclement of the Soul Drinkers.

'The Fists!' shouted Nisryus. 'They're here…'

Eumenes caught sight of something in the ruined building looming over them, its internal architecture laid wide open by Demolisher fire, its floors sagging and shedding drifts of rubble and broken furniture. There was someone on the upper floors – bolter fire flashed from within, the whine of bolter shells zipping through the air and the smack as they hit masonry.

Eumenes saw with a glance that the Fire Drakes covered everything past the rubble cover, their fire fields overlapping with a completeness that reminded him that he was up against professional soldiers. 'Where do we go?'

Nisryus looked up at the firefight bleeding out of the ruined building. 'Nowhere.'

A Crimson Fist smashed through the masonry two floors up and fell, gunning the exhausts of his jump pack to land square in the middle of the scout squad. It was an Assault Marine, with chainsword and bolt pistol, his chest armour scarred and smoking from the hit that had knocked him out of the building.

Thersites was closest. His two bolt pistol shots rang off ceramite and the Fist ignored them, stabbing out with an inhumanly quick lunge of his chainsword. Thersites didn't realise he had been struck until he hit the ground, a huge wet ragged hole where his chest had been.

Selepus leapt at the Fist from behind, his knife stabbing down at the neck join of the Fist's armour. The Fist turned, caught Selepus by the throat and threw him hard against a half-toppled column.

Nisryus crashed against the Fist's leg, knocking the huge Marine down onto one knee. Eumenes dived out from cover, lashing out with a kick to the faceplate of the Marine's helmet to knock him onto his back. Eumenes was suddenly on top of the Marine, his bolt pistol jammed into one eyepiece, pumping shell after shell, point-blank. Splinters of shell casing and ceramite spat up at Eumenes, cutting hot weals across his face as the faceplate split and the Marine thrashed as he died.

The gunshots gave way to silence inside Eumenes's head. It took a few moments for the din of battle to flow back in. The ruined face of the Marine, all shattered ceramite and blood with one smashed eyepiece glaring at him blindly, was all he could see.

A strange warmth washed through him. It was pride. He had killed his first Marine.

He looked up from the dead Crimson Fist. He still had men to lead. 'Selepus?'

Selepus was picking himself back up off the ground. 'I'm fine.'

'Thersites?'

'He's gone,' said Scout-Sniper Raek, kneeling over Thersites. Thersites was letting out a final rattling breath, blood flecking his lips. His tattered lungs were pumping weakly, visible through the red-black hole in his chest.

'We're clear,' said Nisryus, pulling himself from under the dead Marine.

'Good.' They could mourn the dead scout later, when there were fewer people shooting at them. 'Selepus, carry Thersites. Raek, on point. Let's move.'

APOTHECARY PALLAS CROUCHED down, las-shots zipping through the plush audience chamber from the demolished far wall. Here, among the burning drapery and bullet-riddled upholstery, Brother Kirelkin was dying, multiple las-burns scoring his fractured armour. Kirelkin's squadmates in Squad Kelvor were covering Pallas, but Pallas knew right away there was nothing he could do. One of Kirelkin's hearts was punctured and his torso was filling up with blood – his lungs had collapsed and in a few moments he would be gone.

Las-bolts thwacked into the lushly upholstered seating, arranged in rows around a throne from which one of Gravenhold's aristocrats held audience. Bits of burned hardwood showered Pallas as the top of his Apothecary's gauntlet slid back to reveal the thick gleaming needle of the reductor unit inside.

Kirelkin's lifesigns were zero. Pallas thrust the reductor into Kirelkin's throat, feeling the unit thunk forward and snip closed around the geneseed organ. The unit slid back, drawing the precious organ with it.

'Is it done?' asked Sergeant Kelvor. Kelvor's leg had been severed scant minutes ago but already his augmented blood had crusted into a hard seal around the stump.

Pallas nodded.

'Then we're gone. They're trying to surround us.'

Pallas ducked beneath the random gunfire and followed Squad Kelvor into the building, towards where the senate-house loomed.

Another good Marine gone. Many more of Sarpedon's little wars, and there wouldn't be a Chapter left.

Squad Luko and Sarpedon reached the steps of the senate-house first.

Sergeant Luko, his lightning claws smoking from the Guardsmen he had cut through to get there, ran up the steps and stopped with his back against the pillar.

The senate-house had dozens of entrances, to make sure that no one senator had to follow another into the building. Arches ran right around the circular wall of the building, each one carved with the names of past senators. With so many entrances the exterior was barely defensible but inside, hidden now in darkness, was a warren of offices, seating, auditoria and annexes clustered around the senate chamber itself. It would take the Crimson Fists and Fire Drakes a long time to winkle the Soul Drinkers out.

'Clear!' called Luko, and his Marines ran up past him, bolters trained, moving through the archways and into the building.

Sarpedon scuttled up the steps and took cover with Luko behind one of the pillars. Already Chaplain Iktinos and his mob of Marines were coming out of the Ecclesiarchical building across the street, Iktinos's black-painted armour smoking from scars inflicted by a power weapon. The Soul Drinkers were all closing in on the destination and the Fists and Guardsmen were coming with them. Gunfire was drawing nearer and every building seemed to be sporting battle cannon wounds belching smoke.

'Anything in there?' asked Sarpedon.

'No contacts,' replied Luko. 'No one's home.'

The vox crackled. 'Brother Faerak here,' came the transmission from inside the building. 'We've got a situation.'

'Frag,' spat Luko. 'They've got there first.'

'I don't think so, sir. You'd better see it.'

Luko and Sarpedon entered the building through the closest arch, the darkness closing around them. Sarpedon's eyes automatically adjusted to the low light, revealing carved hardwood partitions, handsome bronze sculptures of past senators, inscriptions and prayers of diligence and temperance pinned to the walls. Squad Luko had smashed through the closest wooden walls, Sarpedon and Luko followed in their wake.

Inside the senate-house there should have been a massive auditorium surrounded by private chambers and adepts' offices. Instead there was a yawning pit, a dark ragged shaft sinking through layers of stone foundations and earth, straight down so far Sarpedon couldn't see the bottom. Broken beams and pipes jutted from the crumbling sides, and the shaft cut through several levels of basements so keenly that there were still items of furniture and piles of old senatorial records threatening to topple into the pit.

Sarpedon glanced up – the roof of the senate-house was intact so this wasn't bomb damage. It had been dug deliberately, and recently.

'More xenos?' asked Luko.

'I don't think so,' said Sarpedon.

Then, there was the sound of voices. Someone was shouting down in the depths of the pit in a language Sarpedon could not quite understand; it had the tone and inflection of Imperial Gothic, as if the language itself had mutated. Then there was movement: pale, skinny shapes scrambling up the sides of the pit. There were hundreds of them. Thousands.

The Marines of Squad Luko aimed their bolters into the pit, ready for Luko's order.

'Hold your fire!' yelled Sarpedon. He flicked on the vox. 'Sarpedon to all squads, take cover and hold fire.' The other Soul Drinkers, those now advancing towards the senate-house and those still fending off the Guardsmen and Crimson Fists, broke off and headed for cover. There would be no last stand. They were about to find out if Sarpedon's plan had a chance of success.

Luko looked around at Sarpedon. 'This had better damn well work.'

Sarpedon said nothing. The voices grew louder and sparks of sorcery lit the inside for a split second. Thousands of creatures – humans – were scrabbling up the ladders and handholds, their skin pale, their faces obscured by straps and disfiguring piercings. They had every kind of weapon – knives, clubs, lasguns and autoguns looted from the Entymion IV PDF soldiers, bare hands, teeth. Some figures were floating up the middle of the pit, robed sorcerers with witch-born magic crackling around their hands. The gibbering and screeching grew louder and Sarpedon could make out looping patterns carved into their bodies, hands stripped of skin with metal shards for talons, facial features obscured by scraps of metal seemingly hammered into their skulls.

With a sound like death itself, the army of Gravenhold swarmed up out of the ground.

CHAPTER SEVEN

LORD GENERAL XARIUS watched the holomat projection grimly. Those few who came to know him well soon understood that it was a bad sign for him to be silent, and he didn't say a word as the previous three hours were played out on the holographic map projected into the heart of his Baneblade. The super-heavy tank was hull down in the very shadow of the western wall, ready to grind along behind the Seleucaians behind the advance, that advance had, of course, been postponed until Xarius had regained control of all the forces that were supposed to be fighting for him. The sound of mortar fire and occasional battle cannon shots from forward armour patrols filtered through the massive hull of the Baneblade – Xarius ignored them. He had more important things to worry about.

The holograph was zoomed in on a portion of Gravenhold to the east – the governmental sector, centred around the grand senate-house that stood on the shore of the River Graven. It was covered in scores of blinking icons, dark blue for the Crimson Fists, light blue for the Fornux Lix Fire Drakes, red for the enemy.

Xarius shook he head and wound back the projection, zipping through the last three hours of combat in reverse. It still didn't make sense. It had all happened, certainly – but it couldn't have. It shouldn't have.

The recording was back at the beginning. Xarius watched it unfold again – the blue column of icons snaked from the south-eastern gate towards the governmental district – Elthanion had rounded up the cream of the Fire Drakes' armour, Leman Russ main battle tanks and Demolisher seige variants, even Hellhound flame tanks, to support the Chimeras full of troops. The Crimson Fists had brought their own armour – Space Marines were far too proud to be anything but self-sufficient – mostly their Rhino APCs and some support tanks.

Red blips flickered where the long-range sensors on the *Resolve* had spotted enemy fire streaking towards the convoy. The convoy was mounting a classically stupid drive, completely unsupported, relying on speed to get through unscathed and without any apparent concern about getting surrounded or, indeed, getting back to the south-eastern gate again. Some tanks were destroyed or crippled, their icons dim, their passengers and crew probably picked off by isolated pockets of Gravenholders.

Then the convoy reached the governmental district itself. What followed, even in the clinical holo-display, was a murderously brutal close firefight. Xarius could only assume that the Traitor Marines that the Fists had encountered in the first moves into Gravenhold were holed up in strength, because suddenly the red icons of the enemy were a tight knot of resistance and the light blue of the Guardsmen were dying in their dozens. It was savage. Xarius had seen this kind of fight before, and sometimes found himself too close to them. He could feel the men dying out there. He could taste the smoke in the air and feel the heat of the flames.

There must have been two hundred Traitor Marines. If it had been a case of them against the hundred-strong Second Company of the Crimson Fists the numbers would have told – but the Fists had armour and the support of the Imperial Guard. The Traitors had fallen back, fighting bitterly every metre, to the senate-house itself. The senate-house should have been one of the centrepieces of the recapture of Gravenhold, where the Fire Drakes planted the flag of the aquila on the roof to signify that the city was almost won. Instead, it had erupted with a massive flood of enemy troops.

Xarius had never seen so many Space Marines in one place, but even that was nothing remarkable compared to the army that came out of absolutely nowhere. The sensors on the *Resolve* suggested between ten and twenty thousand enemy troops, a tidal wave of red icons swamping the Crimson Fists and the Guardsmen. The only possibility was that they had been travelling underground, gathering under the senate-house and colluding with the Traitor Marines to launch an immense trap.

What had been a rapid, unstoppable drive by the Imperial forces turned into a rout in a matter of seconds. Xarius slowed the projection down to real-time, watching the enemy pour out across the streets, through the now-ruined Ecclesiarchical offices and the chamber mercantile, spilling down along the banks of the Graven. He switched on the vox-recorder unit, hearing the fractured transmissions of the Fire Drakes as the disaster unfolded.

'...sweet Throne of Earth, there are thousands of them... fire team nine, team nine where the hell is my cover fire?'

'... witchcraft! It's damned witchcraft, they've got the Hellhound crew and they're coming for us...'

'Retreat! It's a frag-up, follow the Fists and get out of here...'

Guardsmen were frantically reciting prayers from the *Uplifting Primer* that every Guardsman was issued with, in the hope of keeping enemy sorcery out of their minds. Fire teams were shooting at one another, either through psychic domination or sheer panic. The Crimson Fists were putting out massive volleys of bolter fire and falling back to their APCs, leaving the Guardsmen to extricate themselves. Xarius saw and heard more than a thousand Guardsmen die in the first few minutes, dragged down by the baying hordes, trapped like rats in closed-off streets, shot by their friends or crushed by the tracks of their own tanks. One vox-burst ended as a Leman Russ exploded, cutting off the voice of its commander in a wave of static. Many others ended in screams. Xarius didn't need anything more to imagine what was going on in those streets – the *Resolve* would probably send him pict-steals of the streets in the morning but he could see, in his mind's eye, the charred bodies and paving sticky with blood.

In his younger days, Xarius would have chased the image away with a good shot of something alcoholic and spicy. He would have pretended that a lord general did not see the men under his command as men at all, but as numbers, weapons, statistics to be stacked and sacrificed until they added up to a victory. But he did not believe that any more. The Imperium was built on death, and it was his job to feel every single one of those deaths in the hope that he could win a victory that did not cost the very lives it was supposed to save. He wasn't a soldier. He was the opposite. He was fighting a war of his own, to keep the suffering from swallowing up what humanity the Imperium had left. It was a war he would one day lose, but that didn't mean he should stop fighting.

Wearily, Xarius flicked off the holomat and felt the claustrophobic interior of the Baneblade looming down on him.

'Hasdrubal?' he voxed.

'Sir?' replied the flag-commander.

'Get this damn coffin back onto the spaceport. The push will have to wait.'

'Yes, sir.'

The engines growled into life as the command tank began to turn and head back out from the shadow of the wall to where it would be safer. Damn the Fire Drakes, damn Elthanion and the bloody Crimson Fists. If a general lost control over his armies he wasn't fighting a war any more, he was just presiding over a disaster. Xarius tried to imagine what kind of disaster could erupt in Gravenhold if he let it happen, and he was glad to find that his imagination wasn't that good.

THE RAZORBACK ASSAULT APC juddered as it crashed over the remains of an administrative building shattered by Demolisher fire. Commander Reinez held on as the vehicle slewed round, gunfire still spattering against its armour.

The back hatch was hanging open and the Crimson Fists were firing out, keeping the hostiles out of the road behind them in case one of them had a rocket launcher or a demo charge. Through the hatch Reinez could see absolute desolation – plumes of smoke, wrecked tanks, piles of bodies, buildings ablaze or already gutted, the broken remnants of the once-handsome governmental district. Fornux Lix Chimeras and Fists' Rhinos ran a gauntlet of small arms fire and suicidal attacks from the corrupted soldiers of Gravenhold, who ran into the streets and seemed determined to take on the surging tanks and APCs with nothing more than bare hands, knives, teeth and fury.

'Inhuaca?' Reinez voxed through the static that accompanied any battle. 'Chaplain, come in!'

'… receiving you, barely,' came the stern voice of Chaplain Inhuaca.

'Where are you?'

'Ahead of you. Approaching the gate.'

'They killed Captain Arca,' said Reinez, unable to keep the anger out of his voice. 'They took the banner.'

Inhuaca paused. 'Then we have much to avenge.'

Reinez flicked off the vox in anger. He had thrown everything he had into taking the heads of the Soul Drinkers and he had failed. He had been thrown back in disarray. He had lost Crimson Fists, most of them veterans and many of them heroes of the Chapter like Assault-Captain Arca. And he had lost the standard of the Second Battle Company, which had been entrusted to him by the Chapter Master himself.

He had seen the Soul Drinkers. He had seen their mutations and their treachery. He had seen the trap unfold, where hordes of the enemy poured out to swamp the Fists and the Fire Drakes. He had faced them, and he had lost.

Reinez fired off a volley of bolter shots at hostiles in the street, seeing their pallid limbs flailing as they died. The Razorback's turret ground round on its bearing and launched a glittering las-blast into a building as the APCs rushed past it, boring through solid marble and sending out a shattered plume of masonry dust. The Marines crowded into the APC beside Reinez fired too, their guns chattering, sending the Emperor's wrath down on the only targets they had after the Soul Drinkers had cheated them out of delivering justice.

'Enough!' yelled Reinez, too disgusted with the wretchedness of the enemy to even look at them. 'Driver! Close the hatch and get us out of here! Catch up with the Chaplain at the gate!'

This battle was over. The APC's rear hatch closed, shutting out the grim aftermath of defeat. The engine revved up and the vehicle surged forward, forgoing firing for extra speed. The enemy couldn't hurt them. It was better to leave them behind and plan to bring the Emperor's vengeance down on them all at once, not waste lives and ammunition on skirmishing with them in the street.

The other Marines knew better than to complain. Reinez was furious, and they knew it because they all were. The shame of defeat had rarely been more acute, even for those who had lived through the loss of the Chapter's fortress-monastery.

The Fire Drakes were faring far worse than the Crimson Fists. They must have left hundreds of dead men in the streets of Gravenhold, with more doomed to die cut off and trapped within the city. But it was the insult that hurt more than the knowledge of those deaths. An insult that had to be avenged, even if it meant Reinez wouldn't get off Entymion IV.

He would kill them. He would kill them all, and it would be his hand that took the head of Sarpedon. He had seen the mutant witch, the arch-heretic, lit by the gunfire in the chamber mercantile. Reinez knew then, crammed into the back of a Razorback with a handful of defeated Marines and fleeing like a whipped animal, that the Emperor's will would only be done on this planet when Sarpedon was dead, and when it was Reinez who did the killing.

IT WAS A TIDE of corruption. It was an endless nightmare of broken minds, men and women robbed of their souls, reduced from humans into a near-mindless horde. The sorcerers were worse – magicians, rogue psychics, witches who sailed above the churning crowds of Gravenhold's unfortunate citizens and directed them like choirmasters. They wore flapping robes of emerald and black, or foetid wrappings of piecemeal leather that dripped bile as they flew.

Runes of power were scorched into the air as they cast their spells, sometimes so bright they were burned into the walls. Their orders, transmitted by thought or magic, rippled through the enemy like waves, drawing the teeming army one way or another. Drifts of bodies built up beneath the windows of Guard-held buildings until the enemy could clamber over their own dead and into the lower floors. Guardsmen were dragged out into the streets and torn apart, tanks were mobbed until their tracks were clogged solid with bone and gore and the Gravenholders pried the hatches open. Guardsmen blew themselves up with demo charges rather than die at these hands – others were mentally dominated by the sorcerers as if for sport, shooting their comrades or jumping out of top-floor windows.

'Are we just going to watch this?' said Luko grimly, hunkered down behind a pillar at the front of the senate-house, watching Gravenhold burning. The rest of the Soul Drinkers were scattered through the surrounding buildings and the Ecclesiarchical offices opposite the senate-house, probably all itching for the command to open fire. The Soul Drinkers had sworn that though they had turned their back on the Imperium they were still dedicated to eradicating the enemies of the Emperor; which definitely included the corrupted Gravenholders. It was an affront to them to be forced to stand by when they could kill thousands of them before being overrun, but Sarpedon was their leader and his word to them was law.

'Yes,' replied Sarpedon. 'We watch.'

'Iktinos here,' came a vox from the Chaplain, in cover on the far side of the senate-house where the river Graven ran in a wide loop around the government district. He had Marines on what remained of the senate-house's upper floors, watching the slaughter unfold. 'The Crimson Fists have pulled out and the Fire Drakes are in full retreat. The enemy is following them.'

'Good.' Sarpedon switched to the scouts' vox-channel. 'Eumenes? Get your squad into the senate-house and into the pit. We're going to where these creatures came from. Report all contacts, fire only when fired upon. Understood?'

There was a pause, slightly too long. The scouts, like all the Soul Drinkers, wanted to fight this enemy, not oblige them. 'Yes, commander,' came the eventual reply.

'Good. Luko will be behind you, find out what's down there and make sure we can traverse it safely.' Sarpedon nodded to Luko, who got to his feet and turned to hurry back into the senate-house where his Marines were watching over the pit in case something else came out.

'Luko,' said Sarpedon. 'Did you think it would work?'

'Honestly?' replied Luko. 'No. I thought it was too much to expect they wouldn't kill us.'

'Something is controlling them, Luko. Something that Tellos was fighting for. As far as they are concerned we're just more of the same, come to die for them. If we look like we're here to fight them instead then they really will kill us.'

'I understand, commander. But I'd be happier if I knew who "they" were.'

'I think we'll find out soon enough. Back up the scouts, and keep your eyes open. No one knows what's under this city.'

Luko saluted with a lightning claw and ducked down into the shadows of the senate-house.

Someone had called Tellos to Entymion IV to fight. Who, and why, were the questions Sarpedon was risking his Chapter to answer. So far Sarpedon had shown his Marines were on the side of the enemy in Gravenhold, they had fought the Guard and the Fists, and let the army of debased citizens run riot through the Imperial forces. Now he had to get close enough to begin the hunt for Tellos.

IMPERIAL HISTORY WAS a fiction. Eumenes had known this even as a child on Veyna, when he heard tell of the Imperial preachers who likened him and his people to vermin to be exterminated. He had seen it when he compared the sanctioned Imperial histories in the *Brokenback*'s Librarium to the recollections of the Soul Drinkers who had lived through betrayal and excommunication.

The history of Entymion IV said the Imperial presence was the first, last, and only human civilisation on the planet. Gravenhold had been planned and built by the first settlers, led by the original explorers and missionaries, to codified Imperial architecture and Standard Template Construct blueprints. There had been nothing there before the city, created on virgin earth for the convenience of the Administratum.

The truth, realised Eumenes as he clambered down the rickety makeshift ladders into the depths of the shaft, was that there had been something here long before the current Gravenhold. Layers of architecture, crushed into contrasting strata of stone, marched past before his eyes. Chunks of recognisable structures loomed out of the crumbling earth wall. Sometimes, Eumenes could just make out, with his still-improving eyesight, carvings or inscriptions in languages he couldn't read. Gravenhold was old – or at least, whatever was beneath it was old.

'Clear!' came the vox from Selepus, twenty metres below.

'Nisryus, anything?'

'They've gone,' replied Nisryus, who was just below Eumenes. 'Most of them won't come back this way. It's confusing down here – the way they think – it's not like human beings. There's something else in there.'

'If you start to lose control, Nisryus, you shut it down,' said Eumenes sternly. 'I don't care how good a precog you are. This city's one big moral threat and I don't want you compromised on my watch, understand?'

Nisryus knew full well what would happen if his psychic powers made him a conduit for some daemonic entity or mind-controlling alien. He wouldn't be the first psychic recruit to be put down by his comrades.

Selepus was on the ground, which was knee-deep in foul water where floated the bodies of the Gravenholders who had fallen during the climb up. Eumenes and Nisryus followed him down, the scout squad dropping into the water. There was only one scout squad now, the survivors of Squad Giryan fought under Eumenes. The eight-strong unit included Eumenes's scouts, Raek the sniper, and scouts Laeon and Alcides from Squad Giryan.

Selepus turned over one of the bodies. Its eyes were covered by a strip of metal that seemed to have been pressed to the skin while red-hot, burning its way through the muscle and melting into the bones of the skull. Rivets were driven into its scalp and it had rusting, jagged talons sprouting from its fingertips. It was dressed in battered leather, the remains of a forge worker's gear.

Nisryus walked up to the body and held a hand over it, letting the sensations of its death flow into him.

'Careful, Nis,' said Scamander. 'They were crazy, even I can feel it.'

'This isn't a human mind,' said Nisryus, his eyes closed. Eumenes saw he was trembling slightly and there were dark lines around his eyes, the marks of psychic fatigue. 'It's xenos. The people weren't just dominated. Someone… someone tore out their souls and put something else in there.'

Several tunnels led off from the bottom of the shaft. Selepus was already at the largest, carefully peering down it. It seemed to have once been a service shaft or sewer, there were lead pipes running along the ceiling and the walls were of slimy brick.

'Clear,' he said.

'Luko,' voxed Eumenes. 'We're going in.'

'Take care, lad,' replied Luko, whose Marines were just reaching the shaft floor. 'I'd hate to have to shoot something through you.'

There was a whole city beneath Gravenhold. Probably several. It was obvious – it was served by half-collapsed sewers that had been dug out to form broad half-flooded avenues under the city. Even with the water it was easy enough for a trained scout to follow the path the Gravenholders had taken – they had crowded the sewers and left scratches on the walls and occasional bodies floating, each bearing the same extremes of self-mutilation as the one Nisryus had inspected. There were tunnels leading everywhere and the horde had been fed from many different parts of the undercity, but the main mass had come from somewhere to the north, beneath the noble estates of Gravenhold. The Soul Drinkers had only seen that part of the city from outdated pict-steals during the briefing sessions on the *Brokenback* – lavish villas, each trying to outdo its neighbour, the largest sporting whole villages of servants' quarters and even the smallest cramming statue gardens and courtyards around houses that ranged from the elegant to the grotesquely tasteless.

It was easy to imagine the aristocracy of Gravenhold too wrapped up in their petty games to bother noticing what lay beneath their feet. Now they were either dead or transformed into a mindless army, controlled by an unholy alliance of corrupt sorcerers and aliens.

The Soul Drinkers moved down the shaft and followed in the scouts' footsteps. Eumenes reported everything he saw to the units behind him, knowing they were spreading out to secure the route his scouts were forging. Sometimes there were inscriptions carved roughly by the builders of the tunnels, graffiti in some pre-imperial dialect.

There were surviving Gravenholders, too, crippled or lost, keening alone in the darkness. Eumenes instructed Raek to take each one down from a safe distance – the scout-sniper was quiet and unassuming, but he was as efficient a killer as Selepus.

Eumenes had moved through the tunnels for almost an hour when he saw the main tunnel ahead was collapsed, leaving a huge rent in the ceiling and a long drift of fallen masonry. The bricks and rubble were smeared with blood from the thousands of bare feet that had charged down it into the tunnels from a huge cavity above. Eumenes could see the ceiling of the cavern above – it looked like a low stone sky, dark rock braced with curving columns of white stone like ribs.

'Stop,' said Selepus.

'Movement?'

'I think so.'

It wasn't like Selepus not to be sure. Eumenes waved for the squad to halt. 'Eumenes here,' he voxed to the squads behind him. 'Stop, we've got contact.'

Selepus was scanning the shadows, knife in one hand and pistol in the other. He indicated one of the side tunnels with the point of his knife. 'It was through there.'

Scamander had his pistol holstered and had his hands held up, ready to fill the confined tunnel with fire. The rest of the squad were clustered in the centre of the tunnel, weapons drawn, covering every angle.

'Don't,' said Nisryus. 'I don't think it wants to hurt us.'

'This would be a bad time for you to be wrong, Nis,' said Eumenes, and then he saw it. There were footsteps in the water, but the creature making them seemed composed of shadow, bleeding into the darkness around it. The barest hint of a lithe, humanoid shape was cast onto the wall before it flickered out of view again.

Eumenes glanced down the tunnel and saw Squad Luko assembling at the next junction back, bolters ready. Luko himself had his lightning claws activated, the power field casting strange reflections on the water.

'Scamander?' said Eumenes. 'More light.'

Scamander brought his hands together and in his cupped palms a white-hot ball of flame appeared. He opened his fingers and the shuddering white light filled the tunnel.

With no shadows to hide in, the alien appeared.

Most Imperial citizens had only seen eldar in pictures or carvings. Even those that were accurate told a lie. The eldar were broadly humanoid – they had two arms, two legs, a head and a recognisable complement of facial features – and so most citizens probably thought they appeared a lot like humans. Eumenes knew different, for he had seen pict-recordings from the battles the Soul Drinkers had previously fought against the eldar and now he finally saw one up close, he understood what 'alien' really meant.

The eldar's proportions were totally, horribly wrong. Its skeleton was jointed wrongly, its pigeon chest flaring into broad shoulders with long arms and fingers like spiders' legs. Its legs were thin but seemed wound up ready to spring at any moment and its face was elongated, with a small mouth and tapering nose. Its eyes were the worst – large, soulless, with huge glittering pupils. The utter inhumanity of the thing was accentuated by the way its skin shimmered and shifted – it was supposed to blend into the shadow but under Scamander's harsh light it squirmed like something trapped, rippling between black and white. On its lower half it wore a tight-fitting bodysuit with curved armour plates, its torso was bare and it carried a strange crystalline pistol in one hand. The other hand held a dagger with an elaborate guard that encased the alien's fist and a long, curved, jagged blade. It was slightly taller than an average man, but the comparison meant little. Every muscle and movement was alien.

There was a second eldar crouching down at the next junction, but though exposed neither one ran. There was an uneasy pause. Eumenes didn't have to tell his scouts not to shoot, but it would only take one threatening move for all that to count for nothing. These were aliens. They were practically born to betray Mankind.

'Good,' said a smooth, dark voice with enough of an accent to tell Eumenes it wasn't from a native speaker of Imperial Gothic. 'Then you are curious, and you are willing to talk, not just fight. Both these things are good. Don't you agree? Youth of the living race, youth of the strong, don't you agree?'

The third alien was different. As it walked into view Eumenes saw it wore full armour, black and glossy, worked into elaborate curves and spikes with plates that locked together to allow full movement. Its weapon was slung over its back, a long crystal rifle. It had a tall helmet with bright jade eyepieces hanging at its belt – its bare face was so pale it looked dead and jet-black hair hung down over its shoulders. 'Forgive my pets, my bloodhounds,' it said, indicating the two other eldar. 'Your soldiers named them "mandrakes" and they fear them greatly, but you have nothing to fear.'

'They're not our soldiers up there,' replied Eumenes. 'But then you knew that.'

The eldar smiled in deference. The expression was as wrong as the rest of it, and Eumenes guessed it was mimicking a human smile to put the scouts at ease. It wasn't working. It had black predator's eyes and a sneering little slit of a mouth, and nothing it did would make Eumenes trust it.

'Please,' said the alien, indicating the path ahead that sloped upwards into the cavern. 'Come with me, sons of the strong.'

'Sir?' voxed Eumenes on the command channel.

'Go with him,' replied Sarpedon. 'Luko, Graevus, join them. Pallas too. If you get the slightest hint of an ambush, get back here shooting. We'll be right behind you.'

Luko's tactical squad and Graevus's Assault Marines, along with Apothecary Pallas, moved down the tunnel. They were wary but their weapons weren't raised. Eumenes waved at his scouts to lower their own pistols, and Selepus holstered his knife.

'Excellent,' said the alien slimily, seeing that the Soul Drinkers were co-operating. 'The prince has long wished to meet with you.'

* * *

'Guilliman's arse,' swore Luko in quiet awe as the Soul Drinkers saw the palace for the first time. They had realised by then that there were cities lying in layers beneath Gravenhold, but none of them had suspected anything might survive this intact. And yet it had, and suddenly what had happened to Gravenhold made a little more sense.

The cavern was not natural. It was a handsome scalloped hemisphere, carved with huge and precise geometry, the dark stone braced with struts of white that formed an enormous vaulted ceiling so high it looked like a dark grey sky.

'They must have known,' said Pallas quietly as the Marines spread out from the entrance formed by the collapsed sewer. 'Whoever was here before the Imperium, they must have built it like this because they knew it would be buried. They had to make sure something survived.'

'Or else it's a tomb,' replied Graevus. Graevus still carried the banner of the Crimson Fists Second Battle Company, rolled up around its standard pole and held in his unmutated hand. He had lost three Marines in the chamber mercantile and he and his squad were badly battered.

The palace itself was even more extraordinary than the chamber it was hidden in. It sat surrounded by lavish stone gardens, marble and jade carved to resemble trees and flower beds, cold and astoundingly lifelike as if a real garden had been suddenly petrified. Marble fountains sprouted flowing torrents of glass. Lawns of emerald crystal were broken by stands of black stone trees with jade leaves.

The building was of dark green veined stone, deeply lustrous, drinking in the light from the glow-globes that hung like fat shining fruit from the stone trees. It was an extraordinary conceit, with bone-coloured marble picking out its battlements, tall fairytale turrets, a massive portcullis of mirror-polished gold and a wide moat full of what had to be quicksilver, churning and swirling around the base of the palace's outer wall. The palace had been built to look like a castle and though it was more a decorative folly than a fortification, the Soul Drinkers, being soldiers, still noted the firing slits and the formidable overhangs of the battlements. They saw the way the corner turrets jutted out to force attackers into overlapping fire fields and the simple difficulty of crossing the moat. If things turned bad, the palace could be a hellish place to attack, especially if it was defended by anything like the forces the aliens could evidently bring to bear.

The alien, with its two mandrake companions loping alongside it, led the way. With Scamander's blinding light withdrawn they shifted in and out of view, their forms blending into the shadows of the trees and fountains. The main path towards the palace wound past statues, oddly stylised depictions of Gravenhold's earlier inhabitants apparently, but not definitely, human.

The golden portcullis ground open as a bridge extended from below the main gate. The interior of the palace was dark with a dim glow from somewhere inside, purplish and uninviting. The Soul Drinkers followed the aliens across the bridge and through the outer wall. The air was as cold as a tomb, the stone sweating slightly, the armoured footsteps of the Marines echoing.

In the courtyard beyond, an expanse of crystalline lawn surrounding the palace's inner keep, hundreds of eldar stood as if to attention. They wore black glossy armour and carried weapons varying from the crystalline rifles to long barbed whips to curved, serrated swords that gleamed with venom. Behind the front rows of warriors were more heavily-armoured eldar with full helmets, thicker and more elaborate armour, and massive halberds with energy blades. There were dark shimmering forms slinking along the battlements above them, more mandrakes no doubt, along with more eldar warriors this time carrying heavier weapons: long-barrelled guns made of something gleaming and black, multi-barrelled versions of their crystalline rifles, and stranger-shaped weapons besides.

The eldar were raiders and bandits, rarely mustering in any number, striking in small co-ordinated bands. It was rare to see so many in one place, let alone in the presence of Imperial troops. The eldar were silent as they stood to attention, eerie and intimidating. There was little doubt how much killing power this army possessed, and the numbers assembled probably counted for only a fraction of their full strength in Gravenhold.

The alien accompanying the Soul Drinkers spoke a few words of the sibiliant eldar language and the assembled warriors parted before the black stone doors of the keep. The doors opened and the alien led the Soul Drinkers into the keep.

Inside, a second large door led into an enormous throne room. Lying prostrated on the floor, facing the throne dais, were scores of the Gravenholders, their faces pressed against the cold stone floor, crouched in silent adoration of the figure on the throne.

Even seated, the prince was obviously tall, and the long halberd leant against his tall throne of green marble was evidently there for more than show. His armour was even more elaborate than that of his elite soldiers – the shoulderpieces curved so high they formed a crescent moon behind his head and dark red silks embroidered with silver billowed from between the interlocking armour plates. A brilliant green jewel was mounted in the centre of his breastplate, illuminating his face from beneath and picking out his long, cruel features. His skin was pale and his shaven head was covered in intricate tattoos, dozens of characters from the eldar language probably recording his many works of depravity.

Behind his throne stood a group of the prince's personal warriors. In contrast to the warriors in the courtyard these were stripped-down, their armour designed more to show off their snakelike muscles and perfect alabaster skin than to provide any actual protection. The reason for their lack of armour was soon obvious. At an almost imperceptible signal from the prince one of the warriors backflipped off the dais and scampered up to the Soul Drinkers with lightning speed and incredible grace, picking its way between the prostrate Gravenholders with such ease it was as if they weren't there.

The lithe eldar exchanged a few words with the Soul Drinkers' guide. Eventually the guide turned to the closest Marine, which happened to be Luko.

'The Pirate Prince Karhedros of the Kabal of the Burning Scale, Lord of the Serpent Void, Victor of the Wars of Vengeance, First Scion of Commoragh and Beloved of She-Who-Thirsts, bids welcome to his allies the Drinkers of Souls, exiles from the Beast Race, loyal to the Prince and devoted to his glory.'

'It is an honour,' replied Luko uncertainly.

'What offering have you brought the prince, that he might know the path of your souls?'

The Marines shot a few uncertain looks between themselves. No one had said anything about an offering. Space Marines were not diplomats, and Sarpedon the Chapter's leader was not there.

Eumenes stepped forward and took the banner from Graevus's arm. 'Here,' he said to the eldar guide. 'We have brought this. The prince's enemies are our enemies.'

The prince saw this, and stood up on his throne, Regally, with the long strides of someone indeed taller even than a Space Marine, he strode across the throne room past the prostrate Gravenholders and took the banner from the guide. It unrolled in his hands and the bloody, bullet-charred standard of the Crimson Fists Second Company stared out at the prince. The red gauntlet icon was embroidered above a scroll listing hundreds of engagements where the Second Company had distinguished itself, a list that should have had Gravenhold added to it.

Pirate Prince Karhedros regarded the banner for several long moments.

'It seems,' he said in flawless Imperial Gothic and a silky voice, 'that my enemies would dearly love to see you dead for what you have taken from them. Those that hate you also hate me, and I hate them. That makes us allies. Bring your warriors to my palace, we have much to discuss.'

Luko looked round at Eumenes. 'Well done, lad,' he said with obvious relief. Then, he flicked on the vox.

'Sarpedon, we're going to need you here. Bring every-one.'

CHAPTER EIGHT

COLONEL SAVENNIAN HAD, at least, answered the summons when Xarius had sent it out. More importantly, he had brought Lieutenant Elthanion with him on the Aquila-pattern shuttle that zipped from the southwestern gate to the eastern spaceport, giving the city and its baleful influences a very wide birth. Along with Colonel Threlnan of the Seleucaians, Colonel Vinmayer of the Algorathi Janissaries and Consul Kelchenko, who effectively commanded the 4th Carvelnan Royal Artillery, Savennian completed the complement of commanding officers under Lord General Xarius.

Xarius met them as the shuttle touched down. Elthanion was still smoking slightly and stank of gunsmoke and sweat, an old soldier in marked contrast to the almost doll-like Savennian, an elderly aristocrat who had gradually shrunk in his old age until from a distance he looked like a regimental mascot in a colonel's uniform.

There had been a time when Xarius would have bawled out both men there and then for dereliction of duty, for wasting the valuable lives of Imperial citizens to go chasing after some Space Marine's personal vendetta. But Xarius knew it wouldn't do any good. Ethanion and Savennian knew damn well they would be lucky to get away without a court martial after Gravenhold was won, and if they stepped out of line again, Xarius would be well within his rights to have them both shot.

So Xarius said nothing, and let his makeshift adjutant Hasdrubal make with the niceties and lead the colonel and the lieutenant to where the commanders of the Entymion IV strikeforce were gathered.

'This,' said Xarius, indicating the artillery train with a sweep of his arms, 'is the beginning of the end.'

The huge circular landing hub in front of him was full of artillery tanks. Basilisks with long-range Earthshaker cannon stabbing upwards, Griffon mortar tanks with elaborate hull-mounted cranes to load their wide-mouthed mortars. Medusas with huge forward-firing guns to crack open bunkers and gun emplacements. Even two Deathstrike missile launchers, devastating strategic weapons which launched vortex warheads – they only got one shot, but by the Emperor they could make it count. The air around them was shimmering with the downdraft of another lander, carrying a pair of Basilisks in its skeletal hull as it descended. Crewmen were scrambling all over the tanks, loading fuel and ammo, finding their favoured machines, checking gunsights and steering.

'This is the 4th Carvelnan Royal Artillery, gentlemen,' continued Xarius. 'Courtesy of the consul here.'

Consul Kelchenko, a fat man in the deep blue uniform of the Departmento Munitorum, nodded smugly. Kelchenko's tiny corner of the Departmento Munitorum was responsible for deploying, fuelling and arming the Carvelnan Royal Artillery, which meant that he was effectively the unit's commanding officer even though he hailed not from the Guard but from the Administratum.

Xarius turned back to the colonels, sitting in a large supply tent that had been cleared out to provide seating for the officers, their various adjutants, and a large holodisplay. 'We now possess the most effective way of killing our own men and creating plenty of rubble for the enemy to hide behind.'

The holodisplay flicked on. Images of the first few hours of campaign flickered past, eerily silent pict-steals of the murderous fighting around the industrial mills and the south-eastern gate. 'The campaign for Gravenhold will require a systematic and relentless drive across the city on a wide front. Our Guardsmen will be advancing into enemy-held areas within moments of artillery barrages. There is ample opportunity for our own men to be shelled, for the line to break apart, for Guardsman to kill Guardsman in the confusion.

'This campaign will only hope to succeed if there is absolute co-operation between all branches. Between the artillery, the men of your regiments, and the observers on the *Resolve*. The battle will be decided at squad level, at which your sergeants will excel because you will have chosen, briefed and directed them according to the extremely close-range combat likely to occur in this environment.'

The holodisplay was showing the Fire Drakes being driven back at the south-eastern gate, fire streaking down at them, bodies and gutted Chimeras littering the broad road. 'But this will not be enough. The Guard advance and the artillery must be co-ordinated with absolute diligence and precision. This operation will be assembled and put into action within the next twenty-four hours so you do not have much time to get your aim in. I suggest you make the most of it.' The holo changed to a map display of Gravenhold and its most prominent features – the River Graven, the arena in the heart of the slums, the massive black iron mills, the lavish homes of the aristocracy.

'Gentlemen, your first impressions. Colonel Threlnan?'

Threlnan stood. 'I believe our first target is the industrial sector. We have been reducing the enemy presence with aggressive patrolling. It will need a major footslog to drive them out and these are large industrial buildings, they won't react well to shellfire. Bringing down a couple of troublesome enemy strongholds is about our limit until we break through into the slums.'

'Which we can happily pound to rubble?' interjected Xarius.

'Yes, sir.' Tactical arrows were appearing as Threlnan spoke, marking out the various paths the Seleucaian units would take. It would be a gruelling, building-by-building grind as the Guardsmen cleared sharpshooters from the towering mills and warehouses. 'If we bypass the mills we'll be handing the enemy a haven too tough for us to crack. Once we drive them into the slums we can push them eastwards with the artillery.'

'Good. Gentlemen, what of the Fire Drakes?'

'I shall allow Lieutenant Elthanion to explain our battle plans,' said Savennian. His voice was thin and nasal, as if he had never had to raise it in his life.

Savennian looked even more brutal than Threlnan and, unlike Threlnan, he had none of the officer's polish to take the edge off it. He was still fresh from battle and he had not had all his minor shrapnel wounds dressed. His heavy dark grey body armour was dulled with grime from engine smoke and spotted with more than a little blood. 'Recon has suggested a large body of enemy light infantry between the governmental district and the south-east gate,' said Elthanion.

'So we noticed,' said Xarius, but choked back the instinct to say more.

'The Fire Drakes are at about sixty per cent full strength,' continued Elthanion, ignoring the insult. Enemy icons swarmed around the governmental district, barring the path of the unit icons representing the depleted Fire Drakes. 'We lost a lot of armour. But we're planning an infantry drive with full artillery support from the start. We'll pound them against the River Graven, then meet up with the Seleucaians to cross the river. Long, hard assaults are what the Fire Drakes do best. The enemy has the numbers but not the quality, we'll break them and chase them into the river.'

Xarius eyed the plans. They were straightforward enough, but the advance from the south-east gate would have had twice the momentum had the Fire Drakes' armour not been so badly mauled haring after the Traitor Marines. Xarius's plan was to have the Seleucaians and the Fire Drakes meet in the centre of the city's southern half, then turn northwards to cross the Graven en masse and surge into the north of the city. The north, with its sprawling noble estates and adepts' quarters, had seen barely any combat and it was anyone's guess as to what might be in there. It was hoped that victory in the south would cripple the enemy hold and leave the north vulnerable, and the colonels' contributions so far seemed adequate. But there was still too much the Imperials didn't know. Xarius wished very dearly that Gravenhold really could be destroyed from orbit, but he knew better than anyone that this battle would be won the old-fashioned way.

'Adequate,' said Xarius. 'Colonel Vinmayer?'

Vinmayer wasn't the source of the problem with the Algorathi Janissaries. He was just a symptom. The Janissaries had, for more than three hundred years, served as a garrison on a feudal world where forming a square against nomadic cavalry or swatting aside spear-armed peasants with parade-ground volley fire was enough to do the Emperor's will. Vinmayer wore a fine powder blue uniform with breeches, shako, gold bullion in neat rows across his chest, a dress sword scabbarded at his waist and only a pearl-handled duelling laspistol holstered on one hip to suggest he belonged in the forty-first millennium. 'My men are the best-drilled you'll find this side of Cadia, sir! Our Seleucaian friends will have nothing to fear, we'll back them up every step of the way. There will be no enemy counter-thrusts, of that you can be sure.'

The arrows on the holo now showed where the Algo-rathi units, hopefully furnished with some Chimeras and a few grim war stories about what real battles were like, would advance into the wilderness left behind by the Seleucaian thrust. Their job was to form a barrier against the most obvious counterattacks, from ene-mies driven into the extreme south of the city's slums where they might reform at the southern wall and drive into the Seleucaian rear. 'As you can see, I have worked carefully with Colonel Threlnan to ensure his every move is shadowed by my men.'

'Good,' said Xarius. 'Then the Janissaries will be where they can be of the most use. Gentlemen, all this is good enough in practice but if we treat Gravenhold like the seat of some petty rebellion then this plan will break down and we will fail. Make no mistake, if the city is not taken by us, in this way, then we will lose the whole planet. The Administratum would rather write it off as lost than have a major military catastrophe on their hands, and I will not have that magnitude of failure under my command. You answer directly to me, and if discipline breaks down in those streets, you'll be busted down so far you'll be carrying ammo to the men you now command. Questions?'

No one made a sound.

'Good. Get these plans finalised, I can see gaps big enough to drive a Baneblade through. Go to your men and see to their morale, they'll take a battering in there no matter how it goes. And for the Emperor's sake, don't forget we're all on the same side. Dismissed.'

'I have... I have one question, sir,' said Consul Kelchenko.

'Yes, consul?'

'What about the Crimson Fists? I had expected their commander would be here.'

Xarius sighed. 'The Fists can join in if they want. Perhaps you might even find some orders they can follow. Now dismissed.'

Kelchenko looked disappointed as the assembled officers broke off to return to their men. Doubtless he had hoped since childhood that one day he would meet one of the armoured heroes of the Imperium. The Marines had that effect. Used right they were a powerful psychological force.

Xarius hoped the Fists would play along. The invasion needed all the help it could get. The Seleucaians were competent and numerous and the Fire Drakes were quality troops, even the Algorathi Janissaries has their uses, but the Crimson Fists could form a cutting edge that Xarius knew could make the difference.

But the Crimson Fists wouldn't listen to him, he knew it. In their own way they were as lost to him as the Traitor Marines they were so eager to kill.

Accompanied by Hasdrubal, Xarius walked back to the squat, monstrous shape of his Baneblade, oddly comforting for all its ugliness. The truth was, when the engines were powered down it was probably the quietest place in the spaceport, and Xarius was an old man who needed some sleep.

BETRAYAL HUNG AROUND the palace like radiation. Sarpedon could feel it. As a telepath, even one who could not receive or read minds, he could sense the heavy dark weight of it tainting everything. The other Soul Drinkers, temporarily barracked in a wing of the palace, could feel it too – they were surrounded by hostile xenos of the kind they were honour-bound to kill, holding off enacting the Emperor's will because Sarpedon knew the aliens were his only link to Tellos.

Sarpedon hated it, too. He hated it more, because he was responsible for it. He had delivered his Marines into the stronghold of eldar far more sinister and cruel than those he had fought before, even on Quixian Obscura where he had first earned his spurs in the eyes of the old Chapter. The mandrakes were silent killers who could probably sneak up on even a Marine in the gloomy depths of the palace. The incubi, as the prince's heavily armoured elites were known, were the equal of an Assault Marine in close combat, and no one knew what other secrets the xenos might unleash at the first opportunity.

The eldar were warriors, aesthetes, pirates, philosophers and killers. But most of all, they were liars.

'Our meeting is fortunate, Lord Sarpedon,' said Prince Karhedros. 'We two are cast out. Hated by our species, no? Betrayed. And forced to fight the cancer that is Mankind. Forced! Surrounded by death, compelled to slaughter. This is your story as well as mine. So we are the same.'

Karhedros reclined on a long couch of carved black wood, some alien creature lying dissected and raw on a low table by his head. As he spoke he picked fleshy scraps from the creature and swallowed them. The circular chamber, on the lower levels of the palace and evidently somewhere beneath the stone gardens, was so lavishly upholstered and strewn with gold-embroidered cushions that it threatened to swallow the silent eldar body-servants that followed Karhedros everywhere. They wore little more than strips of black silk, but that same silk covered their faces completely. They kneeled silently around the room.

Sarpedon declined to take the second couch. With eight legs and power armour, reclining was not an option. 'It is true,' he said, swallowing the filthy feeling it gave him to talk with this creature. 'We are both excommunicate.'

'Ah, yes. A fine way to put it. Your language is painful to us, strong one, but it does have its little gems. Excommunicate we are.' Karhedros glanced at one of the body slaves, who slunk forward and wordlessly poured a long, fluted glass full of something amber-coloured and effervescent. Sarpedon thought the body-slave was a female eldar but he found it difficult to tell with a species whose every muscle and sinew was wrong.

'Try some,' said Karhedros. 'It's not the best, but it's as good as you'll find on this planet.'

Sarpedon accepted the glass from the slave. Even if it was poisoned, his many internal augmentations and redundant organs would filter out anything harmful. It would be more dangerous to refuse it and risk causing suspicion. 'My battle-brother fights alongside your warriors,' said Sarpedon. 'That is enough to convince me we are on the same side.'

'Ha!' Karhedros let out a strange barking laugh. 'I have eyes and ears throughout this city, they more than convince me we are fighting the same enemy. Many died that would otherwise have lived to blight me. We honour our fellow sufferers, Lord Sarpedon, and I feel this city will be won all the sooner. You speak of your brother Tellos, I assume? I understand now where he learned to make war.'

'We fight the same enemy,' said Sarpedon, 'but I still do not know why we fight them here. What do you want on this world? It must have been good enough to convince Tellos.' Sarpedon took an experimental sip of the liquid. It was wine, doubtless looted from some aristocrat's cellar. Sarpedon's metabolism broke down the alcohol instantly but even his unsophisticated palate could tell it was very good indeed.

Karhedros leaned forward conspiratorially. 'I want this city, Sarpedon. I want this world. Think about it. We both wish to hurt the Imperium. For revenge, for gain, for whatever reason. Hurt it. But it is huge. Why, you know better than I what a monstrous thing this empire of Mankind is. I have tried to hurt its citizens, I have. I have enslaved and tormented them by the thousands, but it does not notice! They send warfleets to chase me away but dare not bring me to battle to avenge the insults I do them. They treat me like vermin to be swatted away when I annoy them, but not worth the bother to kill.

'Now tell me, what is the point of that? I have killed more of them than I can count, and believe me I tried to keep a tally, Lord Sarpedon. And then I started to think. What is the Imperium? What is it made of? It cannot be made of its citizens, because I have tortured countless numbers of them to death and not made this empire bleed. What else is there?'

Sarpedon couldn't help considering this question. The Imperium was vast and corrupt. In serving it for thousands of years, the Soul Drinkers had become a part of that corrupt machinery, and it had taken a direct betrayal by the Imperium to force Sarpedon to realise it. It cared only about maintaining its own survival, and certainly had no regard for its masses of citizens. 'Its fleets? Its armies?'

'No, Lord Sarpedon. It took me a long time to understand it, too. The answer, excommunicate one, is its worlds.' Karhedros took another morsel of his meal, this time of pink, gelatinous brain material. The creature had been something like a hairless dog, but it had been elaborately dissected and laid open like a bed of glistening, fleshy flowers. 'The monster you call the Imperium is made of nothing. It does not value its people or its spaceships. The only thing it cares about is the most insubstantial thing of all: the claims it makes to the worlds under its shadow. Take that away, and they swarm like angry insects. And so they become the vermin, Lord Sarpedon. Nothing but vermin.'

'So you want to take a world from them?'

'Of course. What other way is there? I exist, I think, to cause suffering. The Imperium has proven impervious to all the wounds I have caused, and so this is the only way I can do what I am here to do.'

'You know, Prince, that many have tried to make claim to Imperial worlds. Too many for anyone to count, in fact. I once fought them. The Imperium has many rebels and usurpers. Aliens, too. Greenskins, Tau, worse things. And there are some who hold them still, I will admit, but they are few in number and all, if I may say so, have far greater resources than you appear to. You might take Entymion IV and maybe even hold it for perhaps decades, but the Imperium will eventually tire of the insult and send enough Guardsmen to drive you out. Or simply send a battle-fleet to irradiate the planet.'

'But that is the point. Strong one, child of Mankind, you are too close to your species to understand. I will not send my warriors to hold every street and hill like common soldiers! I am not some ork warlord. I do not fight, not when I don't have to. I control. The people of Gravenhold are just mindless slaves now, but when my haemonculi are finished they will be able to act and think for themselves, with my will imprinted on their minds. I and my court will dissolve away.' Karhedros swallowed the last dregs of his wine. He dropped his glass, and a slave darted forward to catch it before it landed on the deeply carpeted floor. 'They will lose their world. It will be reduced to a lifeless ball of rock by their own weapons. But they will not have won, and they will know it. They will never forget. Entymion IV will be a cancer, a reminder of their weakness. Suffering, Lord Sarpedon. It will eat away at so many of them, there will at last be a scar of suffering on the Imperium to which I can lay a claim.'

Sarpedon could feel the prince's emotions bubbling away just beneath the surface. They were horrible, twisted parodies of human hatred and joy, completely alien but so strong that they battered at Sarpedon's mind. It took a lot to register with Sarpedon – though he was a psyker he was virtually a 'blunt', someone who could not receive telepathic information. Prince Karhedros's emotions were intense and offensively alien enough to force themselves into Sarpedon's consciousness. Karhedros was driven and dangerous, but then, Sarpedon had seen and heard enough to have come to that conclusion anyway.

'So you will leave Entymion IV and watch the Imperium destroy it themselves,' said Sarpedon. 'I would imagine that would be very satisfying. But what then?'

Karhedros plucked what looked like an eyeball from the glistening carcass, and popped it in his mouth. 'I will find another world, important but underpopulated, just like this one,' he said as he chewed. 'And then I will do it all again.'

Sarpedon sat back on his haunches. His skin wouldn't stop crawling. Sarpedon had fought all manner of monsters but rarely had he come across a creature who inflicted suffering purely for its own sake. It was a religion for Karhedros, and murder and torture were rituals to the She-Who-Thirsts deity Karhedros had hinted at.

'And the human sorcerers you brought here,' said Sarpedon. 'Do they share this dream?'

Karhedros shook his head. 'Their gods are cruel and brutish. Have you heard them pray? They beg for insanity, so they will have the strength to commit ugliness. I need them to control the Gravenholders. Magic does not come easy to my kind and we do not wish to attract the attention of the warp with our recklessness. This is just another crusade for the sorcerers. I give them the chance to fight in the name of their gods, they want nothing more. Soon they will cease to be useful. I must confess I would rather it was sooner.'

'And Tellos is the same?'

'Your brother Marine? He is not like them. He is honest. He does what he does because he enjoys it. It was why I was so honoured that you came to join him. I trust you fight for the same reason? For the joy and the exhilaration of doing violence to something you hate? No base gods.'

'No, prince, no gods. Where is Tellos now?'

Karhedros waved a hand dismissively. 'He has the run of the city. His purpose is to go where the fighting is thickest and kill what he can. The humans in this city are terrified of him, you know. Absolutely awestruck. I see your race is divided into the strong and the weak, and you strong ones strike such utter fear into the weak. When you are on the same side they clamour around you like children, hoping your strength will rub off. When you oppose them they run screaming. Most amusing!'

'But you don't know where he is.'

'You will know as well as I do that this Tellos is not a creature to be kept on a leash. I am sure you will find him soon enough. The truth is, Lord Sarpedon, your arrival is most fortunate. The Imperials intend to launch a major operation. They were reinforced by artillery and are massing men on both sides of the city.'

'A rolling advance. Artillery and men.' Sarpedon nodded. 'Typical Guard. Old-fashioned and costly, but it'll work.'

'Exactly. There is a chance they might be able to actually win this city if we are not prepared. But that won't happen if my warriors and your Marines hold them up long enough.'

'Long enough for what?'

Karhedros's smile looked almost real. 'Do you really think I will tell you all my secrets at once, Lord Sarpedon?'

Sarpedon had never been so close to an eldar, and never spoken to one at all save to admonish one for daring to exist before trying to kill it. But here he had to converse with one, and act as if he was a heartfelt ally – Sarpedon was sure that he must appear as alien to Kahedros as the eldar did to him, and that it was only this that kept Karhedros from seeing right through him.

If, of course, Karhedros hadn't guessed the truth already, and was just setting up the Soul Drinkers to betray them.

'Now,' Karhedros was saying, 'we have much to do. My advisors are drawing up plans for your deployment. Your Marines will have to move at a moment's notice.'

'They are eager to go,' said Sarpedon, which at least was true.

'Good.' Karhedros indicated the glistening carcass. 'Please, Lord Sarpedon. Try some. It is only right that my allies should enjoy the pleasures I do.'

'It is pleasure enough to fight,' said Sarpedon, which thankfully was diplomatic enough a refusal.

By the time Sarpedon left Karhedros's chamber, leaving the alien dining with his retinue of masked slaves, he felt so filthy and sinful that it took an effort of will just to keep going. He was not a servant of Karhedros, he was not fighting for She-Who-Thirsts. He was here to find Tellos, redeem or kill him, and get out. And if Sarpedon got the chance to betray Karhedros along the way, then all the better.

'LOOKS EVEN WORSE from the inside,' said Luko darkly. The wing the Soul Drinkers were using as a temporary barracks looked out over the stone garden. No doubt it had been an artistic marvel in its day, but now it was dark and sinister. The way the mandrakes could occasionally be seen, bleeding from one shadow to the next, didn't help.

'You hate this place too,' said Eumenes. Eumenes's squad had been barracked with Luko's, which Eumenes felt was fortunate. He liked Luko – aside from Karraidin (who was back on the *Brokenback*, looking after the remaining novices), Luko was the Soul Drinker Eumenes probably respected more than any other.

Luko shrugged. 'Not just the palace. This whole city is wrong.' Luko looked round from the glassless window looking out over the garden. 'Can you feel it?'

'Like it'll turn around and stab you in the back? Like it'll swallow you? Yes, I feel it.'

'It's these damn aliens. You've never faced the eldar, have you, Eumenes?'

'I've read about them. The old Chapter fought them many times. But no, I hadn't seen a live one until today.'

Luko sighed, and Eumenes saw how old he looked. Normally, armed with his lightning claws and revelling in face-to-face fighting, Luko radiated confidence. Not now. 'Most xenos are born just to survive. Some are born to be predators, like the tyranids or the greenskins. You can understand that. It's what the Imperium does – hells, it's what we do. But the eldar are different, novice. They're all born to lie.'

'And we're lying to them? Sounds dangerous.'

Luko smiled grimly. 'I'd rather be back on Stratix Luminae. Back in the Chapter War, even. Anything rather than sit here waiting for them to kill us. The eldar don't know what the truth means – they'll fight alongside you one moment and slaughter cities full of innocents the next. That's one thing the old Chapter would have agreed with, never trust the eldar. I just hope we get to turn on them before they turn on us. Don't turn your back on them, novice, and I mean it.'

The palace wing behind them had once been lavishly gilded but its walls were tarnished and brown, peeling to show the bare stone beneath. Squad Luko and Eumenes's scouts were taking shifts to drop into the half-sleep, not wanting to let down their guard in this nest of aliens but knowing they needed all the rest they could get. A couple of Luko's Marines were stripping their boltguns, while Nisryus was leafing through a battered set of the Emperor's tarot he had taken from the Chapter librarium. Selepus was in half-sleep but Eumenes knew, from experience, that anyone trying to creep up on him would have got a blade in the gut before they got into pistol range. Scamander was resting, too – he needed it more than any of them, because repeated uses of his powers had drained him more than he would admit. His skin was probably still cold to the touch.

'We killed a Fist today,' said Eumenes.

'So I heard,' said Luko.

'He killed Thersites.'

'And you wanted to make him pay? Show him the Emperor's justice?'

Eumenes nodded. In truth he hadn't been thinking of the Emperor at all – he had been thinking of his dead battle-brother and the insult the Fist had done by daring to attack them. But it was close enough.

'Remember how that feels, Novice Eumenes. Eventually it'll be the only thing that keeps you going.'

'But you have more, don't you? I've seen you fight, I've heard you. You love it.'

'One day, novice, you'll be a leader. Everyone can see it. You're the lead scout here and you'll have your own Marine squad if you want it and you get out of this alive. So I'll let you into a secret.' Luko leaned closer. 'I hate it. Fighting is what animals do. It's the most base and ugly thing a human being can stoop to. But you don't chose whether to fight or not in this galaxy. If it's not the Imperium it's the dark gods, or it's the xenos, or it's your own battle-brothers. So I make out that I enjoy it, and most of the time I manage to convince myself as well as the men I'm leading. I can live the lie as long as it's keeping me alive. But take me out of that and make me look at it from the outside, like now, and I hate it.

'I can't tell you why to fight, novice, that's up to you, but if you do it for its own sake then you'll end up no better than that creature you took off the prison ship.'

The two men sat in silence for a few moments, the only sound the clacking of metal on metal as Luko's Marines finished refitting their boltguns.

'Nisryus,' called Eumenes. 'What are the omens?'

Nisryus looked up from his tarot, the dog-eared cards lying in a semicircle around him. The Emperor's Tarot was an ancient tradition but Space Marine Librarians didn't use it very often, they rarely possessed the precognitive skills required to make the most of the Tarot. It was said the Emperor himself spoke through the cards, if only the user listened hard enough. Nisryus held up the first card he had laid. It depicted an archaic Mechanicus war machine, a massive castle that ground across a battlefield on immense tracks, raining death from its battlements. The Destroyer.

'There will be battle,' Nisryus said.

Luko smirked. 'Don't need the Emperor to tell us that.'

Nisryus held up the next card. It was the Jester, inverted. 'A battle you will lose, Sergeant Luko.'

Luko stared for a moment at the card, knowing that of all the Soul Drinkers it could only represent him. 'That is good to know, novice. Thank you.' He sounded serious.

Eumenes saw the Constellation was also inverted, along with the Arrow of Fate. He wasn't an expert but he knew it meant great confusion and reversal, with whole strands of fate changing with the slightest action.

There was a clattering at the door to the wing that could only be one thing and sure enough Commander Sarpedon walked in, his eight talons clicking on the stone floor. He was in full armour and carrying his force staff. 'Luko, Eumenes. Make ready to move out.'

Luko sprang up and shouted heartily to his men, grinning. 'You heard, Marines! Your dreams have come true!' With a flourish he pulled on one of his lightning claws, the bright talons catching the dim light. 'We're going to give this city some real soldiers to fight!'

Eumenes watched Luko marshal his men, and knew he had a lot to learn. He would have to lead, and leadership meant refusing to let your men down.

At least Eumenes knew now what he really wanted. It had flickered in him when he had killed the Crimson Fist, and it burned inside him now he had seen what drove men like Luko. The Imperium took human beings and it turned them into the things they would ordinarily hate, and only the lucky ones among them ever realised it. Sustained by war, the Imperium had ground up whole populations and turned them into soldiers, so they could die in places like Gravenhold to preserve the principles of oppression and tyranny. Eumenes wasn't a Soul Drinker just out of chance. It felt like he was there for revenge against the Imperium, on behalf of the whole human race.

'Your scouts have excelled,' said Sarpedon, standing just behind Eumenes and rising almost twice the scout's height on his insectoid legs. 'But I need you out there, too.'

'Where do you need us?' asked Eumenes.

'Everywhere, Scout-Novice Eumenes. The Soul Drinkers will have to face the Imperial Guard, there's nothing I can do about that for the moment. But you won't be with them. Eumenes, I need you to go out there and find Tellos.'

CHAPTER NINE

THE TRACKS OF the Baneblade ground through the wreckage of the battlefield. Lord General Xarius, theoretically safe in the belly of the super-heavy tank, watched the destruction unfold through the pict-recorders on the outside of the tank that sent images to the many screens surrounding him.

It was bad. Seleucaians lay dead in drifts where the enemy had been dug in, around towering skeletal factories and material silos. Many buildings were blackened husks, all were damaged, some were still ablaze and a few had been completely bulldozed to the ground by the Seleucaian armour.

'Keep up with them, Hasdrubal,' voxed Xarius, straining to hear his own voice above the relentless thudding of the Baneblade's massive engine pistons and the din of wreckage, masonry and bodies being ground to dust under the tracks. The Baneblade lurched as it dragged its bulk over the uneven ground, and over the noise Xarius heard heavy weapons fire chuddering away somewhere nearby. And behind that, ever-present as it had been since the first moments of the operation, was the constant booming of the artillery as it ground along behind the first waves pummelling Gravenhold into dust.

'Yes, sir,' replied Hasdrubal, commanding from within the blunt bulldog nose of the tank. 'Driver! Get us up closer, lean on the infantry line!'

Xarius could see the men advancing. Threlnan had been thorough, sending out his men in waves to make sure that dug-in enemies could be dealt with while the first waves pushed on. Several Sentinels, spindly two-legged walkers that could pick their way rapidly across the shattered industrial landscape, accompanied squads of men creeping warily through the wreckage and gun smoke. Immediately in front of the Baneblade a squad of Guardsmen checked the inside of a burned-out Leman Russ, their lasguns with bayonets fitted ready to impale any Gravenholders using the wreck as shelter to launch an ambush. There had been enough such ambushes already – the Gravenholders really didn't care about dying, and when their original savagery was spent the survivors went to ground to emerge several waves later and kill advancing Guardsmen who thought they had the easy job.

The effect, of course, was to make every Guardsman alert. Las-fire sparked on one pict-screen and Xarius turned to see Gravenholders pinned down in a ruined factory workshop, swapping fire with Seleucaian infantry until a Leman Russ Demolisher blew the whole building apart with a shell from its siege cannon.

Xarius switched to a feed from one of the forward units, the Sentinel-mounted pict-stealer shuddering as the walker lurched forward firing sprays of crimson fire from its multi-laser. Without sound it was an eerie sight. Seleucaians were diving for cover amongst the smouldering ruins of hovels, hurling themselves into the open channels of filth that ran through Gravenhold's southern slums, huddling down behind half-toppled walls. Gravenholders were fighting for every scrap of ground, fighting through the remains of their own past lives. Crumbling buildings full of dirt-cheap tenements had been blasted open, spilling broken furniture into the streets. Rusting groundcars lay on their sides as makeshift barricades, riddled with las-blasts. A Seleucaian officer yelled, the sound cut off from Xarius but the meaning clear, as he waved his men into the dubious cover of a ruined building. An enemy heavy weapon sent ricocheting fire ripping through a unit of Seleucaian veterans who scattered like fleeing rats into the shadow of any cover they could find.

The Sentinel turned to face the gun emplacement – a heavy stubber, belt-fed, with a gunner and an ammo handler – and sent a sustained burst of las-fire into the Gravenholders. One died straight away, the other lost an arm, and the Guardsmen rushed forwards to finish him off.

Murderous street-to-street fighting, hand-to-hand, room-by-room, across hovels reduced to ruins by the rolling bombardment of the big guns. Xarius shook his head, it was always the worst when the enemy were crazy, because then they didn't run away. You had to kill them, all of them, and that was how you got battles like this.

'Threlnan,' voxed Xarius to the Seleucaian colonel. 'Have you got a tac report up yet?'

Threlnan's voice crackled back over the command vox-net – he was with a forward command post, huddled down in a Salamander as his guard of Leman Russ tanks thundered away to keep counter-attacking Gravenholders away from him. 'It's sketchy, sir, but we've got some steady reports coming in from the latter waves. We're getting a decent picture.'

'Good. Send it.'

'Understood. I'll give it you as a burst transmission.'

'Stay safe, colonel.'

'And you, sir. Threlnan out.'

Xarius looked up from his tiny tactical office – above him the ammo-servitors hung from the ceiling, jointed metal arms poised to lug shells into the breeches of the Baneblade's massive guns. Xarius knew the tank's three auto-targeting heavy bolters would be more useful here than the big guns – a stream of fire, targeted by the tank's ancient machine-spirit, would shred any Gravenholders who got close. He doubted the tank's main armaments, the immense mega-battle cannon and the squat-barrelled Demolisher that jutted from the slope of the front armour would even be fired on Entymion IV.

The holo flickered to life, its large display making the inside of the tank feel even more claustrophobic. The map of Gravenhold was streaked with static, the tank's motion upsetting the delicate workings of the holo-projector.

Xarius's position was marked by its own icon. Xarius knew it really signified the Baneblade itself, not him. He was halfway through the industrial district, on ground that had been won early on in the grand push.

The Gravenholders' hold on the area had been weakened by aggressive patrolling and the bombardment had chased thousands of enemies out of the area, leaving only a few nests to resist the first waves of men and armour as they swept westwards from the wall. The Baneblade had been untroubled by enemy counterattacks and the Seleucaians were showing an admirable level of discipline in smoking out the Gravenholders still intent on making their lives dangerous in the shadow of the massive agri-mills. The first waves of the Seleucaians were exhausted and the second and third were the ones now fighting for Gravenhold's slums. The progress was bloody but it was steady. The enemy had nothing that could hold back the tide of tanks backed by men, rumbling through the hovels.

Xarius did a few mental calculations. There were probably something in the region of five thousand Seleucaians lying dead, dying or permanently disabled in the ruined streets of eastern Gravenhold. Xarius was forced to admit to himself that it wasn't too bad, so far. He didn't know yet how the Fire Drakes were doing to the east, or whether the Algorathi Janissaries were running into counter-attacks yet as they formed their line to the south, but the Seleucaians were acquitting themselves acceptably.

Which begged the question, why was the enemy letting them get away with it? The only reason the Seleucaians were here at all, barring a little string-pulling by Xarius, was that one of their sister regiments had been completely wiped out by the presumably alien forces on Entymion IV. There was plenty of horror unfolding in the raw red line of the Seleucaian advance, but there didn't seem to be any aliens involved. Or Chaos sorcerers. Or Traitor Marines. Gravenhold was welcoming them in a little too eagerly.

Xarius scrutinised the holo again. The slums were bad ground to hold – few hardpoints to take and hold, riddled with alleyways and tunnels even after bombardment. A difficult place to make your own, to impose your will over. The city's main arena, positioned in the midst of the slums so the city's poor could flock to its spectacles and vulgar entertainments, was the only building of any real size until you got to the government district.

'Threlnan,' voxed Xarius again. This time he heard more fire in the background of the vox; Threlnan was closer to the fighting.

'Sir!'

'I have your tac report. Make the arena your objective.'

'Sir, yes sir, I've got units making for it now.'

'It's the only defensible structure in the south-east of the city. Priority target.'

'Understood!' Threlnan paused amid the unmistakable sound of small arms fire smacking against the side of the Salamander. 'Priority one! I'll get the Carvelnan artillery to soften up its surroundings and concentrate the third wave on it.'

'Make it happen, Threlnan. We need somewhere to anchor the line.'

'Yes, sir! Threlnan out.'

'Try not to die, colonel.'

'No, sir! Threlnan out.'

THE SOUL DRINKERS were scattered throughout Gravenhold's undercity. The tunnels were not just sewers but underground thoroughfares, crypt corridors, winding alleyways through half-collapsed buildings and whole landscapes of stone and earth. But for the Space Marines' enhanced vision the undercity would have been pitch black – as it was, armour lamps and flares were needed to negotiate the most inhospitable routes through flows of mining spoil and rushing underground rivers.

Gravenhold had not been settled by the Administratum, as its official histories indicated. It had not been purpose-built to manage the agri-crop, its stones laid into virgin soil. Gravenhold was very, very old. There had been several settlements on the same site, and when the Administratum first demolished whatever stood there to lay the foundations for Gravenhold they had not thought to dig too deep. Probably they had used parts of the old city in the construction of the new. Certainly the city walls were riddled with old passageways, burial chambers, and narrow twisting stairways that had nothing to do with the Imperial population. It had been an insignificant detail of history in the grand scheme of the Imperium, but for a great many men it had proved a fatal one.

Prince Karhedros had given the Soul Drinkers their orders, but it was not he who was in charge – that was still Sarpedon, and it was at Sarpedon's insistence that the Soul Drinkers followed intricate crystalline holo-maps or shadow-skinned eldar guides through the underground city. Karhedros had given them key points to hold to keep the massive Imperial drive at bay, and Sarpedon needed the malevolent alien to trust them for just a little while more until Tellos showed up.

Of course, he didn't have to like it. Truth be told, his skin was still crawling from having to talk to the heathen – it was even worse that he was actually in league with it, even if he had no intention of keeping his word when the endgame began.

Luko had been sent to hold a medicae station, a solid building at the northern edge of the industrial district. Graevus was leading a force to the eastern walls to engage the Guardsmen pushing into the city from the south-east – probably, Sarpedon guessed, the Fornux Lix Fire Drakes. Iktinos and the Marines who were now resembling his personal retinue were commanded to lurk on a vital bridge across the River Graven, and throw back the Guardsmen (Fire Drakes or Seleucaians, whichever got there first) who would doubtless try to cross. Karhedros had agreed to give the scouts the run of the city on the pretence that they were gathering intelligence on Guard movements – they would, of course, be hunting for Tellos.

Sarpedon, meanwhile, was headed for Gravenhold's arena.

'You KNOW WE'RE too late,' said Librarian Gresk as Sarpedon's force moved through the dripping half-natural caves beneath Gravenhold's slums. 'The Guard have it already. The arena would have been the first location the Guard drove for. It's the only firm foothold in the slums and they need a point to anchor the line.'

'I'm sure you're right,' replied Sarpedon. Squads Krydel, Salk and Praedon were advancing behind him, guns ready, along with Apothecary Pallas. 'But we're not here to take it. We're here to take it back.'

'Movement,' came a vox from a sharp-eyed Marine in Squad Krydel. The force took cover behind the folds of flowstone and the giant stalagmites, eyepieces glinting in the darkness. Sarpedon held up a hand to indicate they should hold their fire. Even with his limited psychic reception he could feel what was approaching.

The sorceress was carried on a litter by a dozen slave-cultists whose faces were masses of scars and stitches. The bearers's hands had been tied together so they melded into single large fleshy claws suitable only for lifting the poles of the litter. The sorceress herself was a petite thing, with skin the colour of hardwood and eyes so green they shone in the darkness. She was naked, but her body was featureless, as if she was a facsimile of a human being, a women-shaped vessel into which the spirit of something far more malevolent had been poured. Only her face seemed to have been finished, high-browed and full-lipped. Her hair hung in faintly writhing dreadlocks and her fingers ended in long golden claws.

The sorceress waved a hand and from the shadows slunk her cultists, not the mindless creatures of Gravenhold but her own personal retinue. Like her bearers their facial features were sewn up with such crudeness that their faces were just masses of bloodied twine and scar tissue, with malformed eyes staring out of oozing gaps in the skin at insane angles. They wore close-fitting black bodysuits studded with gems as green as their mistress's eyes and they were armed with lasguns, standard-issue. They had either once been renegade Guardsmen or the sorceress had the resources to equip her private army properly.

Sarpedon could make out a couple of hundred cultists. She probably had more.

'The prince had told us to expect you,' said Sarpedon carefully. 'Highmistress Saretha?'

Saretha's mouth opened and a long organ slid out from deep within her throat, a sharp-pointed scaly tongue like the tail of a rattlesnake. She let out a long, rattling hiss.

A slave scampered forward. This one had been permitted to unpick the stitches that had sealed its mouth, leaving a wide drooling slit.

'Highmistress Saretha, Most Chosen Scion of the Lord of Unspeakable Pleasures, though her name be unworthy in the mouths of slaves. You are here as appointed?'

'Yes, highmistress. I am Sarpedon of the Soul Drinkers.'

Another long, horrible rattle.

'The pleasurable dead speak of you, Lord Sarpedon. Through you the Lord of Pleasures gives death to many.'

The sorceress was so corrupted she couldn't even speak. Perhaps her mutated tongue was a deliberate affectation, begged from her god so she could demonstrate her superiority by using a slave to interpret for her. In any case Sarpedon choked back the urge to kill every single one of these vermin there and then, and he knew that his Marines could only do the same for so long.

'I do not stand on ceremony, highmistress,' said Sarpedon quickly. 'The prince wants the arena. I intend to deliver it to him.'

'Indeed, as do I.' Sarpedon had to force himself to look at Saretha when her slave was speaking, and not at the slave itself. 'The Lord of Pleasures has eyes above us. The servants of the corpse-emperor believe they have won it but do not suspect us below them.'

'What are they moving into the arena? Artillery? Tanks?'

'Men. And supplies.'

'The Guard have standard procedures,' said Sarpedon, comforted by the fact that he was talking on military matters, something he could be sure of. 'They'll put the ammunition dump underground to keep it safe from mortar hits. An arena like this will have plenty of space for it, with cells and barracks under the arena floor. Which is where we come in. Saretha, you take the surface. Draw the Guard onto the arena floor. My Marines will take the ammo dump underneath.'

There was a pause, then a short spitting hiss.

'The highmistress defers.'

Saretha began clicking and hissing at her cultists, who scuttled forward with curiously insectoid movements and surrounded her, bearing her into the shadows.

'Throne of Earth, Sarpedon, did you feel it?' said Gresk as Saretha disappeared from sight, her cultists carrying her up towards where the arena loomed over the ruined slums. Even the grizzled old Gresk looked perturbed by what he had just seen.

Sarpedon nodded. 'Chaos. Pure Chaos.'

'Xenos and the dark ones, in league. I didn't think you would go this far, Sarpedon.'

'We could hit out at them now, Gresk, and we'd last a few moments doing the Emperor's work until we died. But if we get close enough we could find Tellos and hurt these vermin badly.'

'But the Guard…'

'The Guard want us dead, Gresk. As long as that is true, they are our enemy. There's nothing we can do about it now. And believe me, Gresk, I intend to hurt that creature just as much as you do.' Sarpedon turned and waved his squads forward. 'Salk,' he voxed, 'You have the point. Take us up into the lower reaches of the arena, no contacts, just get us there.'

Sergeant Salk paused for a split second then moved forward with his squad, ready to lead the way out of Gravenhold's underbelly and into the makeshift Guard strongpoint of the arena.

Sarpedon knew the Soul Drinkers trusted him. But they had to keep on trusting him, just a little bit longer. They were in Gravenhold not because they had to be but because Sarpedon had chosen to be, because whatever happened to Tellos was something Sarpedon had to see with his own eyes and because any force powerful enough to turn Tellos to its cause was something worth fighting. He could explain it to them, but he couldn't be sure they would under-stand like he did. They just had to trust him. That was all.

'We've got something here,' voxed Salk from up ahead. 'Looks like cells cut into the rock. There's a spi-ral passage leading upwards.' The thuds of lifter-fitted Sentinel walkers echoed down along with the distant crumping explosions of mortar fire.

'Good. Krydel, Praedon, stick close. Gresk to the front, Pallas with me. Our objective is the central ammo dump the Guard will have set up under the arena floor. This is what we will do when we reach it…'

'I'VE GOT A SHOT,' said Sergeant Kelvor. He was lying on his front, bolter pointed down through the hole in the inside of the Gravenhold's massive wall, the crosshairs of the scope hovering over the throat of a careless

Guardsman officer who was pausing to consult a map without taking cover first.

'Hold,' said Graevus.

'You're sure?' Kelvor was a very good shot, a fact that had not been compromised by the loss of his leg at the chamber mercantile. He could take the Guardsman as a matter of course, and draw several units of the advancing Fornux Lix Fire Drakes into a firefight instead of winning back more of the administrative district.

'We're not here to fight the Imperial Guard,' said Graevus. 'Karhedros can't watch us here.'

'You're sure of that, Graevus?'

'No. But I am sure we're not fighting for the xenos just yet, so they can win their own battle for the time being.'

'Fair enough.' Kelvor pushed himself away from the hole. Gravenhold's old city walls had been riddled with tunnels and stairways, so although the xenos guide had melted away soon after they had reached the wall the Soul Drinkers still had little trouble in reaching a good sniping spot. The Marines of Kelvor's squad were positioned in firing spots along a section of the wall very high up. The Assault Marines of Squad Graevus were there as a reserve, to face down any Guardsmen who might try to flush out the snipers. In the tight confines of the wall, there was little doubt that Graevus's chainswords and his own power axe could hold off the bayonet-armed Guard almost indefinitely.

But Graevus's small force wasn't about to start risking their lives for Prince Karhedros just yet. Both Graevus's and Kelvor's squads had been badly battered in the chamber mercantile – Kelvor had just three Marines left, Graevus six.

Librarian Tyrendian walked from the shadows inside the wall. He was the final member of Graveus's force, someone who in the old Chapter would have out-ranked Graevus. 'Do you know what I think, sergeant?'

'Enlighten us, Tyrendian.' Graevus, if he was being honest with himself, did not like Tyrendian. He looked too young and too unscarred. Tyrendian was as brave and dangerous as any Soul Drinker, but he just didn't look like the mangled old veteran he should have been. There was something not right about him, something too perfect.

'I think, sergeants, that Karhedros knows exactly what Sarpedon intends to do. He knows we will betray him. The eldar know things they shouldn't, it's what they do. The reason he tolerates us is because he fully intends to betray us first.'

'That is not comforting to know, Librarian,' said Graevus. 'What do you suggest we do about it?'

'Find out what he wants.' Tyrendian knelt down at the wall, careful to keep his armoured body in the shade so the Guardsmen advancing through the city far below wouldn't spot him as he looked down through one of the holes. 'Karhedros didn't come to this city by accident. The eldar don't conquer, they raid and destroy. This city is important to him for some rea-son.'

'Emperor knows there's enough about it the Guard never anticipated,' said Kelvor, who had taken the scope off his bolter and was using it like a telescope to peer down at the Fire Drake units skirmishing with scattered Gravenholders far below. 'There must have been cities here for thousands of years before Graven-hold was founded. Maybe there's something old under all of that. Pre-Imperial, even.'

'If there is, then Karhedros has had enough time to find it,' said Tyrendian. He was watching the Fire Drakes, too. Their line was holding well, the front advancing gradually as the commanders sent reserves through to help clear out the knots of Gravenholders who opposed them. 'I think it's something more complicated than just some old artefact. Look, Karhedros could have the Fire Drakes bogged down in these streets for days on end if he threw enough men at them, but he's practically giving them the administrative district. Either he needs them to be in the city or he doesn't care how far they get.'

'That might be the reason,' said Kelvor, pointing to where the administrative district broke into the highrises fanning out from around the south-eastern gate. The Fire Drakes had used their remaining armour to batter the highrises into glassless steel skeletons standing over avenues full of rubble and the enemy had fled them, but it wasn't an enemy Kelvor had noticed.

Graveus hunkered down beside Kelvor and took a pair of magnoculars offered by one of Kelvor's Marines.

The dark blue Rhinos of the Crimson Fists were grinding through the rubble, following in the wake of the Fire Drakes' advance. The Fists were going back into Gravenhold, this time slowly and deliberately, along the trail blazed by the Guardsmen.

'They're bringing the Fists in,' said Kelvor. 'They must still think there are Traitor Marines in the city.'

'Technically speaking,' said Tyrendian, 'they're right. But the Fists aren't following the Guard, they're coming to get us on their own.'

'Fine by me,' said Kelvor with relish. 'I owe them a leg.'

'How long was it since we and the Fists were brothers?' asked Graevus. Tyrendian and Kelvor looked back at him. 'There was a time when the two Chapters would have gone in together to kill something like Karhedros. Instead we're here killing each other when the real enemy sits back and waits for us to do whatever it is he needs for his plan to work.'

'It's a bad time to start doubting, brother,' replied Kelvor. 'Sarpedon broke with the Imperium because the Imperium is as bad as Chaos. It might not be easy but it's right.'

Graevus sighed. 'That's the point. Think on it. What was it that pulled us apart in the first place? Chaos? Some xenos? No. It was the Imperium itself, just ordinary human beings. The Crimson Fists are some of the bravest soldiers humanity has but we are forced to kill them because the Imperium needs them to be as blind as we once were. If Mankind could just see what we all saw then perhaps these wars would be over.'

Tyrendian raised an eyebrow. 'A Marine who longs for peace? I don't think you would enjoy it, sergeant.'

Graevus scowled back. 'I don't think there's much danger of that, Tyrendian,' he said. 'I just wish mankind could all fight on the same side without having to be deceived into doing it. Fight because it's right, not just to keep the Imperium alive.'

'Looks like they're all on the move,' said Kelvor, quickly counting the Rhinos streaming through the south-east gate. 'I'm sure what you say is right, Graevus, but if the Fists find us they're not likely to let us convince them. Sarpedon should be in vox range if he's close enough to the surface, I'll let him know the Fists have arrived.'

'Good. My squad will take the first watch, yours take the second. Tyrendian, get some halfsleep so you're fresh if we need you. Hold your fire unless we get spotted, Kelvor, I don't want us starting any wars for the prince just yet.'

THE GUARDSMAN SLUMPED to the ground, his throat neatly slit. He hadn't made a sound.

With a practised motion Selepus withdrew the knife, grabbed the body by the collar of its elaborately brocaded uniform and hauled it into the shadows of the abandoned slum building. The building, largely untouched by the brief firefights this area had seen, was a pile of dirt-cheap apartments piled on top of one another, a filthy sagging deathtrap typical of Gravenhold's slums.

In the warren of rooms that made up the ground floor, Scout Squad Eumenes waited out of sight. Scout-Sniper Raek kept watch, his keen eyes scouring the cityscape along the barrel of his rifle.

'Another Algorathi?' asked Eumenes.

Selepus nodded. 'Haven't had one of these put up a fight yet. Something's spooked them, though. Looks like they were just supposed to be watching the backs of the Seleucaians but now they're patrolling deeper and deeper. They're scared of something and they're sending patrols to flush it out.'

'Is it us?'

'No. They don't know we're here.'

'Tellos?'

'Could be.'

The scouts had been trying to pick up Tellos's trail since Karhedros had cut them loose. Eumenes was proud that his scouts were the only Soul Drinkers to have the run of the city instead of running around pretending to follow Karhedros's orders, but theirs was still a daunting task. If Tellos was in the city at all he could be anywhere in or beneath it. The only hope the scouts had was to assume Tellos wouldn't be content to stay in hiding. Tellos's Marines, if they were as crazy as the one Eumenes had recovered from the prison ship, would be eager to go a-hunting through the ranks of the Guardsmen and it was amongst the Guard that the scouts were most likely to find Tellos.

In the southern slums there were plenty of Guard, but little fighting against the Gravenholders, so Tellos could hunt undisturbed. So that was where the scouts had started looking.

Scout Alcides had turned over the still-warm body and was rifling through the pockets and pouches of its uniform. The Algorathi Janissaries wore ridiculous powder blue fatigues with silver brocade. This soldier, like the rest of them, had managed to keep his uniform clean for about thirty seconds and it was now a shade of muddy blue-grey with dirt ground in around the ankles and cuffs. The Algorathi Janissaries, the scouts had quickly ascertained, might have been fine for garrisoning some backwater world but were in over their heads in Gravenhold. It was why the Guard were using them for patrolling rather than fighting, but even so, booby-traps and occasional knots of Gravenholders had started to take their toll. Not to mention the scouts themselves. Alcides pulled a folded sheet of paper from one pouch. 'Looks like standing orders,' he said.

'Let's hear them,' said Eumenes.

'The enemy is underhand and will not hesitate to strike at you with ambushes and other deceit,' read

Alcides. 'Every Janissary is to uphold the spirit of his regiment by remaining absolutely on guard, watching over his fellow soldiers, and most of all remaining dutiful and honour-bound even in the face of such ungentlemanly provocations. Platoons are to be rotated into aggressive patrols to hunt down the creatures responsible and every Guardsman on those patrols will consider their eradication his personal responsibility. The enemy are thought to be heavily armoured and skilled in close combat, they are therefore to be greeted with overwhelming fire whenever they are spotted! Dangerous they may be but they are also few in number, not to mention degenerate heathens who shall not prevail in the sight of the Emperor. Every man will do his duty by the Regiment and by his Emperor, signed, Colonel Vinmayer.'

'Sounds like Tellos,' said Scamander.

'Sounds like us,' added Raek, his aim not wavering as he spoke.

'Whoever it is we're going to find them before the Janissaries do,' said Eumenes. 'Next, we get an officer. Can you manage that, Selepus?'

'No problem with the kill. But getting close won't be as easy, even if these guys are amateurs.'

'Good. We need to move closer to the Algorathi lines, then. Nisryus, I want you up front with Selepus, make sure he knows if anything's going to stumble into us. Everyone else stay back and spread out. We want the Algorathi to do our hunting for us, then we sneak in and take the kill. If it turns out to be Tellos then we'll have to go in fast and hard, and I don't need to lose anyone beforehand. Keep quiet, low, and fast. Move out.'

Without another word the scouts moved out of the
crumbling tenement, all but invisible in the tangled
streets of southern Gravenhold, knowing that they
were not the only army in there capable of putting the
fear of the Emperor into the Guard.

SERGEANT LUKO AND Techmarine Varuk watched
through the cracked window of the medicae station at
the approaching walls of dust that signalled the
advance of the Seleucaians.

'How many?' asked Luko.

'Hard to tell. If they're just Chimeras then there are a
hell of a lot of them. But I think they'll have artillery
mixed up in there, which would probably be worse.
What they'll do to us when they get here is your
department, sergeant.'

Luko smiled. He always seemed the Soul Drinker
who most relished the prospect of a good scrap. 'Tons
of shells followed up with tons of men. It's practically
the Guard's motto.'

Luko walked back from the window. He and Varuk
were on the first floor of the medicae station, in one of
the surgical theatres where devotional scripts were
carved into walls painted just the right shade of dark
green to hide the blood. The station was covered with
carved prayers, devotional graffiti, tiny makeshift
shrines and piles of offerings to the Emperor and his
many saints, both patients and the medicae staff they
relied on tended to be religious types. The theatre contained a large polished metal operating slab, an
autosurgeon with several folded metallic arms like the
legs of a dead spider, and a couple of large tanks of
anaesthetic gas. Gravenhold's elite were well cared for
in airy, spacious hospitals dotted around the north of

the city, but when the city had been normally populated this medicae station would have been heaving with the sick from the slums and those mangled by the ceaseless machinery of the industrial district. The devotional items were a last desperate offer to the Emperor to save them, but scores must surely have met their end in that theatre or in the cramped, bleak wardhouse on the lower floor.

'All squads,' voxed Luko, 'They're coming. Prepare for an artillery barrage and then an infantry assault. They're not expecting us to be here but they'll throw everything at us once they realise we are so I don't want anyone acting like this is their last stand. We draw them in, hold them up, and get out of here.'

'This would be a bad way to die,' said Varuk, almost idly. Techmarines could be an odd lot, before the Chapter broke with the Imperium Varuk, like most Techmarines, he had made the pilgrimage to Mars where he had been instructed in some of the secrets of the Machine God. Exposure to the mysteries of the Adeptus Mechanicus wasn't exactly conducive to normal behaviour. 'Just for appearances. Just so some xenos will trust us a little longer.'

'It's not just so Karhedros will think we're good little Marines,' said Luko, slightly annoyed. 'We don't want the Guard to take this place too fast, otherwise they'll get to Tellos before we do. And besides, if Karhedros doesn't trust us then none of us will get off this planet alive.'

'On Mars they teach you about logic,' said Varuk. 'I've been trying to think how any of this is logical, but none of it is.'

'That's where you and I differ,' said Luko. 'I just fight. You have to think about it.' He flicked back to the vox.

'Squad Dyon, have you got the front of the building covered?'

'It's locked down,' came Sergeant Dyon's reply.

'Good. If you can immobilise one of their tanks with plasma fire you could get them snarled up in gridlock. Squad Corvan?'

'Sergeant?'

'Get a couple of Assault Marines out into the alleyways. We could draw a lot of men into bolter range that way. And my lads, hold the basement. We need to keep our escape route clear and I wouldn't put it past those damn Guard to send some poor boys in through the storm drains. Any questions?'

There were none. 'Excellent. Check your guns and praise the Emperor, we're going to give them hell!'

'Got them,' said Varuk. 'At least three Chimeras with a lot of men on the ground. That engine note is a Basilisk, I'm sure of it, probably two or three.'

'Then we should be downstairs,' said Luko. Just then, the first artillery shot landed just short of the medicae station, kicking up a vicious plume of shattered pavement and earth, and the fight was on.

CHAPTER TEN

SARETHA THE BITCH-QUEEN, the Whore-Priestess of the Dark Prince of Chaos, did not believe in leading from the front.

'Onward! For lust and the end of their world!' she hissed, a spell woven around her words that sent them darting into the minds of her slave-warriors. Around her, leather-clad cultists surged forwards, muscling through the lower reaches of the storm drains towards the surface.

The filthy water in the conduit was chest-high but Saretha was held well above it by her cultists, who would rather die a hundred deaths than allow indignity to touch the skin of their mistress. They loved her, every one of them. And love, like every emotion, created ripples in the warp where her lord Slaanesh lived. The love her cultists had for her was so strong that it created a billowing tide of emotion in the warp, enough for Slaanesh himself to notice it and give His blessing to Saretha. It was why she had been gifted with sorcery, a subtle magic that wormed its way into the minds of men and women and convinced them that they had loved her all along.

The conduit sloped upwards and Saretha saw the drain covers ripped from the concrete by the strong hands of her most able assault-cultists, and the human tide swarmed out of them. She was carried along on that tide, the stench of the sewers mingling with the ever-present sweat and gun smoke on the surface, clashing with her perfumed oils. The voices of her cultists were raised in wordless praise of the Dark Prince and Saretha echoed them, shrieking with lust as she was carried out onto the surface and through the grand entrance gates of Gravenhold's arena.

In a very literal sense, the Imperial Guard of the Seleucaian Fourth Division never knew what hit them.

The arena's many entrances, broad archways around the outer edge of the coliseum, were barricaded against attacks but none of them had been built to withstand a tide of thousands of men and women who were desperate to die. Coils of razor wire were crushed beneath dozens of bodies, all writhing and squealing at the novelty of such pain. The sentries manned mounted heavy bolters to send chains of massive-calibre fire through the horde of cultists, but they just kept on coming, howling with joy as their bodies were blown wide open. The stitches in their lips were torn open as they were finally permitted to scream their pleasure to the sky.

Those gunners who saw Highmistress Saretha could not bear to shoot at her. They could never fire upon something of such overwhelming beauty, something too pure to ever harm. So they fired into the swarm of cultists even as the entranceways were choked with bodies that toppled like a landslide over their guard posts.

These were not just Gravenholders. These cultists mixed the blind fanaticism of the city's slave-soldiers with martial prowess and brute strength. Lasgun fire rattled back from the centre of the hordes as the crowd pressed against the barricades, streaking the old sandstone walls with trails of las-fire.

A squad of Guardsmen tried to engage the cultists, snapping off volleys of lasgun fire to keep the horde out of the arena. But Saretha's beloved did not fight by hiding and scurrying away when death was in the air. Death was the ultimate thrill, the final and most sacred experience granted them by Slaanesh, and the Guardsmen learned this the hard way as the cultist dead were carried forward by the momentum of the charge.

Fire raked back at the Guardsmen. That was nothing compared to the raw, shrieking, bleeding mass of bodies that poured towards them, clambering over one another, stacking the entrance tunnel almost to the ceiling. The Guardsmen fled, and the battle for the arena was on.

SARETHA RODE OVER the shattered remains of the Guard defences. Staked barricades lay in splinters, their spikes impaling a dozen of the ecstatic dead. The walls were painted with blood that shone as brightly as the gems on her cultists's bodysuits. The din of screams was an awful and magnificent music, and for a few moments Saretha just basked in it, the waves of cacophony washing over her. She could lose herself in it, drinking deep of the pleasure that Slaanesh taught was present in all experiences. But she was a fighter as well as an aesthete, there would be plenty of time to indulge her lusts after the battle, for now her duty was to take the arena.

'Weak-souls! Small-minds!' spat Saretha at a group of cultists who had paused to dismember a Guardsman. 'To indulge your basest when there are deaths to be lived through! The Prince spits on you!' Thoroughly chastened, the cultists dived back into the charge, eager to realise their love of their mistress through the sacred experience of battle.

A fire-team of Guardsmen was gathering in the rafters above her, ready to launch volleys of fire down on the cultist mob. Saretha spotted them and, picking a moment of the most extreme pleasure from her memory, hurled it out of her mind at the insolent unbelievers. With the spell still on her lips those memories surged into the Guardsmen's minds. Unprepared for a vision of such pure Chaos, they spasmed violently as their nervous systems overloaded. Bones cracked as their muscles contracted violently, organs ruptured, and they were granted one true glimpse of the Dark Prince's power before they died.

The bodies fell from above to be trampled under the feet of Saretha's palanquin bearers.

The cultists had broken through to the tunnel's exit, where they were emerging in a heaving mass into the arena's dizzying banks of seating. Beyond that was the arena floor where drab green tents were pitched side by side around gun emplacements and vehicle repair yards, muster grounds and medical stations. Guardsmen were running into formation as officers yelled, bringing heavy weapons to bear, forming firing lines to receive Saretha's horde.

So many tiny, closed minds, blind to the promises of Slaanesh. So many lives pleading to be ended, so they could get their one vision of the Dark Prince's power. Death was the final experience, the final moment of transcendental pleasure-pain that converted everyone into a believer in the end.

Highmistress Saretha smiled to herself. This was the part she looked forward to the most, when they made a stand and tried to resist her.

'THEY'VE STARTED,' SAID Sergeant Krydel. An instant later the sound rumbled down through the many layers of cells and chambers: the thud of heavy weapons, the faint white noise of men shouting and screaming, the fizz of las-fire.

Krydel's squad was in front, stalking carefully through the decaying network of cells beneath the arena. The cells had once held the worst of Gravenhold's small but persistent underclass, captured and sentenced to fight for their lives for the entertainment of the workers in the slums. There were also larger cells, stained black-brown with blood, where wild creatures had been held for the prisoners to fight. The place smelt of old sweat and death.

'Then we need to move faster,' said Sarpedon, who was following between Squads Salk and Praedon. Sarpedon would rather have brought some Assault units than the three Tactical squads, but Assault Marines were becoming a luxury amongst the Soul Drinkers after so many had been lost on Stratix Luminae.

Squad Krydel shoved their bulky armoured bodies through the narrow stairwell that led to the next layer up. 'Activity here,' voxed one Marine, Brother Callian.

'Guard?'

'Yes, sir.'

Sarpedon followed, just squeezing his many-legged form through the gap. He saw the floor on the next level up had been scuffed by Guard boots. They must have taken one look at the stairwell and decided it wasn't worth going any further down.

'Why didn't they seal it?' asked Krydel.

'This is recent,' said Brother Callian, kneeling to inspect the disturbance. 'Perhaps they were called up when Saretha attacked.'

'Good luck for us,' said Sarpedon. 'Don't waste it.'

This level had more room and higher ceilings, and larger rooms without bars over the doors led off from the wider corridors. This must have been where the free fighters, men who fought for pay or to earn off a debt, slept or prepared for their fights.

There was an explosion somewhere far above, a dull thud that shook runnels of dust from the packed earth walls. Something big had gone up.

'The Guard cleared out of here in a hurry,' said Sarpedon, 'which means there won't be sentries or booby-traps. Salk, take us up, double-quick.'

Salk was tough in close combat; he had proven that in a short career as a sergeant that had culminated on Stratix Luminae. He was the best choice to have up front in case the Marines blundered into any remaining Guardsmen down here.

The psychic shriek from above shuddered through the earth straight into Sarpedon's soul. It was the filthy, corrupted pleasure-shriek of an individual so debauched by Chaos that they welcomed it into their soul. It had to be Saretha, and she had to be in the thick of the fighting.

'It will be over soon,' said Sarpedon. 'By then it'll be too late. Let's move.'

SARETHA WOULD NOT be touched. Only the consecrated hands of her most trusted cultists, whose touch carried with it the blessings of Slaanesh himself, were permitted to make physical contact with her. The enemy, the weak-minded followers of the corpse-Emperor, were too crude and vile to even contemplate the honour of touching her.

'Die!' she hissed into the face of the closest Guardsman.

And he did, his heart stopping in shock at the vividness of the psychic images that knifed through his mind. The images flooded through his ruptured mind and a dozen more Guardsmen, counter-charging down the rows of stone seating, saw a fragment of what he had seen. They screamed, stumbled, vomited. A few were able to put up a fight as cultists streamed past Saretha and into the middle of them.

Saretha's cultists were streaming down the lower rows of seating, scrambling over the carved benches to get to grips with the rows of Guardsmen who were thinning out their ranks with volleys of las-fire. Return fire was evening the odds but the cultists had to get up close. More Guardsmen were mounting valiant counter-charges from further up the arena's sloped seating area, trying to get close to Saretha herself.

The insult was appalling. Saretha lashed out with her mind again, feeling the dirty little life-lights of the Guardsmen go out as she overloaded their senses.

She turned her attention back to the battle. The cultists were surging closer, clambering over their dead. They were badly thinned out but the dead had done their duty to their god, dying so those behind could swarm closer. The first ranks of cultists were over the lowermost rows of seating onto the dirt surface of the arena. A firing squad of Guardsmen sent a sheet of crimson las-fire into them, cutting them to shreds, but the gap closed in a second and before the Guard had time to take aim again the cultists were amongst them.

The effect was instant. Guard units fell back between the tents and temporary buildings, the weight of their las-fire faltering as they ran from the fanatics bearing down on them.

Cultists tore through billet tents, smashed through the windows of medicae and command huts, swarmed screaming into the Guard camp on the arena floor. An old, battered Chimera APC rolled towards the cultists and exploded, its fuel tank sabotaged by Guard mechanics in an attempt to slow the cultists down. It didn't work.

This was the beginning of the end. Saretha had seen it several times before. The Guardsmen above her had not, and they swore in horror as the fall of their base camp began. They were supposed to be safe, they were supposed to form a strongpoint in the Guard line. Now they were being eviscerated by a foe that even death could not hold back.

'Now take your reward!' called Saretha, her voice coursing into the minds of every cultist. 'See now your reward! Slaanesh sees your devotion and see how he repays you! Take their lives, drink of their blood, draw such pleasure from the slaughter!'

She wished she was young again, new to the extremes of pleasure the Dark Prince promised. She wanted to be down there, among her warriors, revelling in the blood and death. The memory of it filled her with a poignant ecstasy, she could never feel that thrill of discovery again, for she had experienced so much that simple joys like maiming and killing meant little to her. The memories would always be there, but now only the extremes of devotion to Slaanesh gave her the intense doses of pleasure she needed to survive.

But there was nothing to regret. She knew the heights the human soul could reach, and now she herself was more than human. What more could anyone ask?

'Take me down,' she commanded to her palanquin bearers, and they bore her down over the rows of seats towards the brutal close-quarters melee that was erupting in the Guard camp.

One more time into the heart of the slaughter, she told herself. For old time's sake.

'HEADS DOWN, LADS! Now!' Sergeant Luko charged down the stairway into the ward floor as the first shells slammed home. His squad and Squads Corvan and Dyon hit the floor of the medicae's main ward, the walls shuddering around them.

The first shell tore through the upper floors and ripped open the operating theatre. Techmarine Varuk was thrown down the stairwell in a shower of debris.

'...know we're here, we've got to–' Luko's vox-message was blotted out by the second shell that hit the outside of the building and rocked it to its foundations. Slabs of ceiling fell down.

'Don't you curl up and hide, lads!' shouted Luko between the explosions. 'The infantry'll be next!'

Varuk slid onto the floor beside Luko. 'Griffons and Basilisks,' he said as crunching explosions sounded from the surrounding slum buildings as they were blasted apart.

'How many?'

'Support unit. Not a saturation barrage.'

'Good. Then we'll get something to fight.'

With a tremendous crash, the side wall of the ward caved in, the foundations of the building pulverised by a Basilisk shot that tore deep into the ground.

The morning light flooded in, choked a dirty grey by billowing clouds of dust. Luko glanced up and spotted tanks through the swirling debris. And on an urban battlefield, tanks never advanced on their own.

'On your feet!' he barked. 'Guns up!'

The first Guard squad into the medicae building were met with a hail of bolter fire. They didn't stay to duke it out, they broke and fell back, diving behind chunks of fallen masonry as Luko's Tactical Marines sprayed fire at them. The tanks halted and ground behind cover and the accompanying Guard scattered into the shadows. Bad news could travel faster than a bullet and every one of them soon knew that they had stumbled across the Traitor Marines.

Luko knew how powerful a rumour it could be. In the days before excommunication, the Soul Drinkers had turned battles just by the rumour of their involvement. That was why Karhedros needed the Soul Drinkers. If the Imperial Guard thought they were up against Traitor Space Marines then they would falter in their advance, no matter how brave and determined they might be. Officers would wait for reinforcements. Commanders would divert resources. Space Marines were a terror weapon, and Marines who followed Chaos were, if anything, even more terrifying.

'That's enough! I'm not killing these boys for that damn alien's sake,' voxed Luko. 'Dyon, cover us. The rest, fall back to the cellars. We'll give them a firefight then get out of here.'

'I hear that,' said Varuk. Luko heard the unease in his voice. Sarpedon could be enthusiastic about fighting the Imperial Guard when he had to, but here in Gravenhold, at the behest of an alien, it didn't feel right to be killing Guardsmen who thought they were fighting Chaos.

Las-fire was streaking back now, the weight of bolter fire holding back the worst but not for long. Assault Squad Corvan was first into the cellars, Sergeant Corvan's bionic leg clacking against the tiled floor as he hurried down the narrow stairwell. Varuk followed them then Squad Luko. Dyon's fire kept the worst of the Guard firepower off the Soul Drinkers before Dyon followed the others down.

With luck, the Guard would be tied up at the medicae station long enough for Karhedros to be satisfied. In any case, Luko wasn't willing to let his Marines die in a fight over nothing.

The cellar was a grim place, once antiseptically clean but now dark and evil-smelling. The medical waste stored here had been left to decay as the refrigeration units had failed, along with the corpses in the facility's morgue. The back wall and half of the floor of the morgue had collapsed, revealing a passage into Gravenhold's undercity which Luko had earmarked as the Marine's escape route. The Soul Drinkers hurried through the morgue as a couple more Basilisk shots shook more bodies out of the mortuary shelves.

'Dyon here,' came Sergeant Dyon's vox from above. 'No sign of them following. Looks like we scared them off.'

'Make the most of it,' said Luko. 'Get down here and do not engage.'

The uninviting darkness of the undercity was better than the prospect of a firefight with half the Seleucaian 4th Division. Luko led the way downwards, the malodorous darkness enveloping him as the gunfire from above became distant and dim. Squad Corvan took the rear; if the Guardsmen followed them, the Soul Drinkers would need Assault Marines in the rear to hold them off.

'Varuk, get back to Corvan and help him collapse the entrance,' said Luko. 'No need to help them follow us.'

Luko heard Techmarine Varuk calling for krak grenades from Squad Corvan's Marines.

This part of the battle was all but done. Soon Luko would leave the war for Gravenhold behind, help find Tellos, do whatever he had to and get off this damn planet with its aliens and its sorcerers. It couldn't come soon enough.

The shockwave thudded down the tunnel as the entrance caved in. Ahead was a half-crushed tangle of black iron, some forgotten part of a civilisation that no longer had a name. Luko flicked on the power field around his lightning claws just in case, and walked on into the darkness.

'SAY AGAIN?' CONSUL Kelchenko frowned as he concentrated on the vox, the message obscured by static and the sound of the long-range artillery thundering away behind him. A messenger hurried up in the crimson uniform of the 4th Carvelnan Royal Artillery. Kelchenko waved him away as the message repeated.

'Marines, sir… Space Marines, honest to the Throne, I saw them with my own eyes…' The voice was that of an officer with the Seleucaians, bypassing the normal com-channels to talk with Kelchenko directly.

'Calm down, soldier,' said Kelchenko. 'How did you get on this frequency?'

'...my vox-man patched in, consul, I thought normal channels would take too long... need support here, I'm not taking on Marines in this hellhole, not without some of your boys' muscle...'

Marines. Kelchenko had heard them mentioned in a couple of the briefings but he had never really thought about what would happen if the Seleucaian push crashed into them. Kelchenko had heard the stories about what a single squad of Space Marines could do. If there were Marines to be fought in Gravenhold then Xarius's grand push was in trouble.

And then it hit him. He could take them out. The most feared creatures in Gravenhold, and Kelchenko could be the one to destroy them. As far as the Imperial Guard were concerned, Kelchenko was nothing more than a glorified civilian, an interloper from the Administratum playing at soldiers. Never mind that it was men like Kelchenko that kept the Guard supplied with ammunition and rations, never mind that formations like the Carvelnan Royal Artillery couldn't exist without Kelchenko and other consuls martial like him.

And now the battle would be turned by a single order from Kelchenko. Because Consul Kelchenko had brought one of his rarest and most spectacular weapons with him to Entymion IV.

'What are your co-ordinates?'

'Transmitting them now...' For a few moments the vox was lost in static but Kelchenko heard the piercing

tones as the officer's co-ordinates were sent in a burst
of information over the vox-net. '...looks like they're
well dug in, we need this place given a damn good
strike to blast them out...'

'Withdraw your men,' voxed Kelchenko. 'Get them
all out of there. Now.'

'...understood... repeat, message understood...
rather like to know what you're planning, consul...'

'Just fall back and get into cover. Kelchenko out.'

Kelchenko looked down the line of artillery pieces he
had drawn up just inside Gravenhold's eastern wall –
Griffons, Basilisks, even a couple of Hydra anti-aircraft
pieces should the Gravenholders prove to have air
power at their disposal. The artillery tanks were all
blasting away, throwing shells into the city in front of
the Guard advance to keep the Gravenholders on their
toes. But the combined power of every artillery piece in
the city couldn't match the weapon Kelchenko had in
mind for the Marines.

Kelchenko switched to a heavily encrypted vox-
channel.

'Standing by, sir,' came the reply, crisp and clear.

'Good. Stand by for co-ordinates.'

'Co-ordinates received.'

'Good. Go to code black.'

'Sir, we have had no confirmation from Lord Commander Xarius. Are you sure...'

'Quite sure, crewman. Code black and prepare for
launch.'

There was a long pause. Then–

'Launch locked.'

'Good. Go to code red. Deathstrike away.'

The vox howled with a sudden vibration. 'Deathstrike away.'

Kelchenko looked up to see the glittering crescent described by the Deathstrike missile as it streaked over the city towards the heart of the battleline.

'That'll show the bastards,' said Kelchenko quietly. He wasn't sure himself if he meant the Traitor Marines, or the rest of the Guard.

'CODE BLACK ON the Deathstrike, commander,' said Brother Paclo, crouched down in the hull of the Razorback.

'Are you sure? Have they launched?'

'Yes, commander.'

'Damnation. Then they know where the Soul Drinkers are.'

Commander Reinez had been frozen out by Lord Commander Xarius. After the battle with the Soul Drinkers Xarius had taken to leaving the Crimson Fists out of all communications, as if he thought they were a burden on his command. But Reinez wasn't prepared to hunt the Soul Drinkers on a battlefield he knew nothing about, and so he had instructed the Techmarine that accompanied Chaplain Inhuaca to set up a link into the vox-net. The Crimson Fists were monitoring all the command channels used by the officers of the Imperial Guard in Gravenhold, including the encrypted channel that Paclo had just listened in on.

'Gunner, make way!'

Brother Arroyox, functioning as the Razorback's gunner, dropped down and let Reinez pull himself up into the open turret. The Crimson Fists' column was stationary, waiting in ground cleared by the Fire Drakes less than an hour before. The Fire Drakes were progressing rapidly, with the majority of the resistance further east where the Seleucaians were grinding through the slums. The Razorback, an APC with less transport capacity than a Rhino, but with twin turret-mounted heavy bolters, was towards the head of the column containing the remaining strength of the Crimson Fists.

Reinez looked up into the morning sky. It was a drab grey dawn and the trail of fire was clearly picked out against the milky sky, the train of a rocket, arcing up from the east of the city. He followed the trajectory and a practised eye told him the rocket was heading towards the centre of the slums, an area currently contested by the Seleucaians.

'Paclo, are there any reports of xenos resistance in the slums?'

'Not yet, sir. Human-equivalent only, a few sorcerers. Tough, but no xenos.'

'Good.' Reinez flicked to Inhuaca's vox-channel. 'Chaplain, we have an objective.'

'I see it too,' came Inhuaca's stern voice. 'You are certain it is the Soul Drinkers?'

'What else would they be firing at? If it's the xenos then we'll kill some aliens, to which I assume you have no objections. But if it's the Soul Drinkers then I want us to be there when they are blasted out of whatever hole they are hiding in.'

'As you wish, commander.'

'All squads,' voxed Reinez. 'The Guard are smoking the enemy out and we must be there to finish them off. For Dorn and for the Throne, bless your weapons and move out.'

With a roar of engines the Crimson Fists Second Company, humiliated once against the Soul Drinkers, stormed into Gravenhold determined not to be beaten a second time.

SQUAD SALK WAS first in.

'Now!' yelled Salk and his Marines vaulted the improvised barricade across the entrance of the practice ring.

The Guardsmen reacted too late. A squad of them, eight-strong, held the underground practice ring with its heap of tarpaulin-covered ammo crates and lascells. The first thunderous bolter volley threw them to the ground – one was hit, blasted wetly against the far wall and the others dived into cover.

Most troops would have used their surprise attack to get into the practice ring, find cover of their own, keep firing on the Guardsmen and work their way into the room until all the Guardsmen were dead or had surrendered. Space Marines were not most troops. The philosopher-soldier Daenyathos, the legendary tactician of the old Chapter, had written in his *Catechisms Martial* that a Space Marine's strength was magnified when up close, face-to face. Salk didn't have to order his squad to charge across the ring, jumping supply crates, trusting in their armour and their faith in the Emperor to protect them from the frantic las-fire streaking back at them. The veteran Brother Karrick was first in, shattering a Guardsman's jaw with his bolter stock, kicking over a pile of crates onto a second man. Karrick was one of the few of Salk's Marines who had survived Stratix Luminae, he had nearly lost an arm there, but Apothecary Karendin had rebuilt it and Karrick now used it to pick up the Guardsman on the floor and throw him against the near wall.

Brother Treskaen barged one Guardsman to the ground, knocking him aside and blasting a chain of bolter shots through another.

'Back! Back!' yelled the Guard sergeant, a tough-looking shaven-headed man whose left arm had been replaced by a crude bionic.

'Let them go,' voxed Salk from behind his Marines. His chainsword was drawn but he knew he wouldn't have to use it. The Guardsmen fell back under more bolter fire, fleeing full-tilt back into the network of cells and workshops. 'Sarpedon? We've taken the practice ring but we'll only have a few moments.'

'Good,' replied Sarpedon over the vox. 'Can you rig it to blow?'

'Karrick can. Then we need to be gone, there's a lot of stuff here.'

'Make it happen. We'll keep back.'

Salk glanced at the ammo dump. The practice ring was a large circular room cut out of the stone with a floor of beaten earth, where the more well-regarded gladiators would hone their skills between spectacles. The Soul Drinkers' best guess had been right, this was the only place beneath the arena big enough to store the Guard's ammo dump. The Gravenholders had made a habit of lobbing mortars at the Guard's staging areas by the south-east gate and in the spaceport, so they had to keep their ammunition beneath the ground and the arena was the only place in the slums with an underground complex the Guards knew about. There were a couple of hundred crates under large green tarpaulins, they contained las-cells, rounds for missile launchers, heavy bolters and auto-cannons, tube-charges, grenades, replacement lasguns, and all the other bits and pieces needed to keep several thousand Guardsmen armed and fighting.

'Karrick! Rig this up.'

'Yes, sir.' Karrick was an older man than Salk, a Marine who had fought for so long on the front lines that he could turn his hand to any battlefield task. He seemed to have accepted the old Chapter's view that his leadership skills didn't match his ability to fight. Salk was only promoted to sergeant just before the Chapter War and he was glad to have an old warhorse like Karrick to lend his squad some experience. Perhaps that was why Karrick had never been given a squad of his own – because his experience was more valuable within a squad than leading it.

Karrick broke open a couple of crates, pulling out demolition charges and las-cells. 'Give me a couple of minutes. Then we will have to move, this place is all packed earth and the whole floor will collapse at least.'

'Fine. Treskaen! Get a couple of men on the exit. The rest get back to the barricade.'

Salk looked down at the dead Guardsmen on the floor. The Soul Drinkers had once fought on the same side as the Imperial Guard, taking their place in the immeasurably vast army of the Imperium. The irony was, the old Chapter would have had even less compunction about seeing a Guardsmen dead by their hand. They had been arrogant in the extreme – superior to the rest of humanity, the elite, the shepherds manoeuvring the human race towards the lofty goals of the Emperor. The Imperial Guard were just lesser men, normally useful, sometimes obstructive, always disposable.

Now the Soul Drinkers were forced into conflict with the Guard, and yet Salk saw them more and more as human beings than he ever had when he was trained and deployed by the old Chapter. The Soul Drinkers didn't fight to justify their opinions of superiority any more. They fought against the same enemies the Guard should be fighting: the Ruinous Power of Chaos. Instead, the Guard, like the old Soul Drinkers, were compelled to fight the Imperium's wars to the exclusion of everything else. Sometimes they coincided with the war against Chaos. More often they were just to quell rebellion, to terrorise citizens into abandoning their ideals of secession, independence and freedom. The men and women of the Imperial Guard died, not to fight the Dark Powers that were on the brink of devouring humanity, but to keep the ancient, corrupt edifice of the Imperium from collapsing under the weight of its own citizens.

And so the Soul Drinkers had to kill them, when they should have been fighting the same fight.

'It's done,' said Karrick. 'How long do we need?'

'Five minutes,' replied Salk.

'It's done.'

Salk flicked onto the all-squads channel. 'Soul Drinkers, we're gone.'

SARETHA DIDN'T NEED to touch them to feel the pain. Their suffering bled out of them, like a rain of razors against her skin. Her service to Slaanesh had left her so sensitive that emotions strong enough could radiate out and sear her like the heat of a star.

She had almost forgotten how good it could feel.

Her cultists crowded around her, forming a wedge of willing bodies trampling through the tents of the Guard encampment. They were almost at the centre of the arena camp, at the heart of the cultist thrust that had driven the Seleucaian Guardsmen out to the edge of the arena. Las-fire was sporadic and broken – the horror of the assault had thrown the Guardsmen into disarray. Saretha could hear their officers yelling, trying to drag the terrified Guardsmen into a firing line.

Their minds were so closed, thought Saretha. So blind. They really think they can survive.

Another Guardsman died nearby, trampled beneath the feet of her bearers. But they were running out. It was the curse of Slaanesh that victory meant there would be no more deaths to savour, and Saretha, on a deep and half-realised level, was addicted to the suffering of others.

'Forward!' she hissed, her long spiny tongue rattling fearsomely. 'Take me closer!'

She lashed out with her mind, sending a psychic knife slicing through the tents and heaps of equipment, the abandoned weapon emplacements and corpse-choked barricades. She felt the flickering lifelights of her own men go out but the shuddering, blind panic of the dying Guardsmen was in short supply now.

'Damnation,' she snapped to herself. 'We killed them all.'

When the arena was won in the name of Slaanesh, and until the alien came to claim it, she would have to satisfy herself with her own followers.

She saw the last knot of Guardsmen crouched among the far seating behind piles of supply creates, swapping las-fire with the cultists that surrounded them, unable to see even the beauty of their deaths.

And then the world exploded around her.

* * *

LUKO'S LIGHTNING CLAWS flashed as he ripped through the rusting iron bulkhead that blocked his way. His Marines had found their way from the medicae station down into the guts of some old industrial district, all staircases and corroded metal, some layers crushed almost flat by the weight of the city above. It was tight going, but if the Marines could get down here then so could the Guardsmen, with a few demo charges and some guts.

Luko ripped a V-shape into the iron then slashed again, slicing out a triangle from the bulkhead that slammed to the floor.

'We're going to have to cut our way through, lads,' he said, indicating the tangle of metal that lay beyond. 'I make it two kilometres north and seventy metres down to the palace.'

'We're clear behind,' voxed Sergeant Dyon.

'Good. Keep the plasma gun to the rear. Squad Corvan behind me, and get your chainswords out. It'll be tough going.'

Then the shockwave slammed into him, and the darkness erupted from everywhere at once.

TWO EXPLOSIONS WITHIN seconds, like punctuation marks in the battle. The force shook down crumbling hovels in the slums and crystal chandeliers in the mansions to the north. The *Resolve* saw them both from orbit, sudden plumes of destruction amongst the warfare.

The explosion in the centre of the arena sent a shaft of fire a hundred metres into the air, showering the surrounding area with cultists and Guardsmen's bodies. The massive stonework of the arena was fatally fractured and half of it collapsed, the column of fire followed up by a roaring cloud of dust as the masonry crashed down.

The second explosion was a bolt of purest blackness that streaked into the heart of the slum district, blooming into a dark sphere that swallowed up the medicae station and three surrounding blocks of ruined tenements. The silent, hungry void consumed anything it rolled over, and where its furthest extent reached it left men, buildings, and tanks sliced neatly apart.

The vortex missile that had hit the medicae station was normally mounted on the Titans of the Adeptus Mechanicus Legions. It was the only example of vortex technology the Imperium could reliably replicate in any numbers and even then its use was rare. The vortex it created was a chained pocket of no-space, a miniature black hole, an anomaly of physics that sucked anything it touched into the annihilation of the warp. It even sucked in the morning daylight, casting premature dusk over Gravenhold's slums.

THE ARENA FLOOR sunk thirty metres, the cells and training rooms flattened. What remained of the Imperial Guard camp was dragged into the churning mess of pulverised earth and broken bodies, and now lay at the bottom of a huge ragged pit blasted by the detonation of the ammunition dump.

The cistern beneath the arena floor, once used to flood the arena for mock water battles, had been used by the Guard to store promethium tank fuel. It had gone up along with the ammunition and the result was a massive crater where the arena floor had once been, surrounded by a few tottering columns of seating like teeth in a broken jaw.

'There,' said Brother Karrick. The tunnel into which his Soul Drinkers had escaped had collapsed just behind them and now looked onto the bottom of the crater. Smashed tanks lay half-buried in the heaped rubble, tattered bodies were strewn everywhere. In places the dust was stained black with blood, so the slaughter above must have been tremendous.

'Where?' asked Sergeant Salk, who had been the last out of the arena cells and whose squad had narrowly avoided being buried.

'Movement,' said Karrick. 'See it? One of them's still alive.'

'Damn, I thought we'd got them all.' The plan was simple: wait until Saretha's cultists were in the arena and then blow the ammo dump, wiping out her personal army while attracting the least suspicion. It would buy the Soul Drinkers time; the longer Karhedros's army could be forced into a stalemate against the Guard, the longer the Soul Drinkers could hang on and make themselves useful, giving them more time to find Tellos before Karhedros inevitably betrayed them.

It was a shame about the Guard. But they would have died at Saretha's hands anyway and at least this way, death was the worst thing that had happened to them.

'Check it out,' said Sarpedon. 'Be quick.'

The Soul Drinkers spread out across the heaped wreckage, picking their way past upturned tanks and knots of corpses towards the tangle of supply crates and weapon emplacements. Salk saw the way the cultists' stitched mouths were burst open, and he had heard their ecstatic cries from below the arena. They were fanatics, extremists who would never give up. So were the Soul Drinkers, except the Soul Drinkers knew they were right.

'It was here,' said Karrick, stalking past an upturned weapon emplacement built of lashed-together sandbags it was stuck end-on in the heaped rubble, a shattered heavy bolter hanging from its mount.

'I don't see anything,' said Salk. 'Squad? Contacts?'

'Nothing here,' said Brother Golus, who was pushing mangled bodies aside with the muzzle of his bolter in case one of them was just playing dead.

'Clear here, too,' said Brother Skael, sweeping his bolter over the expanse of rubble. The rest of the squad sounded off. There was nothing but death there. Except Karrick wasn't a man who jumped at shadows.

The sound like a striking rattlesnake was the only warning. All Salk saw was a bolt of blackness streaking up from the ground in a shower of debris, spinning through the air as it threw itself at Brother Golus.

The psychic attack that followed it was a wave of foulness. Pure corruption. Salk felt tendrils of something writhing and obscene reaching through him and caressing his soul, a cacophonic choir shrieking in his ears. He saw the blessed debaucheries of the Whore-Priestess Saretha, the mountains of squirming bodies, the taste of refined blood in his mouth, the gentle touch of daemons.

He screamed as he ripped the images out of his mind. His vision swam back and he saw Saretha the Bitch-Queen, the muscles of her naked ebony-skinned body gleaming, her razored tongue punching repeatedly into Brother Golus's chest like a rapier's blade.

Salk dragged himself upward, his hand on the hilt of his chainblade. Saretha's hateful eyes glanced at him and the wave of filth roared through him again – the smell of burning flesh, the feel of cold entrails against his skin, the choir of voices raised in agony, thousands of sensations crammed into one bolt of unholiness.

He moved in slow motion, like a man swimming against the current, the force of Saretha's evil pushing him back. He had faced moral threats before and he knew the depths to which Chaos could sink. But to feel the experiences of the enemy flooding through him, to have memories of debauchery welling up from inside him as if they were his own. He didn't think he could cope with that. He fought on, but he could feel his soul slipping away. He could see the blackness that would remain when his mind was destroyed.

A burst of blue-white light knifed out of nowhere. Golus thudded to the ground as Saretha was hurled through the air, slamming against the burned-out hulk of a Leman Russ tank.

Sarpedon's nalwood force staff was still glowing with energy as his eight legs carried him over the rubble towards Saretha. The Chaos witch sprang to her feet and moved too fast for Salk to see, but Sarpedon was faster; no one, not even Apothecary Pallas, fully understood the extent of Sarpedon's mutations but they had left the Librarian lightning-fast and monstrously strong. With a blur of movement he flipped Saretha onto the ground, slashing out with one of his taloned forelegs. Saretha caught the leg, thinking for a moment that she had left Sarpedon vulnerable before Sarpedon stabbed a second leg through her stomach.

Saretha's blood was clear, like water. Sarpedon lifted her up and caught her by the throat with his free hand.

Salk pulled himself to his feet. He looked down at Brother Golus – the Marine was still alive but badly hurt. The rest of Salk's Marines were on the ground, too, their minds reeling from Saretha's assault. She had nearly taken the whole squad down. Nearly.

Saretha squirmed in Sarpedon's grip, colourless blood spurting from her wound.

'What does Karhedros want?' said Sarpedon evenly.

Saretha hissed violently, her tongue lashing out, but Sarpedon's long reach kept her out of range.

'What does the alien want? What did he promise you? I know you can speak.'

He has you already, came Saretha's voice, a thick syrupy sound broadcast directly into Salk's mind. She was a telepath, of course. She couldn't speak normally because she didn't have to. *He had you from the beginning. You. Your mad cripple. All a part of it.*

'A part of what?'

I can taste the death on you. There are many dead men in the warp who speak of you. Your deformed body, your revenge, as strong as the will of the gods, as strong as us…

Sarpedon was squeezing.

The sacrifice has already begun. Nothing will get off this planet alive. Nothing. Oh, all that death… it was why he chose you…

Something cracked in Saretha's skull. Sarpedon knew better than to try to force something like Saretha into cooperating through mere pain, Salk realised – his grip was tightening involuntarily as he resisted the way her words were worming their way into his soul. She wanted to break him. Even facing death, she wanted to take one more soul for Slaanesh.

He is clever. For an alien.

Another crack, louder this time. Saretha's body fell limp, only her eyes still moved, glinting up at Sarpedon, as if daring him to finish the job.

Salk drew his chainsword. 'Permission to kill it, commander?' he said.

Saretha's body spasmed. Her ebony skin flowed, turned liquid, and slipped through Sarpedon's fingers. She lost her shape, her eyes becoming two burning points in a formless boiling mass, twisting in on itself.

Sarpedon's force staff stabbed out but the mass parted before it. The thing that was Saretha formed up around a bone-white spear that had been her tongue.

When it charged, it came quicker than anyone could see. But Sarpedon didn't need to see. Saretha was a psychic beacon, emblazoned on the minds of everyone nearby. Sarpedon's reflexes were faster than thought.

The force staff shone brighter than a lightning bolt as it slashed down. Its described an arc that hung in the air behind it as the two halves of Highmistress Saretha flopped to the ground in a slithering mess of transparent entrails, the bone-hard spiny tongue split neatly lengthways.

Sarpedon wiped Saretha's clear blood from his eyes. 'Permission denied,' he said.

CHAPTER ELEVEN

'INTERFERENCE MY ARSE,' snapped Xarius, looking up from the reams of cogitator printouts that all but filled his command office, the chattering of an autostylus merging with the rumbling engines of the Baneblade. 'Get him on the vox. Better still, find the idiot and bring him here. I'll give him the old field punishment number one, that little rotmaggot, Munitorum or not.'

When Xarius got really angry, he became quiet and intense. Hasdrubal probably knew the warning signs by now, but that didn't make his job any easier.

'He's somewhere in the industrial area, the second front,' said Hasdrubal. 'Directing the long-range artillery. There's something wrong with the vox-net…'

'Nothing wrong with it when he called the codes in, was there? Worked perfectly well when he decided to start throwing vortex missiles at my battlefield. You don't deploy ordnance like that without the commander's say-so, even Consul bloody Kelchenko knows that. I'm doing him the undue courtesy of assuming he's not just showing off, which means that something spooked him and that's the kind of thing a commander needs to know about. Emperor's teeth, does he think this isn't difficult enough? Maybe he thinks we should be giving the enemy a sporting chance? Maybe it's fairer if we don't all work together. Do you think that might be it, Hasdrubal?'

Hasdrubal had the intelligence not to answer.

Xarius sat back. The office in the heart of the Baneblade was in danger of becoming completely flooded with paper. Transcripts of vox-casts were being forwarded to him by officers all over Gravenhold – he was grateful for the information, but the old, unwelcome feeling of managing a massive human tragedy was well bedded in now. That was what none of them understood: a single battle was an immense disaster. A capital ship lost in the warp, an outbreak of a plague in a hive city, a reactor breach on a forge-world, none of these compared to the toll in human lives that accompanied any major battle of the Imperial Guard. Even when they won, they lost.

Xarius shook his head. 'They've lost the arena, you know. The whole Seleucaian front is unsupported. The enemy could flank them in an instant, they could cut them to pieces. The Janissaries are running from their own damn shadows. And now Kelchenko is throwing my Deathstrikes at some bogeyman or other.'

'With respect, sir, Kelchenko must have had some reason to–'

'Oh, certainly. Aliens, wizards, Traitor Marines, the whole damn city is brimming with them.' Xarius held up a handful of printouts. 'They're seeing everything out there, Hasdrubal. It's a called a battle, it does that to people. The truth is that the much-vaunted aliens haven't shown up yet, which means they're underneath us, waiting for us to walk right over them. That's how they got the arena, mark my words. No one knows what's under this city. I wouldn't be surprised if the real enemy had the run of this place. They're laughing at us, Hasdrubal, and it's morons like Kelchenko that are doing their best to help them.'

Xarius eased his old body out of his chair and clambered out of the sunken office, up into the main hull compartment with its servitor-loaders and clanking engine housings. 'I'm going to get this thing moving so I can find Threlnan, sit him down and work out this mess. We've got enough of the city to redeploy, and if we don't those alien groxhuggers will lead us by the nose into whatever trap they sprung on Sathis at the Cynos Pass. Can we get to Threlnan's position?'

'Yes, sir. But I can direct the driver…'

'Humour me, Hasdrubal. I need to see this battle through my own eyes for a change. Besides, there's more legroom up front. Just get me a fix on Colonel Threlnan. I can make it an order if it would make you happier.'

Hasdrubal ducked into the vox-operator's tiny cubbyhole to scour the vox-net for Colonel Threlnan's location, which was probably somewhere between the first and second Seleucaian waves, if, of course, he hadn't died at the arena. Xarius pulled himself into the tank commander's seat, in the brutal blunt nose of the tank next to the driver, who looked uncertainly up at Xarius.

'Keep up with the infantry and make ready to change course,' said Xarius, noticing the badge of the Steel Hammers of the Seleucaian 2nd. The Seleucaians, Xarius reminded himself, had flocked to join his command to avenge the Steel Hammers who had died at Cynos Pass.

Xarius saw the infantry up ahead, advancing through the battleground that had chewed through the limits of the industrial sector and into the slums. Some of them would be driven on by revenge, the score to settle now including the men and women who had died at the arena. But most of them, Xarius knew, would only be caring about their survival. Xarius knew this because he had been a soldier, too, and all he had ever wanted to do out there was get back alive.

The Gravenholders were relinquishing their city bit by bit, knowing the Guard were too unwieldy to react to them and the aliens that Xarius could feel lurking beneath him. Xarius had to get together with Threlnan and work out a way to get the Seleucaians ready for the final attack, which would cut them to pieces if they were caught unawares. It was, of course, an impossible task.

But then, Lord Commander Xarius had become a lord commander precisely because he could do the impossible. It always cost thousands upon thousands of lives, but that was a price the Imperium had always been most willing to pay.

THE VORTEX PULSE had turned Luko's world into a nightmare of torn metal, a black and swirling madness with a razor-edged wind tearing through it. The world collapsed in on itself, sucked into a black maelstrom that bore down on him and his Marines like a dark sun dawning above them.

The warp-stain rippled at the edges of his mind. As he fell he heard daemons cackling, He saw their tiny, baleful eyes through the darkness. He felt the winds of the immaterium battering against him, and glimpsed the psychic thunderheads of emotion that towered in the warp.

He hit the ground and the warp let go of him to be replaced with a ringing concussion. The world was now full of pain, sparks and white noise.

There was dark reddish stone, smooth with age, beneath him. Walls of the same stone rose around him, soaring up into domes and minarets, decorated with bands of brass and sculptures of strange, stylised faces.

It was one of Gravenhold's previous incarnations, a dark temple-city, this part of which had survived intact beneath a sky of rusting metal. Luko pulled himself up to his knees and glanced behind him.

An immense sphere had been bitten out of the undercity, extending from the surface down to the temple-city. It was a perfect spherical space, cutting through towers and minarets, its sides striped with the various layers of Gravenhold it had sliced through. Where there had once been thousands of tons of metal and stone, now there was just a giant echoing space. A shaft of grimy grey light reached down from where the sphere met the surface.

The space was beginning to collapse under its own weight. Debris was tumbling down, the start of a land-slide.

'Luko to all squads,' voxed Luko. 'Who's alive?'

Acknowledgement runes flashed in Luko's vision, projected by his armour onto his retina. All of his own squad. All but two of Squad Dyon, who had been in the rear. All but one of Squad Corvan. Varuk was alive, too.

'Brothers Muros and Pamaeon are gone,' voxed Dyon.

'Brother Thallion, too,' voxed Sergeant Corvan. 'Tell me that wasn't a vortex detonation.'

'Either it was a Deathstrike missile or a Titan,' replied Luko. 'I like to think we'd have noticed a Titan, though.'

'They must really hate us,' said Corvan.

'The feeling is becoming mutual.'

Techmarine Varuk stomped up, his armoured form and servo-arms silhouetted against the shaft of light from above. 'It's all going to collapse,' he said. 'One half is going to slide and then they'll have a path down. If the Guard are pursuing then they'll be on us in minutes.'

'Agreed,' said Luko, waving his scattered squad towards him. Their armour was battered and scorched, but they were unharmed. 'These damn streets are wide enough for a Leman Russ.'

'There's a canal here,' voxed Corvan. 'Less than a metre deep. Looks like it flows underground and out of the city. There's room for us but I'd like to see them get a tank down here.'

'Good. Then you're in the lead. Soul Drinkers, underground isn't safe any more. That alien owes us three deaths now but we'll have to survive this before we can make him pay. Look sharp and move out.'

CHUNKS OF MASONRY and debris rained down as Gravenhold shifted, filling the huge sudden void carved by the vortex missile. The Imperial Guard waited at the lip of the crater, waiting for the landslide to leave a negotiable path down to the undercity. It was their first glimpse of what waited for them beneath Gravenhold. What should have been solid rock was shot through with tunnels, chambers, whole subterranean cities, abandoned for thousands of years and now infested by the enemy they were here to fight.

Many felt they had been lied to by the Seleucaian officers, who had ordered them into a battle where only the city of Gravenhold was being fought over, not the endless layers of ruins that lay beneath it. The officers felt they had been let down by their intelligence, led into a city that, it turned out, no one really knew anything about at all. Gravenhold itself was bad enough, but at least they knew where it was and how it fitted together. But downwards – there could be anything. And there was nothing more dangerous than fighting a battle through the unknown.

But few Guardsmen had time to voice these concerns. Because just as the landslides picked up enough pace to make a first tentative descent viable, there was a roar of engines from the west. A column of vehicles crashed through the slums, running the gauntlet of the Gravenholders and making straight for the missile site.

Rhinos and Razorbacks crashed to a halt, scattering the Guardsmen assembling to begin the pursuit.

This quarry was reserved for the Crimson Fists.

'TAKE HIM,' SAID Scout-Sergeant Eumenes.

Scout-Sniper Raek didn't reply. Instead, his finger tightened on the trigger and an Algorathi officer's head snapped back, clear and brutal through the lenses of Eumenes's magnoculars.

The Algorathi Janissaries, the scouts had quickly realised, relied on their officers. The Janissaries were an aristocratic regiment at heart, drawn from a world where class and privilege were reflected in their ranks. The masses followed society's leaders, in battle as they did on Algorath itself. Eumenes had never been to the planet of course, never even heard of it before except as the homeworld of the men his scouts were hiding amongst, but he felt he knew the place all the same. There was little question that one class led and the rest followed, it was more Imperial than the Imperium itself.

It also bred men who had a fundamental battlefield weakness. Take out the officers, and their ability to fight was significantly diminished. They could still shoot straight but anything more complicated than sitting tight and keeping their heads down was beyond them.

The Algorathi Janissaries in Gravenhold were currently suffering a severe shortage of officers.

'Nisryus, are they onto us?'

The precog shook his head. 'They could have passed right by but they would have missed us. Which means they're not looking.'

'You're sure? This place is thick with patrols.'

'I'm sure. I can see their future footprints, they're fading out now their plan has changed but it's clear enough.'

'They're moving for a reason. Either they're redeploying or they're running.'

Eumenes pulled back from the window, leaving Raek to watch the squad of Guardsmen who had thrown themselves into cover. The building his scouts were hiding in had been hit by an artillery shell and lost its roof and back wall, but it was well-positioned to watch the wider avenue that cut through the piled-up hovels. The Janissaries had been scouting the avenue, presumably to prepare for a large troop movement. The scouts had slowed that process down but the patrols were still coming.

'Running from what?' asked Scamander, watching the back of the first-floor room.

'Tellos, maybe,' said Eumenes. 'Which is why we're here.'

'I've got something,' came a vox from Selepus on the floor below. 'The third tenement on the the south side. On the roof.'

Eumenes ducked to the window. He could see the building, but there was nothing there.

'I've got it,' said Raek, looking through the scope of his rifle. 'On the corner.'

Eumenes looked closer. There was just a tiny dark shape at the parapet. He looked at it through his magnoculars.

He saw the subtly bladed armour of an eldar. It was crouching down, taking aim with one of their strange crystalline rifles.

'Want me to take it?' said Raek.

'Wait. We don't want a fight with those things, not yet.'

'More,' voxed Selepus. 'Lots more.'

He was right. Dark shapes danced at the windows. With movements too fluid to be real they vaulted out into the open, sprinting and flipping over obstacles so quickly Eumenes couldn't pick any one of them out of the sudden rush of blurring shapes.

They seemed lightly-armoured, all but naked, the pallid eldar flesh white in the morning sun. Eumenes saw blades, whips, as they descended on the Guardsmen whose officer Raek had killed.

Blades sliced. Guardsmen came apart. There were barely a handful of las-blasts before the eldar were crouched amongst the bloodstained rubble the Guardsmen had been using as cover, and Eumenes saw them clearly for the first time; lithe, snake-muscled eldar, their movements so fluid it was hard to imagine they were real creatures. Their scanty purple-black armour contrasted with their pale skin and their too-large eyes shone.

One of them, wielding a whip, yelled an order in their xenos tongue and the eldar melted away, just sinking into the rubble and disappearing.

'Looks like we've found a whole new war,' said Raek quietly.

'Then why are they bothering the Janissaries? The Gravenholders are getting crushed between two fronts in the city. These slums aren't worth anything, that's why they sent their most useless Guardsmen here.'

'They're just in it for the hunt, then?' voxed Selepus. 'Easy prey.'

'No, it's not that.' Eumenes put down his magnoculars. The avenue was now effectively cut off. No Janissary officer would lead his men down there now, not with patrols being reduced to bloodstains on the rubble. That meant the Janissaries would have to avoid the thoroughfare entirely. They would have to head north.

'I think the eldar are herding them.'

LUKO JUST RAN.

Space Marines, the Emperor himself had decreed, knew no fear. That was why they existed, they fought on when other men would run and die, and it was due to this more than anything else that a Marine was the deadliest thing the Imperium could put on a battlefield. But they were not stupid, either. And Luko knew when to stand and fight, and when to run.

The Soul Drinkers could hear the voices of the Crimson Fists, flinging curses into the darkness. They could see the muzzle flashes as the Fists snapped off sighting shots at them, white-hot bolter rounds cutting streaks through the shadows.

'Dyon! How many?' voxed Luko, following Squad Corvan through another waist-deep watercourse.

'Can't tell,' came the reply from Sergeant Dyon, whose squad was last in the formation. 'Looks like Assault Squads, two at least. They're just the vanguard.'

Even a conservative estimate put the number of Crimson Fists pursuing them at most of the surviving Second Company. The Soul Drinkers hadn't been able to stand up to them in a straight fight at the chamber mercantile. Now they were just running like rats across a seemingly endless underground river delta. Dozens of rushing watercourses split off from the main river, and it was across the resulting delta that the Soul Drinkers were forging, hoping to find some way down deeper into the undercity. Luko silently cursed himself for the heretical thought that he was entertaining, he would do anything to see the eldar right now. Whatever side they were on, his Soul Drinkers could do with someone else for the Crimson Fists to fight.

'Got something,' voxed Corvan, whose Assault Squad took up the lead in case they stumbled into something that needed the attention of their chainswords. 'It's deeper but it's heading down.'

Luko's enhanced vision picked out white water up ahead. 'Take it,' he said.

A few strides later he was up to his chest in fast-running water, following Corvan's Assault Marines down into a channel that dove beneath the delta plain into a water-smooth stone tunnel.

Gunfire chattered behind him as Dyon's Marines swapped a few volleys of bolter fire with the Fists. The Crimson Fists Assault Marines were armed with bolt pistols so Corvan's Tactical Marines had the greater range with their bolters, and a few volleys bought them the time to get into the tunnel without losing ground to their pursuers.

White noise of rushing water filled the tunnel. Luko fought to keep his footing; a normal man would have been swept away.

'It widens up ahead,' voxed Corvan.

'Use the space,' said Luko. 'Throne knows what's down here.'

Squad Corvan spread out, as did Squad Luko behind them, several Marines were now wading downstream abreast with their guns held up out of the water. The blackness ahead of them swallowed everything as the tunnel forged downwards.

'Contact! Throne of Earth, what…'

Pistol fire echoed, bolter rounds smacking into the stone walls. Glass broke.

Luko barged forwards past the Assault Marines to see what Squad Corvan had blundered into, water hissing on his lightning claws as he activated the power field.

'Hold it!' Sergeant Corvan was yelling, his power sword a bright stab of light held above his head. 'Hold fire!'

Luko saw what they had found. And slowly he began to understand what Gravenhold was all about.

The rushing river emerged into a wide space, a swirling cauldron of shoulder-high water, too big to see the far walls. Hung in racks fixed into the ceiling were translucent cylinders, and in each cylinder was the smudgy, indistinct shape of a human form. Corvan's Marines had shattered one cylinder with gunfire and its contents lay draped over the rack, glistening with some thick, clear liquid; a pallid, hairless human form, naked and raw.

Corvan reached up and pulled down one arm of the body. There was a tattoo on the bicep.

'It's Guard,' he said. 'Seventeenth Iocarthian Regiment.'

'That doesn't make any sense,' said Luko. 'Iocarth is three systems away. What's he doing here?'

'She,' said Corvan.

'Varuk!' called Luko. The Techmarine forged his way through the water towards him. 'What the frag are these things?'

Varuk struggled through the Assault Marines and took a closer look. 'Not cryogenics,' he said. His servo-arm reached up and a tiny drill whirred at its tip, boring through the side of a cylinder. A threadlike probe spooled out into the liquid, then withdrew. 'Something chemical. Metabolic deadeners, preservatives, conductive saturates. This body was alive until we came along, just.'

'Is this Imperial tech?'

'It's not Adeptus Mechanicus. This is advanced, if it was them there would be prayers and incense everywhere. There might be private industries which could make this, but… well, they've got no business being on Gravenhold at the best of times. And this needs maintenance to keep all these bodies alive. But…'

'But what?'

Varuk examined the base of the closest intact cylinder, where bundles of wires fed into it. 'There should be a power source. This whole place should be lit up like a battleship's bridge. Otherwise they'll shut down.'

'And then what?'

'The bodies either disintegrate or they wake up.'

'Care to guess which?'

'Fifty-fifty.'

'I think we can do better than that,' said Corvan. He had lifted the hand of the corpse and was examining its fingers. The tips were split at the end. Corvan squeezed one finger and a long, thin metal claw, like that of a feline predator, extended. 'Not Guard issue,' he said.

'All this is Karhedros,' said Luko. 'The eldar are raiders. Slavers. He could have taken shipfuls of captives, brought them to Gravenhold, installed them down here. And now he's waking them up.' Luko walked forward a few paces, trying to get a feel to see how many bodies were stored there. He counted a dozen racks, each holding cylinders stacked three deep, stretching off into the darkness.

There were hundreds of bodies. Thousands. And this was just one location. Karhedros had the whole city to hide them under. 'Varuk, how long before they start coming round?'

'Looks like they've been powered down for a couple of days. Some of them are already twitching. I'd guess a matter of hours.'

'Then I think I know what this battle is about,' said Luko. 'Why the aliens are letting the Gravenholders lose the city for them. Why Karhedros wanted us here at all. This isn't about conquest, Soul Drinkers, that damn alien doesn't want to conquer anything. This is about sacrifice.'

TWENTY-THREE MINUTES later, the vox went down across Gravenhold.

The Imperial communications had been patchy at the best of times, cutting in and out at random, but aside from the inevitable confusion of combat, information still found its way through the chains of command up to Lord General Xarius's Baneblade. And suddenly, it was completely gone.

Vox-operators in Guard command squads frantically checked their equipment as their handsets went dead. The forward spotters of the Carvelnan Royal Artillery were cut off from their artillery units and the Imperium's big guns were suddenly silent.

The Crimson Fists, their communications already strung out since they were underground pursuing the Traitor Marines, were suddenly without the vox-net that co-ordinated the charge through the endless subterranean darkness. The attack foundered as the Fists crossed a raging underground river delta, the Assault Squads stranded unsupported on the very heels of the Soul Drinkers. Chaplain Inhuaca demanded they continue, Commander Reinez refused to lose any more of his Marines to an obvious trap. It was clear that both men were livid, but Reinez was haunted by the loss of his standard at the chamber mercantile and was damned if the Soul Drinkers would pick off the rest of the Crimson Fists piecemeal.

The *Resolve* was all but blinded. Communications to the surface were gone. The few spotter-ships out over Gravenhold wheeled in confusion, flitting between bearings and altitudes, trying to find pockets of clear

air where they could send and receive. The clever ones
gave up and returned to the *Resolve*, hoping to make a
visual landing in the cruiser's fighter bays. The rest flew
around until their fuel ran out and they had to ditch.
Some made it into the abandoned agri-wastes outside
the city, but most crashed into the war-torn streets
themselves. Captain Caislenn-Har on the *Resolve* itself
powered up all weapons and put all crew on full alert,
more to reassure the crew that they were doing something positive than for any practical reason. All the
ship could do was maintain visual contact with the
city and try to pick out what was going on from aerial
pict-steals. What had never been a particularly glorious
campaign for the Imperial Navy became a maddening
stalemate, with even intra-orbital communications cut
off so the supply ships and escorts that surrounded the
Resolve were equally deaf and dumb.

The Soul Drinkers were cut off from one another,
too. But then, it was something they were getting used
to.

'DIE ON YOUR knees or send me back to Dorn!' yelled
Librarian Tyrendian, and the catacomb tunnel was lit
bright acid white by the claws of lightning that leapt
from his hand. A dozen creatures were blown apart,
sallow grey flesh and thin blood plastered over the
ancient tomb-niches and worn inscriptions that covered the walls.

Graevus glanced behind him at the Librarian, whose
aegis collar burned with blue-white light that bled
from Tyrendian's eyes.

'Charge!' shouted Graevus and his squad ran into
the gap Tyrendian had blasted. Clawed hands were
reaching from everywhere, as if the Soul Drinkers in

the eastern wall were fighting not a mass of separate creatures but an amorphous, multi-limbed creature surging up the tunnel at them. Graveus lashed out with his power axe, the muscles of his mutated hand carving a great shining arc through them. Old bones scattered as the axe blade bit clean through the stone of the tomb-niches. The Assault Marines behind Graveus stabbed with their chainblades, turning leering faces and blade-tipped limbs into shrieking masses of shredded flesh.

Apothecary Karendin was there, bolt pistol blasting. One of the creatures clambered over Graveus's guard and dove down on Karendin; the Apothecary thrust his medicae gauntlet into its chest and impaled it with a dozen syringes and reductor probes. Combat hormones pumped through it and the thing shook itself to death in a mad welter of blood.

It was bad. Worse than they could have expected. The enemy was coming up from below and this time they weren't on the Soul Drinkers' side. They were making for the surface through the undercity and, in the east, that meant going through the wall and through Graevus, Kelvor, Tyrendian and Apothecary Karendin.

These weren't Gravenholders. These things weren't even human any more. The Gravenholders fought in a mad human flood, but they were still people. These were something utterly bestial. Graevus saw fingers that ended in razor-like blades, mouths that opened to reveal sharp metal tongues like swords, torsos that burst like seed pods crammed with shrapnel, suicide creatures who tried to grab hold of a Marine before their bodies were torn apart by blades and spikes ripping out from inside them.

The Soul Drinkers forged their way further down, Squad Kelvor in the rear as the sergeant fought to keep up on the makeshift prosthetic leg Karendin had fashioned from lengths of wood and bones. The Soul Drinkers' vantage point further up the wall was already swamped, and these monsters seemed to be coming from everywhere at once. The only way out was to get to the foot of the wall and take their chances in the streets of the administrative district.

Graevus literally waded in, stamping down and lashing out at the same time, feeling the weight of the enemy. It was like cutting through dense jungle, like swimming against the current. Brother Vargulis died by his side, faceplate sliced open.

Graevus wasn't going to die here. He was going to get off this dung-pile of a planet. He was a Soul Drinker. He had defied the Imperium and spat in the eye of Chaos. He could damn well do anything, and that included surviving.

The tide gave way to light. Graevus's axe gouged through the crumbling stone and he half-fell into the street, where administrative office blocks crowded up against the eastern wall. His squad fell out with him, Squad Kelvor followed, fighting to keep the creatures from flooding out after them.

'Back!' yelled Tyrendian, and Graveus led his Marines further down the alleyway before another of the Librarian's psychic lightning bolts shattered the ancient stone and a landslide of rubble buried the breach the Soul Drinkers had made.

For a moment there was relative quiet.

Karendin withdrew the probes and reductors of his medicae gauntlet. It was slick with gore. 'Alien tech,' he said darkly. 'Nothing Imperial could have made them.'

'Eldar?'

Karendin shrugged. 'Throne knows.'

Squad Kelvor moved forwards to the entrance of the alleyway. The east wall was behind the Fire Drakes' lines, the Soul Drinkers had tangled with the Fire Drakes at the chamber mercantile and had no intention of doing so again.

'Are we clear?' asked Graevus.

'No,' replied Kelvor. 'We are not.'

Graevus hurried up to the entrance of the alleyway. In front of him was a road wide enough for the magtractors that hauled loads in from the fields or the truckloads of workers leaving through the southeastern gate. The road was filling up with Fire Drakes, running out of the alleyways or the lower floors of the towering administrative blocks. They were falling back, officers yelling orders that kept the men in a steady line. Chimeras rumbled backwards, multi-lasers or pintle-mounted storm bolters facing the way they had come.

Kelvor and Graevus crouched back, but there was no danger of their being seen. The Fire Drakes' line was retreating, several hundred men all training their weapons on the road.

Someone's nerve slipped and a las-shot spat out. A dozen more followed, then a hundred, lasguns on full auto kicking out a storm of crimson bolts and a stinking metallic cloud of burned air. The din of the fire was broken only by the whirring of the multi-lasers as they fired.

The enemy poured like a flood out of the lower windows of the buildings up ahead, burst like fountains out of manhole covers and storm drain gratings. They flowed over obstacles, poured out of alleyways, fell like waterfalls from the crumbling face of the inner wall. Thousands of them. Tens of thousands. Trying to kill them was like a cruel joke, like throwing pebbles into the sea.

The Fire Drakes broke and ran.

'Into the building!' shouted Graevus. 'Up! Go up!'

The Gravenholders were just a garrison force. They were the men and women who had been in the city when Karhedros had come, their minds addled and their bodies pressed into service. This was Karhedros's real army, a slave-army tens of thousands strong, the killing blow from an immense trap that comprised the whole city.

Squad Kelvor quickly broke the closest ground-floor windows and the Soul Drinkers vaulted in. The only safety from the flood was the high, defensible ground of the administrative blocks, the same ground the Gravenholders had struck from in the earliest days of the battle. Graevus followed them in and Karendin was on their heels.

Librarian Tyrendian was the last. With a glance back, he sent out a bolt of blue-white lightning that plunged into the advancing horde, slicing them open in a gigantic wound, reducing a dozen subhumans to charred skin and scalding steam. But the flood quickly filled the wound it left. Tyrendian hauled himself through the small window, and the administrative district of Gravenhold was swallowed up by the slave-army of Karhedros.

THE UNDERGROUND PALACE was just for decoration. It was the topmost tower, built for show, just to prove that whoever had built it could control the skyline of the city at a whim. The wings the Space Marines had used, the courtyard the warriors had ranked up in, even the stone garden with its frozen beauty, these were just the extra flourish that completed the palace of one of Entymion IV's long-forgotten pre-Imperial kings.

The real palace was further down. And while the topmost elements were dark and stern enough, the main body of the palace was utterly brutal. Massive bulbous columns reared up against cliff-like walls of chiselled onyx. Battlements of jade frowned over slit windows like scowling eyes. Ivory inlays surrounded immense verdigrised bronze doors, bright teeth framing a yawning mouth. Karhedros's personal army was stationed in the palace and around its imposing stony hinterland. The wyches lounged by the massive front steps, their languid half-naked bodies giving no hint of the sheer fury and combat skills they employed in battle. Several squadrons of Reaver jetbikes were lined up in the shadow of the front wall, their fanatical riders tinkering with the anti-grav motors or concocting new forms of combat drugs to heighten their senses and reflexes. The eldar warriors were uneasy, barracked in their camp outside the palace, the sentries cradling their splinter rifles wishing they could get a piece of the real battle raging far above them. They would get what they wanted soon enough. They would get far, far more than they imagined. A great many of Karhedros's eldar were on the surface herding the human prey into the path of the slave-army, but there was still a formidable force at the palace.

Inside, the palace seemed even more vast. The ceilings were so high and lost in shadow that to look up was like looking into the night sky. Whoever the king had been, he had wanted to intimidate anyone who came near him. His throne room, larger by far than the audience chamber where Karhedros had first received the Soul Drinkers, placed his throne on a platform backed by huge sweeping wings of dark green stone. The floor and walls constantly sweated beads of water so the air was damp, as if the whole place had risen from beneath the sea, an effect compounded by the dim greenish lights that glowed from luminescent patterns carved into everything.

A hundred of Karhedros's incubi, the heavily-armoured eldar elites who had cost him a great payment of souls and sacrifice to acquire, stood at permanent attention outside the throne room. The throne room itself was the province of the sorcerers and haemonculi. The sorcerers were a dark and hated breed, all of whom had joined Karhedros's pirate fleet to escape the persecution back on Commorragh. They were the ones who gazed into the warp beyond the eldar webway, and sought to draw power from it. The warp was the domain of She-Who-Thirsts so their sorcery was considered the foulest of heresy – but Karhedros needed them, as did all eldar on some strange philosophical level, and though they were tortured and abused they needed him just as much.

The haemonculi were a caste of torturers who set themselves aside from the rest of Commorragh, and pursued the arts of torment. They offered their services to anyone who needed experts in the intricacies of pain, and Karhedros – whose pirates had enslaved prisoners of every species – was an excellent employer. That the haemonculi could become a privileged class within eldar society spoke much of the way Commorragh was. There, suffering was a currency, almost literally a building block of society, to be traded, fought over and stolen. A society based around the concept of suffering was too lofty a concept for the minds of species like humanity to understand, and so the eldar knew that they were the ultimate expression of sentient life in the galaxy.

And Karhedros's kind, those who had embraced what they were instead of fleeing from it, were the ultimate expression of the eldar.

Karhedros himself sat on the throne, watching the sorcerers work.

Their ritual dance began.

'Who will see the end of days? Who will be there when all is come to nothing?' cried a voice from amongst the ranks of the sorcerers.

One of their number ran forward, a gangly, misshapen creature dressed in clanking jointed armour like an insect. 'We see it, we all, with every moment, for time is already ended, and nothing remains…' The eldar in the throne room danced in a complex pattern of intersecting circles, further embellished by the many strange forms of the sorcerers. Magic did strange things to the body and mind. The warp always took its price.

Another sorcerer stepped forward, this time stooped and wizened yet moving with the litheness and speed of a wych. 'Nothing but will, for the will of the sentient mind is all, for understanding is creation, for without it, there is nothing…'

Karhedros watched as the dance became quicker, the circles tighter, like packs of predators closing in on the same prey. The dance was at once a mockery and a refinement of the dance-cycles the eldar had used before the Fall, and were still used by those lesser eldar who hid in their craftworlds. It was itself not magic, but there could be no magic without it because it focused the vast consciousness of each eldar on the part they had to play.

'But what will? What will can make a universe? What intellect comprehends us? What gives us form?' The voice was shrill, the speaker a stunted wretch of a creature carried aloft by her fellow dancers. 'Which dreamer dreamed Commorragh?'

The voices of every sorcerer and haemonculus were raised in unison.

'She-Who-Thirsts!'

Then, the spell began.

Karhedros's kind were wary of sorcery. She-Who-Thirsts was jealous, and magic drew on the power of the warp that belonged to her. But away from Commorragh, Karhedros could take the risks his fellow eldar would never countenance. And besides, the earliest stages of the sacrifice on the surface would be enough to appease her for a few moments.

The circles of dancers were suddenly linked by a purple-blue tongue of fire, streaking through their bodies like a winding sea-snake. The pattern they formed became more and more complex until Karhedros could see the images reflected in its coils: the battlements of the palace around him, then the layers of Gravenhold's undercity streaking past, layers of history dripping with the memories of war and revolution.

The spell tapped into all the death and violence, drawing its power from a hundred generations of war.

The city was a focal point for misery, not a constant, relentless background but sudden bursts of violence that razed one city and built another on the ruins. The pulses of hate were more powerful than weak-minded humanity could ever understand. Reality was weakened around Gravenhold, shot through with cracks that bled pure emotion from the boiling psychic ocean of the warp. It was one of the reasons Karhedros had chosen the planet, it was closer to She-Who-Thirsts than most of realspace.

In fact, if Karhedros listened hard enough, he could hear her calling him.

The shape of Gravenhold was illuminated by the whirling tongues of fire now. The smouldering arena with the massive crater at its centre, the murderous heights of the mills to the west, the sprawl of the slums with their gorgeous taint of misery, the decaying decadence of the nobles' villas in the north.

One sorcerer died, the tongue of fire wrapping around it and shaking it to pieces. The others ignored it and carried on their agonising, spasming dance. Death was a good sign, it meant that She-Who-Thirsts was watching, and had reached out to snatch up the soul of the weakest.

Not long now.

The battle was outlined in fiery reds and purples. The Guardsmen by the east gate were being pushed back in a burning line of dying men. The tide was spreading through the hovels, swirling around the humans in the centre of the slums. They didn't know it yet, but they were preparing for their last stand. The south of the city was populated by the least competent of the Guardsmen, and they were up against a more horrible foe than even the slave-army, but like the rest of the humans, they had no idea what they were up against.

The haemonculi knew their cue. When the dying began, that was where they had to be.

Each haemonculus was a result of his own experimentation – here a sewn-up torso with entrails snaking in and out of artificial orifices, there an extra pair of arms tipped with syringes and scalpels. Hunched backs, multiple glinting eyes, skins turned inside-out and rippling with nerve endings, a hundred different abominations the haemonculi visited on themselves to prove their worth.

Karhedros could taste the pain even from his throne. The haemonculi ran amongst the sorcerers, cutting, killing. One slash of a scalpel-tipped tentacle left a wound so painful it lasted for an age, echoing around in the mind of the sorcerer. Blades were much favoured by the haemonculi and they wrought exquisite slaughter among the willing sorcerers. Knives and scalpels flashed like lightning, staining the blue fire a deep lustful blood red.

As they died, Karhedros saw their souls dragged out of their bodies. The writhing, yowling spiritual heart of an eldar was the purest receptacle of suffering, filled to the brim with the undiluted pain of a lifetime. The sorcerers were shunned and abused, living grim and painful lives even by the standards of Commorragh, and so they were particularly incandescent with agony as She-Who-Thirsts reached through the medium of the spell and ripped their souls away.

In their last moments before annihilation, Karhedros knew they would be grateful. They had become more than they ever could be in life. They were an offering to She-Who-Thirsts, to prove to her that Karhedros's devotion was true.

The haemonculi were almost done. The throne room was buzzing as reality wore even thinner. Karhedros felt the gaze of She-Who-Thirsts upon him and it filled him with awe. It was fitting that he should be the one to make this offering to her, for he was the greatest of Commorragh's children, who were the greatest of the eldar, who were the greatest of all the living things that populated reality.

The fire imploded and the eye-searing scarlet afterglow was swallowed in blackness. The fabric of reality bowed outwards and flowed back and everything rippled as if through a heat haze.

Reality reset itself, and the sorcerers were gone. The haemonculi now stood around a huge circular vortex composed of every colour, shot through with the purple-black of lust – the emotion of She-Who-Thirsts herself, the colour of her desire to consume.

'She-Who-Thirsts!' called Karhedros, standing up from his throne and throwing his hands in the air. 'Consume you shall! Devour! Gorge on their pain! For I give you this world, a world I shall rule in your name! A new Commorragh, perfect in its suffering! For this is my offering to She-Who-Thirsts, the dreamer who dreamed us all!'

A new Commorragh. Karhedros carried on living, which meant She-Who-Thirsts approved.

The first part of the spell was complete. The warp portal had opened. Now all that remained was for the sacrifice to be completed, and the suffering it created would flood into the portal. Soon it would swallow up the whole planet and the new Commorragh would be born.

And Karhedros, the pirate prince of the eldar, would become a king.

CHAPTER TWELVE

'THEY'RE ABSOLUTELY BLOODY everywhere,' said Threlnan.

'Thank you. I like it when tac reports are to the point,' said Xarius. The Lord General pulled himself up out of the tank commander's hatch. Colonel Threlnan helped him down the Baneblade's front armour and onto the ground. Xarius looked around at the shattered buildings and dust-choked air, the darkening sky and the hundreds of Seleucaians hurriedly setting up makeshift fortifications to stem off the tide. Threlnan's command post was in the heart of the slums, in one of the more built-up areas where the buildings were relatively solid, but the place would still fall if enough human waves hit it.

'We're pulling back from the front,' continued Threlnan. 'We drew the front elements back after we lost the arena and I had them just keep going. We're looking at a tight line through the heart of the slums, anchored by the river to the north. Anything solid the men find, they fortify it. We're in for the long term.'

'And the enemy?'

Threlnan took Xarius's arm and led him across the cratered ground towards the shadow of a local Enforcer watchstation, probably the most intact building left in the slums. 'They're mostly coming from the east but they're cropping up everywhere. Damn lot of them came up through the vortex crater to the west of us, although there wasn't much left of them after the Crimson Fists were finished. We're trying to hook up emergency comms to direct Kelchenko's artillery but... well, I think Kelchenko's having problems of his own, sir.'

'And yourselves? How are you going to keep you and your officers alive?'

Threlnan shrugged. 'Get some guts behind a few lasguns, throw down some sandbags, hope for the best. To be honest, lord general, I'm not confident that your coming here was the best move. I mean, the comms being down is killing us and I won't be able to call for extraction if it gets too hot down here.'

'Nonsense! Don't tell me you're not glad to see a Baneblade.'

'Well, of course, sir, but there's a limit to how many of them one tank can kill...'

'It's not for the enemy, Threlnan. It's for your boys. Give them a good old-fashioned symbol of the Emperor's wrath and they'll last twice as long. As for me, you said so yourself, the comms are down all over the city. I'm not much use giving orders from somewhere safe if there's no way anyone can hear me. I'll be doing more good as an extra gun than as a lord commander, don't you think?'

Xarius sat down on a fallen chunk of masonry. The Enforcer watchtower behind him had once been a stern symbol of Imperial authority, it was sheer brutal rockcrete with fire points on the corners and firing slits lower down, and was already populated by most of the heavy weapons units attached to Threlnan's command. The rest of the defensive position was taking shape: a line of ruined buildings was being built up with rubble and sandbags while the gap made by a wide crater-ruined street was being plugged as Hasdrubal drove the Baneblade into position. The fourth side of the position was bounded by a line of Chimeras with flak-board propped in the spaces between them, again manned by Seleucaian troops. A couple of Leman Russ main battle tanks and a single Hellhound flame tank stood in the middle, ready to blast shells or pour flame into whatever enemy managed to break through, And if they got that far, break through they definitely would.

It was a picture that Xarius knew was being repeated all across the Seleucaian line, Guardsmen finding the toughest-looking locations amongst the shattered buildings and racing to fortify them before the swarm reached them. Tiny islands of order in a sea of chaos, nuggets of the Emperor's light in the coming darkness. How many of them would survive?

'What do we know about the other regiments?' Threlnan asked.

'The others? Not much more than you, I'd imagine, which is to say barely anything. There are still shells coming over from Kelchenko so presumably he's got some artillery in reasonable shape. But the Janissaries were under attack from something before the comms went down and it looks like the Fire Drakes are getting the worst of it. Haven't heard from the *Resolve*, but presumably they're fine unless these grox-lovers have learned how to fly.'

'What are the evacuation plans?'

Xarius took off his officer's cap and undid the top button of his dress uniform jacket. His uniform wasn't meant for fighting. 'All evacuation scenarios assumed the main Guard concentrations to be in the spaceport and outside the south-eastern gate. From within the city, and assuming the comms come back on at some point, I'd say we can get maybe twenty per cent of personnel out of this city before it falls. Most of them will be the rear echelons. From within a contested city... no, not many will get out. The *Resolve* had landers and shuttles but can you imagine them getting enough craft close enough, under fire, to lift us out of a contested location like this? The Battlefleet Solar couldn't do it.'

'So we sit tight and hope,' said Threlnan.

'And fight, colonel.'

'I shall find a priest. Have him read a few prayers.'

'Good idea, Threlnan. Best one I've heard today.' Xarius took out his sidearm, a handsome antique autopistol he kept holstered at his belt. 'Do you think you could rustle up a lasgun? Something with a bit of range. This fellow's just for show and he doesn't pack that much of a punch.'

'If I may speak freely, sir,' said Threlnan officiously, 'you really should be back at the spaceport. Hells, you should be up on the *Resolve* by now. There's no need for you to be down here. Leave it to the soldiers.'

'I am a soldier, Threlnan.' Xarius leaned forward, suddenly serious. 'And every soldier here knows what a tragedy this is. It's a shambles. Our mission here was to find what had taken over the city, kill everything that moved and avenge Sathis and his men. It was a simple bloody mission. One city! We even had the gakking Space Marines tagging along! There are a thousand battles like this being fought right now, Threlnan, literally a thousand all over the Imperium, most of them bigger and more complicated. And no one wants to hear about Traitor Marines or cheating aliens or any other excuses. We were given a simple job and we couldn't do it.

'Have you any idea what they'll do to me if I get out of this? They'll look at a whole agri-world and thousands of Guardsmen lost, and all for nothing. I'll be busted back down to spitoon boy. Hells, they'll probably send me to Mars and replace my innards so I can live another century or two, just to pay them off for what happened here. It will be as if nothing I've ever done had happened. I'll be less than nothing. Tell me how the Emperor treats failures, Threlnan. He commands us to put bullets in their heads or hang them at dawn. They won't kill me but they might as well do. I'm not scared of dying, Threlnan, and to tell the Emperor's honest truth I've been looking forward to it for a while now. But I am scared of being nothing. That's what they'll make me after this. Going down fighting alongside these boys here is a good way to go, considering all the other ways there are. That's the choice I'm making. I can make that an order if you want.'

One of the Seleucaians hurried over from the barricades. 'Sirs, the lookouts have spotted something. Looks like they're coming.'

'Make sure each squad has a runner for ammo and wounded,' said Threlnan. 'And… didn't Corporal Karthel teach at a seminary?'

'Karthel? Yes, sir.'

'Good. Get him and three men into the centre, men not manning the barricades can pray with him.'

'Yes, sir. Anything else?'

'Yes. Get the lord general a lasgun.'

Xarius looked up at the Seleucaian Guardsmen. 'Scope and Mars-pattern stock, please, if you have one.'

'You heard him,' said Threlnan. 'Get to it.' The colonel took out his own sidearm, a rugged laspistol with a hotshot pack sticking out of the cell slot. 'They'll need me at the barricades, lord general. Where will you be?'

'Oh, around,' said Xarius. 'Wherever you need an extra man.'

'Best of luck, lord general. By the Throne, for the Emperor.'

'For the Emperor, colonel.'

The sky over the city was darkening, as if Entymion IV's sun was turning its face away.

Xarius knew what it would be like. He had been there before: the stifling tension, the way it knotted your guts up, the way it added years to you before the battle took them away. The knowledge that so many of these men would die. The taste of fate, heavy like a thick blanket over everything. Xarius had been sure that he would die before, many years ago, more than once, when he had shared the battlefield with the men he led instead of directing anonymous unit markers around a holo-map.

It was strangely comforting, knowing he was going to die. The Emperor had had more than His fair share of battles out of Reinhardt Xarius, so Xarius didn't really mind it. He just hoped it wouldn't hurt, not that it was likely to take long, given that Xarius was an old man with brittle bones and a heart that probably wouldn't last a decent drinking session nowadays.

Someone handed him a lasgun. It had a scope but only a wire Rhyza-pattern stock. It was good enough, he supposed. Somehow Xarius had always known that it would end like this, no matter how high he rose or how many campaign medals he amassed, it would always end on a planet he hated, wondering if his gun would take one of them out before they got him. The Emperor had decided, before Reinhardt Xarius was even born, that Xarius would die like that. So it didn't matter. None of it mattered.

The only thing that really mattered was the horde that Xarius could just hear, screeching and hollering a few streets away. If they wanted the life of Lord Commander Reinhardt Xarius, they would have to earn it. However he did it, with las-bolt or rifle stock, with his hands or his teeth, or just by being there, Xarius would make them suffer.

THE FAR SOUTH of the city was turning into hell.

It had started when the sky went dark. Purple-black clouds boiled out of nowhere, blotting out the sun of Entymion IV and casting a ghastly twilight over everything. With the comms down it was as if the planet was suddenly cut off and plunging downwards, the air turning chill, the shadows deepening, the ragged mess of the slums becoming a sharp and menacing labyrinth of ambushes.

Then the news arrived. How it got to the Algorathi Janissaries, huddled in the heart of the slums fleeing from a series of sudden and brutal assaults, was unknown. But suddenly, like bad news always was, it was on the lips of every Janissary. Crouched in cover, some still sticky with the blood of their fellow Guardsmen, they told one another of the massive enemy forces that were bubbling up from the ground elsewhere in the city. Thousands of them. Hundreds of thousands. A hidden army, come to encircle and slaughter every Imperial soul in Gravenhold.

The Janissaries were still being nibbled away. Men were dying by the minute. The last man on every patrol seemed to disappear, snatched away by something swift and unseen. Sniper shots snapped into any Guardsman who showed his head; the shooters fired razor-sharp shards of diamond-hard crystal, and those they did not kill outright were paralysed by the pain. Colonel Vinmayer tried to keep a tally of the dead but they were dying so quickly, and in so many ways, that it was all he could do to keep his men together. Their position was hopeless – a block of half-ruined tenements that had been deathtraps well before anyone had started firing artillery at them – but it was all they had. It was an island of hope in a city that wanted them dead. The Algorathi Janissaries learned urban combat very, very quickly, trying to maintain a perimeter while the men on the outside were being swallowed up by the lengthening shadows.

The comms flickered back on. It was as if the city was waiting for them to take their place in the trap before it let them talk to one another. The communications between the Janissaries and the other forces in the city, with Lord Commander Xarius or the *Resolve*, were still denied, but Vinmayer could at least talk to his men directly.

It was no fun if the men could not share the fear. It was no tragedy if the sons of Algorath could not think they had hope, before they found out that they still had to die alone.

Vinmayer, however, was not a man bred to give up. He had carried the banner of Algorath into its first true combat assignment in several centuries and those unlucky generations before him had prepared their sons for the time when the Algorathi Janissaries would meet their fate in the fire of battle.

He switched to the all-squad vox-channel.

'The company,' he began, 'will form a square. The officers in each corner will be responsible for holding the line. Squads eleven through nineteen will form a mobile reserve, bayonets fixed. The enemy are all alien liars and will falter at the resilience of our formation. I shall take my place in the line where the fighting is fiercest, for so do the sons of Algorath fight. These are your orders. Do not stray from them while but one of us remains. For the Emperor, Colonel Vinmayer out.'

The enemy must have had access to the Janissaries' vox-net, because they used Vinmayer's speech as their cue.

'THEY'RE ON THE move! There!' Eumenes ran down the rubble-filled street, pointing up past the chewed-up skyline. Clouds of thrown-up dust and the crash of collapsing rubble were marking a course parallel to the scouts as something massive and powerful barged its way through the slums.

'Dorn's hand, what is it?' asked Scout Laeon, who was just behind Eumenes.

'The end for the Janissaries, that's what,' replied Selepus.

'They're heading north,' said Eumenes. 'Fast. Keep moving.'

The scouts ran full-tilt through the ruins but they could barely keep up. Even Selepus, who could move through this difficult ground as easily as if he was walking, could only just keep the enemy in sight. The remnants of Gravenhold's shattered lives streaked past, however Karhedros had taken over the city's population it had happened overnight, for here and there collapsed walls revealed a snapshot of lives frozen in time. Tables were laid out for meagre meals. Beds were still made. The families that had lived crammed into these hovels had been snatched away in the middle of eating or sleeping or praying, to become part of Karhedros's army.

'There!' called Selepus. The scouts had come to an area all but shelled flat, affording them a glimpse of the enemy force charging northwards.

Eumenes could see just the suggestion of dark, armoured shapes, and then they were gone.

'Small force,' said Scout-Sniper Raek from behind Eumenes. 'But tough.'

'Eldar?'

'Maybe.'

A hundred metres ahead the terrain broke up, alleyways becoming roads, hovels becoming blocks of tenements. Eumenes reached the edge of one road and skidded to a halt.

'Stop! It's the Guard.' The powder-blue uniforms of the Janissaries, now filthy with dust and mud, were poor camouflage against the dismal dark grey tenement blocks they were using as cover. Eumenes could make out the city block they had chosen, not good to defend, but better than anything within spitting distance.

They had set up a weapons point on one corner of the block, with a couple of heavy bolters and what looked like a lascannon on the first floor of a half-collapsed block. Eumenes spotted men crouching behind makeshift cover in a long, straight line down both sides of the block away from the corner. They had bayonets fixed.

'Selepus,' said Eumenes, 'take Laeon and see if you can get across the road to spot for Raek, I want us across on the east side of–'

A force like a battering ram smashed out of the ruins twenty metres up the road. At first Eumenes thought it must be a tank, barrelling at full speed through the crumbling building and ripping out into the street in a cloud of dust.

The Janissaries had known it was coming but they barely had a handful of las-shots before the enemy was among them, smashing into the line. Blue-uniformed bodies were thrown into the air. Something exploded. Screams were drowned out by gunfire and the sound of armour on stone.

'Closer!' shouted Eumenes. Fear rippled through the Janissaries and they were all shooting at anything that moved, las-bolts spattering against the wood and brick around the scouts. Selepus led the way, hugging the crumbling walls, keeping the scouts in shadow as chaos erupted all around them. Sniper-shots spat from somewhere far off and Janissaries died, shredded by crystal shards.

'Down!' shouted Nisryus suddenly. The scouts had learned to listen to the precog. As one, the scouts hit the ground a moment before something cut the air knife-sharp above them, shrieking on grav-engines over the street and into the Janissaries. Eumenes glanced up, eldar jetbikes, almost too fast to see, streaking in a wide loop back through the Algorathi line. Long curved blades jutted from every surface of each jetbike's long front fuselage, slicing heads from bodies, arms from shoulders, the bare skin of the riders spattered with blood.

Eumenes had seen pict-steals taken during battles with the eldar. They were lithe, lightly-armoured warriors, each specialised in a particular form of warfare. They were deceitful heathens, and the Soul Drinkers had fought them before and after the excommunication, but these were different. The eldar were manipulative and inscrutable. These aliens were just cruel. They revelled in blood. They fought for torment's own sake. Eumenes saw one biker spear a Janissary on the nose of his jetbike then gun the engine and sweep upwards, letting the air resistance drag the man further down the hull, splitting him open. Another had long chains trailing behind his bike that snagged uniforms and skin, yanking two men out of the line then swooping low so they were broken to pieces along the ground.

'Oh, sweet hands of Dorn,' swore Laeon. 'It's them.'

Eumenes scrambled to the edge of cover, following Laeon's gaze.

The force that had first smashed into the Janissaries was playing merry hell. The Janissaries had thrown men forward from the centre of the block but they were just more meat for the slaughter. Eumenes saw purple armour slicked black with blood, chainblades rising and falling, helmetless heads with mad staring eyes.

He saw something more. He saw massive muscles writhing under deathly pale skin. Arms punching into fleeing Janissaries, lifting them up and hurling them through the air off the ends of long whirring chainblades. Blades jammed into the stump of severed wrists.

The Soul Drinkers. The renegades lost at Stratix Luminae, turned mad and brought into the service of a mad alien.

And Tellos.

THE SLAVE-ARMY hit the river first. The River Graven was the anchor point for the northern end of the Seleucaian line, and the massive well-built warehouses by the docks made for an excellent defensive position. The Seleucaian units there who fortified them considered themselves to be luckiest in the city, they were protected on one side by the deep river, while the huge dock buildings could be turned into a formidable fortress. They were the keystone for the whole Seleucaian regiment, forming a fastness to which other units could fall back, a solid foundation for the enemy wave to break against.

They thought they would be the last to fall. Which, presumably, was why the enemy hit them first.

The first truly great battle of the campaign's closing stages erupted on the south bank of the River Graven as ten thousand slave warriors poured into the eastern side of the position. The Seleucaians had covered the roads approaching the docks with scores of firing positions and volleys of las-fire and heavy weapons cut the first ranks of the enemy to shreds. Thousands died in a few minutes, the already dark sky becoming as black as night as las-smoke and debris blotted out what light remained.

The slave-army piled its dead up into bloody ramps of corpses and scrambled up them over the Seleucaian barricades. The Guardsmen saw clearly for the first time what they were fighting, humans who were not human, their bodies deformed into living weapons. Some exploded into shards of bone spikes, others turned berserk and ripped Guardsmen apart with talons or spiny whip-like tongues. The Guarsmen fell back from the first positions in disarray and the slaves swarmed into the shadow of the warehouses, charging heedlessly through crossfires and minefields.

They couldn't outflank or outthink, and normally they would be easy prey for a competent and well-drilled regiment like the Seleucaians. But the slave-army had two advantages: it had the numbers, and it had the element of sheer horror. The Seleucaians had already weathered the unnaturalness of killing soldiers who had once been citizens of the city they were supposed to liberate, but this was something different. These were the slaves taken by xenos raiders over many decades, the sons and daughters of the Imperium who had been twisted into something so inhuman it was blasphemy. The Guardsmen saw their own faces in the creatures they killed. In the monsters that tore their comrades apart they saw friends and loved ones they thought they had forgotten. Karhedros didn't need any alien sorcery to shatter the resolve of the Guardsmen. The Guardsmen did it themselves.

The Imperial Guard communications flickered back on just in time for officers up and down the Seleucaian line to hear the river position falling. The warehouses fell, the disciplined Guard fire breaking down in the face of the assault. Thousands of enemy bodies choked the eastern barricades but they just made it worse, the foul chemical stench of the bodies as they broke down deepening the nightmare.

The Seleucaians were up against the river itself. There, some order was whipped back into the men and they made a last stand, taking cover around the huge mechanical docking cranes, firing from behind giant exposed cogs or banks of container crates. But the ground there was too open, and the Guard fire couldn't thin out the charging ranks quickly enough.

Men turned their lasguns on themselves before the enemy clawed their way over the machinery and into the final Guard positions. The few remaining heavy weapons were surrounded by oozing piles of bodies before they were overrun and their crews torn apart. The final slaughter was the most terrible; so many bodies fell into the river that even the observers on the *Resolve* could make out the Graven running red.

The officers of the regiment heard it all. They heard the lieutenant in charge of the position pull a pin on a frag grenade and blow himself up as the final crane mountings were overrun. They heard the last survivors up on the crane assemblies themselves, sniping at the slave-warriors climbing up the structure towards them. They heard the final prayers of men who might have hours left before their las-cells ran out, but who would definitely die no matter what.

The keystone of the Seleucaian position had fallen. Every officer, and most of the men, knew what the situation was now. There were only two ways out of Gravenhold – die at the hands of the aliens' slave-warriors, or kill every single one of them. The Seleucaians checked their las-cells for the hundredth time, and got ready to do the latter.

* * *

'SACRIFICE,' SAID SARPEDON.

'Sacrifice,' replied Luko. 'It's the only thing that makes sense. And it's happening now, all over the damn city. We're only seeing a fraction of what must be happening but there are thousands of them. They're hitting the whole Guard at once, the Seleucaians, the Fire Drakes.'

Sarpedon had met up with Luko beneath the city as soon as the comms had come back, hurrying from the undercity just beneath the ruined arena to the underground river, roughly parallel with the Graven, to which Luko had fled from the Crimson Fists. The river rushed along beside them, winding through chasms of spectacular rock formations and plunging down sudden waterfalls. This part of the undercity was mostly natural, but there had been some kind of primitive troglodytic civilisation here, probably living off the strange pale blind fish that writhed through the waters. Crude stone burrows were scraped into the earth, and the abstract but somehow still disturbing runes carved into the thick bases of stalagmites suggested a dark and benighted people. Gravenhold had not always been a place of power and riches. Bit by bit the undercity was suggesting a grim, complex history of conquest and downfall.

'The eldar don't conquer,' said Sarpedon. 'They don't hold ground. At most they take slaves and move on. You're right, Luko, he needed this city for something. He needed this battle. He knew we'd turn on him all along. He was counting on it. I can't think of a force in this city more capable of raising hell than us and hell is exactly what he needs.'

'You didn't see them wake up,' said Luko. 'He must have kept them there since he took the city over.

Maybe even longer, if he got under the city before the Gravenholders ever knew about him. Just like a damn alien. You know, I'm starting to get a feel for what you've led us into.'

'Really, Luko? What is that?' Sarpedon folded his arms and sat back on his eight haunches.

'Karhedros lured Tellos here because, like you said, he needed hellraisers, people who could be guaranteed to fight and kill no matter what. He probably would have been content just with Tellos and his slaves to mix it up with the Guard. He must have thought it was his lucky day when we turned up. Hells, we've carved our way through more than our fair share of Guard. We've soaked this city in enough blood. As far as Karhedros is concerned we're his best men. We're on his side, Sarpedon. We're doing just what he wants us to do.' Luko spat. 'Used by a damn xenos.'

'We're here for Tellos,' said Sarpedon. 'Not Karhedros. We will find our brother and do what we have to do. Then, if it is necessary, we will punish the alien for what he did to him.'

'How, Sarpedon? How? I've followed you from one side of the galaxy to the other, I've fought the wars I hate because I knew it was the right thing to do. But I don't think we can win this one.'

'I have given you free rein to speak your mind to me, Luko. That is not a privilege I can extend forever.'

'We won't forgive you, Sarpedon, if you throw us away here for nothing. Remember what happened the last time you forced this Chapter to fight itself.'

There was a pause. For the briefest moment, an onlooker might have thought the two could end up in a shouting match, even a brawl. In the old Chapter, they probably would have. But the Soul Drinkers under Sarpedon and Luko were out of earshot, keeping watch over the banks of the river and the dense forests of stalagmites. The fighting on the surface had begun to spill into the undercity and the Soul Drinkers had to be vigilant for both slave-warriors and Guardsmen even down here.

'I know what you are saying, Luko,' said Sarpedon. 'I came here to find Tellos. Our battle-brothers have died and we haven't found him. But we have found something else, Luko. This Chapter is sworn to do the Emperor's will. Tell me His will is being done in this city. Tell me that.'

Luko had no answer.

'You said Karhedros created this battle as a sacrifice, and we're a part of it. As long as we're a part of it that means we can do something about it.'

'This is not our fight, Sarpedon.'

'That's the point. This Chapter does not fight just to survive. We have done too much of that already. These eldar are devoted to their god, She-Who-Thirsts. They worship and fear it, I could sense it. I just had to get close to Karhedros to know. When this sacrifice is completed, the city is dead. This planet is dead. And Karhedros will be much, much more than just another xenos pirate. It became our fight the moment he promised this world to She-Who-Thirsts.'

'When did you decide this, Sarpedon?'

'What does it matter? What else are you going to do but fight?'

'Commander,' came a voice over the vox, faint through the static, filtering all the way down from the surface. 'Eumenes here.'

Sarpedon turned away from Luko, straining to hear the scout's voice. 'Eumenes?'

'We've found him, commander. Tellos. He just chewed his way through the Algorathi Guardsmen.'

'Where is he now?'

'Slaughterhouse district, near the river.'

'Don't go near him. You can't take him on your own, trust me on that. Can you get back to the government district?'

'Maybe.'

'Good. Do it. I'll gather all the Soul Drinkers who can make it under the chamber mercantile.'

'Understood. Eumenes out.'

Sarpedon turned back to Luko. 'You've got what you wanted, Luko. It's coming to an end.'

'Karhedros has an army to spare in that palace. I'll wager we only saw a fraction of it. Do you really think you can take him on and still have anything left over for Tellos?'

'No, I don't. But the Emperor doesn't listen to excuses.'

CHAPTER THIRTEEN

CAPTAIN THORELLIS VEL Caislenn-Har of the Imperial cruiser *Resolve* walked onto the bridge of his ship, wreathed in a cloud of chemical smoke.

'Navigation,' he said, his voice grating through the heavy-duty rebreather collar that circled his lower face. 'Please, please for the love of the Emperor and all his saints tell me we know where the rest of the fleet is.'

The navigation helm was wrought into the form of a massive cathedral organ, its processing stacks shaped like the pipes and the control console of a long keyboard with hundreds of keys. Data-servitors shaped like gilded cherubs clung to the sides of the organ, whispering strings of co-ordinates to one another. The navigation officer, sitting in the position of an organist, turned sharply at Caislenn-Har's approach, the officer was pure naval academy product, starched collar and all.

'Direct comms are still out,' she snapped, 'but the sensorium has confirmed the positions of escort squadron *Vestal*, primary fueller *Sacred Truth* and seventy per cent of the system support fleet.'

'And?'

'They are somewhat out of position.'

'Good enough.' Captain Caislenn-Har waddled over to his command chair, a massive throne of brass and jade that reared from the scalloped floor of the bridge like the head of a sea monster.

The bridge of the *Resolve* was fitted out in the highest Imperial style, like a baroque nightmare of cathedrals and graveyards crammed onto the banks of an artificial lake fifty metres across. It was onto the surface of this lake that the information from the ship's sensors were broadcast – but now, with most of the comms still down, the surface was just a rippling mask of static. The twin organs of the navigation helm and the communications hub stood on opposite banks of the lake, while behind it a giant tomb complete with guardian statues housed the ship's bridge cogitator. A construction of gold and silver slabs cut into the shapes of stylised clouds hung from the ceiling overhead, on top of which was Master of Ordnance Crinn bent over his readouts and controls.

Banks of cogitator stations lined the walls where petty officers and flight controllers sat, their faces lit eerily green by the data streaming past their eyes. The ship's tech-priest complement were housed in a crown-shaped structure that jutted from the back wall of the cogitator-tomb, constantly rotating like the cog symbol of the Mechanicus itself. The priest currently on duty was enthroned surrounded by silver-plated angels, thick ribbed datafeeds snaking from beneath his robes as they fed information on the ship's systems into his mind.

It was all as ornate and cumbersome as Caislenn-Har himself. The captain himself should have been long dead from multiple and ravenous cancers, but instead the Imperial Navy had fitted him out with so many rebreathers and blood purifiers that he waddled obesely everywhere surrounded by fumes from his artificial lungs.

'I want a full situation report,' said Caislenn-Har. 'Navigation, I want evasive solutions in case all this nonsense is the prelude to a full-scale attack. What about long-range sensors? Could something sneak up on us? Are we bothering to look over our shoulders while all this is going on?'

The navigation officer keyed in a subtle tune and the servitors drifted down on their stubby little wings, whispering a chorus of information as they worked out the various evasive routes the *Resolve* might take. Images flickered by on the surface of the viewing lake, fuzzy, shaky pictures from the *Resolve*'s scanners. The babble of activity got louder as crewmen and officers struggled to make sense of the few working sensors and communicators they had.

'And can we see the city, please? That is why we're here, after all.' Caislenn-Har threw his hands in the air. 'Are they all dead down there? Is the damn place on fire? I don't know because we're completely fragging blind up here! I don't want aerial pict-steals, I want to know where the Guard are!'

'I recognise this,' came Master of Ordnance Crinn's voice over the bridge vox. 'We got some anomalous readings just before the comms went down. Looks like quantum radiation. Probably a vortex detonation.'

'So the Deathstrikes worked after all. Ha! I owe Consul Kelchenko a drink. What else?'

'Orbital comms are still out,' said the officer at the communications helm, the organ's pipes thrumming mournfully as they reported signals not received. 'The emergency channels are up but they're beacons only. We know the *Truth* and the *Vestals* are still there but no details.'

Caislenn-Har leaned forward and tapped his grey-skinned fingers on the arm of his command throne. This was bad. The Navy had been ineffective at best throughout the campaign for Gravenhold but now it was completely blind. The ship might as well not have been there. Anything could be going on down in the city, and judging by the suddenness and completeness of the blackout it probably was. The main task of the *Resolve* had been to watch out for xenos ships coming to aid the aliens that had taken over Gravenhold but as far as anyone could tell the long-range sensors weren't working so the eldar could be right behind the *Resolve* and no one would know it.

'Not good,' the captain muttered to himself. 'Not good at all.'

Something occurred to him. He straightened up and flicked on a little-used vox-channel. The ship's own vox had only just come back on-line and it was through a howl of distortion that a voice answered.

'Ship's archive.'

'This is Captain Caislenn-Har. Are the mem-banks affected by all this?'

'No… no, sir. They're up and running.'

'Good. What's your name?'

'Ensign Castiglian Krao, sir.'

'Ensign, I want to know what could have done this. Weapons, creatures, warp phenomena, anything that could knock out everyone's comms. Can you do that?'

'I'll make a full search, sir. I'll need permission to second one of the tech-priests onto it.'

'You shall have it.'

'Thank you, sir. Ensign Krao out.'

The surface of the lake flashed again and an aerial shot of Gravenhold appeared. Caislenn-Har could make out the glowing black-hearted crater where the Deathstrike had gone down. A cluster of dockyard buildings on the south bank of the Graven was burning and there was a ragged dark hole where the city's main arena had been. A basic overview of troop dispositions was superimposed over the image, Caislenn-Har made out the concentration of Seleucaians in the compact line from the river down to the southern slums, the artillery bunched around a couple of the old mills, the Fire Drakes in the middle of the administrative district in the shadow of the wall.

'Where are the Janissaries?' asked Caislenn-Har of no one in particular.

'Forward sensors back on-line,' came a vox from someone in the *Resolve*'s prow sensorium. 'Severely anomalous readings, running diagnostics.'

'Plasma flux past the limits,' came yet another vox from the reactor core. 'Venting coolant… emergency auxiliary shutdown in operation…'

Caislenn-Har shook his head. His ship was feeling as knocked about as the Guard in the city. Either the sensors were still on the blink or there was something down there pumping strange readings into the ship's sensors. Caislenn-Har wasn't sure which was more likely.

The barely-contained chaos of the bridge played out as Caislenn-Har watched. Runners from all over the ship carried orders or reports to and fro. A gaggle of tech-adepts descended on the communications helm and started taking it apart, levering off its gilded panels, calling down the heavy servitors mounted on the walls to remove the datastacks and remonstrating with the communications officer. A priest hurried in, ascetic brown robes at odds with the massive glory of the bridge, and intoned prayers for the soul of the ship and her crew. Something ancient and electrical finally blew in the cogitator-tomb and ratings hurried in with extinguishers to douse the small fire.

The worse the situation, the more they invented new distractions for themselves. Caislenn-Har wasn't a ship's captain because he was an efficient leader – he wasn't even very ruthless and even before he had become a waddling mass of medical equipment he hadn't been that charismatic. He was there because when everyone else was running around exasperated, he could stay relatively calm and remind them of the tasks that really needed doing. Like getting the ship's sight back, and getting back in touch with the rest of the small fleet.

'Captain?' came a new vox. 'Ensign Krao. We've got our initial results back.'

'Good-good.'

'Well… most disruptive weapons would have inflicted massive physical damage too and, well, I think we'd notice if that had happened.'

'Indeed.'

'And without any nebula clouds or quasars nearby it's not likely to be stellar phenomena, unless Entymion's star had just exploded. Aside from massive technical failure on our part the only remaining options are very unlikely. Sir.'

'Entertain me, ensign.'

'Well, there was one thing.'

'What?'

'Magic.'

'I see. Thank you, Ensign Krao.'

Caislenn-Har flicked off the vox. 'Magic,' he sighed to himself. 'Gakking wonderful.'

Then the view-lake blazed as a large chunk of Gravenhold's wealthiest district erupted into a column of purple-white fire.

'WHAT IS THE weapon that will never fail?' asked Iktinos gravely.

'My soul,' replied Brother Kekrops. 'My soul that will never run dry or falter. That will never be taken and turned against me.'

'Good,' said Iktinos. He moved on down the line. 'Where will the final battle be fought?'

'In the minds of Mankind,' came Brother Myrmos's answer.

'When?'

'We fight it even now.'

'Good.'

Iktinos touched the small leather-bound copy of the *Catechisms Martial* that hung from his waist by a silver chain. The words of Daenyathos, the legendary philosopher-soldier of the Soul Drinkers, were as relevant to the Chapter now as they had been before the excommunication. It was Iktinos's duty that the Marines of his flock should know them off by heart. These were his Marines, the ones with whom he had forged a spiritual bond on Stratix Luminae, and he intended to condition their souls for the struggles the Soul Drinkers would have to endure in the future.

Carnax Bridge was relatively quiet. Seleucaian scouts had tried to cross the previous day when they were at the limit of their westwards push. Their bodies still lay sprawled on the road where Iktinos's Marines had picked them off with bolter fire. The Seleucaians had evidently decided there was some invincible force on the north bank of the River Graven, and had not sent anyone else over.

The bridge was a handsome piece of engineering, a suspension bridge spanning the sheer-sided river with the cable towers in the centre topped with spread-winged eagles. The gate houses on either end were meant to monitor the traffic between the poor south of the city and the wealthy north, and the northern gate-house was correspondingly more lavish. The tall square marble tower frowned with statues and plaques dedicated to the aristocrats to whom the city had owed its gratitude, and inside it was a complex of ballrooms and reception halls to give an appropriate greeting to dignitaries who needed welcoming into Gravenhold's better half.

Iktinos's Marines were stationed in the lower two floors – the two battle-brothers Iktinos had questioned were keeping a watch over the bridge. A mix of Tactical and a few Assault Marines, Iktinos's Marines had lost their own officers and chosen Iktinos to lead them. Normally they would make for an unacceptably unwieldy formation, but Iktinos used them like a weapon. His Marines did not need the tactical independence their previous training had taught them, they just needed to follow him.

'What news?' he asked.

'Very little,' replied Kekrops, an Assault Marine. 'There is a lot of activity on the south side, though. And it looks like a fortification has gone down north of the river, lots of gunfire and explosions. Karhedros is striking back.'

'With what?'

'We haven't seen any xenos, chaplain. More like... humans. Rebels. Maybe even fellow Guardsmen.'

'Hmm.' It was frustrating that Iktinos's Marines had not fought a true fight since the chamber mercantile. He had been tending his small flock only since Stratix Luminae and they had had precious few exposures to battle since then, and battle, of course, was the only place where Daenyathos's words could truly be understood. 'What a fascinating place this city is becoming. Like the Imperium in miniature. Humanity killing humanity with aliens and witches looking on. What would Daenyathos have said?'

'Nothing, chaplain,' replied Kekrops. 'He would have watched until he understood, and then he would have acted.'

Iktinos nodded. 'Indeed. Give the watch to Thieln and Apollonius and enter half-sleep for three hours. This battle may yet reach us and I want you all rested for when the time comes.'

The two Marines saluted and left to summon their two replacements. Iktinos looked out through the grand picture window that looked down on the expanse of the bridge, the Graven was tinted pink with blood and there were dozens of bodies now floating by. He saw some of them were all but naked, with abnormal growths of flesh and metal forming weapons fused to their bodies. Some foul xenos-tech, no doubt. He shook his head. In spite of all, in spite of everything the Emperor had wished and that His faithful had done, aliens and heretics still nibbled away at Mankind's future.

Iktinos had sided with Sarpedon's revolt because even after the intense psycho-doctrination and religious instruction, he had never been completely satisfied with the way the Emperor's will was done. Sarpedon had convinced him that the Imperium was built to serve its rulers and not the Emperor, and everything Iktinos had seen since then had proved that correct. But there was more. The Emperor did not just want humanity to go on surviving. Mankind was not just another animal, there was more to the constant struggle than simply continuing to exist. The Emperor had a grand path for mankind to follow, but instead it was just stagnating, fighting the same wars, living and dying without ever taking that step forward.

It had taken excommunication to suggest the way. Iktinos wasn't sure yet, but he had read the works of Daenyathos and researched the history of the Chapter, and moreover looked into the teaching he himself had received. He was beginning to understand what he had to do, and the first step was to pass that on to his Marines.

He was a Chaplain of the Soul Drinkers, and as such there was perhaps no one in the galaxy who knew the Emperor's Will like he did.

'Disturbance to the north,' came a vox from Brother Octetes.

'Troops?'

'No,' replied Octetes, whom Iktinos had placed on watch at the northern wall of the bridge gate house. 'It's… maybe another Deathstrike…'

Iktinos ran through the ballroom, stomping down into the orchestra pit and over the stage that dominated one end of the room.

Behind the stage backdrop, Brother Octetes was looking out over a view of the north of the city, with its sprawling villas and mock castles competing for obviousness of wealth. In the middle of it all was a strange pulsing purple-black mass, a black glow shot through with purple lightning strobing upwards. 'Iktinos to all Marines,' voxed the Chaplain, wishing that he was still in contact with the other Soul Drinkers below ground. 'Possible moral threat, take cover and steel your souls, this is some xenos trick…'

Then the portal opened.

FROM THE HEART of Gravenhold's northern estates, a lance of purple-streaked blackness ripped up through the ground and up into the darkened sky. Handsome villas were vaporised, their marble walls and gilded friezes dissolving against the raw force of dark magic. Mystical symbols from an alien language flickered in a circle around the crater torn by the magic, echoing the complex patterns of the ritual enacted far below.

The blood that had soaked into Gravenhold, the blood from the thousands dying in its streets, burst upwards and fountained like lava from a volcano, coursing through the streets in a horrendous flash flood, crashing in foaming waves against the buildings. It was as if a massive bullet wound had been torn out of Gravenhold, sending gouts of blood hundreds of metres in the air.

A shockwave rippled out, swamping an area a dozen streets across with evil magic. The magic flooded into the imprints left by savage emotions, leering faces bulged from polished hardwood walls, formed by the arrogance and disdain of Gravenhold's ruling class. The resentment of their downtrodden servants became spectral hands that reached grotesquely from floors and roads. Wherever violent death had blossomed, foul gibbering creatures budded off from the mutating nightmare, capering and screeching down the twisting streets.

The bolt of dark sorcery lanced up through the black clouds, sending thunderheads recoiling. It scoured right through the atmosphere of Entymion IV and boiled up into the black vacuum of space. It streaked past the *Resolve*, blistering the outer hull. Some unfortunate maintenance teams in the outer hull layers were struck mad with visions of alien sorcery, of a great world hanging in the warp where an eldar prince ruled an empire of torturers and magicians.

The magic hit the fueller ship *Sacred Truth* full amidships and sliced it in two. Its enormous fuel cells were breached and exploded, their death a speck of white light in the dark column. Purple lightning arced off the remains of the forward half, incinerating its five hundred-strong crew who were immersed in a torrent of pure madness before they died. Supply ships and landers were scattered by the force of the eruption, spinning out of control into outer orbit or into the deadly gravitational pull of the Entymion system's sun.

In the city, everyone felt it. Pain burst behind the eyes of every Guardsman, followed by a spike of pure evil stabbing at their souls. Lord Commander Xarius saw the fields of dead on Valhalla, endless mounds of frozen corpses that he had put there by ordering the advance. Commander Reinez saw a Traitor Marine he had fought when barely a full battle-brother of the Crimson Fists, and recalled the horror of a fellow Marine choosing to die for the dark gods. Sarpedon saw the face of Michairas, the Marine he had hurled out of an airlock during the Chapter War and who had survived to face Sarpedon again on Stratix Luminae – Sarpedon was filled with shame that he had killed a battle-brother twice over.

Lieutenant Elthanion of the Fornux Lix Fire Drakes saw his men suppressing a rebellion on a far-flung Imperial world, his men dragging women and children from their homes to teach their seditious fathers and husbands about the Emperor's justice. Consul Kelchenko saw his predecessor to the office of consul, an elderly man pleading for clemency as Kelchenko read out the charges of corruption and incompetence that had seen the old man hung and Kelchenko elected to the consulship.

Fear. Shame. Hate. These memories bubbled up from the minds of every human in the city, feeding on the magic now infusing the city. Most men choked them back down, forced them into the depths of their minds where they belonged. For a few they were the last straw and yet more of the soldiers in Gravenhold went insane.

At the very centre of the black column, like the eye of a hurricane, was the true product of Karhedros's spell. It was a tiny window through reality that looked directly into the endless psychic landscape of the warp, and it was growing.

PRINCE KARHEDROS STOOD on the lip of a bottomless pit in the centre of his throne room, a shaft sunk right through the bedrock of reality into the warp. Looking down, he could see a magnificent universe boiling away, seas of molten emotion, floating mountains where roosts of daemons nested. His sorcerers had just opened the gate. The portal was now self-sustaining, the warp energies rushing out of it too vast for it to close.

He could hear a cacophony of daemons' whispers and the screaming of the damned who had become lost in the warp. He could hear the words of gods and amongst them She-Who-Thirsts, first amongst them and the patron of the true eldar. With an open warp portal on its surface Entymion IV would soon be suffused with warp energies and would sink out of real space into the warp in its entirety. A whole world, delivered intact to She-Who-Thirsts.

A human mind would just revel in the knowledge that it would rule a planet where it could mould the continents and populate the continents with subjects drawn from the endless menagerie of the warp. But Karhedros had something more than a human mind. He could understand the cosmic consequences of his actions. He would be a new power in the warp, a creature that had crossed the boundaries between one reality and the next. Whole threads of destiny, so beloved of eldar who cowered away from She-Who-Thirsts, would be snapped. The future history of the galaxy would end and new fates would come into play.

A new Commorragh, no longer hiding from the eyes of the craftworld eldar but a proud beacon shining upon the whole of the warp, illuminating every corner of its reality with the purity of its cruelty and the magnificence of its ruler. No one knew where such an abomination would end. The balance between the warp and realspace could be shattered, one could bleed into the other, and eventually reality as it was known would change into something new. Karhedros didn't know what form any of it might take, but he could feel the savage delight rising in him that he would have been the author of it all.

Karhedros looked over at the haemonculi standing around the portal. Their already twisted faces were contorted with pain. The portal was using the power of their memories to remain stable. They hadn't expected Karhedros would use them that way when they had agreed to join his mission to Entymion IV, but then their minds were too small to understand the true consequence of what Karhedros was doing. They were the torturers of eldar society, each and every one had memories of the most horrendous torments. Many, having experimented on themselves, offered a unique concoction of suffering and cruelty perfect for Karhedros's needs.

Karhedros walked around the portal with its captive haemonculi. The incubi, the heavily-armoured eldar elite who served Karhedros as personal bodyguards and retainers, were standing in black-armoured ranks outside the throne room.

'Captain, our time here is short,' said Karhedros to the leader of the incubi.

'So it has been decided,' said the captain. The incubi were a breed apart from the eldar, and no one really knew what they were or how they thought. 'The call of She-Who-Thirsts becomes ever louder. Now we cannot ignore her.'

'Our hand is now played and the animals on the surface may try to find this place. Grant them death before they see our new world.'

'Of course, my prince,' replied the captain. The swirling column of warp energy cast strange reflections in the eyepieces of his otherwise featureless mask. 'So do the incubi serve their mistress.' The captain – who like all of Karhedros's incubi had never divulged his name – turned sharply and along with his armoured warriors marched out towards the palace gates, where any assault would have to try to breach the palace's frontal defences.

The incubi marched past the wyches, who in contrast waited in a languorous mob apparently without any discipline. It was a completely false appearance, because every single one of them could turn into a lightning-quick killer in a heartbeat.

'And you,' said Karhedros, smiling with what an ignorant observer might think was fondness. 'Children. Blessed of my blood. You killers, you beautiful things.'

The wyches stirred. A couple drew weapons or contorted their bodies as if idly practising the movements of death. One flipped onto her feet. Karhedros couldn't name her, because the wyches chose their leaders anew every day to keep themselves on their toes. 'The games are over, aren't they?' she said. She was as fine a specimen of eldar as existed, with huge green-flecked black eyes and near-white skin pulled taut over snaking muscles. 'We had so little play. And these animals are sometimes good sport, when they have warning. A few of them can fight, and sometimes they don't give up. Is there no more sport here?'

'The games,' said Karhedros, 'are only just beginning, especially for you. You have followed me since I first left Commorragh, do you really think I would cut you down, chain you up and let you never fight again? You shame me. Atone in the streets. Keep the blood flowing. I fear the destruction might end and that will do us no good. Keep the killing hot, blood of my blood. Make them bleed, and I shall see to it that the blood on our new world will never stop.'

The lead wych flipped backwards, drawing a pair of twin-bladed weapons as she did so, she whooped once and the other wyches echoed, following her as she ran for the front entrance. They had permission to kill, those were the only orders Karhedros had ever had to give them.

The eldar warriors were holding the regions around the palace, aside from those that were still out in the city herding the warring human factions towards one another. The palace was hidden and its guardians were Karhedros's best. He could feel the touch of She-Who-Thirsts even now, reaching down from the heavens to caress him in thanks for her dark new world. What things she would show him, for the goddess who wanted to devour the souls of other eldar would instead welcome him as her right hand.

Karhedros ascended the tight winding stairs that led to the chambers once occupied by the palace's king. This king had liked gold and ebony and the walls and floors of his chambers were solid shiny black, covered in delicate inlaid patterns of creamy white. Unusually good taste, for a human.

Akrelthas sat at the large black hardwood desk in the study. Long ago, when Karhedros had been an Archon of the Kabal of the Burning Scale on Commorragh, Akrelthas had been a lieutenant he had almost trusted. Now the Kabal was Karhedros's personal army of pirates and slavers and Akrelthas was still there, Karhedros's eyes and ears.

'Will it stay open?' asked Karhedros.

Akrelthas thought for a moment. 'If the slaves we made keep fighting, as we created them to do. And if the humans don't surrender and die too quickly.'

Karhedros smiled. 'I don't think there's too much danger of that. They have strange ideas about when it is right to die and when they should fight. I understand them well enough, I think. If you place too little pressure on them they become complacent, too much and they give in to despair. But just enough, and they will never give up. Hope is the key. As long as there is a little hope, but not too much, they fight to the death. Every time.'

'You know them well, my prince,' said Akrelthas. 'Perhaps half of them remain and they are resisting hard.'

'And Sarpedon?'

'We do not know. Some of his troops remain on the surface but most are evidently beneath the ground.'

'I should very much like to know where he is. He will be feeling greatly betrayed, and that is something humans take very personally. I should not be surprised if he was heading towards us to fulfil some honour by dying beneath our battlements, which is a complication I would do without.'

'I shall set the mandrakes onto him, prince.'

'Good. We probably have a handful of hours left, ensure the blood does not stop flowing and we shall be done.'

'Of course.'

Karhedros left Akrelthas to his duties. The ancient king had evidently liked to look out over his kingdom because the chambers opened directly onto the palace battlements, which in turn looked onto the immense natural cavern in which the palace stood. The mass of the palace bulged out from one wall with the rest of the cavern stretching out before it, eventually breaking into dozens of smaller tunnels. The ceiling of the cavern hung with stalactites and streams of water spattered down from watercourses on the levels above. Karhedros's eldar warriors were garrisoned on the rocky plain, with a few jetbikes still idling in case anything really did manage to get down there and threaten the palace. The warriors were well aware of their real purpose, however, they were to witness Karhedros's ascension to lord of their new world, because many of them had been there from the beginning. They had been part of Karhedros's pirate fleet when She-Who-Thirsts had first planted in him the desire to leave Commorragh and found the true home of the eldar race.

Karhedros found this underground fortress lacking. It was as good a seat of rulership as existed on Entymion IV, but it had been conceived by brutish human minds. Karhedros would raise a new bastion from the sea, a city-fortress to put the towers of Commorragh to shame, riddled with torture chambers and fighting arenas, pleasure-pits and temples to his goddess. His alien mind could pick out the threads of fate that would lead to him sitting on a throne atop its pinnacle, able to see his whole world at once. Every one of those threads was intact, winding through the next few hours and into the coming dawn.

On the surface, the blood was flowing. Beneath, the portal was sucking the matter of Entymion IV into the warp. As far as Karhedros was concerned, he was already the prince of the warp. All it needed was time.

CHAPTER FOURTEEN

THE JETBIKE STREAKED overhead so close it nearly took Eumenes's head off. He felt the air sliced apart centimetres from his face. A shot from his bolt pistol went wide and the biker wheeled insanely low, jinking between severed stumps of streetlights as he banked his bike around in a long arc for another pass.

The government district had received a thorough bombardment from the Guard artillery after the battle in the chamber mercantile and the scale of the destruction was impressive. Where once there had been seemingly solid blocks of buildings there were now warrens of half-fallen walls and rooms blasted open to the air. Between the Fire Drakes and the Seleucaians, this area was no-man's land and the eldar were all over it, spoiling for a fight, hunting for things to kill. The Soul Drinkers scouts were a prime target, but Eumenes didn't mind so much. He liked being underestimated.

Eumenes snapped off three more shots at the low dark shape streaking around behind him, the shots spanging off charred support columns or drifts of rubble. The bike's long armoured nose flipped over and the bike rolled crazily, using the roll to turn so sharply it was suddenly knifing straight at Eumenes, its rider's teeth bared beneath its green-eyed goggles. Hooked chains streamed behind it, and blades flaring out from the bike's nose sliced off chunks of masonry as the engine screeched into its highest gear.

Eumenes could duck. He could dive to the ground, hoping that the bike would pass over him instead of dipping lower and eviscerating him with the blades hooking down from its underside. He could do what the biker expected, and die. But he did not.

Eumenes stepped out from cover, offering himself up to the biker's blades. The biker had probably seen Guardsmen doing the same, mesmerised by the speed and grace of the jetbike, laid open to a spectacular kill. The biker saw his chance. The bike tipped to one side, the biker reaching out with his own sickle-bladed knife to take the scout's head personally. Eumenes would become a new trophy to be impaled on the spiked chains, a new plaything for when the games were over.

Eumenes, however, didn't fight alone.

The biker suddenly snapped to one side, wrenching the controls as he did so. The jetbike banked too hard and spun out of control, swinging round and round as it careered through the ruins. It smacked into a half-toppled column and broke in two, throwing the nose section and the engine in opposite directions with the biker sailing across the cratered street beyond.

Scout-Sniper Raek slipped out of the shadows a short distance away.

'Good kill,' he said with a smile

'Kill's not done yet,' replied Eumenes. He held out his bolt pistol, drawing a bead on the biker who was trying to crawl away, dragging his broken legs behind him. Eumenes put a bolt through the eldar's neck. 'Never turn your back, Raek, until you see them die.'

The scouts were coming together as a team. Raek's sniper rifle and Eumenes's cunning made for a formidable killing team without adding Selepus's knife or Nisryus's precognitive edge. Scamander hadn't had to use his pyrokinetics for a while, the scouts were moving quickly through the governmental district without needing heavy firepower, dealing quietly with anything that got in their way. The eldar thought they were hunting frightened, stray humans, and more than just the biker had died for that assumption.

'We're there,' voxed Scout Tydeus from up ahead. The vox-channel was still distorted but at least it was working. Eumenes peered through the ruins and saw what had once been the chamber mercantile up ahead – now it and the senate-house behind it were charred shells criss-crossed with smouldering support beams.

'Keep moving.'

As the scouts moved into the ruins of the chamber mercantile they saw some remnants of the battle against the Crimson Fists. A red-gauntleted hand stuck out from beneath a fallen slab of stone. Dead Fornus Lix Guardsmen lay, mouths dry and open, eyes staring. Flies were starting to settle on the dead. Eumenes recognised one dead Soul Drinker as one of Graevus's men, an Assault Marine whose loss the Chapter couldn't really afford. The fresh open wound on the

Marine's throat marked where the gene-seed had been removed by one of the Apothecaries – if the Soul Drinkers got off Entymion IV that gland would be implanted in one of the next novices to be inducted into the scouts. Eumenes himself had one, taken from a sergeant named Givrillian who Sarpedon had considered one of the Chapter's finest Marines.

The chamber mercantile's basements were laid open by an artillery strike, the crater gouging down two floors. Charred paper lay everywhere, the rooms beneath the chamber mercantile had evidently been used to keep all the financial records that Gravenhold generated. Eumenes saw the Marines of Squad Graevus, posted as sentries. There were few of them left now, and Sergeant Graevus was looking the worse for wear himself, his armour was pitted and smoking, and the fittings of his power axe were clotted with drying gore.

'Scout-Sergeant,' said Graevus. 'Good. Sarpedon was waiting for you.'

'From where we were standing it didn't look good on the east wall.'

'No, not good. They went right over us into the Fire Drakes. We had to fight our way through both of them.' Graevus led the way further down, through burned-out studies and libraries.

'The Guardsmen in the south are gone,' said Eumenes. 'The xenos dealt with them directly.'

'There's nothing to stop them any more. Whatever Karhedros is doing with this city, he's nearly finished. Now they can just have their sport. I'll be glad when we're off this damn planet.'

Eumenes looked at him. 'I don't think we're done here.'

Sarpedon was waiting in an almost intact study, antique glow-globes casting yellowish light over walls crammed with mouldering books and the large desk which Sarpedon stood behind, alongside the two other Librarians, Gresk and Tyrendian.

'Scout Eumenes,' said Sarpedon. 'Excellent. We need you to pinpoint Tellos's position.' Sarpedon had an old map of Gravenhold unrolled on the desk. He had already marked the places where the city had been rearranged by artillery or explosions, like the obliteration of the arena and the new crater in the city's north.

'Good to see you alive, Novice Nisryus,' said Gresk.

'Thank you, sir,' replied Nisryus.

'Staying sharp?'

'Very. The fighting helps, I think. I'm not seeing much further but it's getting clearer by the hour. Eumenes will need to know which of the bridges on this map has the twin gate houses before he can tell you where Tellos is.'

Eumenes looked up from the map. 'He's right.'

Sarpedon smiled and pointed at one of the bridges across the River Graven: Carnax Bridge, the same one Iktinos was still holding.

'Then he's here,' said Eumenes. Close to where the slums met the edge of the governmental district was the slaughterhouse district. One of Entymion IV's main exports was the livestock that grazed on its immense grassy plains, some of which were held back to feed Gravenhold's population. Eumenes was pointing to one of the warehouses where they were slaughtered. 'Once the Janissaries were broken we followed his Marines here. I hung back and didn't get any closer but it looks like he's got more than thirty Marines with him.'

'You're certain it's Tellos that's leading them?'

'Half-naked? Chainblades for hands? Yes, I'm sure.'

'Good. You did well not to face him yourself. Tellos has been changing for the worse ever since the star fort.'

'Commander, why... why is he like that? What happened on Stratix Luminae?'

'Two questions, novice, and I am afraid I don't know the answers. Tellos himself probably doesn't know.'

'Will you need me to lead you there?'

'No, Eumenes, we can make it quickly enough. There is something else I need you to do. Rather easier, in a way.'

'What?'

'I need you to find the Crimson Fists.'

'PUT YOUR BACK into it! Throne of Earth, I'm one hundred and seventeen and I'm not ready to give in yet!' Lord Commander Xarius ignored the pain in his joints and heaved another sandbag onto the barricade. Slave-soldiers had scrabbled up the barrier as they swarmed through the ruined buildings that bordered one side of the position, now the sandbag wall was soggy with their blood and the dead lay three deep just beyond it. The smell was appalling, many of the Seleucaian Guardsmen were wearing their rebreather masks.

'Yes, sir.' The soldier next to Xarius heaved up a couple more sandbags, helping to plug the gap where the slave-soldiers had broken in. He had seen the soldier next to him dragged over the wall by steel-taloned hands and ripped limb from limb in front of him. Xarius knew that men who saw such things could clam up, fall almost comatose, and when that happened they might as well be dead.

'Scared?' asked Xarius.

'Yes.'

'Use it.'

In spite of Threlnan's protestations, Xarius had hurried forward with the few reserve men to plug the gap. The men had tried to hold him back but he was sure he had plugged a couple of those deformed freaks before the Seleucaians had formed a second line and massacred the enemy with volleys of las-fire. Now Xarius had his place in the line, preparing the defences for the next surge.

Threlnan's position had been held by about two hundred men half an hour before. Now Xarius guessed they had about a hundred and fifty.

'How is your side looking, Hasdrubal?' voxed Xarius.

'Good, sir,' came the reply. The Baneblade, under Hasdrubal's command, had used its heavy bolters and the odd Demolisher cannon shot to rip the street in front of it to shreds, wiping out the gaggles of enemies that tried to charge down it. The Seleucaians hunkering down beside it had picked off survivors with las-fire. 'We've got enough ammo to keep going all night.'

'I think we're going to have to.'

'And yourself, sir?'

'I'm safe enough, Hasdrubal.' One of the Guardsmen threw another enemy body over the rebuilt sandbag wall, landing with a wet thump on the blood-soaked earth and ash. 'Worry about yourself.'

Likewise the heavy weapons in the Enforcer watchtower kept the third side of the position clear, turning the tangle of ruined hovels in front of it into a blistered, bullet-scarred killing ground littered with bodies. The fourth side was commanded by Threlnan himself – two of the Chimeras forming a defensive line were burned-out but the line had ultimately held.

The small rectangle of bloodstained rockcrete was Xarius's whole world. Beyond it was no-man's land, haunted by enemies who, even if they had once been human, were now alien-wrought fighting animals. Somewhere out there were other islands of Guardsmen, and communications from them occasionally got through to the Baneblade's vox-receiver. But mostly, Threlnan's Seleucaians were on their own.

They had all seen the billowing red-black smoke when the docks had fallen. They all kept glancing up at the shaft of purple-black energy coursing up into the sky. They knew the end was coming soon.

'I'm pretty certain there's a rule against your being here,' said Threlnan. Xarius looked round – the colonel was standing just behind him. His skin and uniform were a charred grey-black. 'There's a directive somewhere about commanders keeping themselves out of harm's way. I'm sure of it.'

'Don't worry, colonel,' replied Xarius, picking up his lasgun again. 'I imagine they'll save that court martial for last.'

'I let a lord commander into the front line, sir. I won't be able to explain that one away.'

'I'll put in a good word for you.'

'Not much good if you're dead. I'm serious, if any of us survive it should be you.'

'Why? This is my fault, Threlnan. That's what the chain of command is for. The buck stops at the top and that means with me. I'm just trying to put it right. And it doesn't look like you're playing the rear-echelon officer yourself, Threlnan.'

'Ah, I can't ask these boys to die on their own.' Threlnan held up the melta-gun he was carrying. 'Besides, it's been a while since I toted one of these. Brings back memories.'

'Acranthal?'

Threlnan nodded. 'Three days and those damned xenos tau never stopped coming. We held that valley until the Navy sent a flyer down to pick us up; I must have gone through a dozen of these power packs before the end. Won me my commission.' Threlnan shook his head, the memories of a soldier's life flooding back. 'And you?'

'Second Battle of Armageddon.'

Threlnan cocked an eyebrow. 'You were there?'

'Tartarus Hive. Nothing like a dying hive city to make you feel small. Calxian Seventh, you know. They made me an officer because I got out alive, that was pretty much how you got promoted by that stage.'

'Well, at least we've both been there before.'

'It's a first for most of these lads, though.'

'Best of luck, sir.'

'And to you. Fight hard enough and maybe they'll put up a statue.'

Threlnan saluted and walked back to his men. Xarius saw the last few bodies being pulled away from the centre of the position, while the two remaining medics tended to the dozen or so wounded. Guardsman Karthel, who had been given chaplain's duty, was doing the rounds taking last-minute confessions and offering the Emperor's blessing to anyone who asked for it. Men reloaded the pintle-mounted weaponry on the Chimeras or ran heavy bolter ammo to the Baneblade's sponson gunners. One trooper took a swig from a canteen, another wiped his gory bayonet blade on the trousers of his fatigues. The nerves were dissolving by now, to be replaced with a grim refusal to die.

'They're coming again!' yelled a trooper on the roof of the watchtower, pointing over the ruined buildings.

'Saddle up!' shouted a sergeant on Xarius's line. 'You! Get your jacket back on. You're on duty, soldier!'

Xarius leaned his old, complaining body against the sandbags, squinting through the tangle of ruins along the barrel of his lasgun. It was still warm from the last volley of shots. Someone moved past him and threw a couple of spare las-cells at his feet. The Guardsman next to him took a deep breath, muttered a prayer and took his position alongside Xarius.

'Gak on a stick,' said a soldier down the line. 'I can see them.'

'More of the same?' said another soldier with mock weariness.

'I don't... no, different.'

'Xenos,' said Xarius wearily. 'At last.'

Then Xarius saw them, too. But they weren't xenos.

At first he thought he saw a woman, but only for a moment. Then he saw the huge ugly claws, the scaled and taloned legs, the pale blue-white skin and the noseless face with its malicious slit of a mouth and black liquid slashes for eyes.

The smell hit him. Musk, heavy and thick, a cloying invisible mist of pheromones. He felt his head swimming and his muscles relaxing, his fingers demanding they be allowed to uncurl from around the trigger of his lasgun. His legs wavered. His eyelids drooped. Did he really need to carry on breathing? Wouldn't it be simpler to lie back and let this beautiful, lethal creature cut him apart?

'Rebreathers!' he gasped, and pulled his own mask out of its belt pouch to pull it over his head. There was a commotion on the line as other men did the same. For some it was too late as they stumbled back, eyes rolling, blind with confusion.

'Medics! Get them out of here!' shouted one of the sergeants. Xarius got the rebreather over his head in time to see more of the creatures advancing, their skins shimmering strangely as if they were just out of phase with the physical world.

He spotted the malevolent reflection of the column of magical energy, pulsing its way into the sky. Warp-magic. The black arts. The xenos were in league with the dark powers, after so many years in command Xarius had suffered his brushes with the agents of Chaos.

'Daemons,' he hissed.

The Seleucaians couldn't take this. Hells, the Space Marines would be hard pushed to fend off a daemonic assault. Xarius had never been in thick of one but he had seen the aftermath, and signed the orders to execute the men who had witnessed enough to break their minds.

The daemons were coming closer, darting between the charred timbers and half-collapsed walls. Some wore scraps of silvery mail or interlocking armour plates, others were completely naked, a horrible parody of female beauty with snaking muscles and teeth glinting in their shark-like mouths.

'O Emperor, though sin calls its siren song and the ways of the corrupt be tempting, shield our souls from perfidy...' Xarius raised his voice as he prayed, hoping the men near him would recognise they weren't fighting rebels or xenos any more and take up the prayer with him.

'...and ...and may your saints come to us, and new saints be born from us...' The Guardsman next to Xarius spoke with a wavering voice as he watched the daemons advance. The Seleucaians, like Xarius, had been taught the simple prayers common to seminaries and chapels throughout the Imperium. Now, suddenly, those words started to actually mean something.

Xarius was leading the prayer, aware of how old and frail he must have sounded calling on the grace of the Emperor as creatures like nothing the Seleucaians had ever seen before moved lethally towards the line. But the prayer was a weapon, it was a shield for their souls, and without it many of them would already have gone mad or died in horror as the pure evil of the daemons's substance made contact with their minds.

There was more movement, further back. Something was bounding closer with sudden, unnatural speed. Xarius spotted long avian limbs pistoning through the shadows, monstrous tubular heads with long sharp ribbons for tongues. Then the daemon cavalry burst out through the ruins, hurtling at supernatural speeds towards the line, daemons were riding the monstrous creatures bareback, claws held out ready to slash and behead, black liquid eyes huge with hate.

'Oh, frag!' shouted the sergeant. 'Fire! Bloody well fire!'

Las-shots whipped out, slicing through the ruins. Daemonic flesh was seared to ribbons and reformed, leaving new deformities on the daemons as they charged. A couple were knocked down, their flesh dissolving as their hold on reality was broken. But the rest – maybe twenty daemonic cavalry – slammed home into the barricade.

Iron-edged tongues lashed out, impaling. Claws snapped off heads and arms. The daemons screamed as they hit and the din was appalling, shearing through Xarius's senses and becoming a wall of hateful white noise.

'Tower!' he shouted, though he couldn't hear his own voice. 'Covering fire! Everything you've got! Everything!'

One of the beasts leapt the barricade right over his head. He let a dozen shots fly on full-auto, searing the mount's underbelly, but it landed intact. The creature wheeled and the daemon on its back plunged its claw into the back of a Guardsman, lifting him high and flinging him back over the sandbags into no-man's land. One Guardsman, his mouth working as he yelled the words of the prayer, jumped onto the daemon's back and stabbed again and again with his bayonet, blue blood spraying all over him. The daemon swivelled round and opened its mouth so widely its jaw must have dislocated like a snake's before it leaned forward and bit half the Guardsman's head off. Another handful of Guardsmen turned their fire on the beast, Xarius lending his firepower to theirs as they speared the daemon with dozens of las-shots. Wet blueish clots of flesh spattered out of the spasming daemon's body as it came apart, its mount slumping to its knees as it melted in a pall of stinking vapour.

Stupid, proud old man. He could have got out of this and yet he insisted on that one dramatic gesture to show what a good man he was. Now he was going to die.

It was the daemons' musk talking. The Dark Powers didn't just send foul monsters to kill everyone, they messed with your mind. Turned you into one of their own. Frag that, thought Xarius savagely, and shook the traitorous thoughts out of his head.

He glanced up and down the line and saw it was in tatters. Half the cavalry had made it over the barricade. A couple were heading for the wounded, the medics and the ad hoc chaplain trying to fend them off with laspistols and bellowed prayers. The men of the line were back-to-back in desperate knots, trying to batter the daemons back with lasgun fire as they were picked off by slashing claws and stabbing tongues. There was nothing to hold back the daemons on foot save for a couple of feet of sandbags and the Emperor's grace, and Xarius knew they had asked about as much from the Emperor as they could. It was down to guts now.

The heavy weapons on the tower opened up as one, and heavy bolter shots stitched down, raking down through the front rank of daemons interspersed with crimson las-cannon shots and explosive autocannon shells. Some of the daemons made it through and into the men making their last stand by the barricade, claws sparring with bay-onets. The white noise was dying down to be replaced with the clashes of steel on claws, gibbering daemonic screaming, howls of dying men, hopeless orders yelled by officers demanding that their men do the impossible.

Xarius wheeled. He was alone. The men on either side of him were dead and he was stranded between two knots of desperate men, the space between them criss-crossed with las-fire. Xarius dropped down into the cover of the half-collapsed sandbag wall, wishing he could disappear, the customary ache from his old body replaced with twitching floods of adrenaline.

Please, Emperor, please make it quick. I don't mind your taking me now. I have failed you completely enough. But make it quick.

A shadow fell over him, edged red by the strobing las-fire. Xarius saw the writhing fleshy horns on its head and the gnarled crescents of its claws. Even its shadow was unnatural, seething and changing. Silhouetted by the fire still stuttering down from the tower, the daemon was a black shape above him. He saw the distorted reflection of his face, staring down from the inky curved surfaces of its eyes.

He knew then that it wouldn't be quick.

A white-hot wall of heat thudded into him, slamming him down into the sandbags. Scalding liquid spattered over him. He scrabbled to wipe it off his face, out of his eyes.

A second shadow fell. Something grabbed the front of his uniform and dragged him to his feet. His lasgun was shoved back into his chest and he grabbed hold of it instinctively.

'Saw you kill that thing,' said Colonel Threlnan. The melta-gun in his free hand was thrumming as its core came back to critical mass. 'Thought I'd get in on the action.'

Xarius blinked the daemon's blood out of his eyes and the shape of Colonel Threlnan emerged. 'Daemons, Threlnan. Not just xenos. Throne of Earth, I've marched you all into hell.'

There were other soldiers with Threlnan, members of his command squad, surrounding the two officers to keep the daemons away with volleys of las-fire. They might have bought thirty seconds or so.

Xarius thought wildly. No matter what, it was over. He only had to worry about his duties as a lord general of the Imperial Guard.

'Hasdrubal!' shouted Xarius over the vox. 'Battle cannon, five o'clock! Thirty metres!'

'But sir, that's where…'

'Bloody do it! Now! And then get into reverse!' Xarius looked back up at Threlnan. 'This place is done. I've seen daemons fly and walk through walls and all kinds of crap, we can't hold them here. Fall back to the tower.'

The grinding of the Baneblade's tracks cut through the screaming.

'We need to move now,' said Xarius.

'Right.' barked Threlnan, vox on the all-squad channel. 'All troops, back to the tower. Now. Tower, covering fire. Get the Chimeras back to block us in.'

The thirty seconds were up. Threlnan, Xarius and the surrounding troops broke into a run, las-fire snapping half-blind. The Seleucaians who could were doing the same thing, and the position was gone completely. The daemons running in through the buildings were sprinting unchecked into the heart of the position.

'The Emperor be my guide!' someone was yelling. 'The Throne be my beacon!' Xarius saw it was the makeshift preacher, Karthel, who was kneeling over the wounded with a laspistol in each hand. He was trying to fend off the daemons scrabbling towards the wounded.

The medics were with the troops running for the tower.

Someone screamed and a daemon impaled the man just behind Xarius with its claw, lifting him clean up into the air where he wriggled like a stuck fish, blood spurting. A stray las-shot took down someone else. Guardsmen's hands kept pulling Xarius forward and suddenly all those years were catching up with him, the weight of decades trying to crush him down to the floor.

Threlnan fired again and the daemon's midriff was vaporised. The dying Guardsman thudded to the floor. No one tried to help him. Like the wounded, like the crazy, he was just one step removed from dead.

The sheer grey sides of the watchtower, now peppered with las-shot holes and spatters of gore, loomed up ahead. Seleucaians were scrambling in through the open front doors, tripping over one another. Some of them were firing from the cover of the doorframe, teeth gritted as they sprayed full-auto lasgun fire at anything that wasn't human. If a single daemon got in, the slaughter would be even more terrible.

The Chimeras were trundling closer, ready to block the doors once enough men had got inside. All the Guardsmen knew they weren't important enough to wait for. Once the doors were closed, that was it.

Threlnan fired again, the wash of heat almost knocking Xarius onto his face.

Xarius heard the Baneblade tracks stop grinding. That was the only warning anyone had.

The mega-battle cannon mounted on the Baneblade was the biggest gun in Gravenhold save for the single remaining Deathstrike launcher. The explosion was so loud it wasn't a sound at all but a wall of force that threw Xarius the rest of the way into the watchtower. One Chimera was shunted sideways by the shockwave, slamming into the watchtower. Men were thrown to the ground. A daemon's body shattered against the doorframe, spraying shimmering gore everywhere. The heat came next, singeing uniforms and hair, blistering paint, howling over everything. Choking dust and smoke billowed like a sandstorm.

Xarius turned over painfully, every joint a throbbing nugget of pain. He was lying just inside the watchtower. As his senses swam back he saw the huge crater where the ruined buildings had been, now just a massive bowl filled with rubble and splintered wood. Fragments of shell casing were stabbed into the rockcrete, glowing hot. Bodies and parts of bodies were cast around, just more ruins.

Xarius guessed that half the daemons were gone, vaporised in the blast.

Hands grabbed hold of him and dragged him further in as the last few Guardsmen followed, caked with blood and dust. The Chimeras were out of action but the Baneblade would do just as well, reversing into position to block the doors, gun barrel swinging back round.

'Threlnan!' shouted Xarius, barely able to hear his own words. 'Colonel!'

But Colonel Threlnan of the Seleucaian 4th Division was lying on his face, a shard of shell casing speared through him. Blood was spreading from beneath him and Xarius could see his lungs through the massive rip in his back, see them as they stopped pumping.

'Close them,' said Xarius, his voice barely making it out of his body. The doors were heaved shut as the Baneblade backed closer. Xarius could see men still out there, blinded or crippled, writhing through the wreckage. One Guardsmen fell brokenly from the front hatch of a shattered Chimera, crawling towards the watchtower as the doors closed.

The watchtower had been too small to hold the hundreds of Seleucaians, which was why it had only formed one part of the position. Now there could only be fifty or so Guardsmen left. Plenty of room for everyone to die.

Xarius tried to drag himself to his feet as the Guardsmen barred the doors. There were wounded and dying men lying all around the bleak, bare rockcrete ground floor, which was featureless save for the narrow stairway leading to the upper floors and a couple of cells for prisoners. One of the Seleucaians helped Xarius up.

'Is there a medic?' asked Xarius. His ears were ringing and he could barely hear himself.

'One got through, I think,' replied the Guardsman.

'Good. Good, get some painkillers into these men. And into me, if there are any to spare.'

Xarius could hear gunfire still stuttering from the upper floors. He heard the daemons, too, keening madly as they tried to climb the sheer walls. Eventually, Xarius knew, they would succeed.

Xarius looked at the Guardsman who had helped him, it was a sergeant.

'What's your name?

'Sergeant Gabulus, sir.'

'Good. Gabulus, we need to get all the men off this floor. They'll come through the walls.'

'I think the wounded are too…'

'They will come through the walls, sergeant. I know about these things. It's my job. Move them. All of them. And get some guns on the stairs.'

Xarius was too shaken and numb to feel anything apart from a faint annoyance that he wasn't dead yet. It wasn't so bad, dying on the barricades. But now he had to go through another last stand, a wretched final handful of death before it was done.

He had been right all along. He had asked too much of his Emperor. It wouldn't be quick after all.

CHAPTER FIFTEEN

THIS WAS NOT like killing the Janissaries. It was on a different level than hunting even the eldar, expert hunters themselves. Eumenes could feel the danger, the place was steeped in it, drumming silently in his ears, a faint metallic taste in his mouth. Everything was brighter and sharper. The fissures that crackled in the earth, massive wounds torn by the Deathstrike impact, filled the air with the smell of heat and destruction. Eumenes could feel it on his skin like a knife held just above him, ready to strike.

Selepus was so silent it was hard to see him even if you looked right at him. Eumenes had to be careful not to lose the scout in the cratered wasteland. Most of Gravenhold was ruined but the area around the old medicae station was absolute desolation. The scouts took cover in shell craters or behind slabs of ground that had been lifted up by the vortex impact. The area

had been carpeted by shellfire on the orders of the
Crimson Fists, and a greater weight of death had fallen
on this section of the slums than on any other. The
bleak heart of Gravenhold was laid open, raw and
bleeding to the dark sky. The bodies were unrecognisable twists of carbonised flesh. The abandoned tanks
were melted heaps of slag. Palls of smoke bled from
gouges right down through the layers of Gravenhold's
history, and in places the strata of the city could be
seen. At long last Gravenhold was displaying its tormented history to anyone who looked.

Not that there were many to see it. The Imperial
Guard had mostly been smart enough to get the hell
out before the Deathstrike hit. The Gravenholders had
died in greater numbers, thrown into charred heaps by
the force of the vortex blast. The smell of cooked meat
mingled with the smoke and ash.

The scouts were approaching the vortex crater
itself. Eumenes had heard it was bad but he had
never seen destruction on this scale from a single
weapon. A shockwave had levelled two blocks in
every direction and over the crater itself still hung a
dense cloud of dust, the remains of pulverised hovels. More permanent structures were just lonely
blackened skeletons. As the air thickened and visibility dropped the bodies became fresher,
Gravenholders and then slave-warriors with massive
wounds from large-calibre guns or close combat
weapons. The blood oozing from their wounds mingled with the dust to form a greyish-red gunk that
pooled beneath the tangled heaps of bodies.

Selepus was crouching down by one body, a night-
marish creature with a ribcage that gaped open to
reveal a maw filled with fangs. It had been all but

bisected by a huge wound, still wet and rapidly caking with dust.

'Chainblade,' said Selepus quietly.

The winds blew and the dust swirled, descending like a thick dark blanket over the ruins. The shape of the crater itself was just ahead, like a deep black pool that seemed to suck the rest of the ruined cityscape towards it.

The Crimson Fists had followed Luko's Soul Drinkers through the crater into the undercity, only to be forced back out when the slave-warriors had awoken and coursed out onto the surface. The Fists had held the tide back, plugging the bleeding wound. Without them the slave-warriors would probably have surged eastwards and wiped out what remained of Imperial artillery.

The Soul Drinkers could listen in to the Guard transmissions, not that there was much to listen to with the Guard army cut to pieces and being ground into the dirt. But the Crimson Fists were something else. By now they had stopped talking to the Guard and their own vox-channels were too secure. No one knew what they were doing or how many of them were left, only that they were probably holding the area of the Deathstrike hit, waiting to link up with a friendly force and blaze their way out of Graven-hold.

Eumenes crouched down by Selepus, knowing that even in the half-light a sharp-eyed Marine could pick out a scout's silhouette against the swirling dust. And they were all sharp-eyed.

'The crater is deep enough for them to hold,' said Selepus. 'The enemy don't have artillery so it can be defended.'

'Agreed,' said Eumenes. 'It's where I'd be. Aggressive patrols, though. Hunt and kill stuff.'

'Assault Marines?'

'Tactical. They'll want to keep the assault troops in reserve in case the eldar decide to make a battle of it.' Eumenes turned back, he couldn't see his fellow scouts but he knew the pattern they would be using, spread out amongst the upheaved ground and piles of crumbling ruins. He waved Raek forward. Raek slunk out of the shadows and slid down on his stomach next to Eumenes. 'Raek, we'll need you to cover and spot for us.'

'Just you two?'

'That's right. Between your eye and Nisryus I want to know of any surprises that are coming our way. Scamander will be our artillery. Tydeus, Laeon and Alcides are backup.'

Eumenes paused, looking again towards the crater. If he was a commander with the best troops in the galaxy, he would want the Fists out in the ruins, sweeping the area, killing anything that shouldn't be there. If you have a weapon like a company of Space Marines, you use them. In Eumenes's mind he could see patrol routes snaking between knots of hard cover, the places where one fire team would leapfrog the other, the fields of fire they would keep.

Space Marines were good. They were the best. But the Soul Drinkers had been the same before the excommunication and Eumenes had studied them as well as he had the way the Chapter currently fought. They were tough, fearless, and disciplined, but they were not creative. They all thought the same way. Eumenes had sat through dozens of pict-recorded tactical sermons and he knew the principles laid down in the *Codex Astartes* of how a Space Marine should fight. He knew how they thought.

'Can we do this?' he asked quietly.

'Yes,' said Raek, drawing his sniper rifle down off his back and putting his eye to the scope.

Selepus nodded. The others didn't reply, which was enough.

'Because it doesn't matter if we come back from this one,' said Eumenes. 'You know what they can do. They did it to Thersites. They know we're here already.'

'Got them,' said Selepus. Eumenes followed his gaze but couldn't make anything out. For now he trusted the scout; Selepus didn't have a habit of being wrong.

'I'll be thirty seconds behind you,' said Eumenes.

Selepus slid forwards and was gone, worming his way through the hard black shadows in the direction of the crater. Eumenes followed, feeling the field of fire from Raek's sniper rifle sweeping over his back.

Eumenes could feel the Fists watching, because the Crimson Fists would be out there trying to hunt the scouts down. Instinct painted every open angle and field of fire over the twilit desolation. Eumenes could all but see the landscape painted with life and death, the places he could hide and the places where a Tactical Marine could see him and direct a volley of pinpoint bolter fire to leave him a steaming bloody mess.

Then he saw the Fist. He was part of a Tactical Squad patrolling in loose formation, each Marine a strong-point in a widely-spaced line. To Eumenes the Fist's field of vision was like a wide-beam spotlight that would kill anything it touched – if Eumenes wasn't invisible then he was dead.

Now he had the position of one Marine, Eumenes could pick out the others. Five Crimson Fists, a fire team:

one sergeant, one with a flamer, and three with bolters. Perfect for running down knots of slave-warriors, herding them into flamer range with bolter fire with the sergeant's chainsword finishing off the survivors. Not, perhaps, so ideal for a squad of Soul Drinkers scouts with a very specific mission.

Eumenes saw Selepus well before the first Crimson Fist did. Even then it was no more than a shadow on a shadow, a faint suggestion of movement blurring behind the Marine as he scanned for targets. It was the knife that let Eumenes know what was coming. Selepus's combat knife, flashing in that familiar arc towards the Marine's throat where even power armour couldn't save him.

The Fist was as quick as the silver slash of the knife. Faster.

An elbow connected and suddenly Selepus was visible, as if the darkness was lifted off him and he was shockingly obvious, reeling back with his knife still in his hand but a spray of blood spurting from his nose.

Eumenes's grip on his bolt pistol tightened. He was a damn good shot but he couldn't take down a Crimson Fist on his own at this range, even if the shot hit home he would draw a punishing weight of fire before he managed to squeeze off a second shot.

The Fist and the scout were grappling. Selepus was stabbing up at the Marine, seeking the few gaps afforded by the power armour. The Fist was lunging down with the butt of his boltgun, looking to crack open Selepus's skull, smash his jaw, cave in his ribcage.

The other Crimson Fists were running to help. Not even Selepus could hold them off on his own.

Eumenes hurried forwards, risking everything for an edge of speed. He wondered what he would say when they took Selepus's geneseed and buried him in the newly-finished vaults on the *Brokenback*. A good scout. A worthy Marine. An example of the future of the Soul Drinkers and a man who died in the service of his Emperor. How many men died such a death? How many died free, and for a reason?

Selepus rolled away and tried to disappear again. It was almost successful. The Marine snapped off bolter fire at him and the shots strobed through the darkness, lighting up Selepus as he wriggled away.

By now the Marines knew they weren't fighting more slave-warriors, which meant that they would move to take down Selepus with everything they had. It also meant they would know he wasn't alone.

'Three closing in,' voxed Nisryus. 'Then the sergeant.'

Eumenes saw the Fists appear on the dark horizon a moment later, stalking towards the battle-brother who had so nearly died under Selepus's knife.

'Raek?'

'I can take one.'

'Not good enough.' Eumenes kept moving, skirting around the open ground. He knew now that if Selepus made it out then it would be a bonus. Eumenes wanted some of his men to survive to take up the power armour of a fully-fledged Soul Drinker, but even that was a goal he could ultimately fail as long as the mission was completed.

Eumenes saw his chance. A fissure curved around behind the Crimson Fists squad, and Eumenes finally saw what he had been looking for: the final member of the squad, the Fist with the flamer. If Selepus doubled back and fled, the flamer Marine would incinerate him as he tried to escape. Tactically sound Marine thinking straight out of the *Codex Astartes*. Eumenes followed the faint glint of cobalt blue power armour, pistol heavy and ready in his hand.

Bolter fire was streaking out from the other Marines, picking out a zone where Selepus would be pinned down and in cover. Head down, scrambling for safety, he was so much dead meat as far as the sergeant was concerned, a heretic begging to be spitted on a chainsword as he cowered. If the Fists had realised they were up against Astartes scouts then the sergeant would know exactly what he was facing, the exact make and thickness of the armour, the weapons and training of the enemy. Eumenes didn't have to look to know the sergeant would be rushing forward, chainsword raised, already knowing how it would feel as it ripped through armour plates and into Selepus's chest.

Eumenes kept going. The flamer Marine, the unnaturally tall figure silhouetted black-on-grey in the dirty half-light, hadn't seen him.

Now. Now or never.

Eumenes took aim and fired. His bolt pistol barked and the shell smacked into the Marine's shoulder guard, spinning him round enough to tell him where the shot came from but not enough to knock him off his feet.

'For Dorn!' the Fist yelled, and to Eumenes the gout of flame seemed to ripple towards him in slow motion, flowing over the torn ground, reaching for him like something hungry and alive.

Eumenes threw himself to the ground and rolled, flames licking over him, grabbing at his armour, sending searing red tongues over the skin of one cheek and hand. He had hit the ground hard but he kept firing, a spray of shots smacking up into chunks of broken masonry or whistling wide.

The Fist knew his target was dead. He must have seen Eumenes's body picked out by the glare of the flame. He knew that Eumenes was just a scout, outgunned and outnumbered, one of the hated Soul Drinkers ready to die a screaming mess of charred flesh and bones.

'Now,' gasped Eumenes into the vox.

Raek's bullet thunked into the Marine's throat with a horrible wet sound. The Crimson Fist was knocked backward onto his knees, the momentary shock keeping his hand from squeezing the flamer's trigger lever.

Illuminated by the glare of the flames pooling on the ground, the Crimson Fist had been, almost literally, an impossible target for Raek to miss.

Now, there were just a few seconds left.

Eumenes scrambled through the fire, ignoring the pain searing through his hands as he dragged himself through the burning fuel. The Fist hadn't gone down yet. Eumenes threw himself onto the Marine, knocking the flamer away and pushing the Fist onto his back in the dust.

It was a neat wound, right through the flexible throat armour and through the windpipe. Even a Marine had to breathe, and this one would be dead in a couple of minutes. The blood was already clotting in hard red jewels around the wound but it was too late. Only a fellow Marine knew how to kill another Marine, and in Raek's case the target had been the tiny sliver of weakness between the faceplate of the helmet and the collar of the chestplate.

But killing wasn't enough.

'He's down,' voxed Eumenes. 'But he's not dead. We might get something out of him before he dies. We need to get him back to the palace, now. Use the entrance under the senate-house, take the sewers three kilometres north. Make this loyalist vermin suffer for Lord Sarpedon.'

The Crimson Fists knew their battle-brother was down. Fire was snapping towards Eumenes now. Eumenes rolled off the dying Marine, trying to gauge if there was a safe path back towards the edge of the dust pall and into the ruins where he could disappear. It didn't look like it.

He looked back at the Fist. He was still breathing in long, terrible gurgling breaths.

'For Dorn, brother?' said Eumenes quietly as bolter shells thudded into the ground beside him. 'Dorn was never a slave. Dorn never served tyrants and butchers. Nor do we. When you die, brother, you will not be at the Emperor's side. You will be burning in a coward's hell, watching Dorn lead us. We might be excommunicate, but the Emperor turned his back on you a long time ago, and come the end you will know it.'

The Marine took his last breath. It was enough that he had heard. It confirmed what Eumenes had realised when he had talked with Luko at the palace, he hated them. He hated them for what they represented, and for what they could be if they only saw what he saw. Wasted lives disguised as heroic sacrifices. Slaughter and butchery disguised as triumph. If the Emperor could, Eumenes knew, He would step down from his throne and crush the Imperium Himself, winning it back from the tyrants in a second Great Crusade.

Eumenes would have been happy to die then. He had killed two Space Marines, how many men could say that? But he knew he would be more use alive.

The Fists were firing almost blind, the remnants of the flamer's burning fuel their only target. But they were closing fast and soon and once they saw him Eumenes was dead. He scrambled half-crouched through the shadows, knowing that any second a bolter shell could blow his thigh open and leave him writhing in pain, shatter his spine and paralyse him for those last few seconds, blow out the back of his head and kill him before he hit the ground...

He jumped the melted stump of a wall, ducked past charred support beams sticking like burned ribs from the ground. Bullets whistled and cracked around him.

'Traitor! There,' the sergeant was yelling. 'You can't run from Dorn. You can't run from your blood.'

Eumenes hit the ground. He could feel the Crimson Fists close behind him, searching for their target. He could feel the paths of their bolter shells before they fired them, spearing through him and bursting in the ground beneath, blowing him into bloody chunks. He knew how it would feel, the red wash of pain followed by nothingness.

White-hot light erupted in a great flaming sheet behind him, the heat throwing him down again into the dirt. A wall of fire sheared up from the ground, carving crazy swirling patterns in the dust, edging everything in sudden unearthly white light.

It was the artillery. It was the biggest gun the scouts had.

Eumenes saw Scamander standing bolt upright, hands held out, the fire rippling out of him, licking out of his eyes, tapering from his fingertips. Eumenes jumped to his feet and ran headlong, not caring any more who saw him. He vaulted the last few knee-high melted ruins and barged into Scamander, throwing him to the ground.

Scamander was ice-cold. Eumenes couldn't imagine he was still alive.

Nisryus and Raek ran up to Eumenes. The wall of flame was still burning but it was flickering, without Scamander it would be gone in a few moments. Tydeus, crouched just behind them, loosed off two shots from his grenade launcher to add to the confusion.

'Just go,' gasped Eumenes, throwing Scamander's freezing body over his shoulder. He got his head down and ran, letting the dust and shadows envelop him.

One scout left behind. One probably dead. But the mission, Emperor willing, was done.

Eumenes wasn't worried about the craft of warfare any more, about the teachings of Daenyathos or the unique freedom of the Soul Drinkers. With the bullets of the Crimson Fists still streaking wildly through the darkness, he kept his head down and ran.

'AGAIN,' SAID REINEZ. Seated in the back of his Razorback, Reinez fairly itched with the desire to get back into the city and hunt down the Soul Drinkers. Now they had found him, killed one of his Marines, and escaped. The Fists had killed one of the scouts in return, but tit-for-tat killings weren't enough.

The Techmarine ran back the vox-recording, operating a mem-slate fixed to the back of his gauntlet. Sergeant Iago's squad had lost the surviving traitors but he had at least had the prescience to keep the recording of Brother Tehuaca's last communication.

'I can clean it up,' said the Techmarine. 'Lose some of the static.'

'Isolate the voice,' said Reinez. 'I have to be sure.'

The Techmarine made a few adjustments and played the recording again.

'...back to the palace, now. Use the entrance under the senate-house, take the sewers three kilometres north. Make this loyalist vermin suffer...'

The voice was young. A novice. Emperor's soul, that meant they were recruiting again.

'Again.'

'...to the palace. Use the entrance under the senate-house...'

'That's enough.' Reinez sat back. 'Send Chaplain Inhuaca in here.'

'Yes, commander.' The Techmarine, the servo-arm on his backpack scraping the ceiling of the Razorback, ducked back outside. The Razorback was Reinez's makeshift command vehicle, parked in the centre of the Fists' position in the great Deathstrike crater. The Fists had been effectively stuck there after blunting the tide of subhumans who poured up out of the ground. With the Imperial Guard shattered and the enemy with the free run of the city, Reinez could not just drive his Marines around the city without a target.

Now he had one.

'Commander? What news?' Inhuaca's skull-mask looked into the Razorback.

'We've found them. A palace underground. It's where Sarpedon has been hiding. It's where my standard is. We can reach it through what's left of the senate-house.'

'This is unexpected. What plan of action do you suggest?'

'Forget the Guard,' said Reinez. 'Load the tanks up, drive there at top speed and throw every fragging thing we've got at them. Any objections?'

'None, commander.'

'Good. Tell the men that Dorn and the Emperor have given them their battle at last.'

SOMEWHERE IN THE bitter, bloodstained industrial mills of eastern Gravenhold, Consul Kelchenko died.

It had only been a matter of time. The massed batteries of the 4th Carvelnan Royal Artillery could shatter city blocks from miles away but they could not defend themselves from the hit-and-run tactics of the xenos raiders, especially when the attacks were interspersed with waves of blood-mad slave warriors.

The artillery had ceased to exist as a cohesive formation about fifteen minutes after the first slave-warrior incursions. The xenos who had duelled with the Seleucaian patrols early in the battle now broke cover and cut the artillery line to pieces. Some of them were half-naked acrobat-warriors who seemed to dance rather than fight, flipping through the rubble and taking heads with a flourish. They ran alongside horrible creatures, like skinless attack dogs, that slunk through the shadows and wolfed men down whole.

There were torturers who stalked artillery crews, using retinues of deformed and animalistic eldar to drag men back to their masters. The few men who had any idea what was happening said the torturers had a lab or a temple somewhere, and were using the battle as cover for some kind of sacrificial experiment. The screams certainly carried far enough to suggest the story was true.

A hovering creature slipped out of the shadow of the mills and did for three Basilisk crews, killing them in a few minutes of panic and pain. It appeared mechanical from a distance but up close the bundles of red wet muscles were obvious between its armour plates, as its underside yawned open and its shear-tipped limbs dragged screaming men inside. No one paused long enough to speculate on what it could be, and the few that saw it and lived thought it was just another xenos experiment in the infliction of suffering.

By then the 4th Carvelnan Royal Artillery was no longer a part of the Imperial forces in Gravenhold. Its co-ordinated barrages were impossible now, with one tank crew too desperate for their own survival to talk to another. The functioning tanks still sent single shots arcing over the tormented city, hoping that the mostly random fire would at least help the Imperial Guard who still had a chance for survival. The Carvelnan Artillery had never been a unit of great prestige or with any notable history to speak of, but there were many stories of immense bravery written in the shadow of Gravenhold's mills. There were crews who fought off slave-warriors with laspistols and bare hands as they chambered one more Earthshaker round. Some men volunteered as runners to find help, or just orders, from command posts that no longer existed.

There were, of course, plenty who ran, or went crazy. Some tried to drive their tanks back through the mills, through the arches under the eastern wall and back into the safety of the spaceport. But the spaceport was overlooked by the wall itself which was now home to roosts of eldar warriors. These eldar had strange winged jump packs that let them flit from one battlement to the next, so they could get the best shots with heavy weapons that fired bolts of blackness. The armour of Basilisk self-propelled guns and Manticore missile launchers did little against the xenos weaponry and soon the way to the spaceport was blocked with burned-out artillery pieces. Men drowned in pools of burning promethium. Artillery shells cooked off in the heat and turned the eastern mills into mazes of toxic smoke and guttering flame.

A few Basilisks were dug in and turned into impromptu pillboxes, and a dozen isolated last stands were enacted. Many crews let the slave-warriors over-run their vehicles before blowing them up, sending hundreds of the enemy and dozens of friends to the judgement of the Emperor. In some places the small contingents of infantry actually mounted a meaning-ful defence, driving waves of attackers into kill-zones where the artillery could blast the enemy into a thin crimson mist with short-ranged shellbursts. One such defence took place in one of the towering agri-mills, amongst the grain silos and conveyor belts where the labour servitors still went through the motions of their daily work ignorant of the carnage around them. This was the site of the Carvelnan Royal Artillery's last rea-son for existing – the second Deathstrike launcher, this one armed with a multiple warhead with scores of cluster bombs designed to reduce whole infantry divi-sions to body-strewn wastelands.

No one was sure where Consul Kelchenko was. The last anyone had heard he was in his command Sala-mander tank, driving along the line checking the efficiency and morale of the gun crews. Wherever he was, he managed to get a vox-message to the Death-strike crew. It lasted just a few seconds, and not everyone was sure it was really him, but he recited the launch codes, and that was enough.

Perhaps it was another officer, faking the codes and determined to send one last reminder of Imperial spite into the heart of the enemy. Perhaps it was some alien or cultist imitating Kelchenko, or Kelchenko himself controlled by xenos sorcery. More likely it really was Kelchenko, knowing that his life was measured in minutes and wanting to leave some meaningful legacy on the surface of Entymion IV.

In truth, no one cared. The officer in the Deathstrike launcher gave the order and the missile was launched, carving a violent crescent of fire across the boiling dark clouds. The target area was the villas in the north of the city, presumably where the xenos were waiting to stream southwards and claim the whole of Graven-hold for themselves. The Deathstrike broke up above the north of the city, the individual warheads falling in a brilliant curtain of light.

It was the last valiant display of the doomed 4th Carvelnan Royal Artillery, a final act of destructive beauty in the face of crushing defeat. The warheads plummeted into the villas of Gravenhold's elite, smash-ing through the roofs of estates and miniature palaces already warped by the magic of the warp portal. A few detonated around the column of black magic still pour-ing up into the sky – some shot into the column itself and became white streaks of fire, spitting up into space. Clusters of explosive blossomed into huge blooms of flame, sending tidal waves of fire through the streets.

A few wayward slave-warriors were incinerated. The daemons had mostly moved southwards to the killing fields of the slums and administrative district, and only a few discorporated in the inferno.

Eldar casualties were nil. A few of them felt the impacts, far below in the upper reaches of Karhedros's palace. None of them was nervous enough to think it was important.

After this final gesture of defiance from his artillery, Colonel Kelchenko was caught somewhere in the labyrinth of industrial mills, his Salamander crippled by xenos energy weapons. He fled the wreckage, firing wildly with his laspistol sidearm while the lightning-quick gladiatorial warriors of the eldar rushed at him from every side. He screamed obscenities at them, but cowardice took over when the first blade cut him. By the time they had surrounded him he was on his knees, crying and pleading, promising he would give up his Emperor, betray his men, serve them for a lifetime and more if they would just let him live.

But the blades didn't stop, and after twenty minutes there was finally too little of him to survive. The last few artillery pieces lasted a bit longer than Consul Kelchenko, but as the night over Gravenhold became a solid black mantle in the sky the big guns were silent and the east of the city had completely fallen to the enemy.

THE STREETS OF the slaughterhouse district ran with blood at the best of times. But now the channels cut into the rough stone streets overflowed with blood, not from slaughtered livestock, but from the men of the Fornux Lix Fire Drakes. Some time in the last few hours the south-eastern gate had finally fallen and the Fire Drakes had been forced further into the city. They had pushed a vanguard as far as the slaughterhouse district, but they in turn had been cut off and slaughtered in the streets. The rest of the Fire Drakes were still in the administrative district, probably holding the high-rise office buildings as they fell floor by floor to a mix of xenos and slave-soldiers. Maybe daemons, too.

Sarpedon looked over the scene. Fire Drakes were lying draped over ruined walls or simply face-down in the streets. Bodies were piled behind cover where units had made final stands, but mostly they were spread out and scattered. It had been a short, brutal, one-sided fight. The looming warehouses of the slaughterhouse district enclosed stockyards that backed onto the River Graven, and normally offal and slurry from the day's slaughtering would have been dumped into the river. Now the river was in much the same state, but the foulness was human instead of animal.

Sarpedon led the Soul Drinkers out of the burned-out accounting house. It was through the charred cellars of the accounting house that the undercity connected to the surface – it was the closest the Soul Drinkers could get to Tellos's last position. The rest would have to be over the surface. Almost all the Soul Drinkers in Gravenhold had managed to meet up with Sarpedon's force for the final assault on Tellos's Marines. Luko and Varuk had slogged their way through the undercity, Salk and Tyrendian had made it from the eastern wall. Eumenes's scouts were still in the city fulfilling their own mission, and Chaplain Iktinos was still on the north shore of the Graven where Sarpedon suspected he would be most useful – other than that, all of the surviving Marines in Gravenhold moved out into the slaughterhouse district, bolters raised or chainblades held at guard, ready for anything that Gravenhold might throw at them.

'Bolter fire,' said Luko quietly as he led his squad just behind Sarpedon. 'And chainblades.'

Sarpedon didn't answer. As a psyker he was receptive to extremes of psychic activity and Gravenhold was throbbing dully with it, an ache that had been building up since the column of black magic first ripped up into the sky. Reality was breaking down and it was taking Gravenhold with it. It was subtle at the moment but it would get worse. The colour of the sky, the faint whispers Sarpedon thought he could feel just out of earshot, the heavy, electric feel to the air. And every now and then he sensed a spike in activity, a flurry of something coming through from the other side. Karhedros had opened a window into the warp, of that Sarpedon was sure. And the inhabitants of the warp were coming through.

Daemons. Maybe worse. He had to get the job done and get his Marines out as soon as possible. The Soul Drinkers were badly battered and even they couldn't survive for long if the city was flooded by the footsoldiers of the Chaos Gods.

She-Who-Thirsts. Just another name for one of the Dark Gods, worshipped by aliens too corrupt to see they were damned.

'This is fresh,' Luko was saying, kneeling to examine one of the dead Guardsmen. 'Not more than twenty minutes gone.'

'The target is up ahead,' came a vox from Sergeant Salk. 'One of the warehouses. Looks like the fight started here, there are dead everywhere.'

'Good,' replied Sarpedon. 'All units, converge on Salk's position. Stay alert. We all know who these Guardsmen ran into.'

Sarpedon rounded a corner carefully, bolter drawn. A burned-out Chimera stood just past the cover and Sarpedon's eight legs took him quickly up on top of it. He could see the warehouse in question, with the Soul Drinkers moving quickly and efficiently to surround it.

Sarpedon saw Sergeant Kelvor keeping pace in spite of the rudimentary prosthesis Pallas had rigged to replace his severed leg.

He had asked so much of his Marines. They had never let him down. He hoped he would not let them down by throwing their lives away on this dying world.

Sarpedon hurried down the street into the shadow of the warehouse. The bodies were strewn about here in a horrendous mess of severed limbs and loosed organs. The Fire Drakes had probably seen the warehouse as useful cover until they walked into a lattice of bolt pistol fire followed by a chainsword charge more murderous than anything they could have imagined. The doors of the warehouse were scored by a few las-blasts but not many – the Fire Drakes, decent troops that they were, had been shredded before they had been able to put up a fight.

'Do it,' voxed Sarpedon.

Sergeant Graveus hefted his power axe and smashed the doors aside with a single swing. His squad and the few surviving Marines of Squad Kelvor were in first, followed by Luko and Dyon. Sarpedon's augmented eyes adjusted automatically to the dark as he followed Luko in, several squads of Soul Drinkers charging beside him, all prepared to meet the counter-charge of Tellos and his renegade Marines.

The warehouse contained a forest of rotting meat, hung from rows of meat hooks that ran the length of the single cavernous room. The stench was horrible and Sarpedon's many respiratory filters kicked in. The rows of meat slabs were strung in several layers, all the way up to the high ceiling of the warehouse, all of it long spoiled and foul.

Sarpedon moved forward, moving a side of meat away from him with one of his forelegs. It spilled writhing maggots onto the dirt floor as he passed.

No wonder Tellos had chosen to hide here. He had wanted to surround himself with death.

'Clear here,' voxed Graveus.

'Here too,' said Sergeant Dyon on the far side of the room.

'Clear,' said Luko, moving carefully between the slabs of meat beside Sarpedon. 'But they were here.'

Up ahead the slabs of meat had been cut down with chainswords and were lying in a trampled, maggoty layer on the floor. This was where Tellos had hidden out, making murderous forays out into Gravenhold, returning to kneel in prayer to the Blood God.

The Soul Drinkers reached the far end of the warehouse. The far wall had been torn through, leaving the warehouse open to the courtyard beyond which backed onto the River Graven itself.

'They came through here,' said Luko. 'Just a few minutes ago.'

'They didn't know we were coming,' said Sarpedon.

'How can we be sure?'

'Because Tellos would have come out to face me. No, they're heading for that.' Sarpedon pointed towards the twisting column of purple-black energy, fat with the power of the warp. Lightning was streaking down it, and all around blood was falling in a rain of crimson tears to mark the death of Gravenhold. 'Tellos has earned his way to the warp. That's where he's headed. That's what Karhedros promised him. Which means he has to get across the river.' Sarpedon turned to Luko. 'How is the vox?'

'It's getting worse. It's fine short-range but I don't think it'll reach much further.'

'Then try. Someone has to let Iktinos know they're coming.'

CHAPTER SIXTEEN

THE FIRST IMPERIAL forces into the north of Gravenhold were the Crimson Fists, crossing somewhere beneath the river in the tunnels and sewers that ran under the city. The Soul Drinker scout would pay for his poor discipline, just like all the Soul Drinkers would. Already some of the traitors's xenos allies had been spotted, creatures with shadow-black skin that could not hide from the eyes and bolters of the Crimson Fists.

Reinez was at the head of the Crimson Fists alongside Chaplain Inhuaca. The battle-brothers were quiet and tense, bolting down their anger with the discipline of a Space Marine. Reinez knew the feeling – their thoughts were turned towards revenge. In most soldiers, that would make them lax and jittery, their anger taking the edge off their skill in battle. But Space Marines were different. When the hatred grew, they fought better. When the pressure was on, they rose to meet it. It was why the Space Marines were the best soldiers in the galaxy, and why the Crimson Fists were amongst the foremost of the Adeptus Astartes. They had a lot to hate.

They had lost Captain Arca and Brother-Librarian Haxualpha, along with enough battle-brothers for the Second Company to bear the scars for a long time to come. They had lost the standard, sacred to the Chapter and to Rogal Dorn himself. They had been beaten and humiliated by traitors. They had taken out their anger on the Gravenholders and slave-warriors, and on the few aliens they had fought. But it wasn't enough to wipe away the shame. Only the death of the Soul Drinkers would do that.

And so the battle-brothers were silent as they advanced through the grim dark undercity, their hatred bubbling just under, waiting to be unleashed when the enemy dared to stand before them.

They hadn't been able to get any of the armour down the pit inside the ruin of the senate-house. The Razorbacks, Rhinos and Predators were back on the surface. But the Crimson Fists had Devastator squads whose firepower had been stymied in the close quarters of the chamber mercantile, firepower that Reinez was determined to see make a difference now. The Soul Drinkers weren't at full strength – they were scattered around the city, as battered as the Crimson Fists and thinking they were safe in their lair. The Fists were a rock-hard sledgehammer of disciplined, hate-filled men who would die rather than give up.

'We are close,' said Chaplain Inhuaca. He had come to the same conclusion as Reinez, the tunnels led towards the column of power in the north of the city.

Sarpedon was working some foul sorcery and even Reinez, who had no psychic ability, could feel the power in the air. It was sorcery that required great preparation and concentration, which meant that Sarpedon would be preoccupied and vulnerable. It would be his last mistake.

'Get the Devastators to the front,' said Reinez. 'Follow up with the assault units. Inhuaca, lead the charge.'

'It is an honour, commander. I take it you wish to face Sarpedon yourself?'

'If we have the choice,' replied Reinez. 'Otherwise, feel free to kill him. Just try to keep his head. I would hand it to Chapter Master Kantor myself.'

'Then if we have an agreement, I would face their Chaplain. The one who killed Arca.'

'Feel welcome to him.'

The tunnel opened up ahead. Darkness yawned. Reinez's vision cut through the gloom and picked out a high cavernous ceiling, a sky of stone. He glimpsed battlements, polished stone glinting in the half-light.

'For Dorn, brothers,' said Reinez to the Devastator units as they moved up ahead, their heavy weapons shouldered, ready to lay down the hail of fire that had been denied in the confines of the city.

'We've got targets,' voxed Brother Kroya, who had taken over Caltax's Devastator squad.

'Sergeants, take positions,' voxed Reinez. The sergeants of the second company sounded off, taking their positions in the wide tunnel – the big guns at the front, Inhuaca and the Assault Squads, then the Tactical Marines who would cover the assault with massed bolter fire.

'Good. Kroya, engage. Crimson Fists, for Dorn and your Emperor, flood this city in heretic blood.'

CAPTAIN CAISLENN-HAR rumbled and wheezed as his servo-assisted body waddled through the tight, dark corridors of the ship's astropathic suite. Nestled in the heart of the ship and heavily shielded against all psychic interference, the astropath quarters were avoided by most of the Emperor-fearing crew. Astropaths, though sanctioned by the Imperium and essential to its functioning, were still psykers and most of the crew did everything they could to stay away from them.

Caislenn-Har found the idea of being here at all to be distasteful. There was more than enough psychic madness happening on the planet below. But needs must, he thought, as he lumbered past the many devotional seals and inscribed prayers with which the ship's astropath had warded his quarters.

'Captain. It is a pleasure.' Astropath Torquen's voice was ice-cold and drained of emotion. It clearly wasn't a pleasure at all. Caislenn-Har imagined that nothing pleased Torquen very much.

The captain squeezed his bulk through the doorway and entered the astropath's inner sanctum. Torquen sat at a lectern that filled most of the tiny room, a spider-like servitor clinging to the chest of his robes and turning the pages of a massive prayerbook. Torquen's face was little more than a skin-covered skull with a lipless reptilian mouth and twin vertical slits instead of a nose. A strip of dark red material was tied around his eyes. Astropaths were almost all blind, a result, it was said, of the ritual on Terra itself where they were converted from powerful but uncontrolled psykers into powerful telepathic ducts. From the walls of the cell led cables and wires that plugged into Torquen's scalp like the strings of a puppet, monitoring his brainwaves. Torquen was the ship's main instrument of communication, because only telepathic messages could reach across the immense interstellar gulf.

'Torquen,' said Caislenn-Har. He was still wheezing, his body wasn't suited to walking around the ship. 'No doubt you are aware of our situation.'

'Is it as bad as it sounds?' The servitor turned another page and Torquen's fingers slid automatically over the writing. The writing was not raised; Torquen could feel the ink on the paper, reading the devotional texts as he had been trained to do, keeping his mind pure.

'Probably. All contact with the planet has been lost. We can't even see the city any more.'

'And then there is the… disturbance.' Torquen waved a hand idly, indicating the ribbon of black sorcery rippling through space, too close for comfort. 'I can feel it, though I do not know what to make of it.'

'Nor do we. Which is why I am here.'

'I wondered why you would visit me yourself. You do not trust this message to the ship's comms.'

'No.'

'Very well. Who is the target?'

Caislenn-Har shrugged. 'The nearest world with a sizeable population. Somewhere relatively important.'

'That is unusual. There is normally at least some particular individual or organisation to be contacted.'

'I doesn't matter who it's sent to. They'll hear it whoever receives it.'

Torquen paused. 'I see. And the contents?'

'I suppose I had better make this sound formal,' said Caislenn-Har. 'Please begin, "For the Attention of the Orders of the Emperor's Holy Inquisition…"'

'WE HAVE RECEIVED no orders to relinquish this position,' said Chaplain Iktinos. 'Therefore there will be no retreat. Is this understood?'

The Marines kneeling around Iktinos did not need to answer.

They were on the ground floor of the Carnax Bridge's northern gatehouse, surrounded by the magnificent finery of Gravenhold's elite. The ballroom that made up the lower floor was used to receive dignitaries who came through the city from the south-east gate and it was designed to impress. Immense chandeliers seemed too fat and heavy to hang from the ceiling, tapestries hung on the walls depicting Gravenholder nobility hunting through the forests around the city. Everything was gold and imported hardwood, a symbol of the decadence and decay eating away at the heart of the Imperium.

'Good.' Iktinos glanced up from the kneeling Marines, looking through the grand windows that looked down the elegant iron span of the Carnax Bridge. There were Soul Drinkers on the bridge, and Iktinos could see with one look that they weren't on his side. Their armour was filthy and dented, their helmets gone and their faces wild-eyed. Most of them carried chainswords thick with clotted blood.

'Take your positions. Make a firing line. Steel your souls.' Iktinos drew his sacred crozius arcanum as the Marines he led formed a line of bolters at the windows. The crozius was a Chaplain's badge of office and a weapon in its own right, surrounded by a crackling power field that would shear through armour.

Iktinos was a Chaplain, a guardian of the Chapter's collective soul. He was just beginning to understand the place of the Soul Drinkers in the Emperor's plan, a grand design for Mankind that needed the Soul Drinkers to be free of the Imperium before they could play their part. Iktinos would lead them in that plan, but first he had to survive.

'…aplain… in your direction, be ready to…' Sarpedon's voice crackled over the vox, distorted by howling static.

Iktinos switched it off. This was his fight, these were his Marines. They would die for him, they would die for the Emperor's plan.

'In range,' said Brother Kekrops, squinting down the length of his boltgun.

'Hold.'

'Counting… thirty-two.'

'Then they outnumber us. Good. Where will your soul be thrice-forged like steel?'

'In battle,' replied Kekrops levelly. 'Where the fires are the cold flames of hell.'

'When will our work be done?'

'Not until the end of time,' said Brother Octetes, who knelt in the firing line with his meltagun ready to fire. 'Not until the Emperor is with us again and all the worlds are one.'

'How will the enemy be known?'

'By their works,' replied Brother Apollonius, who was crouched behind the firing line with his chainsword drawn. 'For when the End Times come, they shall line up against the Emperor and beg us for death.'

'Good. Open fire.'

The windows of the ballroom shattered and the Carnax Bridge was a rushing river of hot shrapnel, sheeting into the renegade Marines. Bolter shells spanged around the supports of the bridge, criss-crossing the killing zone with lethal ricochets.

But it wasn't enough. The enemy were Soul Drinkers, driven mad by horrors most could only guess at. It took more than bolter fire, more than discipline.

Iktinos saw Tellos throwing one of his own Marines aside, trampling another underfoot to close with Iktinos's Marines. Bolter shells passed through Tellos's pallid, gelatinous flesh, punching through his horribly exaggerated muscles without slowing him down. His hands were rusted, gore-crusted chainblades, his face an unrecognisable mask of scars and hatred.

This was the reckoning. Two groups of Soul Drinkers, both forged on Stratix Luminae. One, Iktinos's men, had been enlightened, realising a bond that would take them to the ends of the galaxy doing the Emperor's will. The others, under Tellos, had been lost and damned, drowned in violence until their wills were not their own.

Two men. One enlightened, one insane. It was good that it had come to this, thought Iktinos. This battle would have been fought out eventually anyway.

Tellos dived into the firing line first, his fellow renegades on his heels.

Brother Octetes got one blast off from his meltagun, vaporising the arm of a renegade before Tellos was on him. The chainswords went through Octetes's torso as if Octetes's armour wasn't there, spearing out through his back. Tellos did little more than shrug and Octetes was sheared in two, gore showering everywhere, Tellos revelling in the gout of blood. He flung the two halves of Octetes aside and strode further, swiping off Brother

Thieln's arm even as Thieln pumped a volley of bolter shells into him.

The other renegades were into the ballroom and it was a murderous close-quarters melee where neither side was willing to die easily. Iktinos felt almost detached from his body as he raised his crozius and charged in. It was as if he was not himself any more but a part of a greater plan. He was a messenger, a symbol, a pawn of the Emperor himself.

The eagle-headed crozius crashed into the torso of a renegade, crunching through armour and the Marine's inner chestplate of fused ribs. A bolt pistol shot thunked into Iktinos's shoulder pad but the impact barely registered with him. He could feel forces controlling him. He could feel the words of Daenyathos welling up from his memory, the patterns of the *Catechisms Martial* fitting the movements of his limbs that sent the crozius shattering the skull of the renegade at his feet and hacking down through the arm of another.

This was the way it would be in the End Times. Brother against brother, and yet no hatred. Just a total sense of purpose, a conviction that Iktinos was playing a part in a grand drama that would always end in victory, had ended, was ending, always.

Brother Apollonius was duelling with Tellos, giving ground as Tellos's chainblades lashed against his own sword time and time again. Sparks were flying. Iktinos watched them dispassionately, noting the bestial strength that forced Tellos's blade through Apollonius's chainsword, the metal teeth that flew from the shattered blade like shrapnel, the way Tellos simply stamped down on Apollonius's leg and the ugly angle of his leg as it snapped.

Tellos didn't bother to kill Apollonius. He just stepped over him, and turned to Iktinos.

Chaplain Iktinos knew that this fight was written already. It was the will of the Emperor that he bring his crozius down onto Tellos, carving down in a great glittering arc that would shear him lengthways in two with such ferocity that even Tellos's mutated flesh could not save him. Tellos's death had always been there, in the northern gatehouse of the Carnax Bridge, replaying over and over again for countless eternities, waiting for Iktinos to take the stage and place himself in the role of the Emperor's servant.

The crozius rose, sparks pouring from its power field. Iktinos put his whole weight behind the downstroke, feeling the strength of the Emperor himself sending the crozius down into Tellos's mutated body.

Tellos caught the crozius in the crook of his crossed chainblades. Iktinos's blow stopped jarringly, sparks cascading off the power field.

Suddenly Iktinos was back in his body, not watching the combat from afar but face-to-face with Tellos, feeling his arm forced back by Tellos's obscene strength, tasting the blood in the air, ears full of gunfire and screams and the whirring of the blades that were about to eviscerate him.

Tellos swung around, forced Iktinos's crozius arm down. He hooked an elbow over Iktinos's head, forcing it down as he brought his armoured knee up into Iktinos's faceplate with shuddering force.

Iktinos reeled back, his senses swimming. Solid red pain flooded his mind.

Tellos crossed his blades and this time closed them like pincers around Iktinos's arm. With a twist he lifted Iktinos clean into the air and threw him with such force that he smashed through what remained of the window frames and flew out onto the blood-slicked surface of the Carnax Bridge.

Iktinos's crozius arm was broken before he landed, the bones snapped in a dozen places by the force of Tellos's grip. But he could use his other hand just fine, take up the fallen crozius, leap back into the fray and deliver the Emperor's justice to the mutant and traitor who had dared kill his battle-brothers.

Tellos's boot stamped down on Iktinos's good hand, splitting the ceramite of his gauntlet. Red gunshots of pain were broken fingers.

Tellos looked down at the stricken Chaplain, his face silhouetted against the purple glow from the warp portal in the city behind him. Iktinos could just see the eyes, two red black-red pools slitted with hatred.

'You didn't think you were the one, did you?' said Tellos. 'The one to finish what Daenyathos started?'

Iktinos struggled. Tellos had him pinned down and he was unarmed. This traitor, this monster, had him at its mercy.

'How you cling to your faith,' continued Tellos. His voice was thick and dark as blood. 'And yet you say you are free. Did you think you would fight to the end of time, Iktinos? Did you think your acolytes here would be there at the Emperor's side? What do you think He wanted for Mankind? He wanted freedom. Only one of us here is free, and it's not you.'

Iktinos had a soul strong enough to go through hell and still let him counsel to the spirits of his battle-brother. But even so his blood ran cold. Tellos was not just a madman. He could see right through Iktinos, through the skull-wrought faceplate of his helmet and right into his soul.

'Tellos,' gasped Iktinos through the pain and shock. 'What did you become?'

Tellos smiled, actually smiled, the mutated flesh of his face opening up into a wide rictus like a shark. He raised his chainblades, poising one over Iktinos's throat and the other over his heart. 'Blood for the Blood God, Chaplain. That's all there is.'

'Tellos!' yelled a voice. Tellos looked up from his butchery at someone further down the bridge.

Iktinos twisted his head until he could see down the bridge. There, standing in the middle of Carnax Bridge, completely alone, was Sarpedon.

'XENOS FILTH!' BELLOWED Reinez. 'Die! For the Imperium and the divine right of Man! Die!'

The palace gardens were a battlefield. Eldar warriors streamed from the doors to be cut down or blown apart by missile launchers and heavy bolters. Crimson Fists fell to energy weapons on the battlements or horrible skinless beasts that coalesced from the shadows to drag them down with teeth and claws. Jetbikes banked at insane speeds, their riders lashing out with energy blades at Marines only to be snatched off their mounts by well-placed bolter shots.

Chaplain Inhuaca led the Assault Squads in a charge that had left a third of their number wounded or dead before smashing into the main body of eldar warriors. Chainblades carved through exotic armour and sheared through the barrels of crystalline rifles in a mass swirling melee against the gates of the palace. The eldar, cheating xenos though they were, could not stand up to Inhuaca's charge and were forced across the bridge leading to the palace's quicksilver moat. With their backs to the wall the eldar were dying in prodigious numbers as the rest of the Fists followed up, swapping fire with the eldar on the battlements, supporting Inhuaca's assault as they tried to crush the defenders and breach the gates themselves. The moat was choked with eldar bodies and some of the Assault Marines were walking across the bodies to get to grips with the enemy.

It was magnificent. It was beautiful. Those Fists who died would be remembered, and it was an honour that their last memories should be of a true honest battle against the foes of the Emperor.

No more lies, promised Reinez to himself as he ran head down behind the shattered walls and strange stone trees of the palace gardens, crystal shards slitting the air around him. No more betrayals. No more trickery. This was the Crimson Fists' time, a time full of nothing but battle. It was the way of the Adeptus Astartes, force would prevail where cunning did not.

The Space Marines of the Imperium did not misdirect their enemies or weave them into plots full of betrayal and deceit. They destroyed them, absolutely. It was the way of Rogal Dorn. It was the way of the Crimson Fists.

Reinez led the Tactical Squads forward towards the gates, bolter fire streaking up at the battlements, eldar scurrying for cover or tumbling off the wall to land crunchingly far below. Shadow-skinned eldar ducked out of the darkness to pick off Marines with fire from their crystalline pistols or impale them on wicked curved blades, only to be lit up by strobing gunfire and smashed aside by bolter impacts. More eldar, close combat specialists who wore next to no armour but moved with astonishing speed and grace, tried to join the warriors at the gate but Reinez bellowed the order to fire. Fifty bolters shredded the eldar, swatting them aside and spattering the obsidian walls of the palace with their blood.

Still moving, the Crimson Fists turned the palace gardens into a brutal crossfire. Eldar reinforcements lay dead, delicate bodies burst open by bolter fire. Jetbikes burned. Power armour turned aside crystal shards fired by eldar snipers from the palace windows, and the Marine's reply was heavy weapons fire. A plasma cannon blast filled the chamber beyond one firing slit with superheated plasma, exploding outwards in a plume of yellow fire.

Reinez led the Marines over the last few metres of palace gardens and joined Inhuaca at the gate. The Chaplain's crozius arcanum smoked as its power field burned away the blood that encrusted it. The eldar warriors were making a last stand behind one of the wall buttresses, swapping pistol fire with the Assault Marines.

'Squad Zavier! Squad Padros!' yelled Reinez. 'Flank those groxfraggers!'

Two Tactical squads ran onto the far side of the moat and, with the Assault Marines, caught the eldar in a savage crossfire. Eldar bodies were slammed against the wall by the force of the gunfire as the Assault Marines strode in to finish off the survivors. Assault-Captain Arca had been beloved of the Chapter, and the Assault Marines had revenge on their minds.

Sarpedon was hiding behind xenos, letting them die to keep the Fists away from him. A coward and a witch, a traitor and a disgrace to the blood of Dorn. All the eldar filth in the galaxy wouldn't save him now.

'Safest place in this damn city,' said Reinez to the Chaplain.

'Agreed. At last we know where our enemies are.'

'Ready?'

The Chaplain inclined his head. 'Always.'

'Devastators! Get this door down!'

The Devastators had been waiting for the order. A trio of krak anti-armour missiles streaked up into the door, reducing it to splinters of charred hardwood. The golden portcullis beyond barely lasted that long as Reinez smashed the bars aside with a swing of his thunder hammer.

Reinez and Inhuaca charged into a storm of crystal gunfire that filled the courtyard. Reinez's armour had been forged by the finest Chapter artificers to have survived Rynn's World and the crystal shattered against it. Some splinters forced their way into his flesh but he had suffered infinitely worse and he strode through the storm, the Crimson Fists following in his wake. The courtyard was bounded by walls on the battlements of which were the warriors who had fallen back from the outer walls, more of them died to bolter fire and missile blasts as the Crimson Fists made rapid work of the courtyard.

The inner doors opened and the eldar that charged out were heavily-armoured, wielding halberds with powered blades that sliced through the armour of the first Crimson Fists to face them. Reinez was in the front rank and caught a blade on the haft of his thunder hammer, feeling strength he had thought beyond the eldar forcing the blade closer to his face. He dropped back a step, pivoted on one heel and brought the hammer smashing up into the face of the eldar – he saw the eldar's facemask, featureless except for its shining green eyepieces, crumple as the hammer's head shattered the side of its helmet and he threw the eldar aside.

Xenos elites. He had fought their kind before, Aspect Warriors who embodied one particular facet of the eldar way of war. These were different, stronger and more heavily armoured. Reinez swept out again, found his thunder hammer parried and a volley of laser stings slicing into his chest armour from a helmet-mounted projector. A white flash of pain stabbed into the wound but Reinez choked it back, kicking out and smashing the knee of the warrior who had stung him. He brought his hammer up and smacked the pommel of the handle into the eldar's forehead, knocking it to the ground. He swung the hammer again at the eldar's head, presented to him like a target in the Chapter training rooms. The eldar was decapitated neatly, another's arm being broken by the hammer's upswing.

There weren't enough of them. They were up against the whole Second Company of the Crimson Fists, and the eldar were forced back into the palace itself.

'Take them!' shouted Reinez to Chaplain Inhuaca and led the way past the battling eldar into the palace. The eldar could evidently see well in the dark but a Space Marine's augmentations lent him even keener sight, cutting through the gloom.

He wasn't here to kill all the xenos. That could wait. He was after Sarpedon.

The palace was a maze. The dynasty that had built it had evidently been unbalanced because dead ends and insane proportions were everywhere, staircases that soared into nowhere and corridors that ended in sheer dark pits.

Reinez led half of the Marines down into the palace, leaving the rest with Inhuaca to keep the eldar from pursuing them. His instincts took him downwards, down tight twisting stairways and through ambushes of eldar warriors. The eldar had not been expecting them and the defence was piecemeal and desultory, gaggles of them ready to die under Reinez's hammer and the bolters of his battle-brothers. The momentum never let up, Reinez knowing that Sarpedon's best chance lay in sending enough troops out to swamp the Crimson Fists while the eldar and Soul Drinkers organised a proper defence.

Down, further. Deformed eldar torturers led packs of fleshy, mutated creatures that shambled forwards through the gunfire, and the Marines had to take them apart with bolter stocks and combat knives. Brother Arroyox was lost, dragged down by the eldar's creations. Reinez shattered the torturer's torso with his hammer and led the way on, saying a silent prayer for Arroyox's soul.

The palace dimensions grew greater, as if a race of giants had built it. Soaring vaults of obsidian. Sweating greenstone walls that reeked of brine, galleries of faceless statues. The eldar were few down here, and Reinez knew they weren't just hiding, even he could feel the air of reverence in the lower levels. He was on sacred ground where few eldar were permitted, and so few had been down there to face the Crimson Fists when they attacked.

He passed the cells of the torturers, where the remains of Guardsmen and Gravenholders lay dissected on tables of bloodstained onyx. Skins were pinned up on the walls. One chamber held two bodies, evidently Guardsmen stripped naked and chained to the floor. It looked like they had been pumped full of combat stimulants and forced to fight one another with bare hands, dying horribly for the entertainment of whoever led the xenos.

Reinez knew that Sarpedon had fallen far. He was only just now understanding exactly how far. He was a heretic mutant who delighted in cruelty, one who had become like the decadent alien in the depths of his debauchery. The annals of the Crimson Fists would record with pride the purification of Dorn's blood that would be achieved when Reinez killed him.

The corridors and anterooms opened up into an immense vaulted reception chamber. A pair of vast studded doors dominated one wall, where the palace opened up into a lower cavern. A second pair of doors, smaller and of veined green stone, were set into the opposite wall. Though not a psyker, Reinez could still feel the power behind them, the aching swell of dark magic billowing up from the depths of some dark soul.

'There,' he said. 'Meltagun.'

Brother Olcama ran forward with his meltagun as the rest of the squad took their places by the doors, ready to sweep into the room and pump bolter fire into whatever they saw. Reinez was ready to charge past them, knowing that only a witch, a debased psyker like Sarpedon, could be beyond there.

Olcama opened fire. White-hot gobs of molten stone spattered as the meltagun's beam bored through the stone. The walls creaked. The door shuddered as the heat forced its molecules apart and then, with a sound like a caged thunderclap it burst open.

Shards of razor-sharp stone span everywhere. Reinez was prepared for that. He was not prepared for the hurricane of magical energies that ripped out, suddenly uncontained. Brother Olcama was picked up and thrown into the huge far doors, plunging through them even as the shockwave ripped them off their hinges and cast them into the vast dark cavern beyond. The Crimson Fists were lifted off their feet and thrown backwards by swirling tendrils of purple-black magic. Their fingers scrabbled for purchase on the smooth stone floor. Reinez was picked up and thrown, raging his frustration. He hefted his thunder hammer and brought it down into the floor, gouging the head deep into the stone. It drew a deep molten furrow as he was flung back but the hammer braked him and he held on, feet dangling as if hanging, staring into the maelstrom of sorcery beyond the door.

There was something in there. Someone. Kneeling as if in prayer in the eye of the storm, surrounded by the energies of the warp portal.

Reinez dug his feet into the floor and hauled himself towards the door, using the hammer to lever himself along. He couldn't see if any other Fists were with him. He couldn't worry about that now. He was the only one who could do it, they had all known that.

Another step. Another metre. It was pure hate keeping him going. Everything he had ever learned, every prayer of rage, every moment of battle, it all fuelled the hate.

He reached the threshold and pushed himself through the door. The paint was flaking off the ceramite of his armour, the clenched fist symbol on his shoulder pad peeling away. It felt like the skin of his face was going with it. With a final effort, he pushed himself through the storm of magic and into the eye of the cyclone.

The figure looked around. It was a tall eldar, with a drawn, pallid, ageless face, pure black pupils. It was bald and its scalp was covered in intricate black tattoos. Its elegant purple armour was hinged like the carapace of an insect, drawn into blade-sharp curves and crescents. It knelt by the edge of a pit that seemed to lead through the floor and straight into an insane galaxy of light-filled nebulae and shifting formless stars. Reinez knew instinctively that the eldar had created a door to the warp, the dimension of madness and evil where the dark powers lay.

Eldar and Chaos. They had been tearing Gravenhold apart since before the Crimson Fists had arrived. Now here was the heart of it, far beneath the city.

Several more eldar stood, motionless and blank-eyed, around the edge of the portal. They were evidently the same kind of torturers that Reinez had encountered on his way down, their skin cut and stitched as if they had experimented on themselves. Black power flickered from their staring eyes. They had given their souls to keep the portal open.

The tall eldar rose to its feet, taking up the long halberd that had lain on the floor in front of it.

'Lord Sarpedon,' it said in a deep and slightly accented voice, its Imperial Gothic crisp and prayer-house perfect. 'I see you have seen the truth at last. I have been ready to receive you a second time, but I know you will not now be so accepting of my hospitality. For your betrayal, you may have the honour of fighting Prince Karhedros, and of being offered to She-Who-Thirsts in defeat.'

Reinez stepped forward, gripping his thunder hammer in both hands. 'Sarpedon is a heretic and a traitor to the blood of Rogal Dorn,' he snarled. 'A creature should know who kills it. I am Commander Reinez of the Crimson Fists, scion of Rynn's World, a son of Rogal Dorn, servant of the right hand of the Emperor.'

The eldar looked Reinez up and down, noticing his normal legs and the deep blue of his armour. 'My apologies,' it said slickly. 'You all look alike to me.'

There was nothing left but the hatred. The xenos, the traitor, the heretic, all wrapped up into one smirking enemy. Reinez couldn't have held back if he had wanted to.

The eldar was fast, fast enough to turn away Reinez's first blow and spin away from the second, the silvered haft of the halberd deflecting the head of the hammer with its crackling power field. Reinez powered forward, swinging wildly, frustrated with every step by the eldar who could see each move before Reinez made it, bringing the halberd around in silver arcs that threatened to slice off Reinez's head.

Strength wouldn't work. This alien was the very soul of deceit, and its feints and parries would bring Reinez down. But it didn't matter. This was the only victory to be had on Entymion IV, and Reinez's duty to the Emperor and the Imperium of Man demanded he fight for it.

'Your etiquette demands that you know who kills you,' the eldar was saying. 'Very well. I am Pirate King Karhedros, lord of the new Commorragh, favoured of She-Who-Thirsts, the Void Serpent, the End of Worlds, Archon of the Kabal of the Burning Scale, and future lord of the planet on which you stand.' Karhedros swept out a leg and knocked Reinez down onto one knee. The Space Marine barely kept the halberd's crescent-bladed head from slicing into his throat, turning it aside with one armoured forearm. 'When your nightmares bleed into the warp, they will be of me. When your dead souls are sucked into oblivion, they will witness me in my glory as they are consumed. I am the future of the eldar race, the culmination of a thousand fates.' Another thrust and the halberd cut through Reinez's chest armour, plunging deep through ceramite and bone, slitting through one of his lungs. 'I am a god born before you, one with the warp, sired by She-Who-Thirsts to herald the rebirth of my race in the true kingdom of the warp.'

Reinez bellowed and swung out, the hammer's head battering Karhedros back in a cascade of sparks. Enough of the force had got through Karhedros's guard to leave his armour split and blistered down one side.

Reinez breathed out a mist of blood as his lung filled up. He felt his artificial third lung taking the strain. Many more cuts like that and it would be over. He didn't let up, forcing the eldar back around the edge of the portal, towards where one of the torturers stood catatonic.

Reinez barrelled forward, knowing that his greater strength and momentum was his only advantage. He crashed into Karhedros, trying to force him back to the edge of the portal. Karhedros stepped aside and Reinez stumbled, letting his hammer swing out for balance.

Karhedros darted to one side and blocked the swing of the hammer just as it was about to knock the head off the torturer.

Reinez got his balance back and grinned savagely. The eldar had to keep the torturers alive. That was why he was in the portal room at all, to make sure they remained until the portal swallowed up the planet.

Now he knew what Karhedros feared.

The eldar's eyes widened with shock as Reinez swung again, this time low, the hammer catching the torturer full in the midriff and catapulting it far across the portal to fall, broken and showering gore, into the bottomless pit of the warp.

This time Karhedros came back in a frenzy. It was not about affirming superiority over the crude, ignorant human any more. It was about the survival of his ascension. The two warriors fought savagely, sparks flying, cutting and bludgeoning until blood spattered from a dozen wounds each. Karhedros ducked and backflipped, Reinez smashed huge holes in the floor so the shockwave battered Karhedros further.

Reinez knocked another torturer into the portal, Karhedros unable to protect himself and the vessels of his sorcery at the same time. An edge of desperation entered the eldar's fighting style: he was trying to hack deep gouges into Reinez, cut off his arms, stab him through the heart. But it wouldn't work. Reinez, as a Space Marine, was the embodiment of raw force focused for victory. Karhedros had been trained to fight with elegance and finesse. Reinez, ducking a swing of the halberd, came up inside Karhedros's guard and headbutted him, following up by ramming the pommel of the hammer's haft into Karhedros's abdomen. Karhedros stumbled back, wide open for just a split second.

Karhedros expected the hammer strike to the head. Reinez didn't oblige. He charged forward again, reaching round with his hammer hand to pin Karhedros's arm against his side. With his free hand he grabbed the eldar's throat and lifted him up off the ground.

Karhedros struggled. The pirate king was reduced to a helpless xenos, just another foe of Mankind staring into the truth of the Emperor's Justice.

'I was hoping to find Sarpedon here,' said Reinez through a mouth of broken teeth. 'But an enemy is an enemy.'

He pulled back his arm and threw Karhedros into the air with all the strength of his enhanced muscles. As the eldar fell back down he drew back the hammer and swung double-handed. The hammer slammed into Karhedros's midriff as he fell and Reinez smacked him halfway across the room, Karhedros yelling a final curse in the tongue of the eldar as he tumbled in a slow arc into the portal.

Reinez watched the eldar fall. He was still alive when he passed from realspace into the pure madness of the warp. He saw shadows coalescing from the shimmering nebulae and swarm towards the eldar, dark spectral hands reaching out, shadowy maws full of teeth gnawing at Karhedros's body.

Reinez was sure he heard the creature scream as it was devoured. The warp was brimming with mindless, hungry predators and without his world, without the blessing of his god, the Pirate King Karhedros was just so much prey.

Reinez watched until there was nothing left of Karhedros, just a swirling pit of darkness. It took several minutes. Then, Reinez walked around the portal and threw in the remaining few torturers. As the last one followed Karhedros into the warp the whole room shook and the walls of swirling dark energy were suddenly pale as death, shot through with white lightning. Reinez stepped back sharply as the edges of the portal began to crack and crumble.

Reinez placed a hand experimentally into the swirling walls of the cyclone. Most of the power was gone. With the spell broken, the vortex of energy was about to collapse – it meant he could get out, but it also meant there might not be much of a city left to escape to very soon.

He holstered his thunder hammer and, head down, ran back through the wall of power to join his battle-brothers.

The battle for Gravenhold was over. Now all that remained was to escape.

CHAPTER SEVEN

CHAPTER SEVENTEEN

TELLOS KICKED IKTINOS aside, satisfied that the Chaplain was no longer a threat, and walked towards Sarpedon.

Sarpedon was alone on the bridge. The rest of his Soul Drinkers were on the south shore, watching the standoff. Tellos raised a chainblade and the sounds of conflict behind him dimmed as the Soul Drinkers loyal to him backed off from Iktinos's Marines.

The sounds of battle elsewhere in the city were faint against the wind and the dull rush of the River Graven below. Otherwise, there was nothing.

Sarpedon walked forward slowly. His force staff was slung at his back and his bolter was holstered. Tellos held his chainblades low, the closest thing he could do to disarm.

'Tellos,' said Sarpedon. 'We thought we had lost you.'

'And you are here to see if you really had?' Tellos had mutated further since Sarpedon had seen him last, his musculature swelling to grotesque proportions, his face was obscured by his lank hair and deformed flesh but there was still the hint of a grim smile there. 'How noble. Daenyathos would approve. Risk your battle-brothers to placate your guilt. Wage war to prove you did everything you could. You are not so different from the old Chapter, Sarpedon. Just killing the same enemies in a different order.'

'And you, Tellos? What do you stand for now?'

'The same thing you claim to fight for. I am free.' Tellos held his arms wide, his still-churning chainblades spraying clots of congealed blood. 'Once you realise that we are all blood, just blood waiting to be spilt, then you really know what freedom is. We are free of honour and duty. We can do as we please, and it pleases us to kill.'

'I know I lost you at Stratix Luminae. I let you go too far. If it is me you hate, Tellos, remember what your battle-brothers fought for. They would have died for you. If there was a way we could have rescued you, they would have defied my every order to get you back.'

'You think this is as simple as revenge? I did not become what I am because I was betrayed. God of Blood, Sarpedon, if you had not left us there we would not have seen the way! We cut through thousands of those creatures to get out. All that blood, all that death. We heard a voice from the warp, calling us. That was when we understood. Everything is blood, Sarpedon. Ourselves, the enemy, you, me, the earth, the stars. And when you realise everything is blood, you know that blood only flows one way. I have seen how it will end. How everything will end. It is blood and death and madness. We are only playing our part. Soon the whole galaxy will look like this city.'

Sarpedon walked a few paces further, his weapons still holstered. 'I know that Chaos came to you, Tellos. We captured Brother Lothas, he said the same things. The Blood God has touched your mind. But Chaos is a lie! You know that, you fought it often enough! You took a vow with the rest of us that Chaos would be the enemy. It is not too late. We can cure your mutations now. And we can cure your mind. It will not be easy, but we can bring you back.'

Tellos shook his head. Droplets of blood sprinkled from his lank hair. 'Is that why you are here? To bring me back? You left me and my brothers to die, and the rest of the Chapter knows it. Are you sure you're not just making sure they know what a fine leader you are?'

'If the Chapter didn't want me they would let me know soon enough.'

'Oh, that they will. Can't you see the cracks already? I knew they were there since before the excommunication. I was the first. My men followed me instead of you, even when I spoke the words of the Blood God. I have seen how this Chapter ends, too, and it's the same blood and chaos that rules everywhere else. You can't control the Soul Drinkers forever, Sarpedon. You can't control them now. Now they're not the lapdogs of the Imperium they need something to keep them fighting and every one of them is searching for something different. Try them. Ask them. You'll have to kill them all, one by one. And then Chaos will have won. It's already happened, you are just too blind to see it.'

'Perhaps you are right,' said Sarpedon. 'But that's the difference between you and me. You were always eager to fight because you knew you would win. Do you remember how you once were? A hero for the future. And you knew it. But now you fear that we might fail, you have given yourself over to the dark gods. I don't care if failure is inevitable, Tellos. I never did. Our purpose is to fight on against the enemies of the Emperor because the fight itself is justification enough. I can show you. We all can. Do not just give in.'

'I saw the end of the galaxy,' said Tellos, almost sadly. 'All my brothers did. We saw it written in the blood of our enemies. We are on the winning side now. That is all that matters. Everything else is just so much dust. Cling to your honour when Chaos rules everything because that is all you will have.'

'Then if you really are lost, Tellos, there is only one way this can end.'

'Ha! Then you see. Everything ends in blood. You will learn, one day.'

Sarpedon took the force staff down off his back, leaving his bolter. With a mental command he willed its force circuit into life, the circuit spiralling round the inside of his armour to channel his psychic power into the nalwood staff. 'For the Emperor, Tellos.'

'Blood for the Blood God, Sarpedon.'

IKTINOS PULLED HIMSELF over onto his front. The painkillers dispensed by his armour were cutting through the fog of agony but he could still barely move. He saw Sarpedon and Tellos charge at the same time, the two mutants slamming into one another. Flashes of lightning lit up the ironwork of the Carnax Bridge as Sarpedon's force staff smashed against Tellos's blades. Behind Iktinos, his Marines and those renegades who had followed Tellos watched the duel.

Iktinos was the one who would have to lead the Chapter towards its role in the Emperor's grand plan. But it was Sarpedon who would have to fight the battle for the Chapter's soul.

'He was too far gone,' said Librarian Tyrendian. Beside him on the edge of the River Graven stood Graevus and Salk. 'We should never have come here. Let the Imperium deal with him.'

'Your commander is risking his life,' snapped Graevus. 'Tellos was our responsibility.'

'You think so? Look at the Imperial forces here. They couldn't defend a single street of this city as they had to. We could have just flown the *Brokenback* in and blasted this city off the face of the planet. There would be precious little to stop us. Wipe out Tellos, his renegades, the aliens, everything.'

'Tellos fought his way off Stratix Luminae without us, Tyrendian. It would take more than that to kill him. This is the only way.'

'I hope you're right, Graevus.'

'He is,' said Salk.

Luko crouched down in the burned-out southern gatehouse, watching through an empty window frame as the fight unfolded. He saw Sarpedon duck a chainblade, counter with a thrust to the chest. The head of the force staff punched into Tellos's chest but Tellos just swivelled out of the way, the staff passing through his gelatinous flesh.

Luko's muscles twitched in time to Sarpedon's attacks and parries. Luko wanted to be out there, fighting with him, but he knew that this was not just another fight against another enemy. Sarpedon took

Tellos's fall personally. He had to make amends personally, too.

He had to win. It had to be over, cleanly and for all. Otherwise Luko knew that this scene would repeated over and over again until Sarpedon was defeated or the Chapter was dead.

'Kill him, Sarpedon,' whispered Luko to himself as Tellos struck back, stamping down on Sarpedon's single bionic foreleg and shattering it in a shower of sparks. 'For all our sakes, make it final.'

'Let me see.' Eumenes lay down in the smouldering rubble of the docks alongside scout-sniper Raek. Beside him lay Scamander, still cold to the touch but breathing and occasionally conscious. Nisryus kneeled nearby, keeping watch.

Raek handed his rifle scope to Eumenes. From where they were, in the bloodstained ruins of Gravenhold's river docks amid the remains of a terrible struggle, the combat was just visible down the river as a series of flashes as Sarpedon's force staff hit home.

Eumenes peered through the scope and saw Tellos's hugely overdeveloped back, the cords of muscle writhing beneath his pallid skin as he swung a blade that slammed against Sarpedon's guard and knocked him against the railing of the bridge. Sarpedon was fast and strong but Tellos was nothing but raw power. The Hell was no use, Tellos was too far gone to be distracted by fear.

Eumenes looked up from the scope at Nisryus, kneeling with his back to the rest of the scouts. 'Nisryus. Can you tell who will win?'

Nisryus looked round. 'No. They must be too far away.'

Eumenes looked back at the fight. Sarpedon was on the defensive, his back legs bowing under the pressure as he leaned out of the range of Tellos's blades. Tellos took advantage and pressed home, crossed blades pushing down on the force staff. Sarpedon's back was against the railing.

Sarpedon turned the force staff and tried to prise Tellos's blades apart. The blades snapped apart suddenly and sliced down through the railings on either side of Sarpedon.

Sarpedon reached out and got his arm around the back of Tellos's neck as he fell backwards, and the two of them pitched over the side of the Caltax Bridge into the River Graven.

SARPEDON AND TELLOS hit the river bed still locked together. Sarpedon tried to hold on, hoping for some advantage, any advantage that would let him get in the one single telling blow to finally drop Tellos. The foul waters swirled around him, filling his mouth and nose with the stench of filth and blood. Tellos writhed to get out of his grip, to open up enough space for his chainblades to cut Sarpedon apart.

Tellos reached back and slammed an elbow into Sarpedon's chest. The two Marines flew away from each other, almost lost in the underwater gloom. Tellos twisted in the water and his feet connected with the bridge support, stopping him and bringing him round to face his opponent.

Sarpedon reached down with his legs and his talons found the rockcrete bed of the river. The force of the blow had knocked most of the air out of his lungs and he would have to strike now or be forced to surface for air. That would leave him open, blind and vulnerable.

There would be nothing he could do against an attack from below as he tried to gulp down breath.

There was one chance. Tellos probably knew it, too. Whatever the Blood God had shown him, it had purported to be a vision of the future. No doubt Tellos thought he knew how this fight would end. Sarpedon would have to prove him wrong.

Sarpedon dug his talons into the rockrete and pushed himself forward. Forced into slow motion by the rushing water, the two prepared to clash. Sarpedon took his force staff in both hands, ready to stab it like a spear. Tellos was braced against the bridge support, both chainblades up, ready to impale Sarpedon with the force of his own momentum.

Sarpedon sped up. The water rushed in his face, bodies and chunks of debris rushing past. He could see the red hate in Tellos's eyes, the mark of Khorne the Blood God, most bestial of the Chaos Powers.

He tensed for the strike. He could see Tellos's blades churning the blood-laden water pink, could almost feel them carving through his armour and into his body.

With all his strength, Sarpedon struck.

He was a fraction too high for Tellos's blades, which passed under his body and finished destroying his bionic leg. The force staff passed over Tellos's shoulder, spearing right past him into the bridge support beyond.

Sarpedon's force circuit burst white-hot as his psychic strength was channelled through the staff into the support. All his anger, all his frustration, everything he had ever felt was poured into that one strike.

The iron and rockcrete of the support base shattered. The weight of the support thudded down into the river bed and toppled forward towards the two Marines.

Sarpedon dug his talons into the rockcrete again and forced his seven remaining legs to pull him back from the support. But Tellos's body, bloated with muscles, was too unwieldy to get out of the way. He reached out for Sarpedon, trying to grab a leg and drag him back to share his fate, but Sarpedon's mutant body was just that split second too quick.

Tellos disappeared beneath a massive dark cloud of rubble and debris as first the support column, then the Carnax Bridge itself, came down on top of him.

APOTHECARY PALLAS SAW the bridge coming down from the south shore, just beside the gate house, The whole central section sagged and the suspension wires supporting it snapped like a volley of gunshots. The whole section tipped and pitched into the sea, kicking up a huge plume of dust and water as it crashed into the river bed.

For a moment there was relative quiet. Then Pallas heard something moving in the water just below him. He looked down over the edge of the sheer channel and saw an arachnoid leg reach out of the water and spear a talon into the surface of the rockcrete. A hand followed, then another leg, and Sarpedon was pulling himself out of the water, scaling the wall of the channel.

Pallas reached down and grabbed Sarpedon's hand, hauling him up onto the bank.

'Thank you, Brother Pallas,' said Sarpedon, breathing heavily.

'Are you hurt?'

'Yes. But nothing that won't heal. And I'll need another leg.' He indicated the remains of his bionic foreleg, now a chewed-up mess. Pallas looked Sarpedon up and down – there were chainblade scars all over his armour, a massive dent in his chestplate and a dozen minor wounds where Tellos's attacks had got through his ceramite. His arachnoid legs were bleeding in a dozen different places. But a Space Marine could survive worse.

Sarpedon looked towards the north of the city and saw that the column of dark sorcery was now a swirling white vortex, shot through with lightning. 'Good. It looks like Commander Reinez has done his duty, too.'

Luko ran from the gatehouse. 'Commander!' He pointed down to the river, where the water still churned under the fallen bridge. 'Is he dead?'

Sarpedon followed Luko's gaze. 'Probably not. But I have faith.'

Luko cocked a cynical eyebrow. 'You think the Emperor will kill him for us?'

'No,' replied Sarpedon. 'But I have faith in His Inquisition.'

TWO HOURS AFTER the warp portal began to collapse, every communications device on Gravenhold was activated. Vox-sets on dead soldiers and burned-out tanks, the communicators of the Soul Drinkers and the Crimson Fists, even the comm-relays of the support ships still in orbit.

The same voice spoke from them all. It was the voice of Techmarine Lygris, chief tech-specialist of the Soul Drinkers and the de facto captain of the space hulk *Brokenback*. He was coming into close orbit to send transports down, and any Imperial ships who wanted to be shot out of the sky should stay in his way.

* * *

THE BROKENBACK WAS followed in by the Crimson Fists' strike cruiser *Herald of Dorn*. The *Herald* quickly ascertained that a single cruiser could barely dent the huge space hulk, and much less survive the barrage of firepower it could probably bring to bear. Even given that the Soul Drinkers were a hated enemy of the Crimson Fists, the *Herald* hung back long enough for the *Brokenback* to depart before sending its own Thunderhawk gunships down to retrieve Commander Reinez and his men.

Reinez was furious. He thought that the *Herald of Dorn* should have sacrificed itself to keep the Soul Drinkers in Gravenhold a couple of hours longer, and give him and his men a chance to reach them. He eventually made a report to this effect to Chapter Master Kantor, who reminded Reinez that he had lost the sacred standard of the Second Company, and no longer had the right to demand the deaths of his battle-brothers.

THE LAST CRIMSON Fists' Thunderhawk over Gravenhold, responding to an Inquisitorial request, made a detour over the slum district and lent its firepower to a struggle between surviving Guardsmen and a pack of daemons which had entered the city through the warp portal. The Thunderhawk picked up Lord Commander Reinhardt Xarius from the roof of an Arbites watchtower. The men around him had to force him into the custody of the Crimson Fists, who reported later that Xarius had demanded they leave him there to die.

THIRTEEN DAYS AFTER the *Brokenback* jumped into the warp and the Crimson Fists withdrew from the system, Inquisitor Ahenobarbus of the Ordo Hereticus arrived with his personal warfleet and declared the planet Entymion IV to be Diabolis Extremis. The warp portal had by then collapsed and taken most of the centre of Gravenhold with it, forming a massive wound in reality that bled daemons and raw energy into the planet's atmosphere. A plume of warp-stuff jutted from the planet like a solar flare and monstrous creatures ran wild through the ruins of the city and forests beyond. Entymion IV was terminally ill, and only one sentence was appropriate.

LORD COMMANDER XARIUS watched as the sentence was carried out. Inquisitor Ahenobarbus, his body completely encased in the gold-plated power armour he wore as a badge of office, sat beside him on a similarly gilded throne on the reception deck of his flagship.

Xarius was not shackled or locked away, but he knew he was nevertheless a prisoner. Ahenobarbus's personal guard of female Imperial Guard veterans would have been only too happy to kill him. He sat on the reclinium couch and watched as the cyclonic torpedoes soared away from Ahenobarbus's gun cruisers, on their way to deliver the Emperor's judgement on the dying world.

'In Exterminatus Extremis,' intoned Ahenobarbus, his voice booming deep and metallic from the mouthslit of his facemask. 'Domina, Salve Nos.'

'I should never have got off that rock,' said Xarius bitterly.

'It is right that the guilty be alive to face their judgement,' replied Ahenobarbus floridly. 'If it is possible.'

'Have you decided what it is yet?'

Ahenobarbus thought for a moment, resting his chin on gilded knuckles. 'Your crime has been adjudged incompetence in the seventeenth degree, for which the punishment is execution. It has been deemed appropriate by the Orders of the Emperor's Holy Inquisition that this sentence be commuted to eternal service, particulars to be decided.'

'Penal legions? Death world garrison?'

'Those possibilities are being discussed. Amongst others.'

Xarius sat back on the couch. It was what he had expected. Still, maybe he would find a place better worth dying for than Gravenhold.

He allowed himself the small consolation of watching Entymion IV die.

THE BROKENBACK WAS long gone by the time Ahenobarbus arrived. Lygris had connected up enough of the engines of its component ships to make it fully warp-capable and it was currently streaking through the warp, heading for an anonymous tract of space on the other side of the galaxy.

Eumenes watched the Soul Drinkers disembark from their transports onto the fighter deck of one of the *Brokenback's* many warships. The Apothecaries were tending to the wounded, including Scamander, who would survive, if only just. Chaplain Iktinos, though wounded himself, was holding a sermon on the deck, and Marines knelt around him. They had lost several against Tellos's renegades holding the north end of the bridge, but others had evidently joined them.

Sarpedon was talking with the sergeants, confirming the numbers of the dead and wounded, planning already for how the Chapter would be reorganised to take into account the officers and men who had been lost. There would be funerary rites to conduct, gene-seed to place in storage, novices to educate in the lessons that Entymion IV had taught the Chapter. Again, the Soul Drinkers had taken a battering, but again, they weren't dead yet.

Eumenes was disembarking from the last transport, which had swooped low over the docks to pick up him and the surviving scouts. The scouts had a debriefing from Captain Karraidin to look forward to. Karraidin would no doubt be frustrated that he had not been down there with them, but soon Pallas would complete the bionic replacement for his ruined leg. Although, of course, there were many more lost body parts that needed replacing now.

Eumenes looked round to see Nisryus climbing down from the cargo ramp of the obsolete fighter-bomber that had served as one of the transports. 'Scout Nisryus,' he said.

'Scout-Sergeant?'

'You could tell which way the fight would end, couldn't you? You foresaw it.'

'I did. I saw that Sarpedon would lose.'

'So… you were wrong at last?'

'No,' said Nisryus. 'I think that we all lost.'

TELLOS CROUCHED ON the heap of dead that filled the now-dry River Graven. After he had dug himself out of the rubble the warp portal had collapsed completely and the raw stuff of the warp was oozing through the north of the city, bringing insanity with it. Imperial Guardsmen and slave-warriors alike, driven crazy by the influx of warp energies, had roamed the city looking for something to kill. Daemons had poured through the breach, eager to revel in death and destruction. Those who strayed too close to Tellos had died and were now piled up beneath his feet. The dead were drawing more and more of the living, eager to take part in the latest game of slaughter. So Tellos waited there for something else to come and face him.

He saw the first torpedo streak down through the black clouds and spear into the ground just outside Gravenhold. The shockwave shook the whole city as the torpedo bored its way through the planet's crust. Lava fountained up as it penetrated the mantle and the pressure was released on an endless torrent of magma surging up from beneath the crust.

A hot red plume whipped up into the air. It was blood, thought Tellos. The blood of a planet. More blood for the Blood God, because everything, eventually, was blood.

Thirty seconds later the warhead detonated, timed to go up at the same time as the other torpedoes which had speared the planet all over its surface. The detonation forced the planet's radioactive core into critical mass and the nuclear fire that resulted flash-burned the surface of Entymion IV away.

The bodies burned. The city burned. Tellos burned, letting the pain wash over him, become a part of him, searing away the altered flesh and leaving only his bare soul burning. He had seen this, too. He had seen how his weak body would be stripped away to prepare it for something stronger, something that would bring the dead of empires to the throne of the Blood God.

Everything was blood, in the end. As his soul flitted through the warp to become one with the Blood God, he saw the galaxy drowned in blood, screaming, dying as Chaos took it over.

And then, as Entymion IV finally died, there was nothing.

ABOUT THE AUTHOR

Ben Counter has made several contributions to the Black Library's *Inferno!* magazine, and has been published in *2000 AD* and the UK small press. An Ancient History graduate and avid miniature painter, he is also secretary of the Comics Creators Guild. *Crimson Tears* is his fifth novel.

WARHAMMER 40,000

DAN ABNETT

RAVENOR RETURNED

A MIND WITHOUT PURPOSE WILL WALK IN DARK PLACES

Coming soon from the Black Library

RAVENOR RETURNED

A Ravenor novel
by Dan Abnett

'You.'

The voice was so low, so very, very deep, the single word resounded like a seismic rumble. A curious hush fell across the vast free trade salon. People began to look. Some picked up their drinks and moved away. They knew what this was.

The implanted eyes of all the Vigilants present also turned to stare at the confrontation, green and cold. But they would not intervene. Not unless the Code of the Reach was broken.

'You,' the voice repeated.

To his credit, the man in the lizard-skin coat had not turned around. He was sitting at one of the high tables, conducting some business with a pair of far traders. The traders both looked up nervously at the figure standing behind the man in the lizard-skin coat.

'I... I think you're being addressed,' one of them muttered.

'I've no business with anyone here except you two gentlemen,' the man in the lizard-skin coat said loudly. He picked up one of the napkins on which the traders had just been scribbling cost estimates. 'Now this figure here seems very high–'

The far traders pushed back their chairs and stood up. 'Our business is done,' one of them said stiffly. 'We don't want to get involved in... whatever this is.'

The man in the lizard-skin coat tutted and got to his feet. 'Sit down,' he told the traders. 'Order another flask of amasec from the tenders on my account. I'll just deal with this and we can resume.'

He turned around. Slowly, he lifted his gaze until he was looking up at the face of the man who had interrupted his meeting.

Lucius Worna had been in the bounty game for fifteen decades, and every second of those savage years showed in his face. His head, shaved apart from a bleached stripe, was one big scar. Livid canyons split through his lips and eyebrows, and formed white ridges on his cheeks and jawline. His ears and nose were just eroded stubs of gristle. The blemish of old wounds overlayed one another, scar tissue upon scar tissue. The carapace armour he wore had been polished until it shone like mother-of-pearl. Even without its plated bulk, he would have been a big man.

'I have a warrant,' Lucius Worna declared.

'You must be very pleased,' the man in the lizard-skin coat said.

'For you.'

'I don't think so,' the man in the lizard-skin coat said, and began to turn away again.

Lucius Worna raised his left paw and displayed the warrant slate. The hololithic image of a man's head appeared in front of it and gently revolved.

'Armand Wessaen. Two hundred seventy-eight counts, including fraud, malpractice, embezzlement, illegal trading, mutilation and mass murder.'

The man in the lizard-skin coat pointed one lean, well-manicured finger at the slate's image. 'If you think that looks remotely like me, you're not very good at your job.'

Behind him, the far traders chuckled. 'Get on your way, bounty,' one of them said as his confidence returned. 'Any fool can see that's not our friend here.'

Lucius Worna kept staring at the man in the lizard-skin coat. 'This face is Wessaen's birth-face. He has changed it many times, in order to evade the authorities. He escaped death row incarceration on Hesperus and absconded from that planet by smuggling himself offworld a piece at a time.'

'I think you've had too much to drink,' one of the traders laughed.

'I don't really care what you think,' replied Worna. 'I know what I know. Armand Wessaen had himself physically disassembled by a black market surgeon on Hesperus. His component parts – hands, eyes, limbs, organs – were grafted onto couriers, hired mules, who conveyed them off planet. Wessaen himself, wearing a body made up of all the transplants removed from said mules, followed them. He later slaughtered the mules instead of paying them what he'd promised, and harvested his component parts back, reassembling himself. All except… the face. There's one mule still to find, isn't there, Wessaen? That's why you're trying to arrange passage to Sarum.'

Worna glanced sideways at the far traders. 'That's what's he's after, isn't it? Passage to Sarum?'

The traders looked at each other. One nodded, slowly.

'This really is nonsense,' the man in the lizard-skin coat smirked. 'My name is Dryn Degemyni, and I'm a legitimate businessman. Your suggestion is… is little short of farce. I cut myself apart, did I? Posted myself offworld, bit by bit, attached to others, and now I'm sewn back together?' He laughed. Some onlookers sniggered too.

'Not sewn. Surgically rebonded. A process paid for by the four hundred thousand crowns you embezzled from the Imperial Guard Veterans' Association on Hesperus while you were acting as their treasurer. They sponsored this bounty, as did the families of the mules you used and killed.'

'You're just annoying me now,' said the man in the lizard-skin coat. 'Go away.'

Lucius Worna adjusted the setting of the warrant slate. The headshot changed. 'Just the face left. And this is the face of the mule you used to smuggle your features out.'

The far traders suddenly began to back away. The hololithic image now plainly showed a perfect match for the face of the man in the lizard-skin coat.

The man sighed sadly, as if all the air had drained out of him, and bowed his head.

'Armand Wessaen,' Worna intoned. 'I have a warrant for your–'

The man in the lizard-skin coat flicked out his right arm and stabbed the bounty hunter in the face. Lucius Worna recoiled slightly and dropped the warrant slate. The flesh of his right cheek was sliced open to the bone. There was blood everywhere.

A shocked murmur ran through the onlookers. No one quite understood what had just happened. They'd barely seen the man in the lizard-skin coat move, let alone produce a weapon.

With a resigned shrug, ignoring the terrible wound, Lucius Worna lunged at his quarry.

Wessaen darted aside, easily avoiding his big, clumsy opponent. He moved like quicksilver, and as he ducked under Worna's reaching arms, he lashed out with a sideways kick.

This should have been as successful as kicking a Baneblade. Wessaen was slender and un-armoured. It seemed insanity for him to try and take on a giant in a suit of powered battle plate in close combat.

But the kick connected, and Lucius Worna was flung sideways, thrown by a force even his suit's inertial dampers couldn't deal with. He crashed into the high table, knocking over the drinks and two of the chairs. Then the man in the lizard-skin coat was on his back, right hand raised to strike at the nape of Worna's neck.

Just for an instant, the onlookers glimpsed that hand and understood. It was folded open, like the petals of a flower, hinged apart between the middle and ring fingers. A double-edged blade poked from the aperture. A graft weapon. An implant. The hideously folded fingers seemed to form a hilt for the blade.

Worna reached around, grabbed the shoulder of the lizard-skin coat, and flung the man over his head.

The man somersaulted in mid-air, controlled his fall, and bounced feet first off the far end of the high table with enough force to slam the table's opposite edge up into Worna's chin. Worna staggered back. Wessaen landed on the salon floor and renewed his attack.

The onlookers in the free trade salon crowded in closer, astonished by what they were witnessing. Some of them had seen the bounty hunter at work before. You didn't mess with that, not hand-to-hand, unless you were crazy, or suicidal or–

Or something else entirely.

Something laced with grafts and glands and implants. Something so augmetically re-engineered it would take on a monster without hesitation. In any fight, there was an underdog. Despite all physical appearances to the contrary, that underdog was Lucius Worna.

This was something the crowd wanted a ringside seat to see.

Worna threw two heavy punches at the man in the lizard-skin coat. Each one would have demolished his skull if it had connected. But Armand Wessaen seemed to slide out around them, leaving empty air. He landed two strikes of his own: his graft blade slit through Worna's left eyebrow, and his left fist actually dented the mother-of-pearl surface of Worna's chest plate.

Worna stumbled away from the force of the blows.

Wessaen's left hand produced a cisor from the pocket of the lizard-skin coat. The warmth of his hand woke the large, black beetle-thing up, and its exposed mandibles, razor-sharp, began to chitter and thrash.

'You've picked on the wrong man tonight,' he hissed as he came in again..

Worna swung around. Again, his punch hit nothing but space. Wessaen had danced nimbly to the left, and stabbed the graft blade up under Worna's left shoulder guard. He tugged the blade out, escaping the blind retaliation. Now blood was spurting down the bounty hunter's left bicep guard.

Worna pivoted at the hips and clawed at his adversary. Wessaen backed away with abnormal speed, executed a deft tumble, and came back on his feet behind his cumbersome opponent. The cisor ripped into Worna's lumbar plating, the mandibles chewing through it like it was tissue paper.

Worna pulled away, but no matter how tightly he turned, he was just a thundering hulk in heavy armour, and Wessaen was always behind him, jittery-fast. Wessaen was glanding something potent, and hyperactivity pulsed through his hard-wired, reconstructed body.

Worna made another desperate grab. Wessaen kicked him in the face, and then followed the kick with another stab of the graft blade. The blade punched through the bounty hunter's midriff armour.

Where it stuck fast.

Wessaen swallowed.

Worna grabbed the man in the lizard-skin coat by the right wrist and wrenched the graft blade out of his belly. As the cisor chattered in, Worna caught that wrist too.

Wessaen's eyes went glassy-wide. Glanding, he was faster than the massive bounty hunter, and almost as strong. Almost.

Struggling, Worna raised the man's right wrist until the graft blade was in front of his face. They were locked, quivering with matched fury. Worna slowly leaned his head forward.

And bit the graft blade in half.

Wessaen squealed. Lucius Worna laughed, a deep booming laugh, and spat the broken blade out of his mouth. He let go of Wessaen's right hand and yanked on the other wrist, straightening Wessaen's left arm as he brought his free fist up under it.

The left elbow of the man in the lizard-skin coat snapped the wrong way with a bone-crack that made the onlookers wince.

The cisor fell onto the floor, and began to eat the carpet. Wessaen started to squeal again, but the squeal ended abruptly as Worna's right hand punched him in the face and sent him flying across the floor.

'End of story,' said Lucius Worna.

Oblivious to the blood streaming from his wounds, Worna clanked towards the fallen man. Wessaen lay in a twisted heap, his broken arm limp and dislocated like a snapped twig. He was moaning, blood pattering from his mashed lips.

'I have a warrant,' Worna boomed, his voice like tectonic plates scraping together.

Closing his bitten-off graft weapon so that his hand refolded, Wessaen fumbled into his lizard-skin coat and wrapped his fingers around the summoning whistle.

His last resort.

It had cost him a fortune, more than all his body enhancements in fact, and he'd not used it before. But he knew what it did. And if there ever was a moment for it, this was it.

It wasn't actually a whistle. It was a smooth piece of rock that had been hollowed out by a technology unknown to the Imperium. But blowing through it was the only way a human could activate it.

Wessaen blew.

All the onlookers winced. Glasses shattered on the salon tables. The huge bio-lumin tank-lights suspended in clusters from the salon's high roof flickered. Every forparsi in the chamber fell down, ears bleeding.

Ten metres from Armand Wessaen, the nature of space-time buckled and popped apart. The surface of the air itself bubbled and began dripping, like the emulsion of an old tintype pict exposed to flame. A seething, iridescent vortex, whisked up from molten, pustular matter, yawned into being, and the hound stepped out of it.

Just a skeleton at first, dry-clicking into view. Then, as it came on, organs materialised inside its ribcage, blood systems wrote themselves into being, muscle grew, sinews, flesh. It solidified, clothing its reeking, yellow bones in meat.

It was hyenid in structure, its forelimbs long, its back sloping off to short hind legs. Its skull was massive, with a pincer jaw and long yellow fangs that could shred anything, even a man in ceramite armour. It stood two metres tall at the hunched shoulders.

Its eyes were white, the hair on its hunchback a bristly black.

The eager onlookers now recoiled. The traders and merchants in the salon began to flee in blind panic, along with the tenders. Not just from the sight of the monster, but also from the smell of it. The gross stink of the warp.

Worna turned to face it, drawing an execution sword from his harness. He knew it would be over fast, just as well as he knew the outcome wouldn't favour him.

Wessaen began to laugh, despite his injuries. 'You picked on the wrong man, you frigger! The wrong man!'

The vortex faded. Now fully manifest, the hound padded forward, about to spring, intent on the prey it had been summoned to destroy.

The Vigilants swarmed onto it from all sides, lashing into it with their hand-and-a-half-swords. Blades rained and sliced. The hound coiled and turned, but by then it was already too late. In less than twenty seconds, the Vigilants had hacked it into bloody slabs and shreds.

The Vigilants turned, as one, to face Worna. In unison, they rested their bloodstained swords on the floor, tip-down, their hands folded over the pommels.

'Oh, Throne, no...' gurgled the man in the lizard-skin coat.

'Code,' Worna said. 'The Code of the Reach. No weapon is permitted that has a range longer than a human arm. And *that* came from more than an arm's reach away.'

Worna picked up the cisor. It wriggled in his hand, chittering. 'The mule wants his face back,' he said.

And that was when the man in the lizard-skin coat really learned to scream.

'HOLY THRONE,' REMARKED Ornales. 'I honestly don't think we need a piece of that.'

The free trade salon stank of blood, and other things less savoury. Under the watchful gaze of the Vigilants, tenders were hosing the floor down. A few traders had been lured back in with the promise of free drinks. Business was still business at Bonner's Reach.

'No, I think we *do*,' Siskind told his first officer.

'His type comes with trouble.'

'Only for the ones he's going after,' said Siskind. 'Come on.'

'What do you want?' asked Lucius Worna, barely looking up as they approached. He was just finishing packing the various tagged and numbered pieces of

Armand Wessaen into the individual cryo-caskets his servitors held ready.

'I want to retain your services,' Siskind said.

Worna straightened up and looked at the ship captain directly. 'You sure? Some people don't like what they get. If this is a midnight wish, then forget it. You're drunk. Go to your bed.'

'A midnight wish?' Siskind echoed.

'Look at your chron, master,' Worna rumbled, returning to his labours. 'The Imperial calendar is about to flick over one more meaningless digit. A new year. If you're partied up, and fancy to settle some old score, sleep on it. I'll still be here in the morning.'

'No,' said Siskind. 'I know what I'm doing. I want the services of a bounty tracker. I'm prepared to pay.'

'How much?' asked Worna.

Siskind glanced at Ornales. 'Twenty thou. Plus a ten per cent stake of whatever cut we make.'

Lucius Worna dropped a still-twitching hand into one of the icy caskets and closed the lid. He looked at Siskind. 'You got my attention,' he growled. 'What sort of cut are we looking at?'

'You know, you're still kind of *bleeding* there...' Ornales said timidly, indicating his cheek.

'Yeah,' Worna replied. 'You gonna sew me back up, pussy-boy?'

'N-no, I just–'

'Then I'll get to it when I get to it,' Worna said. 'What sort of cut?'

'Six, maybe seven million in the first year.'

'At ten per cent? That's a real lot. What's the job?'

'I need you to hunt for me.'

'That's what I do.'

'I was meant to meet a body here, here at Bonner's Reach. A good friend. Name of Thekla.'

'So go look around.'

'I have,' Siskind replied. 'He's not here. He told me he would be, at Firetide, but he's not. If he'd gone out on some trade run, he would've left a message here for me on the personal spindles. But he hasn't.'

'Why's it so important?'

'I know he has enemies.'

'Yeah?'

Siskind shrugged. 'I want to employ you, Worna. To find my friend, or find the bastard who killed him before he got here. There's a lot riding on it.'

'And who might this bastard be?' Worna asked.

'Gideon Ravenor. An Imperial inquisitor. Is that a problem?'

'Not even slightly,' said Lucius Worna.

The story continues in
RAVENOR RETURNED
by Dan Abnett

Available from the Black Library
www.blacklibrary.com

READ TILL YOU BLEED

DO YOU HAVE THEM ALL?

WWW.BLACKLIBRARY.COM